Political prisoners are set free. Exiles return home. Mandela walks from prison. A new flag is unfurled. In streets and on squares people dance to the rhythms of freedom. Former overlords and underlings meet as equals. Bones are dug up. The need for atonement, the difficulties of reconciliation and the ambiguities of love are confronted.

After decades of captivity in the stultifying enclosures of the old order, South Africans now live in the liberated space of democracy.

From this post-apartheid vantage point fiction writers reflect on the advent of freedom. The dramatic consequences of the historic changes of 1994 are thrown into sharp relief in this volume of stories.

In some thirty-one previously unpublished narratives, by gifted South African practitioners of the short story, an irrevocably changed and still changing world is brought into view. The birth of the new society is symbolically celebrated while high expectations jostle with apprehension and creeping disenchantment. Light falls on once obscured dimensions of social and interpersonal life as writers meditate on meanings and ironies of emancipation.

ANDRIES WALTER OLIPHANT is a writer and critic who lectures in the Department of Theory of Literature at the University of South Africa. A former editor of *Staffrider* magazine he currently chairs the Arts and Culture Trust of the President and is a recipient of, among others, the Thomas Pringle Award for Short Stories and the 1998 Book Journalist of the Year Award.

At the Rendezvous of Victory and Other Stories

Compiled and edited by
ANDRIES WALTER OLIPHANT

Cover design and typography by Nazli Jacobs
Set in 10.5pt New Century Schoolbook
Printed and bound by NBD,
Drukkery Street, Goodwood, Western Cape

First edition 1999; second printing 2000

ISBN 0-7957-0093-8

Contents

Introduction

ANDRIES WALTER OLIPHANT

This anthology of stories attempts to provide a perspective on narrative responses to recent changes in South Africa. These changes centre on the advent of democracy after centuries of minority domination. Originally conceived around the theme of independence, the anthology developed in scope to take into its purview a variety of themes concerned with social change and emancipation.

This means that the writing anthologised here, while taking the question of national liberation as a starting point, engages with and articulates a range of related experiences. The nuances of life as experienced in times of transition find narrative expression here in such a way that emancipation with all its ironies and contradictions emerge from the post-apartheid historical context to enter into the perennial discourse on freedom. It takes on the form of aesthetic as well as ethical engagements.

Given this, the vantage point from which these narratives are articulated is decidedly post-apartheid. There can be no doubt that 27 April 1994 is a watershed in South African history since the inception of colonialism four centuries ago. The change which followed has, and continues with varying degrees of intensity, to exert pressure on all aspects of local life. In the domain of literature, expectations of dramatic aesthetic change that would uncouple contemporary writing from the preoccupations of the past, have been voiced with growing ardour since the beginning of the decade.

Accordingly, South African writers, especially those who adopted a critical stance towards minority rule, have been assailed with questions demanding to know what they would write about now that apartheid can no longer serve as the master theme for local writing. This, as Njabulo Ndebele (1992:24) succinctly puts it, is often approached with the one-sidedness of simplifications produced by the epistemologies of division: 'With the monster of apartheid gone, what will Black writers write about? This question has thus far been thrown at Black writing. White writing has thus far not been able to recognise its own precarious position.'

This tradition of enlisting the racial differentiations on which the colonial order in South Africa was based to categorise local writing found expression in Richard Rive's (1981) and Piniel Shava's (1989) interpretations of Black Writing. Black Writing, according to this view, centered on an opposition to racial and colonial domination. White Writing, on the other hand, J.M. Coetzee (1988) states, had the colonial experience of settlers as its focus. Both forms of writing, we can see, reacted to, and drew on the realities of colonialism. The liberation of South Africa has stripped not some, but all South African writers of the relatively stable frame of reference which prevailed for so long. Thus the advent of majority rule produced a cultural situation in which the divided aesthetics of the past were rendered obsolete.

Consequently, narratives of the racial Other, which informed colonial writing, or of the oppressed Self in the writing of the colonised, are no longer possible as stories of social actuality. The collapse of this order shifted the ground to open the field of local writing to an infinite number of alternative possibilities and themes. In this way the social changes forced aesthetic reconsiderations on writers. Among the new themes, the most obvious is the challenge to narrate the process of transition and with it the changes which have swept over South Africa recently. Such narratives, far from starting on a blank slate, it seems to me, must necessarily engage with the past. This is inevitable, since it is only with such historical reference that the present conjuncture establishes its identity as different to the past. It should then come as no surprise that an interplay between present and past is readable in this collection.

In different ways many of the stories explore the relationship between the present and the past. Written from the perspective of contemporary South Africa, they narrate the present as a direct consequence of the past. The new emerges, so to speak, from the womb of the old. In the process the past itself is opened to reinterpretations through a dialogue engendered between the new-found freedom and any number of unresolved problems inherited from the past. This kind of exchange, difficult if not impossible before the end of colonialism, is the matrix through which the nature of change itself is explored. Accordingly, a sense of the present and its challenges, its expectations, its ironies, its ambiguities and creeping disillusionments, are conveyed. This, the reader who works through this collection will realise, is the temporal and contextual framework through which the implications of emancipation come into view in these stories.

Against this background, at least eleven interrelated themes emerge from this anthology. I wish to cursorily draw attention to these. A few cautionary notes are, however, necessary. To begin, the themes identified are not exhaustive. Further, what is picked out, highlighted and grouped together are often partial aspects of stories which differ and relate to one another in a variety of ways. In some cases, stories stand in contrast to each other; in others, their relationship is complementary. Some narratives, through their specific place in the anthology, comment directly and indirectly on each other; a few provide perspectives unrelated to stories surrounding them. This can be glimpsed from the thematic clusters outlined below.

One: in the stories of Peter Horn, Maureen Isaacson and Peter Rule, encounters between the present and the recent past, in specified as well as allegorical contexts, are narrated.

Two: related to this is the theme of change itself and the uncertainties and terrors it sometimes holds, as expressed in the stories by David Medalie, Barry Levy and Tania Spencer.

Three: in the stories of Sandra Lee Braude, James Matthews and Ahmed Essop, changes in the relations between people in work situations or in the larger context of social interaction, brought about by shifts in power, are explored.

Four: these social interactions stand in a contrasting relation to the stories by Ken Barris, Ann Oosthuizen, Diane Case and Miriam Tlali. Here intimate relations, characterised by domination, come under scrutiny in the context of a changing world. These two themes are straddled by Elleke Boehmer's story which looks at love against the backdrop of a situation that promises change but does not result in the realisation of expectations.

Five: the terminal nature of the self-isolation in which privileged sectors of the South African society lived, drawing their identity from European references, is brought into view by the stories of Etienne van Heerden and Rachelle Greeff. In Zoë Wicomb's contribution the post-apartheid context relating to some of these issues is made explicit.

Six: related to this are the issues of post-apartheid African identity as these emerge in the stories of Phil Ndlela and Gomolemo Mokae.

Seven: this in turn articulates directly with questions of persistent ethnic prejudices and attempts to establish a notion of equality among South Africans as reflected in the stories by Sandile Dikeni and Colin Jiggs Smuts.

Eight: in the stories of Rustun Wood/Karen Williams and Nadine Gordimer, the mixed fortunes of former combatants involved in the struggle for liberation are narrated. Beverley Jansen's story, which tells of two school boys who find an unexploded hand grenade from the war of the past, with which they terrorise their fellow pupils, is ironically linked to this theme.

Nine: in Johnny Masilela's and Mike Nicol's fiction we encounter two contrasting literary views of change. In Masilela's piece a sense of optimism and excitement is registered in the celebration of the newborn. In Nicol's story a view emerges which sardonically places contemporary change in the ironic light of the past.

Ten: the ambiguities of forgiveness, atonement and reconciliation can be read in the stories by Achmat Dangor and Graeme Friedman.

Eleven: in the stories of Rayda Jacobs and Norma Kitson, expatriates and exiles return home with great expectations only to be confronted with a society that has changed but struggles to shake off a tenacious past.

Viewed from this perspective, the overarching theme of independence is inflected by many subtle shades in this collection, all of which, in different ways paint a nuanced picture of the implications of liberation and change. The stories illuminate the extent to which South African writers engage with the unfolding changes, adopting different postures and angles. It suggests a society which along with its writing is becoming increasingly differentiated. Hence, the ironic title of the collection, taken from Nadine Gordimer's contribution which deals with complexities of political power and social transition, serves to delineate the concerns of this anthology.

Short-story writing in South Africa remains a diverse and vibrant genre. It is practised with skill by many gifted writers. This is borne out by this anthology.

REFERENCES

Coetzee, J.M.: *White Writing: On the Culture of Letters In South Africa*. Radix. Sandton, 1988.

Ndebele, Njabulo: 'Literature and Nationhood' In *Staffrider* Volume 4. COSAW Publishing. Fordsburg, 1992.

Rive, Richard: *Writing Black*. David Philip Publishers. Cape Town, 1981.

Shava, P.V.: *A People's Voice: Black South African Writing in the Twentieth Century*. Zed Books. London, 1989.

The day the rain clouds returned

JOHNNY MASILELA

We hear that the crops withered that year. That the cattle and the goats, skinny and weak from the scorching heat of the sun, nibbled at dying leaves. And that the chickens pecked at goat droppings.

The tribespeople scanned the skies with their eyes, hoping for the gathering of the rain clouds.

When the clouds failed to gather and the rains did not fall, Mabhoko the king ordered the village induna to blow on the horn of the bushbuck, fashioned by the village woodcarver specially for such purposes.

Voo! Voo! Voo!

At the sound of the bushbuck-horn, the tribespeople knew there was to be an imbizo, the important gathering at the royal homestead.

At the king's kraal the tribespeople were called to join the elderly king, his wives, his children and his children's children around the anthill, to plead with the ancestors to send rain.

But maibabo! those resting in the bowels of the earth did not send the rain clouds.

Then we hear that word went round that by the hillside, in the house of Masilela, the old man's daughter-in-law was soon to give birth to a child.

The wise men of the village, those who could read the future from dried bones and the fly-whisk, anounced that the unborn carried with it an important message. For how could any woman expect a baby in such difficult times?

Then we hear that when nails, growing from a hand as gnarled as the cracked soles of a herdboy, snapped off the umbilical cord, the winds started blowing from the direction of the faraway seas. The baby started to cry.

The elderly midwife, she of the hands that were rugged, cupping the umbilical cord, emerged from the thatch-roofed hut, a toothless smile flashing across her moon-shaped face. Her eyes looked sunken, the whites glowing like pebbles scattered on the bed of the great river Mogalakwena. Her head was shaven clean and shiny, the beadwork of her neck coverings holding her neck erect, like that of the ever vigilant ostrich.

Then suddenly the winds blew strong, but at intervals, and the tribespeople looked at the skies.

The midwife hurried from the hut to bury the umbilical cord at the foot of the anthill. Then she rose from behind the mound of soil and put back in place her ruffled wrap-around.

When the wind tugged at her dress and shook the old woman with sudden violence, the tribespeople lifted their eyes to the skies once more and watched with wonder as rain clouds started forming and re-forming themselves into wondrous shapes.

The elderly midwife hurried from the anthill to the gathered tribespeople, to break the news of the birth of the newly-born, the wind sweeping her wrap-around this way and that way.

She announced the news, at the same time flailing her hands, still wet with a little blood from the umbilical cord, in mid-air. The midwife ululated, singing praises to the newly-born, and to the ancestors of the land of Mabhoko. For was it not those who rest in the bowels of the earth who had made this birth of another warrior possible?

'Eu! Eu! Eu! Eu!' the elderly midwife chanted through toothless gums, pointing towards the thatched hut. 'In giving birth, our daughter-in-law has triumphed. She whose father was wise enough to accept the lobola herd from our house, the house of Masilela, descendants of the great Dlambili clan.'

'Dlambili! Dlambili!' the tribespeople responded.

When the wind subsided for a brief while, it seemed to allow the clouds more space to somersault and reshape themselves. When it gushed forth again, the leaves of the trees rattled and the rain clouds high above shook and surged.

'Eu! Eu! Eu! Eu!' the midwife ululated and waved her rugged hands in the air, wriggling her waist like the barbel in the waters of the great Mogalakwena, a toothless smile lighting up the wrinkled moon face.

She twisted and turned her waist in the agile ways of the maiden dancers of the land of Mabhoko, and then zigzagged her way back to the thatch-roofed hut, stirring up spurts of dust with her cracked feet, all the while drawing intricate patterns on the ground.

'Eu! Eu! Eu! Eu!' the village women howled.

The men cleared their throats and whistled, emitting sounds echoing the call of the weaver bird and laksman.

The young music makers holding the bullhorns pursed their lips, the maidens lined up behind the drums, caressing the stretched cowhide with their smooth palms.

Vooo! Vooo! Vooo! Vooo!

Those with the bullhorns drew their lungs full of breath and blew a tricky but popular tune, triggering ululations from the women and whistles from the older men.

Doom! Doom! Doom! Doom! the maidens pounded the drums, their long fingers tracing invisible patterns on the taut cowhide. The villagers leapt into the air, some landing on the hard ground on one knee, while the younger and stronger warriors turned somersaults and hit the dust with bare backs.

A flash of lightning lit the sky, followed by a loud rumble. The men rolled their fingers into fists, moved them in half-circles, this way and that way, and haibo! at the same time throwing one muscular leg after the other into the empty air.

They provoked the village women, these muscular warriors of the land of Mabhoko. The women, young and striking, broke into the sensual qobosha dance.

Half-naked maidens lunged into the qobosha, heaving their breasts outwards and inwards, as the dance dictates. Outwards and inwards, and then suddenly the knees are bent, as if to settle their buttocks on their bare heels. Outwards and inwards they thrust their breasts, outwards and inwards.

'Haibo!' the village menfolk gasped at the rhythmic movement of the pointed breasts, and the buttocks that were being lowered far down and then lifted back into position.

In the thatch-roofed hut, the one with walls decorated in patterns and images, the meaning of which was a closely-guarded secret among the tribespeople, the baby continued to cry.

With a gnarled and rugged hand the midwife carefully placed a herb-twig into the log fire in the hut. It burned into black ash. The scorched herb was removed and cooled off inside a broken calabash containing a little rainwater, thereafter to be pounded on a millstone into a black powdery paste.

The midwife put a handful of ground herb in her mouth, spat the blob into her palm and rubbed it over the baby's scalp, at the same time communing with the ancestors in a monologue half drowned out by the cowhide drums, the bullhorns and the rumbling thunder.

The baby had fallen silent.

Those conversant with the ways of the land of Mabhoko, the rolling hills and distant valleys, could follow what the elderly midwife was saying. She was saying:

In the name of the kingdom of Mabhoko
The house of Masilela, of Dlambili
We announce to our ancestors
The arrival of the little warrior.
We ask you to protect the little one
From those whose pastime it is to
Cast bad spells on the innocent.

'Dlambili! Dlambili!' the gathered tribespeople answered.

A flash of lightning zigzaggged above the distant hills, rumbling thunder followed. The clouds rolled and surged in the sky, turning daylight into a smokey grey.

The rain fell, first in scattered but large drops. Then a heavy downpour came, in steady, grey beats.

The great river Mogalakwena swelled with muddy water.

On its banks the likawaans lay belly-up. When the raindrops touched their soft undersides, the creatures leapt and splashed into the roaring river.

On hearing the sound of water and the rumbling thunder, the herdboys in the veld hung their goatskins around their shoulders and guided the cattle and the goats to a clearing among the thorn trees for an early cud.

At the Masilela household the cowhide drums and the bull-horns and the dancing were brought to an abrupt halt by the pouring rain. Wet to the bone, the villagers headed for the dry safety of their own huts.

For that whole day and night the rain came down, relentlessly. In the maize and sorghum fields large puddles formed. The hillsides started to drip with water. The land of Mabhoko sucked up the moisture until it was soaked.

By nightfall the river Mogalakwena was lashing the land, uprooting trees and drowning animals in its massive current. Until finally, it burst its banks in flood.

And that, we hear, was how I, Zanemvula the rain child, was born on the day the rain clouds returned to the land of Mabhoko, the land of failing crops and half-naked maidens with pointed breasts.

The finger of God

GRAEME FRIEDMAN

'I have been away such a long time,' I told him. 'But I don't know where I've been away from. That's all I can say.' I scratched my head which is what I always do when people ask me about my past. I think I'm trying to scratch something loose but nothing ever falls out. Or nearly nothing. What I was thinking was that this black guy in his BM is dressed only smart, hey. I thought maybe he'd been to church but then he wasn't from around here, he was on his way somewhere. He had on a white shirt with a fancy tie and his dark suit jacket was hooked up there in the back of the car.

'I woke up one morning in the town over there,' I said. 'At the railway station.' I stretched my arm out, pointing past the tin shanties of the township, over the dusty veld and those little dust devils and the dry donga where maybe a million years ago a river used to flow, but now we just throw our empty beer bottles there and Dominee De Klerk has to step around them when he comes fossil hunting on Saturdays. Jas, it was quiet, I tell you. Sunday afternoons! Everyone here in the township was sleeping off their visits to the shebeens last night and there in the white town all the men were tired from too many beers in front of the rugby yesterday and from being woken by their wives to go to church in the morning. 'There, over there, you see by the Dutch Reformed Church,' I said, 'there by the steeple that sticks up sommer like a finger pointing at God. Ja, man, I've been wondering now for a long time, is that our finger pointing at God, or is that God's finger just pointing nowhere?' I thought that would make him laugh but no, the blerry oke just stared at me with a face like a rock. 'Which reminds me,' I said, 'of that rock over there in South-West. They call it the Finger of God. You seen it? Namibia. I've seen it. Ja, I know. It's one of the few memories that have dropped out after I've scratched. It's near that little place – man, what's it called – Asab, ja, but it's fallen down. It doesn't point to the heavens any longer.' I stuck my finger in the air, 'now it points over here, sommer straight at the Klein Swartberg. Ja, this place sits in the middle of the country like a dried-up old pampoen. That's the Karoo for you.' The black guy was still looking up at me, his hands tight on his steering wheel like he was going somewhere at a helluva speed. 'I looked for a job, you know, all over town. No one would give me work, so I came over here, to the township, and the black people gave me work in this garage. It's only got this one pump as you can see – but now, what was that? full up, you said? high-octane? – I think they thought it would be clever to have an old white man like me to work here. They were being wise, I think.' I laughed. He just looked confused, his face all screwed up like he was about to make a shit or something. 'Ag, that's just my little joke, man. You see, my boss' name is Wiseman. I think they made a joke by giving me this job. They didn't think I'd stay. Wiseman has three garages now. One in town, this little one, and another one just down the road there in Laingsburg. So I thought, why not?

This man just carried on checking me out. I swear if his lips weren't so dark they'd have gone white 'cos they were so tightly pressed together. That look on his face, it was sort of like he was waiting for me to slip up or something. But not so casual as them, man. Me, I just opened the petrol cap and cleared the pump reading and put the hose in and switched it on automatic and then went on telling those staring eyes my story like those eyes of his were pools I was throwing stones into and when the stones hit the water they just disappeared. Ja, just like that. But I carried on talking anyway.

'In the beginning,' I said, 'they all wanted to know, who are you? You're an educated man. You're always quoting people. Shakespeare, I like to quote Shakespeare. But man, they were only small quotes, like 'Bubble bubble toil and trouble' or 'Now is the winter of our discontent'. I've got culture, you know.

Maybe I was a teacher, I told them. But I don't remember. I know things about history and geography and the world. I know a lot about Denmark for some reason, but hell, I can't say why. I speak English, Afrikaans, and Zulu and Sotho. That's unusual for a white man, I know. So maybe I was a teacher. In town they say I am an Afrikaner because of the way I speak, and maybe they've got a point, hey. I dream in Afrikaans ... I think I'm maybe sixty-five now.'

I was looking in the other direction now, to where the National Road leaves town on its way to Laingsburg, where the klonkies sit with their bare brown feet and wave at the cars, trying to sell their wire goodies with the windmills that don't even turn when it blows. 'There where the road makes its way to the Witberge, we went there last spring. Wiseman drove us in his Mercedes. Jas, he even let me drive for a little bit. There you come out of the Karoo into this lekker little plek where the daisies just stand up in their purples and whites, and the vygies and fruit blossoms, they all just jump out of these fields of green wheat. Ja, it's a sight, I can tell you. Afterwards, Wiseman took us for tea at the Lord Milner, there by Matjiesfontien. He says he likes my educated company.'

The pump clicked off and so I went over to squeeze the trigger, little bit, little bit. Wiseman is very sure about that: when they say fill it up, that means to the very top. Every cent counts. I've said to him, 'Ag, they hardly ever fill up over here. It's ten rand here, twenty rand there.'

I went back to the customer. 'Would you like me to check your oil and water, sir?'

This guy was wiping his face like he wanted to make it clean and when he took his hands away his eyes were these red slits, and I thought he must be squinting into the sun but then I saw that the sun was behind him. I thought maybe he was a bit deaf or something, so I just put the volume control on my voice up a bit like you have to with the old tannies in town and said, 'Oil and water?'

'Yes,' he said. Then he leaned forward to release the bonnet. 'And the tyres. Do you have a clean toilet?'

'Ja, over there. I clean it myself. Twice a day. But I must get the key from the office. I call it the office, see, but it's really just that little hut over there by the Coke machine where I can sit and have my tea or when it's raining, which it doesn't do much of here in the Karoo but when it does, jislaaik, you don't want to be in low-lying areas. Like the Laingsburg floods.'

'The key,' he said to me, and got out of his car.

I went to fetch it. He seemed to be in a big hurry. I came back and handed it to him. 'I keep it locked, see. It keeps the place cleaner. They know I know they're going in there. And since I have to clean it ...'

He started hobbling to the toilet. Sort of shifting along like a crab with a broken leg or two. This was the first time I had any idea he was all fucked up like that. He was hunched over, very small, like he'd been crunched up by something – you know, like you scrunch up a piece of paper before you throw it in the bin. He was gone a long time, and after I'd checked his oil and water – which were fine – I put some air in his tyres. Two bars. Then I cleaned his windscreen, front and back. Maybe he'd give me a tip. They like to do that, some of them. While I was drying the back window I started thinking of another time Wiseman took us north up the National Road to Seven Weeks Poort. That place is God's own seat, I tell you. Blerry giant rocks that go straight up to the sky, you just look up at their brown and white faces with your own mouth catching flies. Then their faces come together like they're smooching, and between their lips you can just squeeze your car through, with just enough room for the river. When there's heavy rain you can't go up there.

The customer came back, limping badly like you see those okes after they've run into a tackle by old Ox Venter who plays prop for the rugby team there in town. He hobbled past the big cactus plant that Wiseman wanted me to chop out but I said no, it looks pretty, and then past the old wagon made of kiaat and knoppiesdoring that I've been fixing up in my spare time. He leaned up against the car. He was smoking a cigarette. More like sucking it 'cos his lips didn't work so well.

'You shouldn't smoke by the pump,' I said.

He just looked at me from behind the smoke. Then he started to talk. 'My name is Vusi Nkosi,' he said. His mouth was shaking, and the sounds that came out sort of fell about a bit like they were drunk. I had to listen very carefully.

'I work for the Government now,' he said, 'but in the eighties things were different.' And then he tells me this story about the terrible things that were done to him. How he was chased and then caught, and then taken somewhere and questioned and tortured, and as he's talking his voice is getting clearer but I don't know if he's speaking better or I'm just getting used to it. 'One had my left leg and the other my right,' he said. 'The third man, the Captain – I'd never seen him before – he came into the room just before they put me out the window.' He looked away. Jislaaik, I thought he was going to start crying. He bit his lip and then looked back at me and said, 'The Captain, he was standing back, behind the others. 'Can you fly?' they wanted to know. 'Can you fly?' 'No!' I screamed.'No!' He said that so loud I looked around. Man, that scream was loud enough even to wake Wiseman from his hangover. 'It was night time but I knew I was high up – there were some lights down below. The cops were laughing, as if they were having a party.' Then he looked away again, at the cactus.

I thought he was going to start jumping up and down, you know, like he'd sat on that blerry plant, and I was a bit worried he'd fall over. But he didn't move. He just looked me back in the eye and said, all calm like, 'You know how it is when you're about to fall, you put your hands out to catch yourself? I wanted to do that, only my hands were tied behind my back, and all that was being put out to catch my fall was my head.' He laughed but I didn't think it was so funny, man. Then he said, 'One of them says in Afrikaans, "Joost, let's see how strong you are. Let's see if you can hold him by yourself." In those days I was a lot bigger than I am now.'

He was showing me with such big arms, I said, 'Like Arnold Schwarzenegger?'

'Yes,' he said, 'I suppose so.'

'Hell,' I said, 'you wouldn't say that now.'

He gave me a look, all narrow eyes, like he thought I was joking with him. I just looked away, over towards the town, there by the nicer side where sometimes I go walking to see the rich people's houses with their green lawns and smart cars in the driveway. Hell, green lawns in the Karoo, it's a treat to see them, I can tell you. Our mayor could go and live there but he doesn't. He still stays in the same old shack he's lived in for donkey's years.

'No,' said the black man, shaking his head, this head that came out all crooked from his neck like a tortoise's, 'you wouldn't say that now. No one would say I look like Arnold Schwarzenegger now.' He thought for a bit, his eyes back on that cactus plant, then he looked back at me. 'So this white man, the one called Joost says, "Ja, okay, let's see. Let go your leg, man." As if it was his leg. I wanted to say, that's my leg. But it wasn't my leg, it belonged to them, like the rest of me. So the other man, I never heard his name, he let go of the one leg.'

I looked down at his leg. Which one was he talking about? They looked okay to me. But the way he walked it was like he had a wooden leg, or one side of his body was dead like he'd had a stroke or something.

So this guy cleared his throat like he was going to carry on with his little speech, and he did. 'Then the Captain,' he said, 'he's been quiet inside the room, he sticks his head out the window and says to me in Zulu, "Vusi, time to talk, man. This Joost's a bietjie pap. I wouldn't trust his grip for too long. He's too weak to hold a big man like you." And then he laughed.'

'Shit, man,' I said.

'Well,' this guy said, 'the Captain was right. Joost was too weak to hold me. Or maybe he could've held on longer and they were going to drop me anyway.'

All the time he was talking he was looking into me, like he wanted to find something there. I wanted to say, go ahead man, I've been searching since I got here in '94 and I haven't found anything.

He shook his head again. 'My body has held onto a memory

21

of those policemen. Just before Joost dropped me the Captain said, "Well, what's it to be, Vusi? To be or not to be? That is the question." I hit a flagpole on the way down. It broke my fall, and my back. Some other policemen found me at the bottom. The security cops said I tried to escape by jumping out of the window.'

'Jeez, man,' I said, 'and after you told them you couldn't fly.' Well, I know how that sounds now, but I didn't know what else to say, him all banged up like that. He just gave me another one of his looks, staring at me for a long time until his eyes began to swim in tears so that he couldn't have been able to see the outside of me very clearly, never mind the inside. Then after a long time he got back into his car and drove away.

'Hey,' I called after him, my voice getting eaten up by his dust cloud, 'you didn't pay! What about the petrol, man?' I was angry I can tell you. Any shortfall Wiseman takes off my salary. A tank of that BM's petrol is two week's earnings for me.

Bitter fruit

ACHMAT DANGOR

It was inevitable. One day Silas would run into someone from
the past, someone who had been in a position of power and
had abused it in a way that had affected Silas's life directly, not
in the vague, rather grand manner in which people said everybody had been affected, because power corrupts even the best
of men, they said. Those men had done all kinds of things they
could not help doing because they had been corrupted by all
the power someone or something had given them.

Bullshit, Silas thought. It's always something or someone
else who's responsible, a 'larger scheme of things' which exon-
erates people from taking responsibility for the things they do.

Silas watched the man, the strands of thinning hair combed
all the way across the head to hide his baldness, the powdery
residue of dry and dying skin on the collar of his jacket, the
slight paunch, the grey Pick 'n Pay shoes, the matching grey
socks.

The man leaned forward to push something along the check-
out counter and turned his face towards where Silas stood
holding the can of tomatoes in his hands like an arrested gesture. Yes, it was Du Bois. The same dead, fixed stare in his glass
eye, the same alertness in the other, good eye. A bit slower
though, Silas thought, as Du Bois moved his head from side to
side observing the cashier ring up his purchases.

Silas went closer, accidentally jostling a woman in the queue
behind Du Bois. Silas watched Du Bois push his groceries along,
even though the cashier was capable of doing this on the con-
veyor belt. Typical pensioner's fare. 'No Brand' cans of beans,
cans of tuna, long-life milk, sliced white bread, instant coffee,
rooibos tea, denture cream.

So the bastard's losing his teeth, Silas thought, picturing

23

Lydia's face-of-anger, were he to return home without groceries.

Today's Sunday and the shops are open only until 1 o'clock. She'd suppose out loud *she'd* have to do the shopping the next day because Silas's job was too important to allow him to take time off from work.

Silas abandoned the trolley and followed Du Bois out of the store. Halfway down the length of the mall, past shop windows that Du Bois occasionally stopped to look into with familiar ease, Silas began to ask himself what the hell he thought he was doing following a retired security policeman about in a shopping centre? What Du Bois did he did a long time ago. Seventeen years ago to be exact. And Silas had learned to live with what Du Bois did, had absorbed that moment's horror into the flow of his life, a faded moon of a memory that only occasionally intruded into his everyday consciousness. Why did it matter now, now in fact that the situation was reversed, when Silas could use the power of his own position to make the old bastard's life a living hell?

The man's smell, that faint stench of decaying metabolism, was in Silas's nostrils, like a hunter suddenly upon its wounded prey. Du Bois had stopped at a café, had pulled a chair out from under the table, ready to sit down. Silas stood close to Du Bois, facing him, and suffered a moment of uncertainty. Shit, this man looked so much older than the Du Bois he remembered. Then he looked, startled, into Du Bois' equally startled living eye.

'Du Bois?'

'Yes?' Du Bois said and looked Silas up and down, his bewildered manner changing to one of annoyance. He sat down, uttering an elderly person's weary sigh, trying to draw the attention of other shoppers: Look, here was a young man bothering an old man, a pensioner.

'Do you remember me?' Silas asked.

Du Bois leaned back in his chair, his air of open-armed, I'm being put-upon vulnerability quickly brought a security guard closer.

24

'Should I?' Du Bois said quietly, caught the eye of the security guard, then raised himself from his chair and pushed his trolley towards the exit.

Silas watched Du Bois disappear into the bright sunlight, watched the security guard watching him. Silas turned away. The rage he felt was in his stomach, an acidity that made him fart sourly, out loud, oblivious to the head-shaking group of shoppers who had gathered to witness a potential scene. The guard spoke into his radio, the café owner pointedly dragged the chair back to its neat place beneath the table. Silas's rage moved disconsolately into his heart.

He drove home and without saying a word to Lydia, took a six-pack of beer from the fridge and went to sit on the grass verge on the corner of Honey and Lily. He was aware of Lydia looking up from the paper, then pushing it aside to watch him as he passed the window on his way to the gate. He drank a beer with long gulps, burped, and continued to drink with slow, slaking swallows, until his eyes swam and his face flushed warmly.

He stretched out his legs, smiled at the passers-by. This busy intersection reminded him of the township, where you could start off by yourself with a few cans of beer and soon, by the very peace of your solitariness, summon a whole group of Bra's to join you, squatting in a circle and drinking beer and talking Bra-talk, a mellifluous flow of gruff observation and counter-observation, no topic serious enough or dwelt upon sufficiently to maroon the hazy passage of a pleasurable, forgetful afternoon.

No one pressed you for answers or confidences, you soon forgot the problem that had driven you and your pack of beer into the street, just one of the manne, deserving of your privacy. Until a wife or a mother, or a formidable duet of mother and wife came along to tell you that this was no way to resolve your problems, drinking in the street like a kid, or worse still, a tsotsi who took to petty crime because he couldn't face life. The worst-case scenario was the arrival of the cops, all cold-eyed and admonishing, revving the engine of their van

25

until you and your friends slowly dispersed, a herd of dumb, resentful beasts being driven from a favoured water hole.

Lydia was more astute. She sent Mikey to remind Silas that they were due to take Mikey to his grandmother's for the day. Silas, into his third beer, tried to ruffle his son's hair, teased him about how it was time to cut the mince shorter, that Afros had gone out of fashion long ago, when Michael Jackson dropped it as a hairstyle. Mikey smiled that condescending smile adolescent boys reserve for slightly drunken fathers. Silas didn't mind. This was the peace he had sought, some ordinary weakness to drive the anger from inside of him, an emptiness filled with mortal belching and pungent farts, things that Lydia and Mikey, and indeed Silas himself could cope with.

Lydia drove, fast and resolute on the freeway, slow and careful when they took the off-ramp to Soweto. An afternoon haze of smog turned the sun to brass. Silas remained in the car outside the high wall of Jackson and Mam-Agnes's Diepkloof home. The car wouldn't be safe if left unguarded outside the yard. In any case, Lydia was on night shift and they couldn't stay long. Jackson, his face burnished the colour of dark wood by a day of drinking in the sun, swaggered out through the gate, his oversized shorts flapping around his sturdy legs.

'Sielas, Sielas, they'll steal you and the fucken car,' Jackson said, delighting in the musical tone this emphasis gave Silas's name. Silas went inside and had a beer with Jackson. Agnes gave the two men gently chiding looks, while Lydia became stony-faced. Silas gulped his beer much too quickly. They drove back towards the city. His loud, exaggerated belches brought no reaction from Lydia, who concentrated on her driving, glancing at her watch all the time.

'I saw Du Bois today.'

'Who?'

'Du Bois, Warrant Officer Du Bois.'

Lydia said nothing. Her fingers gripped the steering wheel a little more tightly.

'Where?'

'In the mall.'

'Is that why we have no groceries?'

He looked out of the window. They had emerged from the township smog. Clouds darkened the sky. He opened the window, letting in a gust of moist, refreshing air.

'I recognised him immediately. Old and fucken decrepit, but Du Bois all right. It was his eye, that glass eye. And that arrogant voice.'

Lydia looked at him, then returned her attention to the traffic. Silas tried to engage her eyes, but she stared straight ahead of her.

'You spoke to him?' Lydia asked after a while, her enquiry casual.

'Yes.'

Again he looked at her. She was steering the car down the off-ramp towards Doornfontein, bending her body with the curve of the road.

'I didn't mean to. I followed him out of the store, then suddenly found him sitting down, as if he was waiting for me.'

Lydia straightened as the car straightened, peering into the side-mirror as she entered the slow city traffic.

'Christ, Lydia, it just happened, I just ran into him. A fucken accident.'

Lydia pulled the car half-way up the driveway, switched off the engine and got out. Silas sat for a moment, then followed her into the house. Lydia was already in the bedroom, pulling off her clothes.

'Lydia ...'

'I'm going to be late, Silas, I'm on theatre duty tonight.'

Silas sat on the bed, watched her change her clothes. The white, staff sister's uniform soon gave her a new and formidable freshness. She seemed to curse her own distraction, hitched the skirt up and pulled on a pair of black pantyhose. Her legs assumed a contained kind of sensuality. Then she pulled down the skirt, smoothed it, pinned the badge with her name embossed in gold onto her blouse, grabbed her bag and the car's keys. She said a hasty 'Bye' and left Silas sitting on the bed.

He heard the door close, the customary quiet click of the latch. Lydia had always been so quiet, so precise. He heard the car start, the engine rev, heard it settle down to an idle.

He went to the kitchen and opened a beer, pouring its contents into a tall, tilted glass, until it was almost full, then held the glass upright, continuing to pour, slowly, until a delicate head of foam gathered at the mouth without spilling over. Overcome by a sudden, bloated feeling, he abandoned the glass and the empty bottle on the long, austere dining room table and sat down in an ancient easy chair which creaked and added to the air of silence in the house.

The hot day and all the beer he had drunk made him feel drowsy. He raised his head to the sun sinking behind the tall buildings which marked the boundary to Berea, and imagined the sun shining in through the high, square window of their home in Noordgesig, a township on the edge of Soweto; recalled the small-house peace of the day winding down, the noises in the street, remembered such half-drunken Sundays when the sun in the square window gave way to cold shards of moonlight and Lydia waking him up to go to bed. Then the moon was caught in the bars of the window and Lydia's voice was hoarse, vibrating like a singer's voice too rich to be played so loudly through a set of worn out speakers.

'Run, run, you pig,' another voice said, while another voice laughed above the sound of an idling car engine, and Lydia's scream was far away.

Silas woke from his beery sleep, his mouth dry and the sky dark. He heard the car's engine running, looked through the window and saw the empty seat and the door ajar. He stumbled outside, light rain on his face, switched off the engine, looked around, saw Lydia sitting in the wicker chair on the stoep. He must have rushed right past her. Silas closed the door and locked it.

'Lyd, you all right?'

'No, Silas, I'm not all right.'

He approached her with a sence of foreboding. Lydia was in one of her implacable moods. Like when Biko was killed, and the day Silas confessed his one and only infidelity, and when she found out he had been in the underground and had never told her. Now he put his arm around her and felt her coldness.

'Christ, Lydia, you're cold, let's go inside.'

She raised her legs onto the chair and hugged her knees to her chest.

'Silas, I'd forgotten ...'

'I'm sorry, I didn't intend to run into him.'

'You chose to remember, you *chose* to come home and tell me.'

'You know I couldn't hide anything from you.'

He took his arm away, went to sit on the wall of the stoep.

'Christ, Lydia, it's not something you easily forget, or ever forget.'

'All these years we never spoke about it.'

'There was no need to.'

She looked up at him, her eyes scornful.

'No need to? What do you mean, no need to?'

'It was a time when, well, we had to learn to put up with those things.'

'What did you have to put up with, Silas? He raped me, not you.'

'It hurt Lydia, it hurt me too.'

'So that's it. Your hurt. You remembered your hurt.'

'Shit, Lydia, I didn't mean it that way. I was there, helpless, fucken chained in a police van, screaming like a mad man.'

'So you didn't hear me scream?'

'Of course I did, how do you think I knew?'

'How do you know it wasn't a scream of pleasure, the lekkerkry and fyndraai and all that, the things you men fantasise about?'

'Fuck you, Lydia, I know the difference, I know pain from pleasure.'

Lydia stood up, her angry reaction slowed by the coldness in her body.

'You don't know about the pain. It's a memory to you, a

29

wound to your ego, a theory,' she said thrusting her face into his. 'You can't even begin to imagine the pain.'

They stood facing each other for a moment. Late-summer rain was cooling the night down. He slumped down in the wicker chair.

'Ja, I suppose imagined pain isn't the real thing. But I lived with it for so long, its become real. Seventeen years. The pain of your screams, his laugh, his fucken cold eye when he brought you back to the van.'

'What else do you remember?'

'That Sergeant Seun's face, our Black brother, the black, brutal shame in his face.'

'You don't remember my face, my tears ...'

He closed his eyes almost as she closed hers. When Silas opened his eyes Lydia had gone indoors, and was busy dialling on the phone. He followed her.

'Who're you calling?'

'The hospital, tell them I can't come in tonight. It's late to call, but a courtesy anyway.'

He took the phone from her and asked for the matron in charge, told her that Lydia was ill, that he'd call the next day to tell them how she was.

'I don't know, some kind of fever,' he said, then slowly re-placed the phone.

Lydia stood by the kitchen sink, drinking a glass of water. He went in, leaned against the fridge.

'Lydia, we have to deal with this.'

'With what?'

'With what we went through, both of us.'

He saw the smirk on her face.

'Yes, for fuck's sake, I went through it as much as you,' he said.

'You're screaming at me, you know how I don't like being screamed at.'

'I'm sorry.'

She went into the front room, he wanted to follow her, but felt that she might think he was pursuing her. He leaned up

30

against the fridge, felt its throb against his back, slid down until he was squatting on his haunches. He remembered how they made them tauza, squatting on their haunches like this and frog-jumping so that anything they had concealed in their anuses would drop out. He closed his eyes and smiled. Lydia was back in the kitchen.

'You're amused.'

He got to his feet.

'I remembered that they made us do that.'

'What?'

'When we were in detention, tauza! to check if we'd hidden anything up our arseholes.'

'And did you?'

'Shit, what could you hide in your anus?'

'A penis.'

'Hell, Lydia.'

'Well we have to, all the time, hide penises up our fannies, the recollection of them being there. Even the ones we never invited in.'

'Christ, Lydia.'

'Christ what Lydia?'

'We have to do something about this.'

'What, talk to the Truth Commission?'

'Well, why not?'

'You think Archbishop Tutu has ever been fucked up his arse against his will?'

'Lydia, what difference does that make?'

'The difference is he'll never understand what it's like to be raped, to be mocked as you're being raped, that piece of useless flesh you call a cock transformed into a hot knife.'

'Not all men are insensitive, Lydia.'

She stood close up to him.

'Do you want to know what sensitivity is?'

She raised her dress, pulled down her pantyhose, let it fall to her feet.

'Here, feel.'

She took his hand and placed it on her vagina.

'No, Lydia, no.'

'Go on, put your hand in, your whole fist, feel the delicate membrane, those child's lips that a woman's poes has, that is sensitivity!'

She took his finger and forced it into her vagina, winced as his finger nail touched something soft. He pulled his hand away, walked onto the stoep, leaned back and thrust his face into the rain until it ran saltily into his mouth. When he lowered his head Lydia was standing on the stoep, barefoot, sipping his abandoned beer.

'Shit, Lydia, that must be really flat.'

'I want to taste like a man, all sour.'

'I'll pour you a fresh beer.'

'I want it to be flat, like a man's breath.'

She sipped, pulled her mouth in distaste.

'Would you kill him for me?'

'Who?'

'Du Bois.'

'Lydia ...'

'If you were a real man, you would have killed him on the spot, right there in the mall, his blood running all over the floor.'

'You're joking.'

He realised his mistake. Now she would mock him even more.

'Joking? He took your woman, he fucked your wife, made you listen to him doing it. I became his property, even my screams were his instrument. Now, you're a man, you believe in honour and all that kind of kak ...'

'Lydia stop it.'

'You know what he called me as he was fucking me?'

'For fuck's sake, Lydia!'

'He called me a nice wild half-kaffir cunt, a lekker wilde Boesman poes.'

Silas grabbed Lydia by the arms, and shook her. The glass of beer fell from her hands. She kissed him on the mouth. He held her close to him, his tongue exploring her mouth. She tasted of hops, the bitter fruit of tepid beer. She gasped, then

32

leaned up against him, her head against his chest, weeping, making gentle dancing movements with her feet.

He cradled her head, astonished by how much taller he was than her. He glanced down the slenderness of her back, saw the slow pool of blood spreading on the floor, saw his heavy shoes immersed in its dark glow, saw her feet dancing, delicate little steps, on the jagged edges of the broken beer glass.

Mind reader

MAUREEN ISAACSON

It is exactly twelve months since forty billion fire rockets detonated their light into the heat of a darkened Cape sky, as Daniel opened his mouth in an arc of pleasure, as Siena shuddered, as outside people screamed their joy. The new order was born.

Baby Karl still refuses to emerge. He can smell the air in his parents' house, Number Seventeen, Block Seven. It is weighed with the smell of morogu and pap; it is pendulous with waiting. Siena has refused induction. Karl's will, like his mother's, is of wrought iron. He rides her ebb, feels the dark currents of his dad, snuggles deeper. Daniel is yesterday's hero, a sad playwright who defied the censors of the old order and who has now been overlooked for promotion at the State Theatre.

Today is Independence Day. New BlockSun X scarcely protects the fried egg nipples of Siena and comrade Thuli. The sun beams a ferocious radiance onto the beach where they have escaped the celebrations. 'When Karl does eventually arrive, I will need someone to continue the work of the Organisation,' Siena is saying, as the contractions begin.

Five hours later, Thuli puts to use the knife she has brought along to slice the watermelon. Snip goes the umbilical cord. Splash goes the sea water. Two teeth glimmer like milk in the uncertain twilight. Eyes open and something is communicated. *Take me to my father.* Daniel's heart releases its burden but he does not understand how the baby's telepathic powers will further the ends of the Organisation, as Siena has prophesied. *More lotion on my left buttock, more mashed apple, pass my rattle, please. Agoo.* As there is nobody to continue her work, Siena leaves it to Daniel to warm Karl's milk in the early hours of the morning and later, to prepare his sandwiches for school. There is no need to ask what Karl wants.

Karl knows too much. He knows before his teachers do what they will say and why. They declare him a genius. Yes, perhaps he can discern dissidence and espionage and help the country to achieve true liberation, says his father. Nobody must ever know of his gift.

He is a remote child, detached yet obedient. He delivers the information requested by his parents but is unable to penetrate minds that have locked their knowledge away. Also, he fails to discover what has happened to the fifty comrades who went missing on the night of his conception. 'I tried,' he says, after each new mission, and returns to his room.

He spends a great deal of time looking into the mirror. His eyes, vague with the desperation of searching for a young woman, any young woman, do not register a true reflection. He does not see that lying too long in Siena's womb has left his face as flat as a compass. He attempts to slick back the hair that grows like khakibos on his oversized head but he does nothing to soften the glow of his nose. Obsessive clothes-pressing and fingernail-paring offer no guarantee against rejection.

His voice rises like high tide when he speaks to girls. He knows too well what is going on behind their pleasant ways and cunning smiles. Loneliness turns his interest to the aerodynamic construction of water towers and the interior workings of space craft. He delves into the mysteries of time and brings forth information from a future where men are unable to speak without musical accompaniment.

He meditates on a small black spot on the ceiling of his bedroom. Large pustules fight for dominion over his forehead. He spills gobs of spunk into handkerchiefs, which he washes and dries near the river. His school results make the newspaper headlines and at fourteen, he matriculates with twelve distinctions.

On his fifteenth birthday, before the Independence Day celebrations begin, he is called to the Freedom Mental Hospital.

Here he is told he will train as a psychiatrist under Dr Motau. 'It will take a mind such as yours to help us restore the sanity that was shattered by the old order,' says the doctor.

'Memory is the map. Through memory we can learn to understand and control the threat to democracy,' he is saying when a man in torn pyjamas shouts to him, 'Hey boy! I thought I told you to come in through the tradesman's entrance!'

'Here is an example of an excess of memory which is unable to integrate with the present,' says Dr Motau. He force-feeds these patients with videotapes of the events that led up to the Independence. Treatment is more severe for amnesiacs, the old regime supporters who now claim always to have possessed a spirit of liberalism. Dental drilling and hair waxing jolt the memory. 'For the severe cases, and there are many, the perpetrators of human rights abuses who believe they were freedom fighters, we have more specialised treatments.' Doctor Motau does not elaborate.

After a week, Karl will be expected to suggest a cure for all of these ills. His proposal will be passed on to Dr Garcia, the hospital head, later to Government. Doctor Motau refers to his superiors as 'the powers that be'.

Karl senses a nagging dissonance in this doctor's excessive willingness to please but the man's mind is shut tight, like a security gate. How can he tell that this is Karl's first encounter with people such as these patients, people who live in the memories of his parents? Theirs was a different fight, the fight that is still unmentionable in the new country.

Karl studies books about the mechanism of the mind. He tries to think of 'solutions' that will aid the hospital in its research, with no success. He waits for time to pass.

One day a radiance bursts through the gloom of his vision. It emanates from a young nurse with lyrical hands. He follows her, careful to remain well out of sight. Her perfume reminds him of the garden where he played as a child. Now he smells the sweetness of the roses, now he scrabbles on his knees under the loquat tree. It is afternoon and soon his mother will call him in for tea.

Down three flights of stairs and then another, down a long corridor and into a darkened wing, he treads lightly, borne on hope. His destination, as it turns out, is a ward. Here people sit on chairs arranged in a circle and stare into space. 'Vitamin time!' says the nurse.

He hides behind a screen and watches her inject an orange liquid into the bruised veins of her patients. He counts fifty needles. Karl looks into the minds of the patients. Like over-exposed film, their stories are imprinted there. These are the fifty missing members of the Organisation! He must leave at once. A floorboard creaks and the nurse catches his eye.

A letter of dismissal arrives on his desk. Doctor Garcia has signed it. He is not surprised, but he does not expect what he gets; incarceration in a rage-red room and worst of all the waiting, in between the ultraviolet lights and the standing after the feet flogging. When his mind is 'clear', Karl is regressed to a prenatal state. Back in his mother's ebb again, he recalls the history of the Organisation. He remembers its revival, its plans for the future, but the censor encoded in his early years is still operative. He does not talk, nor does he win.

Six weeks later, Karl's mind is empty; it is like a blank in a pistol where there should be a bullet. When he is released he has forgotten everything he knew, which means he has forgotten who he is. Now that he is nobody, he has nowhere to stay and nothing to do. His home is a tall oak tree surrounded by veld, which is skirted by a low, threatening sky. His hair is matted, as if woven into a nest for the birds who are his fellow tenants. He thinks their thoughts, which are mainly about worms. He flaps his arms and fancies that he is made of feathers. His shadow bites him. He pecks at the fetid waters of the nearby river. The days are as bland as porridge. Hunger twists his colon. How long can he continue to live this way?

Once, when Karl was still able to think, he believed that there were no coincidences. Now a stanger sits beside him under his tree.

'Don't do it! Don't leave your job,' he tells the man. 'You are about to receive a promotion.'

'You are a mind reader!' shouts the man; 'I must take you to meet my uncle.' The impact of sudden kindness shocks Karl back into memory, then out of it.

The man's uncle is head of an unnamed committee. He allows Karl to live in his disused coal shed. Karl paints an oak tree on the wall. He executes simple tasks in the uncle's office: floor scrubbing, boot polishing, tea making. *The Organisation is a danger to the country.* Dusting, shining, onion peeling. *Destroy the Organisation.* Clothing, washing, ironing, mending. *Who are you, Karl?* He does now know the names of these people. He is sent to another office where things are no different. Fetching, carrying, more cleaning. *The Organisation must die. Root out its members.* Karl is now able to extract information from the area of his cortex that was damaged by his captors. He is able to receive messages. *Congratulations, Karl, you have earned the title, New Freedom Fighter. Here is your weapon.*

Back at Number Seventeen, Block Seven, the cracked white horse that once rocked Karl's small body stands to attention in his old room. It is late July. Icy winds freeze the eyes. Rain has soaked up the colour of the fields outlying the megalopolis. The mirror that once showed him how far he was from handsome now reflects a bitter rural scene beyond the garden. It is 8.30 p.m. Daniel is in the kitchen, warming his feet before the stove where the hot chocolate has begun to boil. Siena climbs into bed at the same time as the steel of the AK 47 presses its coldness on Daniel's temple.

Now Daniel is marching, his hands beat the air above his head like angel's wings, as he moves to join his wife in the bedroom. Daniel and Siena look into each other's eyes. Together they choke on their son's name. Finally it escapes into the air with desperation, announcing its liberation with an ugly double squawk: 'K-a-a-a-a-r-l!' Would it make any difference if he knew that their grief over his disappearance has terminated the work they do for the Organisaton? *Destroy the Organisation. Pull out its roots.* The boy ushers them into the afterlife. First Daniel. Then Siena.

It is ten fifty-five. At precisely 11 p.m., his dying will begin. 'Mother! Father!' will be his involuntary cry. In the morning, the park-keepers will find his body. When they dump it into the small vacant box and then into Number *7X69616@Death* in the New Freedom Fighter section of the ever-expanding cemetery, the thud will scarcely be heard. Perhaps a gull will swoop overhead; perhaps the silence will be unrelieved. There can be no assurances.

Souvenirs

PETER RULE

This is Terence's story, and it happened two weeks after
South African armoured cars raised crimson-brown columns
of dust as they returned across the Angolan border after Operation Palmiet. It comes to me in the dead parts of the night,
more often now that you have gone. Here I am pinned down
like a man before on-rushing headlights, held by nothing but
my own weight. Or some sound reminds me of his laughter –
a woman at a party who has drunk too much; bare hands
squeaking on a glass before it shatters.

It begins with her. Like a stranger in an unfamiliar country, someone not yet accustomed to the terrain, she was new
to puberty. She had wide eyes, pupils black as the burnt undersides of stones, high eyebrows. There was something about
her mouth, the way it pulled up at one corner and dimpled her
cheek. Her face shone, I remember, even as she tried to avoid
attention. She wore a trinket around her neck. It was something bright, perhaps plastic, glittering in the shallow pool at
the base of her throat. Standing at the entrance to the head-
man's hut, we felt the slow bludgeoning of the sun on our
heads and shoulders.

We were after a gang that had ambushed a police vehicle,
killed the driver and fled with sacks of post. Nothing makes
soldiers as mad as letters gone missing. But, understand me,
I do not use that to justify what happened later, this was just
a routine patrol in Sector 2.0. As we entered the kraal we noticed her among the toothless, wizened elders and children
with bloated bellies and listless fly-plagued eyes. Of course,
there were no young men to be seen. There she was on the pe-
riphery of our vision, perhaps trying to efface herself. She
stood very still, one arm held across her midriff, fist closed,

the other hand touching the trinket at her throat. Her eyes were downcast but for a quick flashing look. The breeze tugged at the crown of her woolly, ochre-tinged hair.

Nice legs, someone said. She got tits, too.

She flinched, I recall – hearing the snake in the undergrowth of the occupier's language? Terence giggled, his head jerking back characteristically. I called him Terence. He was the one who walked in front of me on patrol. His gait was imprinted on the backs of my eyelids. But the others taunted him with the nickname 'Terr', saying that he spoke like a kaffir-boetie. No, no, he would insist, his head joggling, trying to win us with his serious, earnestly green eyes. He had a long, sallow face with a small round mouth. I imagined him singing soprano in a choir before his voice broke. Perhaps that was all that he was: a boy with a broken voice, a rifle and a distant mother. Yes, we *are* here to protect them against the onslaught, he would insist.

Terence really believed that we had a mission to civilise the natives, to banish the evils of Communism from their midst, to save them from themselves. He spoke like someone in the rescue services who climbs trees to deliver stranded cats. His eyes shone through his peculiar deliberate way of blinking as he explained all this to us. In an earlier age he would have been a missionary with a wide-rimmed hat, home-knitted socks and a compass. He was our souvenir.

They say no one has been past, said the lieutenant, emerging from a hut. They say their own sons are at some funeral ceremony. But it's in their nature to lie, even when they don't have to. Look around the homestead. Try to find one of them who will talk, but be careful.

The interrogation developed naturally from an exchange of words – she was not forthcoming – to a more intimate encounter. She fought back at the beginning. She hit Jannie below the eye, cutting him so that they had to hold her arms down behind her as he laboured, bleeding onto her. I remember the fat beads of sweat in her eyelashes, the narrow muscles running crazily in her upper arms. The smell of her cunt through the close air of the hut. Jussus! said Jannie.

She screamed only the first time.

When it came to Terence, he got himself tangled among her limbs and his own loose trouser legs. He was all elbows and knees, gooseflesh on the red back of his neck, one frantic hand tearing the trinket from her throat. I remember his pale, contorted face, his teeth bared in the roundness of his mouth. He managed only to spill himself across her thighs.

Struggling to button up his fly, avoiding our eyes, he hurried to the doorway. There was just that one short, high-pitched bark of laughter.

But when we turned to look, he had gone.

What about you? you ask me, curling your legs up into your body, your back to me. But I can read the taut angles of your back. Were you next?

I tell you that it is not my story, it is Terence's story.

And what about the girl? Isn't it *her* story? Your voice is flat but there is disgust in your spine as you jerk yourself up and throw each particular thing into the bag and slam the door so that the walls shudder and the rafters creak, leaving me here. You did not allow me to finish, so I write this for you. Not that you will come back. But I believe you want to know.

You who liked the uniform when I came home on passes and said the short hair suited me and wanted to make love on the night before I returned all those years ago. You who said you could smell the rain and dust of Ovamboland in the creases. The uniform is gone, pawned to a second-hand clothes shop the day after Mandela walked free. But sometimes I can still smell the place, taste it at the back of my throat, see the shimmering heat on the horizon when I close my eyes. And I can still hear the two of them, his laugh and her cry. The truth is they never even exchanged a word.

Why didn't I tell you before? I always seemed to be telling you, but my tongue did not move against the silence. There are certain things that take time to emerge from the body, pictures stored behind the eyelids that begin one day to fall, clattering. Clattering. And with all this stuff in the newspapers about uncovering the truth you get to thinking about what exactly happened and why it happened and what the truth of it is.

The girl was there while her brothers were not. It was nothing personal. How you hate it when I talk about what is and is not personal. Even in your absence I am sure of your response. How can you rape a girl and say it's nothing personal? Did your uniforms give you some kind of indemnity so that you were no longer yourselves, so that what you did was not personal? I explain it as a vicarious 'contact', to use the military term, with her brothers at large in the bush. It was, after all, a war that we returned from. And not a glorious war. No, a war fought in another people's country against their sons and daughters. And the Generaal and the Kommandant stood up and spoke about the 'aanslag' and how we were there to fight the global expansion of demonic Communism. The rhetoric wore thin like the soles of boots on an eternal, mindless parade. Most of us just wanted to get it finished and return to our real lives. I remember how the mud used to cake in the sun after the rains, and then crack and curl slowly from the edges as the sun claimed its moisture, and then crumble in the attrition of the relentless heat. And the flies feasting on the wet of your back.

He was silent as we walked back to base. Not the kind of silence which is just an absence of words — all of us had to observe silence on patrols. Rather, it was something in his body, his walk. He seemed to have lost the wobbliness of his head. He was stiffer. I wondered if he had grown up at last, this boy who kept photos of his mother and sister in the cover of his pay book, who read the good book every night. Had he at last shed his naïvety?

Back at base he played cards with us in the tent, an unlit cigarette at the corner of his mouth. He smiled when we ribbed him about his Woolworths vests and those parcels from his mother with neat compartments of home-made biscuits and Reader's Digests and raisins and melted chocolate. But he said nothing and made none of his usual attempts to lead us to reason. His quietness spread to us. There were the sounds of cards slapping on the upturned trommel in the heat, an occasional belch, or phlegm hawked in the nostrils. The smell of sweat and cigarette smoke. No one ventured a clinched string of curses at his luck or the customary jokes about Pik and PW and Nujoma, the leaking boat on the Cunene and the crocodile, but no one left the tent either. Everyone focused on the game as if it were not just rearranging a pack of pocket-worn cards stained with rifle oil three thousand kilometres from home.

I don't remember how the game ended.

Much later the tent quivered around me with the explosion next door. I struggled out with the others. We found Terence with one leg folded up to his chest, the other extended straight down along his rifle. His head was bowed as if in prayer. He had curled a narrow, ugly, long-nailed big toe around the trigger as he held the barrel againt his chest. No, the trinket – a plastic astrological symbol, probably made in Taiwan and bought on the streets of Windhoek by a brother or boyfriend – was not lying between his feet like some tribal fetish.

And I know you will not come back, that this thing which I carried inside me for so long like a corpse has now come out of me and that it is intolerable to you. But what I wanted to tell you, what I wanted you to know about Terence, about how I found him lying there, was that he wore the trinket on his person. Around his neck.

Free range

DAVID MEDALIE

Simon was a man who took care. His parents and his brother had all died before they were sixty five and he had no intention of following them to what he considered an unacceptably early grave. Being an atheist, he had no hopes of an after-life; all the more reason, then, to remain alive as long as possible, before oblivion put an end to it all. Simon had longevity as an earnest ambition. He became strategic about his lifestyle and diet. He would buy only the meat and eggs of free-range chickens and he never ate the skin. Red meat was out of the question. Biltong he considered to be nothing less than salted suicide. He avoided dessert for so long that eventually he came to believe that it was only for greedy people and so his objections to it became moral as well as nutritional. As he grew older, life seemed to him more and more a matter of fending off dangers.

Simon always advised people to choose their parents carefully if they wanted a long and healthy life – it was his favourite joke. Despite the poor genetic inheritance that his parents had handed on to him and which had not spared his brother (who was younger than he), Simon was adamant that there would be no determinism in his genes, only redemptive possibilities. He set what he was born with against himself as an antagonist and fought against it. His efforts met with success. He began to look upon his dead brother with sad regret and a faint contempt for his passivity. Simon achieved a cholesterol level that would make people twenty years younger than he feel satisfied; his blood pressure was better than normal for his age. He was not overweight. He grew enamoured of the notion that he had played an active role in ensuring that his late middle age was not blighted with illness. There is no greater solace, he believed increasingly, than taking control of one's own life. Let others dream of Elysium; for him the most potent myth was the one in which the little boy put his finger in the dyke and stemmed the catastrophic flow.

But his satisfaction was short-lived. Simon found that he began to be oppressed from another direction. Having conquered indolence through regular exercise and appetite through a strict diet, he found that he was left with the unbearably threatening fact that he lived in one of the most dangerous cities in the world. He dreaded reading the newspaper and yet he read every page of it, morbidly. Not a day seemed to go by without someone – usually an elderly person who lived alone, as he did – being murdered in his or her home. Every day people were hijacked. The lucky ones survived, the others were killed. Johannesburg seemed to Simon to have become a place of siege, where the have-nots lay in wait and the haves lay in fear. As he took his vitamin supplements, his garlic-and-celery pills, his fish-oil tablets, as he continued to ensure that he drank one glass of red wine every night, all he could think was that in statistical terms he was more likely to be murdered, living in Johannesburg, than any person living in any other place, except where there was an acknowledged war. That made him tense; then he considered that tension affects one adversely, so he grew tense about being tense; that made him think that Johannesburg was killing him through fear, if not through crime. The teeth were snapping shut. What to do? What to do?

After a short period of morose self-pity, he became vigorously active on his own behalf. He sold his expensive motor car and bought a modest second-hand one that suited him very well. Modest second-hand cars, he determined, are also in danger, but they are statistically less likely to be hijacked. Simon decided to put statistics on his side, rather than against him. Then he set out to make his house more secure. He already had bars on the windows, but they were not very sturdy; also, they were on the outside of the windows. He had them replaced with much thicker ones on the inside, which were cemented into the window sills. The rationale for this, according to the expert advice that he sought, was that it is extremely difficult to saw through bars or lever them away from the wall through broken glass, which was what the would-be burglars or assailants would have to do. That was very expensive, but Simon did not hesitate in having it done – it was an investment in his future. Then he had a wrought-iron door put in the passage which separated his bedroom from the rest of the house. It had a special key which could not be replicated. He locked this door at night. This meant that if intruders got into his house, they would not be able to get to him in the bedroom.

This was not all. The next thing was to have a sophisticated alarm system installed. There were panic buttons in every room in the house and scanners with red eyes that winked at him conspiratorially whenever he moved. He felt that he was being watched by his own house, which was a strange feeling; but soon he grew accustomed to it and considered that he had transformed his comfortable domestic existence into a sentry, standing guard on his behalf. It was not enough, in these straitened times, for his environment to offer him comfort only. It had to be watchful too.

Then he bought a gun. This was a difficult decision and he agonised over it for a long time. What put him off was not so much the thought of having to use it or even of having to kill someone in self-defence; it was, rather, the statistics which suggested that people who owned a gun were in danger of being killed by that same gun, either through having it go off accidentally, or through having it used against them by someone else. But eventually he was persuaded by the argument that the mishaps occurred only when gun owners used them carelessly or injudiciously or ineffectively; so he determined that he would be guilty of none of these. He went for lessons and learned how to shoot. He turned out to be good at it, which was both surprising and encouraging. Then, having taken expert advice as to what would suit him best, he bought the gun. He kept it near him and treated it with reverential care, seeing himself more as its custodian than as its owner. The distinction was a fine one, but Simon upheld it, for it might save his life.

Other precautions were available to him. He went out at night less and less; then he almost never went out after dark. He accepted lunch invitations, but never dinner invitations. He decided that he would not go to the city centre unless it were really necessary. Then he realised that it never was really necessary, so he did not go there at all. He began to avoid areas that he considered unsafe. His old friend Leon lived in one such area, so he tried to get Leon to come to him every time they met. When Leon tired of the lack of reciprocity in these arrangements, Simon stopped seeing him altogether. He accepted sadly that Leon's disappointment and the fading of the long-standing friendship were the price of self-preservation. When Leon was mugged outside his flat a few weeks later, Simon felt sorry for him, yet vindicated at the same time.

He found that he needed to leave his home less and less. He cancelled his subscription at the gym and bought several pieces of gym equipment instead, including an exercise bicycle. He discovered that some of the better stores would deliver food and groceries, so he opened accounts and bought exclusively from them. He knew that he was becoming a recluse, but who is not a recluse during a siege? He knew also that his wealth was protecting him from harm. Indeed, he could think of no better use for it. If his money was what people were after, then his money had better do something to protect itself. He had not been passive when it came to his health; he was certainly not going to be passive when he needed to defend himself. Over and over he told himself that he lived in the Murder Capital of the world. Murder Capital. Murder Capital. These were words of fearful fascination, like Beelzebub or Mephistopheles.

After the gun came an electrified fence around the property, as well as a Rottweiler called Nemesis. Simon knew that he could not allow himself to relax or become complacent, not even for a moment, for, when life is threatened daily, vigilance must infect daily life; but he did grant himself some credit for realising, before he became a victim or a crime statistic, that the danger was not an amorphous, generalised threat, but rather something that required an expeditious intervention in his own life and living arrangements.

Then he was invited to a meeting of the residents of his suburb, where the problem of soaring crime in their area was to be addressed. At the meeting, an accountant (who lived four houses away) and a restaurant-owner (who lived in the next street) proposed a drastic scheme. Simon was astounded to hear what they were suggesting: he had not considered for a moment that such a thing could be feasible. The idea was that they seal off the suburb and restrict it to residents. Simon liked the plan from the start, but he felt convinced that it would, regrettably, either be impractical or legally impossible. The acountant and the restaurant-owner assured the people at the meeting that it was neither. The suburb was small; it had no main thoroughfares running through it; it was possible to limit access through three points of entry, each of which could be manned by armed guards. Anyone who was not a resident would have to sign in under the supervision of these guards, who would record the person's name, number-plate and the make and colour of the vehicle. Another suburb had recently been granted permission by the municipal authorities to fence itself in in this way. That suburb had already recorded a dramatic fall in crime.

The residents were asked to think it over. A fortnight later, another meeting was held at the restaurant-owner's house. Although it was at night, Simon broke his rule and went to it. An armed guard was employed to look after the residents' cars while the meeting was in progress. Simon believed that, if it were feasible, everyone would support the initiative. He found that he was wrong. The accountant and the restaurant-owner had the support of an orthopaedic surgeon, a retired insurance broker and two optometrists. But they found vehement opposition in an oncologist, a clinical psychologist, a physiotherapist, another accountant and two dentists. Simon did not speak up on behalf of the plan, but he turned repeatedly to the couple seated next to him and said, 'What else can we do? Something has got to be done. What else can we do?' Afterwards he found that they were amongst the opponents of the scheme. The accountant and the restaurant-owner asked the meeting for a mandate to investigate the practical and legal situation. They undertook to speak to the committee from the suburb that was already successfully enclosed and to establish the best course of action. A vote was taken and the mandate was granted by a narrow margin.

At the next meeting, the situation was more acrimonious and the two sides more entrenched in their positions. The oncologist said that the moral implications bothered him more than the legal ones. Officialdom might grant them permission, but that didn't mean that they ought to proceed. He argued that the roads in the suburb were public property; they should not treat them as their own private property. Nor should they use the power of their affluence – he should say their *relative* affluence – to cut themselves off from the rest of the country, especially since it was the new South Africa, where barriers were supposed to be coming down. The proposed enclosure of the suburb would not be dealing with crime – it would be driving it elsewhere. South Africa had only recently come out of the laager: he had no intention of allowing anyone to drive him back into it. The clinical psychologist said that she would not live in such a suburb; she would sell her house. Simon was not persuaded at all by what they said, for the restaurant-owner kept repeating bluntly that 'what this is about is saving lives', and he found that to be the most eloquent and cogent argument of all. At that meeting the anti-enclosure side narrowly won the vote, much to his surprise. Their arguments seemed to him to be full of delicate qualms, quite out of place in an emergency. The accountant and the restaurant-owner vowed that the matter would not end there.

Simon berated himself for not volunteering to do something as well; after all, he had the time. But he had never been that sort of person. He would sign petitions if he needed to and he would contribute towards the building of the wall which, if they prevailed, would enclose the suburb, and towards the guards' salaries, but he was prepared to leave it to others to make the arrangements. For months he had read letters to the newspapers in which people lamented the descent of Johannesburg into a state of anarchy, describing (invariably) how they had greeted the advent of the New South Africa with euphoria, but now they were bitter and fearful and thinking of emigrating. He sympathised with these sentiments, but he never wrote any letters himself. If a feeling is prevalent, he believed, it will find expression. Others more articulate than he would give vent to the widespread disquiet.

Then, when people began to write letters to the local newspaper about the dispute in his own suburb, Sterling Park, he felt suddenly that it was simply not good enough to hold that attitude. His apathy was reprehensible. He had not submitted meekly to his unenviable genetic endowment, he had done everything to protect himself when the security situation worsened. Now he should use that same determination on behalf of the beleaguered suburb. His resolve was strengthened by an incident two streets away in which a man, returning from work, was hijacked in his driveway and shot twice. He was in hospital in a critical condition. The local newspaper that week reported the incident prominently and included statistics which showed that the situation in the suburb was deteriorating; but it also carried a letter by the oncologist, reiterating his objections to the proposal to enclose the suburb. He concluded by referring more explicitly to the affluence of the residents. Money, he said, cannot buy everything – at least, it shouldn't be allowed to. Money should always be held responsible.

Something in this letter stirred Simon. He decided to write back. It would be the first time he had ever written a letter to the press. The fact that it was a local newspaper with a relatively small distribution was somehow consoling to him. He also liked the idea that he was writing to his neighbours about something that affected them all. He saw his letter as an act of community. He felt unusually public-spirited. This is what he wrote:

Sir
The letter by Dr Jenkins, published in your Letters Page on 24 March, requires a response. Dr Jenkins is hopelessly out of touch with public opinion. He is concerned about the rights of the public, but what about the rights of those who are killed or assaulted or robbed daily? This does not bother him unduly. Dr Jenkins forgets that we live in the Murder Capital of the World. We have to find ways of dealing with this emergency. Building a wall around Sterling Park is a sound and practical idea. We should give it our full support. Surely anything is better than being killed for our possessions, or becoming the victim of an act of irrational hatred?

He thought of signing it 'Concerned Resident', but, in the spirit of his new activism and social commitment, he signed his name and included his address. He suspected that his letter would not be published – no doubt, many of the residents would write in to take issue with the oncologist, and their letters would probably be far more forceful and persuasive than his. But, to his surprise, it was published the following week. He read it over several times and felt quite proud of it. Except for the fact that the 'unduly' appeared as 'unduely', which bothered him because he did not wish people to think that he couldn't spell correctly, he saw nothing in it that was unworthy. It was short, to the point, and full of sound logic.

The following week he was flattered to find that a number of people had written in response to his letter. One person, identified only as 'Worried About Crime', wrote that Simon's letter, in focusing as it did on the very real peril that they faced, showed that Dr Jenkins and those who supported him were satisfying their own ideas of morality and conscience at the cost of other people's lives. Another letter-writer, after stating briefly that she agreed with Simon, went on to recount at some length her experience of being hijacked one morning on the way to work. Simon felt gratified that his letter could have prompted such responses. He had begun to keep a file of all the articles and letters relating to the controversy and he added the latest batch, noting with pleasure that the number of letters in favour of the proposal far outweighed the number of dissenting responses.

A meeting of the supporters of the proposal was held at the accountant's home to consider strategy. People congratulated Simon on his letter and this time he did stand up to speak, emboldened by the success of the letter-writing. He said that he thought they should canvass opinion in the suburb to ascertain the attitudes of those residents who didn't come to meetings: they needed to know whether or not the majority of the residents of Sterling Park was behind them. People supported his suggestion and it was decided that a questionnaire would be distributed to every resident. Simon felt pleased with himself. There was something intoxicating about being part of a swelling consensus; he regretted that he had not involved himself in community activities before. The meeting ended with one resident offering to draw up and photocopy the questionnaire, another offering to put one in every postbox in the suburb, and Simon found himself volunteering to collate all the results once the questionnaires were in. Consequently, it was decided that residents would be asked to place completed questionnaires in his postbox. Then someone proposed that a name – something catchy – should be found for those who were working to bring the proposal to fruition. Several possibilities were considered, but they finally settled on CLASP (Campaign to Limit Access to Sterling Park). Simon went home feeling proud and surprised: he had been elected onto the committee of CLASP.

After that, things moved quickly. The questionnaires were drawn up and distributed and posters urging people to support CLASP and save lives appeared on tree trunks and lamp posts. The completed questionnaires began to trickle in. Simon became more interested in the contents of his postbox than he had been for years. At first almost all the respondents were in favour of the proposal, but after a while an increasing number of votes against it came in. Simon calculated the total every evening, and although those favourably disposed were still ahead, he noticed that their lead was narrowing. What alarmed him was a note that he found one day amongst the questionnaires, addressed to him (although his name was wrongly spelt). It said: STOP WHAT YOU DOING WE WILL KILL YOU. A few days later there was another one: IF YOU DO THIS YOU DIE. Simon didn't know what to make of them – was it a joke? He showed them to the restaurant-owner, who told him to ignore them. He tried to heed this advice, but found that he couldn't. He became anxious about what he would find in his letter box and the pleasant curiosity that he had begun to enjoy dissipated.

One day he went out briefly and returned to find a message on his answering machine. A thick and muffled voice, scarcely distinguishable, said, YOU DIE SOON, YOU DIE. YOU MUST STOP WHAT YOU DOING. Simon went to the police with the notes and the recorded message. They were so uninterested in his complaint that he had to urge them to even take down the details. The less concerned other people were, the more his anxiety grew. He began to sleep badly. When he did manage to fall asleep, Nemesis would bark and he would wake with a jolt. He got up repeatedly during the night to make sure that he had set the alarm before he went to bed. He kept opening the drawer next to his bed to check that the gun was close at hand.

The questionnaires continued to trickle in. Simon watched the lead that CLASP had established at the beginning grow smaller and smaller. For a while the two sides were equal, then the votes against enclosing the suburb drew ahead. Every day the situation grew worse. Nonetheless, he continued to believe that it would turn in their favour again. He could not accept that there were more people who sympathised with the views of the oncologist and the clinical psychologist than those who felt that staying alive was the most important thing in life. How could so basic and primal a need not overrule all else? Eventually the questionnaires stopped coming in and Simon had to present the final tally. CLASP had lost by nineteen votes. After imparting the news, he awaited what he believed to be the inevitable response: a renewed campaign, more letters, door-to-door discussions with those who had votes against it to persuade them to change their minds. He was prepared to participate fully in all of these efforts. However, he was astonished to find that nothing of the sort was proposed. The members of CLASP accepted their defeat with dismaying resignation. Even the accountant and the restaurant-owner gave in. The accountant said he would sell his house and move – either to the suburb that had enclosed itself, or into a town-house complex where there were armed guards and surveillance twenty four hours a day. The restaurant-owner said his wife had been urging him to emigrate; he thought after this that perhaps she was right.

Simon went home full of flat, chilly sadness. He wished that he had never had anything to do with CLASP at all. To see all his enthusiasm and energy come to nothing was devastating. He felt bitter and angry. If people were attacked or murdered in Sterling Park after this, they would have no one but themselves to blame. But what if the victim were someone like him, someone who had fought for the plan? Then it would be his unreasonable, impervious neighbours, full of moral niceties, who would be culpable. The very community that he had sought to protect would then be an accomplice in the crime.

There was another message on the machine. The same indistinct voice said, WE COMING FOR YOU. YOU MUST DIE SOON. Simon unplugged the phone and the answering machine. He went to the corner café, which stayed open till late at night, and bought what he had scorned for years: chocolates, salty potato crisps, marshmallows, ice cream and biltong. The biltong didn't look very good – it was greyish and gnarled, but he bought it anyway. At home, instead of doing his exercises, he sat in front of the television and began to eat what he had bought. Hours went by. There was nothing good on the television, but he watched it anyway. Then a late movie came on. It was Audrey Hepburn in *Wait Until Dark*. For years Simon had refused to watch thrillers, as a matter of taste and principle. But he watched this one, with the lights switched off. The television cast rushing shapes and shadows on the wall behind him.

Walking the road of death

PETER HORN

The road was deserted. Something was wrong. He mumbled
that he had to do something about it. If only I were ... But he
was unable to complete his thought. Sometimes his thoughts
were going off into nowhere at all. He had noticed that and
every time it happened, he became very angry. It was as if a
sheet of black rain enveloped his thinking and all images in
his mind went dark. Then a blinking knife cut through his
darkness, gleaming in the light of the moon, and it was light
again, but his thoughts were gone, he could not remember
them at all. A knife and blood.

Somebody was very pale, but he did not remember who.
There were bars all around him then, but that was a long
time ago.

This is the place where they are fighting all the time, he
thought. 'I shouldn't walk here,' somebody said, 'I shouldn't
walk here, it was too dangerous.' But the road was deserted.

Nobody walked. No cars were driving anywhere. Nobody
was shooting either. But something was wrong. He saw the
blood running down the street, the massive wall of a wave
breaking over his head, and all the houses were on fire. As he
focused again, the street looked quite normal again, except
that it was totally empty. Nobody. Nobody at all.

Most houses along the stretch of road which was visible to
Stofile were gutted by fire, most walls showed a profusion of
bullet marks. He thought that that was weird. Crazy. Unusual.
A few cars were standing abandoned along the sides of the
road, one had been burned out.

Strangely enough, none of them seemed to have been van-
dalised. The tyres had not been removed, and from one even
the radio was still blaring. A very serious voice said, 'Yes, yes,

but there is the provision in the constitution that every person shall have the right to life.'

Another voice, the voice of a woman with an African accent, was heard laughing, 'Now that's a good one, that is really a good one. You are not suggesting seriously that ...' There was a moment of silence, and then the earnest voice was heard again over a confusion of voices: 'But why do you say that? Don't you think that that is a central and important provision of our new constitution? It is my considered opinion that without the right to life all other provisions are meaningless.'

At that moment the radio, which had been on since two o'clock at night when the driver and his wife were shot, suddenly became silent. Probably the car battery had run empty. With the last human voice gone, an eerie silence hung over the street. Not even the twitter of a bird disrupted this silence. Stofile peered into the car, noticed the two motionless figures, and said, 'Hell, no, this is Andile!'

He banged on the car roof and said, 'He! Andile, wake up, man, wake up, it is morning.'

Andile did not move. The blood which had soaked his shirt had dried to a dark black-red.

Stofile was confused. He went over to the other side, and opened the door. The body of Andile's wife, Nodoli, slid towards him in slow motion until it sprawled on the dusty road, her head thrown back, her arms next to her body, with her legs still caught in the car. The red puncture in her head released a lazy welling of fresh blood.

'What is wrong with the two of you?' Stofile cried. Then he sighed, 'They don't have a head. Why do they sleep here in the middle of the road, and on a weekday in the bright morning sun? Hey, are you not ashamed to be drunk on a sunny morning like this?'

At that moment he heard the police sirens. He looked around and then moved slowly towards a house without a door and a blackened burned door frame. When the casspir turned the corner, he had disappeared into the house. As soon as the police vehicle came into view, there were scattered shots. Some of them seemed to come from the hostel on the low hill at the end of the road, others from the houses further up the other side of the road. As the casspir moved down the road, more and more shots ricocheted off the armour with a loud clang. Some of the shots hit the houses and added a few new scars to their pocked surface.

Stofile mumbled, 'I am no rabbit! I won't run away and hide in the bowels of the earth. I am not the running kind. They can't frighten me any more. Not me, Stofile. What is all this about? Has the world come to an end? Is everything going to burn to the ground? This is all wrong and crazy.'

There were shots from the casspir as well, but they were aimless. The marksmen on both sides were invisible except for an occasional puff of smoke from a window of the hostel.

'You fools, you bloody fools,' whispered Stofile as he was lying on the floor behind an opening which used to be a window. 'If you go on like this, the sun is going to go black and the grass is going to wilt. Babies will die instead of being born. Our oxen will walk into the caves of yesterday.'

As the casspir reached the car, the radio came to life again with a strongly rhythmic song, and as it ebbed away the same very serious voice started talking again: 'Well, in this part of the discussion we are going to look at economic activity, labour relations and property.' An angry voice interjected: 'What property? I don't have any property! We blacks have been robbed of our heritage. The new constitution is merely making sure that nothing changes. You are going to remain the haves, and we are going to remain the have nots.' The serious voice said, 'Now, now. I am sure you are exaggerating. What about your car? And as far as I know you have a very nice place down in Yeoville. Now that is property, and as such it is protected by the constitution. Like everybody else's.'

The voice faded, as the radio crackled for a moment and then went into a high-pitched whine. The casspir had stopped, but none of its crew appeared. Instead the gun fire intensified, and bullets came whining through the window opening and the burnt-out door. Stofile cowered on the floor, sweating. The marksmen from the hostel and those from the township renewed their fire and for five minutes there was a nearly ceaseless noise of shots. Then the fire died down on all three sides, and into the silence the very serious voice could be heard saying: 'Well, the effect of that could be a great deal of litigation swamping our courts. If in every case we will have to go into the history of the acquisition of the property, that will keep thousands of lawyers busy for many years.' The angry voice interjected: 'That is probably the reason for this clause. Whites want to hold on to their ill-gotten gains, if necessary with the help of the law, lawyers and the courts. Why not proceed from the premise that all land in this country belonged to the original inhabitants and was stolen by the white settlers. The onus would then be on the settlers to prove their claim to any land they hold.'

Several shots hit the car, but did not silence the learned voices. At that moment Stofile thought he had noticed a movement in the deserted house. In the half darkness he couldn't see clearly what it was, until the boy slipped in next to him, cowered behind the window-shelf, and laid down his gun. He was not more than twelve, judging from his size.

'Why is everyone making such a noise?' Stofile complained.

'Are you a bird? Do you want to fly away?' asked the boy contemptuously. 'No need. Nobody is going to shoot a madman.'

'I am not a madman,' protested Stofile.

'Only madmen walk this road,' said the youth. 'Everybody knows that you are crazy, and that's why nobody shoots you.' After a pause he added, as if to explain, 'You are neither ANC nor PAC nor IFP. So there is no reason for anybody to shoot you.'

'But I am,' said Stofile.

'Which of the three?' asked the youth.

'I am all three of them,' said Stofile.

'There, you see, you are crazy as a coot,' said the youth. 'You have to be either the one or the other. Or you would fight yourself all the time.'

Stofile turned away from him, sulking.

In the silence they could hear an advertisement for furniture and electrical appliances which were on sale at a special low price. Then the radio shifted into one of those mindless pieces of bubble-gum music, which made the morning appear listlessly jolly and filled with a friendly emptiness. The casspir still stood next to the car with the bodies of Andile and his wife.

The shooting had stopped for the moment. Everybody seemed to be waiting for the next move of the others.

'Oh, why am I laughed at by the birds?' Stofile cried out softly. 'Why does nobody show me and my white hairs any respect?' Suddenly he started to jump up and shout: 'I am not crazy, and you, little boy, should show me some respect. Do you hear me? I am not, I am not, I am not!'

'Shut up,' said the boy. 'Be quiet, or they will shoot us.'

As if to corroborate his view, the police started shooting again. Stofile ducked quickly behind the windowsill. One shot ricocheted off the back wall and came screaming towards them and buried itself deep in the muscles of the boy's thigh. The boy screamed, grabbed his gun, knelt behind the windowsill, and started to fire wildly through the window frame towards the casspir, but suddenly collapsed back onto the floor again, moaning and crying.

While the police went on shooting in all directions, the casspir's back doors were suddenly flung open, two policemen with bullet-proof vests emerged and dragged the body of Andile into the casspir, his shoes dragging through the dust of the dirt road, then returned into the gunfire which had erupted again in full strength, to fetch the body of his wife, Nodoli. This was no time for niceties. They grabbed her arms, her head dangling between her shoulders.

One of them started to run towards the house in which Stofile and the boy were hiding, but suddenly fell to the ground clasping his arm. Two other policemen stormed out of the casspir and dragged him too, back into the casspir. The driver revved the engine of the casspir, and did a fast turn on the road which was still under fire from all sides. Then the casspir retreated at full speed, its sirens blaring into the distance. In the ensuing silence the voice of the radio was back, declaiming

that every child shall have the right to a name and nationali-
ty as from birth, to parental care, to security, basic nutrition
and basic health and social services.

'Did you go to school?' Stofile asked the boy.

'Yes, why?'

'Do you understand what the voice in the language of the
white man is saying on the radio?'

'Yes, I do, in a way, but it is all rubbish, just bloody boere
propaganda.' He spat disdainfully: 'Bloody hogwash!'

He lifted himself up on his knees again, aimed his gun, and
fired. The radio was silenced.

'You must not believe what they tell you,' the youngster
said. 'It is all bloody sell-out propaganda.'

The boy's shot was answered by a few more desultory shots
from the hostel and the township, then there was silence
again. While they were waiting for the shooting to start again,
Stofile asked the youth: 'So, what is your name? I am Stofile.'

'I am Lenin,' said the boy earnestly. 'That is my MK-name.'

'What is "Lenin"?' the old man asked. 'I have never heard
that name before. It doesn't sound Xhosa.'

'Lenin is the great revolutionary. The great African freedom fighter. He died some time ago, but he started the Great
Revolution,' the boy said.

'Why are you not in school? Why are you carrying this gun
and shooting at people?'

'They stole our school.'

'Stole your school?'

'Yes, they stole it. People who have been driven out of here.'
He pointed vaguely down the street. 'They need to have houses, so they took from the school whatever they needed to
build their shacks. One Saturday morning the buildings were
all still there, and that same day in the evening there was
just an empty space.'

'How is that? How can an entire school disappear in just
one day?'

'Well, there are a lot of homeless people around here, and
everyone took what he could.' Then he added as if it were an

afterthought: 'But this school was no good anyway. It was all this Bantu Education, where they taught you how to be a good "boy".' He spat out the word 'boy' as if it was poison. 'Just bloody sell-out propaganda like all the rest.' After a while Stofile said, 'I think we can go now. Shall I carry you or can you walk if I support you?'

'Hell, no, I can't walk out onto this street. They are going to shoot me immediately.'

'But you are losing blood.'

'If I walk out onto the street, I am going to lose even more blood. I am going to be stone-dead.'

'Not if I carry you. Nobody ever shoots at me.'

'I am going to wait until it is dark,' the boy said, but he carefully avoided looking down at his leg. He did not want to see how the blood seeped through the legs of his trousers and formed a pool underneath him.

'But aren't you in pain? You need a doctor. Mind you, not that I trust these doctors any more than you do. They kept me in a prison for years. They said that I was crazy, but I am not. I tell you, I am not.'

'Yes, it hurts,' the boy said, 'but that is the price you pay for your liberation.'

They remained silent for a while. Then the boy suddenly jumped up, and limped onto the road, screaming, 'I will get you, you bloody bastards. One settler, one bullet.'

A few shots were fired from the hostel, and falling on his belly, the youth returned the fire, and then crawled back into the burned-out house.

'If somebody is crazy in this house, it is you,' Stofile said. 'Running into the street and shooting at nobody in particular. I mean that is asking for it. Do you want to be killed? What did you do that for? Now the shooting will start all over again, and they will not let you get away, after they have seen that you have a gun. They shoot at everyone with a gun.'

The boy looked at him sullenly, but did not answer. They sat, their back against the wall for a long time, not talking. Then the boy said, 'It hurts a lot.'

Stofile looked at him. He got up and walked out of the door onto the road. As he stepped out, the shooting started again, and he retreated quickly. Then the shooting stopped.

'It doesn't look as if we can leave here. At least not by the front door. Which way did you come?'

'Through the kitchen in the back.'

Stofile walked through the passage to the kitchen. The kitchen was empty. All furniture that had once stood there had been removed, even the sink had been yanked from the wall. The walls were blackened by a fire. The door was missing, and as Stofile moved towards the empty frame, more shots were fired. One missed him by a few inches. He quickly withdrew again into the passage.

'There is no way we can get out of here,' he told the boy. 'Now why did you have to start shooting, you moron?'

The boy did not move, but his face was contorted in pain. After a while he said, 'I am very thirsty.'

'There is no water here,' Stofile said, but he got up. 'I will go and look.'

'Don't leave me alone here,' the boy begged.

'No, I will come back. But I don't know where I will be able to get water.' He went to the front door again, and stepped out into the road. Again there was a short burst of gunfire, but Stofile went ahead, walking right into the shower of bullets, then the marksmen seemed to have recognised him and stopped shooting. Stofile walked unsteadily towards the hostel, mumbling to himself: 'Bloody fool, could have gotten myself hurt. All because of this mad schoolboy with a gun.' He knew there was no water anywhere nearer. When he approached the hostel he could see the guns trained on him from the windows. But he went on regardless.

The gate to the hostel was heavily barricaded. He stood in front of the gate and shouted, 'Water! Give me some water! The boy's hurt. He is thirsty.'

'Go away, you old fool,' somebody shouted from inside. 'That boy is ANC. We know him. He is a boss trouble-maker. The sooner he dies, the better.'

64

Stofile started banging on the gate: 'You idiots. You bastards. The boy is hurt. He wants water.'

Somebody fired a shot, not at him, but down the deserted road. Stofile looked around, but there was nobody he could see. Then somebody poured a pail of water over him. 'Run, you madman,' somebody shouted, 'or we are going to shoot. Run, run!'

Stofile turned away, his shoulders slumping in defeat, and trotted back down to the house where Lenin was waiting for him. While he walked there were a few more shots, but they were carefully aimed away from him, along the sides of the road. Just to show that they would not tolerate anyone else walking out of the house.

The comrades on the other side kept their fire, until he had reached the house and entered. Then they fired a few volleys towards their enemies in the hostel.

The boy's eyes were veiled and feverish, and he moaned softly when Stofile entered the house again. 'No water,' he said, 'sorry, but the people at the hostel don't like you. They say they know you, and that you are a boss trouble-maker. They wouldn't be sorry to see you dead.'

The boy just breathed: 'Water, dad, water. Please, get me something to drink.'

Stofile stood at the window and looked at the boy. His mind was racing. A wave of black water engulfed his brain and all images in his mind went dark. Suddenly he screamed, 'Stop!' and let out a howl which diminished into a screech. He raced out into the blinding sun of the deserted street, and while he confronted his own blinking knife in his head, his thoughts were gone and he could not remember them at all. Blood. His clothes were strangling him, and there in the open road he started to tear his shirt off his chest, pulled down his trousers and stood there naked in his gleaming blackness. For a moment he swayed in the sunlight, then he broke down, fell on the road and rolled about in the dust until his body was the red colour of the road. In the end his body just lay there, immovable.

The boy had raised himself on his knees, and watched him

through the empty window frame. He was shivering, and there was fear in his eyes. He saw the body there on the road, lying still, for a long time. I can't go out there, he thought. I can't. They are going to shoot me.

He attempted to get up, but the wound in his thigh was hurting so much that he collapsed again onto the floor.

I can't walk out into this street. They are going to shoot me immediately. If I walk out onto the street, I am going to be dead. Anyway, I can't walk. And I definitely can't carry him. He is much too heavy.

The boy was lying there, moaning. When he had regained some strength, he hauled himself up again, holding onto the windowsill. Without stepping on his right leg, he pulled himself upright and started to hobble towards the door.

'He, Stofile,' he cried, 'what happened to you?'

Stofile did not answer. His eyes stared at the boy, not comprehending the situation. But one of his legs started twitching, and then he lifted himself up on one arm. Slowly he rose from the red dust of the road, a red naked body with dull eyes.

'Are you hurt?' he asked.

'Don't you remember?'

'What?'

'How the police shot at us?'

Stofile looked at him in a puzzled way. 'The police?'

'Yes!'

Somebody was very pale, but he did not remember who. There were bars all around him then, but that was a long time ago. He did not remember the police or this boy. ·

'Come,' he said to the boy, 'I am going to help you'.

'But they are going to shoot me.'

'Nobody is going to shoot at Stofile.'

He came over to the door, took Lenin's arm, placed it over his shoulder, and started to walk with Lenin limping along.

As they walked away from the hostel, the street was entirely deserted. The two lone figures on the street made a good target. But there was no shot until they had rounded the first corner.

66

The promised land

BARRY LEVY

The sun beat down, a hot knife, peeling the skin. It was their third week here, a Friday morning and something they had taken to, all of them, that is, the three of them, when they had nothing better to do – lying on the beach, sapping up the sun. Just like when they were younger and the kids were smaller and they were all together on holidays in Cape Town, or Durban, which Australia's Gold Coast reminded them most of. True, this was no promised land in the sense of Jerusalem, Israel, but who wanted to go there and stay forever anyway? Israel was good for a visit, a poke-around to see where the money you were donating was going to, a glimpse into your history. But to stay, no, it would be like jumping out of a frying pan straight into a fire. Instead of pogroms, now they died in wars. There wasn't much difference, maybe it was worse. If there was a chance of avoiding bloodshed then it had to be taken, especially when there were children involved, Ben Isaacs thought, as he lay back on his gigantic towel on the white, grainy beach sand.

So many generations of useless cruelty; all you had to do was look back at your own parents, may their souls rest in peace, escaping the pogroms of Russia, Lithuania, arriving in wet and overcrowded London and farmed out like plants to the colonies: South Africa, the New World, land of gold. And yet they had made it, most of them anyway. It showed a certain resilience, a certain enterprise. Chutzpah. Your father with his city clothing shop, which you turned into an even bigger clothing store with two suburban branches. They had given you the money to control your future, choose your destination, escape the violence that was burning South Africa; that would roast your own white skin if you did not make use of your chances.

You had to take advantage of every opportunity, like your parents had done, saving themselves from the pogroms and who knows, maybe even the gas ovens; at any rate, certain bloody death under Hitler's boot-heels, by getting out of Eastern Europe when they did, by leaving with next to nothing to start somewhere else. On another continent, in another world. It had to be done. You didn't want your children to have to live through the violence. Not in their own backyard. That was why Israel was fine in theory, but in practice, in reality, a last, a very final last resort. And definitely not if you had the money and still wanted to make the most of your life, what was left of it, turn it into a quiet, peaceful little fling before the lumbago, the arthritis got too bad and you couldn't move at all. Then, when that happened, maybe Israel. Then it would make no difference. But for now, based on what he had seen on a previous trip, a 'business-reconnaissance' trip about a year ago, to add weight to the word of his brother Max who had already moved here about five years ago, and who had implanted the vision in the first place even before that, this would be it, their Promised Land, land of milk and honey. Maybe it wasn't as close to everything as they were used to, the shul, Jewish schools, Israel, Europe, America, and there weren't as many of their own, yet there were enough to remind them of who they were. Anyway, at least it was peaceful, hot but peaceful. The Gold Coast, Surfers' Paradise, somehow it had a ring about it not quite of an exotic island, but of something fresh and of youth; a new world, a world that you felt you were at the beginning of and had a place in, not like South Africa where you were born and bred and yet only now, at sixty years of age, were beginning to discover that maybe it wasn't your own country after all, that maybe it wasn't the beautiful, unshakable haven you had thought it was. It had been good to you, but would it be the same for your children? One fed up, had already left, for the United Kingdom. But who wanted to end up there, cold, miserable, stiff upper-lipped or too crazy; not the place to finish out your days, you could better spend your days trapped in a cold shower. Had you only done this sooner maybe Stephen would still be with you, maybe he would still come now? There was still a chance the incessant damp in London would bear him down and he would come back to you, in this land of no extremes. He would enjoy Australia, there was no doubt. There was lots of room for people with enterprise and ambition and new ideas to build their way up. So he would write and keep on writing and sending him papers and brochures and more brochures to show this was as near enough to the promised land as anyone could ever get. After all, it was no good being an idealist, and he would urge Marlene to write too, to tell her brother so. Only seven years younger than Stevie, there was a greater connection between them. What she would have to say would make him think, would twist his arm a bit. Australia wasn't really that far away. Not in today's world anyway.

Marlene Isaacs had drifted off to sleep. When she awoke, through her still barely open, squinting eyes, the light from the sun streaked into her pupils; it was almost like she could see a beam of sunlight stretching from her eyes to heaven; it was like she had been chosen. It was hot here, maybe too hot, but it was important to be able to send pictures back to the friends you had left behind of a well-browned body, a body that showed you really were in paradise. That life was easy, exciting, untroubled, a cradle rocking smoothly in your direction. The beach was getting crowded, even for a weekday morning, but she would not let that bother her. It had been a long time since she had lain around like this with her mother and father, all three of them together, sunning themselves, taking dips in the salty, wavy ocean, and just sitting there on the sand doing nothing but looking into the sun and at the shiny silvery water. Not at least since she was fourteen, on Durban's North Beach, and still too shy to move too far away from her parents, to the top end of the beach where Stevie sat with the gangs of teenage boys and girls who hung out there. Most of them were from Jo'burg, but many of them you didn't know, from suburbs you would not ordinarily find yourself in. Now they were all there, in one big clump, from all suburbs, rich and poor, some of them you knew or had seen around and many who were strangers, some you weren't even sure if they were Jewish, hanging around waiting, meeting, making arrangements. That's where you met Arnold, older and shyer than most of the others, a year-and-a-half ago, when you were seventeen. Arnold, so serious that when you let him sleep with you on that holiday, you knew the word would never get around; you knew inside there would be something permanent between you; not just a holiday fling. Now it was time to test the waters, those feelings. On the other hand, being honest, it was also a good break. But it also meant sitting around with the old folks again, like when you were fourteen, waiting for a miracle to come along and ask you on a date, or at least up to the wooden railings where everyone met. Or to the restaurant above for a toasted sandwich and milkshake.

There was no shortage of well-shaped bodies here, you had to say that, you had never seen so many in one place before, muscles rippling everywhere, bodies shining oily and golden, heads of hair bleached white in the sun. Nice to touch, but not Jewish. There were dangers here. Slowly you would get to know people, you were pretty confident of that. There was an air of ease, friendliness here. And in the end did it really matter if they were not Jewish? This was too nice a place to be despondent. It would happen. Definitely when you started varsity in a few weeks. The University of Queensland. It sounded strange, so that you had to repeat the name over and over to yourself, to convince yourself it was real. That you really were here, that you really were going to university, and that it was in Queensland. The campus was big, you'd seen it; there had to be a range of people to choose from. Wits would have been okay, but the truth was the campus was overcrowded, over-built, over-volatile. Even on visits there with friends, with Arnold, to special events, you felt the tension, you saw the signs on the walls – SUPPORT THE ANC! THE FREEDOM CHARTER! AMANDLA! – and read in the papers of police charges on the campus, of spies, of students clashing amongst themselves, of a new breed of black student who would stand on you if you came too close. It oppressed you like a heavy, prickly blanket. The secret fears of having to go to Wits University were over now; they, your parents, had understood without saying a word. You disagreed on many things, especially politics, they were so much older than you, too old when they had you. But deep inside they understood. You knew that now. As much as they had done it for themselves, they had done it for you. After all, their lives had almost been lived, yours only now awakening, something you could feel in the way you thought about things, as though from above, no longer from the side or even below. The world was beginning to take on new meanings, it was beginning to expand, but you had a better view of the surface. Arnold, you had to admit, had had something to do with it, he was a thinker, but not the thinker you wanted to be around for the rest of your life. It was time to see for yourself, to move on, to live away from the old folks, to see if the world could offer up any more than sweet old Arnold, who could be so cutting and dry it hurt ... like the build-up to leaving Jo'burg, telling him how good it would be to be away from the Afrikaner mentality, from apartheid.

'At least there's none of that crap over there,' you had said.

'No, they got rid of their Aborigines a long time ago – poisoned and shot them!' he had stabbed back smugly.

'Well, it's different now, everyone there is equal ... Anyway, I don't know enough about it to know if what you're saying is really true.'

'True enough for H.G. Wells to have written about it. To make a point of mentioning it as the world's worst genocide, the extermination of Tasmania's Aborigines.'

'What about Hitler?'

'Well, before Hitler, how bad do you have to get?'

'Well they're okay now ...' Why did you always have to go on the defensive? 'It's different there now, everyone is equal.'

Ja. Oh ja. Just perfect. A true egalitarian society. Well, for your information, Marlene Isaacs, because it looks like no one else is going to tell you, thirty percent of Aborigines are homeless or live in third-world conditions; infant mortality among Aborigines is four times higher than among white Australians; Aborigines still suffer from diseases whites thought were extinct; and the life expectancy is seventeen, *seventeen* years less than for other Australians.'

'Just because you're studying sociology, you think you know everything, don't you!'

'You don't have to go to varsity, you know ... all you have to do is read!'

'Anyway, at least no one's getting bashed and burnt and shot in the streets every damn day.'

'So, nor is anyone over here ... not in the white suburbs, anyway.'

It was true. All the violence you had heard about, you had read of in the papers. You had imagined you saw it with your own two eyes, but it wasn't here, it was in the papers, over there, in the townships, in the country towns, between themselves. Between themselves and the police. You had put down the paper and had said it was full of bloody deaths; weren't there better things to report? The only violence you'd ever really seen, a black woman, a friend of a neighbour's new maid, being thrown into the back of a big metal police van your mother called a Black Maria. You remembered the way the woman was picked up by a burly white policeman, as though she weighed nothing, was nothing, and was hurled head first into the van, that sensation inside of you of flesh tearing against metal. But you didn't really see the result of the violence, the woman's face, the blood in the steel cage; it was black in there and the thick steel gate was slammed shut. All you had felt inside of you was something you couldn't explain, something that hurt, that made your stomach turn, something you had to get away from, forget.

She looked around her and saw a blur of bodies, passing, sitting, running, shouting. She looked into the sun and it seemed to strike straight back at her so that she had to blink and turn her eyes away. It was hot, too hot. It was melting her. For a while longer she lay down flat and let the sun burn her, as though it were some kind of penance or atonement she had to perform. She picked up a handful of hot, dry, white sand and let it flow slowly out of the bottom of her fist. She turned her head to watch the steady stream of grains and imagined her hand was an hour-glass and that she was watching time run out. The last grains scratched and tickled her hand, it woke her out of the semi-stupor she seemed to have fallen into. Suddenly she sat up, crossing her legs.

'I'm going back to the flat.'

'Why don't you stay a little while longer?' Her mother was leaning back against a small canvas sand-chair, square under the shade of their rainbow-striped beach umbrella. 'We'll only be here another half an hour or so,' thinking it was strange for her daughter to want to leave the beach so soon. She lived for the sunshine. Maybe it was this unfamiliar new country getting to her. Eventually she would get to know people; they would start going to shul.

Ben Isaacs agreed. 'Stay a bit,' he said. 'What's the hurry? We'll come back with you.'

'No, I'm hell'va hot. I want to go now. I've had enough,' she pressed, feeling like their fourteen-year-old again, looking for a way out. 'Anyway I want to phone the estate agent about that unit in Toowong.' She liked the names of the places over here, there was something exotic about them, like Coorparoo, which sounded like it belonged to an island somewhere far away. She really was at a new beginning, she thought.

'You sure you're alright to walk by yourself?' Fay Isaacs, growing round and flabby at the waist, asked, looking towards the rows of apartment blocks and the crowds on the beach.

'Of course, it's only five minutes away. This is the Gold Coast, you know, not a jungle.'

'She's right, she'll be okay,' her father said and went back to the paradise he was grappling with somewhere between the foamy waves and the number of young blond-haired males that still gave him a shock.

'Okay, we'll be up soon, we'll get some cold meat on our way for lunch.'

.

Fay Isaacs watched her daughter walk off, a thin see-through purple sarong wrapped around her body and a towel draped over a shoulder, the sand flapping out of the back of her sandals like angels' wings. She had a good body, she would find someone ... in time. Young people knew how to look after their bodies these days. That was the good thing about the Gold Coast, Surfers' Paradise or whatever you called it. You got dressed up when you went out at night, you could sense the competition. In the day it didn't matter, everyone was casual, just a smart towel and a sarong and no one batted an eyelid. Ben was right, as he had been with most things, this was a good place, sunny, relaxed and peaceful, even if at times you did feel somewhat swamped. But then, this wasn't Jo'burg, nor was it America, or Israel, or Sydney even. So it was to be expected. Ben's brother Max had assured them that they would meet people like themselves ... in time. Ben, slower at making friends, was confident too. He had met some of them already. What was important was that Marlene should meet someone, people she could get along with. Jewish people. Maybe they should move up to Brisbane with her, see her into the right circles. Universities anywhere could be tricky places. At least over here things weren't crumbling. There was space to move in, a future, and Marlene would grow with it. Who knows, maybe Arnold would come out and then the two of them would at least have one another. No, she could do better than that! There was something about people who thought they were too clever ... at least over here people were more down to earth, not so ready with answers. They didn't all claim to be professors. It was what was happening in South Africa that made everyone so clever, think they were experts in all things. Especially the youngsters, an opinion on everything. This isn't right, that isn't right ... no, it was getting too crowded, you felt it creeping into your own backyard. It hadn't happened yet, but it would. Sooner or later. And it wasn't that you denied anyone. Everyone deserved the right to live and eat and have a shelter over their heads. Only not in your backyard, not right on top of you. Live and let live, that's what you had been taught and that's what you always said, but not on top of you, like a blanket. There was no future for Marlene over there. Stevie had done the right thing, only they should have listened and packed with him. Maybe he would have seen sense and they would all be together now in one place. There was nothing wrong with it here. He would see. But for now it was Marlene who was the worry ... getting her into a little flat of her own, somewhere near the university, maybe a little car ... that would make her feel good about herself. Independent. She'd meet people ... in time. The right people.

Suddenly anxious, flushed, like a wave of hot moist air had been poured over her shoulders, Fay said, 'Ben, I think it's time to go. I'm burning.'

'In a minute, just a quick dip in the water.'

Fay Isaacs nodded and looked across the little mounds of sparkling white sand stretched out and dotted with people. Time was running out, she thought, this was their last leg. At least it should be restful. And filled with air you could breathe.

Ben stood ankle deep in the waves, the tide receding making him feel like he was on an escalator going in the opposite direction. It made him feel unreal, like he was on a cloud. God had been good to them, he thought, and looked into the sun. It was far too bright and made him squint and look down again. Oblivious of the shrieking children around him, he walked a little deeper into the water and bent down, allowing the crest of the small waves to break over his shoulders. They were stronger than he expected and threw him backwards. In the lull between the waves, he patted some of the water over his head and eyes with his thin, ageing hands. At last, he was thinking, the kind of retirement he had always wanted. He breathed in a salty, satisfying breath. The place was already beginning to feel like home. Better! No governments to argue with, no customers to please, no people to fight with. No fears of losing your own home, of having your possessions, your own children stripped and stolen from beneath your feet. Live and let live, he had always said that. Blacks had their rights too, but not right on top of you. Over here there were no threats. Everyone got along, and if they didn't, they spoke about it without strangling one another. It was for her that they came, but it was time too. Things were getting ugly, the economy wasn't moving, no one was buying. People were stabbing and shooting one another. Marlene would find her way, eventually. She was a clever girl, cleverer than he had been at her age. And if she found the right person he would help out. Maybe even open another clothing store ... He glanced across the glistening water. It was early days yet. Too early. Time would tell. You still had to get used to the strange names of some of the places. Like, what was it ... Too-wong? In-door-oo-pilly? That one would take a while to get used to. Where did they find such names? When his daughter lived in those suburubs he would learn their names. She was the educated one, she would teach him. There was nothing more a person could ask for than food, comfort, an education for your children, and health. She was a good kid, Marlene, she'd get over Arnold, find someone stronger, nicer, better equipped to take care of her. This would be their land, a place they could call their own. He turned his back on an incoming wave and broke into a light jog to get out of the water. It was the first time in years he had run.

Marlene unlocked the door to their ground-floor apartment; all she wanted to do was lie down in peace and stretch out on the bed before they arrived home. Then it would be on the phone to arrange a time with the estate agent in Brisbane. There wasn't any great hurry ... yet, but it would be nice to know you had a place, near the university, and could settle into the area before you began. T'wong. It sounded nice. The kind of name you'd like to print on the back of an air mail envelope and think of your friends wondering what sort of paradise you'd landed yourself in. She banged the door closed behind her. Inside the flat was shadowy, as though the sun had suddenly been eclipsed. She switched on a light in the dining room, the first room as you entered. At least the air in the flat was cool, a relief to be out of the sun. She threw her towel over a chair and for a moment thought she heard a noise, like rats across a carpet. She stood still and listened. It stopped. Perhaps it was nothing, just the unfamiliar noises of a new home. She made to move on and then there was a second, harder noise, like footsteps. It was impossible that her parents could have arrived home before her. She called out anyway, 'Ma ... Dad ...' No response. Not a sound, only the sharp flow of her own breathing. Assured it was nothing, she walked on, turning into the passage towards her room. As she passed the kitchen something that sounded like a knife or spoon dropped onto the tiled floor. She poked her face in to see. As she did so she heard a cracking sound in her head. But it was like something apart from her, loud and exploding, somewhere in the distance. Then suddenly there was a deep pain, as though every fibre in her head had joined together into a single point that had been pricked by some rough yet sharp object. For a moment she became aware of blurry blond figures in front of her, then there was a shout, boyish but loud and firm, followed by another cracking sound, only this time it felt much duller. There was a sensation of something tearing, then flowing like milk, or honey, in her hair. The apartment was turning around and it seemed like someone was hammering in the flat above, only it could have been in her head, right at the very top, in the cranium.

Ben and Fay Isaacs walked into the flat, tired and noisily.

'Ello-oooo,' Ben called out. 'We're ho-omme.' It was always good to announce your presence, who knows what you might come up against with the kids of today?

He walked straight down the passage into his bedroom and flopped heavily onto the double-bed. It wasn't a far walk from the beach, but now he felt especially tired, strangely claustro-phobic, as though someone had placed a blanket over his body. Maybe it was the humidity? The sun? He would just have to get used to that.

Fay, in the kitchen, unwrapped the cold meat they had picked up at the delicatessen. She did not put it on a plate but left it on the creased white butcher's paper, as though to breathe, on top of the kitchen table. She was hungry and tempted to cut off a little piece, but restrained herself. She would go to the toilet quickly, then fix up a salad, and call everyone when it was ready. She looked briefly at her reflection in the long glass of the back-door and thought of the weight she had put on since they'd been here. She noticed that the door, which led out onto a little back garden, was slightly open. A prickly tingle ran through her body and then she remembered, of course, Marlene. Still so security conscious, she smiled embarrassedly to herself. Nobody here had bars in their windows and walls around their houses. She looked around outside, standing for some reason on tiptoe, but could not see Marlene. 'Marl …' she called out on the way to the toilet and took a quick peek into her daughter's room. 'Maybe she's just slipped down to the shops,' she said aloud.

The door to the toilet would only open a little way. Probably a faulty hinge. Fay Isaacs knew nothing of these things but looked at the hinges anyway. They were painted white, like the rest of the flat. They looked fine. She pushed harder. Nothing. Just as she was about to call out for Ben to come and see, the door suddenly flung open with a breaking sound, her full weight pressing against it. You expected better in an apartment you were paying so much for, she thought, and looked down, trying to squeeze her way in.

The sarong was half draped over the browned flesh and the limp foot she had been pushing the door against was pinned against the wall. Her stomach contracted. It was like someone had shot her in the heart, but with the bullet coming through her stomach and somehow shooting straight upwards again. Lodged behind the thick curved pipe at the back of the toilet she saw her daughter's face. Only it wasn't her daughter's face. It was black and blue and puffy and there was a black lock of hair that swept from the back of her head into an eye. She saw the toilet and her daughter in one place and then they spun around and there was blood on the wall spinning at the back of them. Beneath her bare feet Fay could feel grains of beach sand grating like broken glass.

'Be-en!' The shout that came from her was loud, but because Ben did not respond, it turned into a scream that reached from the bottom of her stomach, coming automatically, over and over again, like waves. Then Ben was at her side and suddenly she was heaving words. 'Look what they've done to our baby, Ben ... our baby ... look ... For what? For what?'

Ben knelt down, his knees were trembling, he felt them giving in, like they would not carry his crouching weight. Inside, he knew what he saw, but he shook his daughter's legs and hip and arms anyway, but not very hard, as though he did not want to harm her, or wanted to wake her very gently from a deep sleep. In the back of his mind the thought kept occurring to him that they would have to do something with the body. There was nothing he could do about it, the thought just kept coming, wheeling around and around in his head. Inside, at the back of his throat, it was dry like a stone quarry. There was no voice, no anything. He fell on to his knees over the body and mumbled 'home' so that only he could hear it.

Cropping angles

TANIA SPENCER

The early-winter sunshine curled like smoke into the room where she stood hunched over the table. She moved the cropping angle one inch in, covering his ear. She pulled a face.

She wasn't happy with the crop but it was the only way to fit the photograph on the cover. At the rattle of teacups in the doorway, Ellen looked up. Ghita carried in a tray.

'Not a moment too soon,' she said and flicked the switch on the light box.

While Ghita poured the tea Ellen opened a brown-paper packet on the tray and began placing muffins on the side plates.

'Blueberry, yum. Wasn't it my turn to buy?' she asked.

'Yes,' Ghita nodded. 'But we'll let you off this time seeing as you're hard at work.' Her faint accent, picked up during a British Council scholarship a few years back, gave a London inflection to her voice.

'Nice red, Ed,' Ellen teased with a mouthful of muffin.

Ghita looked down at her jacket, passing her fingers lightly over the cold gold buttons. 'Yes, Woolworths, believe it or not,' she smiled.

'I saw one very similar in last month's Vogue. It had double pockets on each side,' Ellen said looking surprised.

'That reminds me, thank you, I must pass on that copy,' and Ghita scribbled a note on a yellow Post-It. Walking over to her desk, she stuck it below her computer screen. It read 'Magazine Club – Janet.'

Then, stirring her tea, she asked, 'And so, how did the pics for our medical feature come out?'

'Not bad. I think we've got something,' replied Ellen slowly, taking her tea and perching on the desk in the sunlight. As she lifted her cup, the grass bracelets slipped down her thin arms, tanned and silvery like her short hair. She hadn't been thinking much about the feature.

Not since that morning, when Gladys had stood at her door clutching her old black umbrella with both hands. As the door had opened, she'd grinned uncertainly. The Jack Russell leapt and yipped at her skirt. She tried to pat her but missed. 'Gladys, where have you been? Its been two months now,' she had said, irritated. Gladys had said nothing. Stepping inside, she sat down gingerly, smoothing her skirt with her fingers.

Ellen resurfaced in the conversation. She said mildly, 'It's amazing I got anything at all. Imagine allowing me only twenty minutes to take pictures of a hospital, for God's sake. Real in-depth stuff.'

She swallowed a mouthful of tea loudly, grateful to be led away from Gladys, grateful to be right about something. 'While he was giving me the Gettysburg Address about not politicising health issues, tra la la, there, hanging on the wall behind him, was an oil painting of a woman without a stitch of clothing on.'

'No,' Ghita said.

'Yeah. Very voluptuous. Blonde. Very pink. Suspended in the black background were the faces of five leering men. He probably thought this was a medical classic.' She took a bite of her muffin before adding, 'I would have had my revenge but unfortunately he declined to be photographed in situ.'

She peered closely at her muffin, and asked, 'Do you think this blue colourant is bad for you?'

'What you don't know, won't hurt you,' Ghita replied. 'To change tack slightly, we've still got to get permission from the Traffic Department to close off the street for Friday night's party. I'm going to do that at lunchtime if you want a lift to town.'

'Thanks.'

Her eyes had already skipped across the university lawn to the Natal Midlands beyond the window. She found herself back at the narrow, red path Gladys's boys had been walking along. It was late and the wedding party had been good. With a bellyful of beer and meat, Jabulani and his younger cousin were looking forward to bed. As he walked behind Themba, Jabulani smiled at the thought of Sibongile.

She'd definitely given him the look, he thought sleepily. *And* she was a nurse. She'd want him to wear a condom. He'd deal with that when the time came. He was still smiling when Themba froze.

And then he saw them too.

A group of five men running noiselessly towards them. Jabulani leapt to the side of the path into an adjacent mealie field, with Themba just behind him. Both cousins ran blindly, stumbling over the ploughed clods, blundering through the plants with leaves blue as blades. In their wake, spurts of maize blossom puffed in the moonlight.

'Penny?' Ghita said over the rim of her teacup.

'It's nothing,' Ellen frowned quickly. It was nice that they worked so well together. Even nicer that they split spring bulb orders, shared Nina Bawden novels and an interest in transitional art. Right now they were in the throes of arranging a street party for the lane in which they both lived. Ghita kept calling it a lane.

They'd been planning it for weeks and had invited all their neighbours: among them the Telkom family, the shy Seventh Day Adventists, the Zaïrean theology student, the woman from Public Works and her partner, the biochemist who'd recently returned from Australia, and the policeman and his wife who made noisy love and had even noisier fights. Rain permitting, Friday night would find them all outside enjoying the New South Africa. Although they weren't crass enough to put it into quite those words.

They'd arranged a sheep-on-a-spit and a local violinist who could fiddle up a storm. Someone had even offered to make a fireball out of tightly bundled hessian soaked in petrol. Once it was lit, everyone would set upon it and kick it up the street.

It sounded dangerous. Ellen was still wondering about this

when Ghita asked if Gladys could help with the salads on Friday morning.

'Then there won't be very much more to do other than set up the PA system in the afternoon.'

'Gladys? Well, until this morning I hadn't heard from her in two months.'

'Two months?'

'Yes. She's done this before but never for this long. She lives out at the mountain and there has been a lot of trouble there,' she offered. Then she shrugged, 'But you just don't know.'

At first the boys' breathing was just ragged. But when it dawned on them that they could not outrun these men, it changed and became guttural and high pitched. Like a buck in that last sprint. Jabulani realised and began to unbutton his shirt as he ran, screaming back to his cousin to do the same. Then he ripped it from his torso and threw it to the side in a tight ball. It opened over the mealie plants like a table cloth as he slipped away. He was still running when he heard his cousin's scream.

In the early hours of that morning, Jabulani brought his mother to the field to look for her eldest sister's child. She came with two elderly neighbours. As soon as he had pulled the tall plants to one side and pointed, Jabulani turned on his heel and left. Gladys wasn't to hear from her son for many months, until someone said they'd seen him. He was at Jozini, training to become a policeman.

She found Themba lying face down in the field, still wearing his smart white shirt. Although it wasn't white anymore. There was a big gash down his left shoulder blade and his neck was hacked. Gladys cupped one hand around his shoulder and pushed down with the other as she turned him over. When he was born, seventeen years before, she'd had to push his one little shoulder back inside her sister when he'd got stuck. And now she couldn't even recognise him. No one said anything as Gladys knelt beside him. Her gingham doek had slipped off and her hair floated around her head like black coral. A low keening came out of her throat as she held his hand and rocked backwards and forwards in the patchy light. For Themba had no ears, no nose, no lips, no eyes, and no genitals.

Gladys and the two old men sat there with him until the sun came up and the police eventually arrived. She heard their radio crackling from the other side of the mealie field.

'Sarge, I think we've got something here …' said the young one with the soft voice.

Then she stood up with her red, red knees and went home to pack some of her things.

It hadn't been a surprise, she said. A few weeks earlier she'd come home one evening to find her house empty, the door open and her twins hiding in the veld. When she called, they came back slowly. While she held their small shaking bodies, neighbours came out of their houses to say that some men had come looking for the older boys, Jabulani and Themba. They wanted to know why they had not been attending the meetings.

'Since then we sleep outside, out there in the veld. At night I take my babies, my girls and my husband and we sleep there in the trees.' She put up two fingers. 'For two months now, we live like this. Every night. Another lady I know, they put petrol and burn her in her house where she sleeps.' Gladys shook her head, clucking her tongue, 'With these people you don't know, you just don't know.'

When Gladys had finished her story, Ellen could not think of a thing to say. She sat there smoothing her thoughts, plucking at a Lifeline counseling course she'd done years ago. Something about post-traumatic stress syndrome. She could ask Gladys if she was having bad dreams, she supposed. Bad dreams? She put her hand over Gladys' hand and said nothing.

The next evening wreaths of smoke hovered above the street, above the drone of voices, clinking cutlery and the sizzle of marinade being brushed onto the side of a sheep. In the middle of the road stood a long line of variously sized tables with smart white table cloths.

A fireball leapt into the air. Someone whooped. It moved slowly in its velvet trajectory before landing softly, shaking off sparks like a wet dog as the next person kicked it back up into the air.

It is dangerous, thought Ellen, as she stood watching from the upstairs window. Behind her the walls trembled with pink light and she thought of Gladys. And how you just don't know.

A new dispensation
SANDRA LEE BRAUDE

Zipporah Feigel walked through the parking area under the building and, turning right, entered the staff quarters.

Heavenly Heights, in the prestigious suburb of Killarney, had been built some forty years before, and its design reflected the philosophy of the time. There were six floors in the building and twenty-four flats, all of them spacious, with multiple bedrooms and bathrooms. The residents were mainly old and wealthy, with just a couple of the flats rented out to those who didn't fall into this category. There were more women than men – widows whose husbands had succeeded in business in Johannesburg and had left them with a solid income and too little to do. So they filled their time with shopping and having their hair done, playing bridge and doing voluntary charitable work. Sometimes they entertained in their luxurious homes, which were filled with comfortable, stylish antique furniture, and were well cared for by maids.

Zipporah was one of the few who didn't have a full-time maid. She no longer worked and had decided that she could run her flat with the help of the part-time char provided by the building. It was this part-time char she was on her way to see.

A long, green-painted cement corridor stretched in front of her, dim and badly lit. She walked to the fifth door and knocked. There were sounds inside, as of someone in pain. She pushed the door open and walked in.

The room couldn't have been more than four metres square. Against the opposite wall, beneath a high-placed window, stood a bed on bricks. The place was crowded with furniture – an old wooden cupboard, a kitchen table and two kitchen chairs, an electric hot-plate, and a wire strung across one of

86

the walls on which clothes hung. Caroline lay on the bed, moaning.

'Caroline?'

'Yes, ma'am,' she whispered between moans.

'What is wrong?' asked Zipporah, thinking about the fact that she had to go out.

'The baby, it is coming.'

'I didn't realise it was due so soon!'

Caroline let out another moan. It took a few minutes for her to reply. 'Yes, ma'am. The baby it is coming.' Her face was pallid. Drops of sweat collected on her brow.

'What can we do?' Zipporah asked, her mind racing, then: 'I'll try to get an ambulance.'

It took some time for her to get through to the hospital. By the time the ambulance arrived, the arrival of the baby was imminent. Zipporah watched as the stretcher-bearers loaded Caroline onto the stretcher. Then she returned to her flat and reluctantly began to clean.

Two days later Caroline was back, carrying a small bundle. She undid it and showed it to Zipporah. A tiny boy, its skin soft and delicate, with minute waving fingers and unfocused blue eyes with a depth of black in them.

'Why, he's adorable,' breathed Zipporah. 'What will you call him?'

'Sipho,' replied Caroline. 'He is my only son. There are two older girls. I cannot have another one.'

'You don't need another,' Zipporah said enviously. 'How are you going to look after him?'

'I am going home, ma'am,' said Caroline. 'I can go home for three months and then I can come back.'

'Will you bring Sipho back with you?'

'No, ma'am. There is a woman at home who will look after Sipho. I will be able to come back to my job.'

After three months she returned, thinner and darker of skin, with a hungry look about her eyes. She brought photographs of Sipho, dressed in his best.

'Don't you miss him?' asked Zipporah.

'Yes, ma'am, I miss him. But I shall go home every month to see him. I must work. There is no money otherwise.'

She took out the vacuum cleaner and started to clean the carpets. Zipporah heaved a sigh of relief. She was no longer encumbered with that job. But several weeks later, problems began to arise. One morning Caroline looked as pale as when she had been giving birth to Sipho.

'There is trouble, ma'am. I have got notice.'

'What do you mean – notice?'

'The caretaker, he has told me that my job here is ending. I must leave at the end of the month.'

'But why? I don't understand.'

'He says that since I had the baby, I don't work the same way any more. He says that people don't want me.'

'I can't see any problem with your work. Who doesn't want you?'

'Dr James, I think, ma'am. He says he has his own maid. He doesn't need a char.'

Zipporah began to ask around the building. Caroline was correct. Dr James, a divorcee, had a maid of long standing. He had only recently moved into the building but he had nonetheless been elected as one of the Trustees. Now he objected to paying for a char when he had his own maid. In fact, he had already reduced his levy payments by a hundred rand a month. This, he calculated, was the amount paid by each owner in the building for cleaning services. Dr James's needs were few, and he had brought with him Violet, a maid of long standing. When approached, he was adamant.

'I have no intention of paying a hundred rand a month for a service I neither need nor want. Violet does everything for me. As far as I'm concerned, Caroline must go.'

'She needs the job,' Zipporah pleaded. 'She's not qualified to do anything else, and besides she has a young baby.'

'I'm sorry about that,' Dr James responded, 'but it has nothing to do with me.'

The situation looked hopeless. Caroline continued to do her

88

job grudgingly. Zipporah slept fitfully, waking in the mornings with pains all over her body, as though she had been beaten. What to do? What responsibility was it of hers? But how could she possibly let Caroline go? She felt the urge to fight stir in her.

She had already had a couple of disagreements with the Trustees elected to manage the building. The committee was headed by a self-appointed Chairman in his eighties. He and his wife and a nondescript third, along with Dr James, believed their positions gave them power. It seemed useless to quote the provisions of the Sectional Title Act under which the building was run, even though according to the Act, the Trustees held the position of servants, not masters.

The following morning Zipporah phoned her lawyer and explained the situation to him.

'We are desperate,' she said. 'Isn't there anything we can do?'

'If what you tell me is correct, then the building cannot just dispense with her services. She has been there for many years and is permanently employed. If they persist in this dismissal, she has a right to approach the CCMA.'

'CCMA?'

'Council for Conciliation, Mediation and Arbitration. It's a legal body that deals with unjust dismissals.'

For the first time, there was hope on the horizon. The following day when Caroline rang the doorbell, Zipporah answered, fully dressed.

'Come,' she said firmly. 'We are going to the CCMA.'

The CCMA offices were downtown. It wasn't easy finding parking, but at last they managed. Zipporah's heart pulsed with emotion and righteous indignation. Caroline followed her. They entered a large office, filled with people sitting or standing quietly around the walls. Zipporah had no intention of standing around for hours awaiting attention. She walked boldly up to an official, who was filling in a form, on the far side of the counter, and said, 'Excuse me.'

For a few moments he took no notice of her, then he looked her up and down. His attitude was belligerent. She hesitated.

'I've brought my maid – Caroline Mokoena.'

His look was scathing. He thinks I'm one of them, she thought, one of those who comes to complain. Well, he's wrong!

She took courage. 'This is Caroline Mokoena,' she informed him. 'I've brought her here because she needs to file a complaint with the CCMA, against her employers – the owners of the building in which I live.'

Now he looked at her with different eyes, appraising, questioning.

'You want to help this woman?'

'Yes.'

'Fill in these forms, then come back to me,' he said, smiling.

The forms had to be delivered by hand to the Chairman of the Trustees of Heavenly Heights. A man of heavy stature with a rogue-elephant disposition, his face turned purple and his eyes bulged when Zipporah delivered the CCMA papers to him. He accepted them angrily.

'This is nonsense!' he growled.

There was a lightness in Zipporah's step as she returned to her flat. 'Justice, justice, justice,' she murmured to herself. That was surely what it was all about? Justice, and compassion for the underdog. Caroline was poor, and had a baby to support. The Chairman was rich and powerful. She, Zipporah, was taking sides.

That night she logged onto the Internet and sought information for her cause. 'Justice' was too wide a term, bringing in tens of thousands of responses, but eventually a combination of the words 'labour' and 'equity' brought her what she was looking for. She made notes on the proposed Labour Equity Bill. It hadn't yet been passed, was still in the process of discussion and formulation, but it had in it what Zipporah was looking for. There was enough material for her to prepare for the hearing.

The day of the CCMA hearing dawned. Caroline arrived early at Zipporah's flat, neat in a two-piece outfit, but looking drawn and tense.

'I am ready, ma'am,' was all she said.

The drive into town was silent, Zipporah trying to concentrate on the traffic and simultaneously remember all that she had read about Labour Equity. She parked. Still in silence, the two women entered the building and rose in the lift. The waiting room on the eighth floor was crowded. There would be many hearings that morning. Most of the claimants were black workers, but there were other people, too, distinctly professional-looking, carrying stuffed briefcases. Lawyers, probably. Zipporah suddenly felt edgy. What right had she to take on a case for which she wasn't qualified?

Time dragged. Wasn't it Einstein who said that time is relative, if you sit on a hot stove it seems to go on forever? But even forever passes: at last they were summoned to the desk.

A young woman stood waiting: short, podgy, without makeup, her hair drawn back in a ponytail. 'Come this way,' she said.

Zipporah and Caroline followed her down a long corridor. As did the Chairman, his wife and the Superintendent of Heavenly Heights in tow. They entered a large room with a long corporate table lined with chairs.

'Please sit down.'

The young woman took her place at the head of the table. Zipporah and Caroline sat on one side. Their three opponents found seats on the other.

'I expect you know what this is all about,' said the young woman. 'The CCMA is not a court, but a place for discussion and mediation. You apparently have a labour problem. We will try to work it out here. My name is Jane Brown, and you may call me Jane, Ms Brown, or Commissioner – whatever you wish. Now, would you like to open the discussion?' She turned to the Chairman.

In his slow, heavy fashion, the Chairman began, 'Caroline has been given notice. It costs the building a lot of money to have her, and we don't need her any more. She has a young baby and doesn't do her work properly. That is why she has to go.'

91

Then the battle started. It was not a discussion. It was war. The heat rose. The Commissioner was obviously taken aback. She had presided over many mediations, but this one was different, more vitriolic, more bitter than the others. At last she raised her hands.

'Enough,' she cried. 'I can't have this. Please remember that this is a place for mediation. It's not a courtroom. We are not trying the case here. We are simply attempting to arrive at a reasonable agreement. I'm going to leave the room for a short while, to allow you to take control of yourselves. When I come back, we shall discuss the matter further.' She left the room.

A silence fell. The factions whispered amongst themselves, but didn't speak to one another. After a short while the Commissioner returned.

'I think I understand what this is all about,' she said, 'but I have to tell you that unless you agree to compromise, this matter will have to go to court. And then you'll probably all lose. So I suggest that you sign an agreement, whereby Caroline Mokoena remains in her job. After all, the reasons given by you,' she nodded at the Chairman, 'don't fall within the confines of current labour law. If you persist in your approach, you will be liable for unjust dismissal.'

Yes! Yes! Zipporah's heart jumped. They had won! Caroline would remain in her job and, from now on, all that would have to be done would be to see that her working conditions were improved. Yes! Yes! They had won! She had won!

So a compromise agreement was signed, and Zipporah and Caroline followed the Commissioner and the opposition out of the CCMA precincts.

The Chairman and his wife were furious, the Superintendent apologetic, the Commissioner cold, and Caroline? How did she feel?

'Thank you, Mrs Feigel,' was all she had to say.

Zipporah went on holiday overseas and in the excitement of travel almost forgot the episode. But in the time she had been away, a new spirit had emerged in Heavenly Heights, and the moment she returned, she found herself again in the fray. One of the flats had been let out to an Advocate van der Merwe – a youngish man, who had acquired a reputation at the Bar, and his new wife, a labour consultant. They brought with them not only youth, but an undisputed knowledge of the law and an aggressive attitude towards employees. It seemed that Zipporah and Caroline might have won the first battle, but now the real war was beginning.

Dr James was still adamant about reducing his levy, which he was obliged to pay in full like everyone else. Some of the owners were up in arms about this: the cleaning services had been available ever since the building had opened its doors. They raised objections. He was insistent.

'What do we want these women for?' asked Dr James at a meeting of the owners. 'They cost us money. They're just a remnant of the past. We employ our own servants. Let them go.'

'How can you even suggest that?' asked Zipporah heatedly. 'Two of these women are old, and the other two have young children. As things stand in the country at present, they won't get other jobs. What you are trying to do is send them into penury – maybe even into starvation.'

'I'm afraid that's not my problem,' Dr James said. 'I'm simply saying that I object to paying the extra money.' When the meeting was over he commented to Zipporah, 'You're a pain in the arse!'

'And you are the arse!' she countered.

The building split into factions. The superintendent walked around the building, knocking at each door and collecting signatures on a hand-written sheet of paper:

We the undersigned do not or do require future servicing of our flats by female staff.

The majority of owners wanted – *did* require the service in the future, so Dr James continued to subtract a hundred rand from his monthly levy.

One morning Caroline arrived at Zipporah's flat, looking very worried. 'Mrs Feigel, we have joined the Union,' she said.

93

'What Union?'

'Mrs Feigel, there is a lot of talk amongst the people here, and we have decided to join the Union which fights for the rights of domestic workers.'

'That's good, Caroline. This is the only way you'll have the strength to get what you want. You need to stand together. Has everyone joined?'

'Yes, Mrs Feigel. All the people who work for the building. Me, the other three women, and the men.'

'All of them?'

'Yes – all the cleaners and the security men.'

'Good.'

'And, Mrs Feigel, they've made me shop steward.'

'That's great, Caroline. I think you'll be very good,' Zipporah said after a moment of stunned silence.

There weren't many people in Heavenly Heights who were happy about the new state of affairs. The predominant feeling was that there would be trouble, that the workers would demand large increases in salaries. The Chairman spoke to the staff and explained his problems to them.

'We haven't got money to pay you more,' he told them. 'You see, we have to waterproof the patios, and it's going to cost twenty thousand rand for the tiles alone.'

The staff were furious. 'What is he saying?' one of them asked. 'Twenty thousand rand for tiles? What about me – my pay is eight hundred rand a month. My son goes to university. I have to pay for him!'

'Stick together,' advised Zipporah.

'Yes, in unity is strength,' Caroline agreed.

But sticking together was not easy. One morning Caroline brought the news that the two security men who answered the front door-bell and watched the cars going in and out of the underground garage, had backed out of the Union.

'But why did they do that?' asked Zipporah.

'They got some money,' Caroline said, curling her lip.

'More money? From whom?'

'Dr James gave them some.'

As time went on, Zipporah had to acknowledge to herself that she was in a difficult position, one of her own making. Here she was, the affluent owner of a flat in a prestigious building, siding with the workers, against the other owners. There was a growing animosity towards her.

'You're a Communist. People don't like Communists. You should know that,' one of the friendlier people in the building explained.

Zipporah was outraged. 'Of course I'm not a Communist! I never have been and would never want to be,' she defended herself. Then she became defiant. If that was how people saw her, that was their problem, not hers.

The Union representative, Bongile, arrived at Heavenly Heights for a meeting with the Chairman but, at Zipporah's request, came to see her first.

'Why are you doing this, Mrs Feigel?' she asked.

'Why? I'm not quite sure. Maybe it's because I'm a woman, and want to protect the women who work here.'

After Bongile had gone, she remembered she had once heard about a rabbi whose wife accused her maid of stealing some jewellery and laid a charge and took her to court. When the day of the hearing came, the rabbi dressed to accompany his wife to court. 'I don't need you,' she told him. 'I'm quite capable of speaking for myself.' 'That I know,' said the rabbi, 'but who is to speak for the maid if I don't go?' Then Zipporah knew why she was acting in this way: it was to speak for people who had never had the opportunity to speak for themselves.

The meeting between the Chairman and the Union representative was inconclusive. 'We have to meet again,' Bongile reported back to the members afterwards, as they sat hunched around a table in the small basement room. 'He is a very difficult man, the Chairman of this building, and he doesn't listen to what I have to say. But I am sure that we will come right with him.'

Tensions continued to rise. An owner met Zipporah in the lift and complained about Gladys, the char who had cleaned her flat over many years. 'I don't understand her. She's so ungrateful! I've always been good to her, giving her extra money and my old clothes, and now she comes to me and tells me that I'm not treating her like a human being, that she has no pension and nowhere to go! As if it's my fault!'

Another referred to the cleaning staff as 'monkeys'.

These were all little battles in a larger war, in which the issues were serious – employment against dismissal; jobs against penury; selfishness against social justice; the Trustees against the Union. The cleaners were simply pawns in a much bigger game, one motivated by money and power. The Chairman and his Trustees had both, and were determined to use them to their own advantage.

A letter from the Trustees advised the owners:

We have co-opted Mrs van der Merwe onto the Board of Trustees. She is most useful in giving advice on how to deal with the labour problem that is threatening Heavenly Heights, and she charges the Body Corporate only one half of her usual fee. We are grateful to her. The Union is demanding a minimum wage of R1 300 per month. This we have rejected, and so the situation is currently unresolved, but the staff has now talked of an increase of R90 for all. We have intimated that this would be more reasonable, but must wait to see how the amount is accommodated within the several other demands of the Union.

All other demands – permanency of employment, overtime pay, maternity leave and pensions – were rejected. *We just cannot afford these things*, wrote the Trustees.

Caroline was very stressed by her responsibilities as shop-steward. 'What do I do?' she asked desperately.

'Phone the Union. Speak to Bongile. See what she has to say. You can use my phone any time you wish.'

'Thank you, Mrs Feigel,' said Caroline. She pulled a worn slip of paper from her overall pocket and dialled the number written on it in pencil. A few words in Sotho, then she put the phone down. 'Bongile isn't there.'

'Well, try tomorrow.'

But tomorrow proved the same, and the following days.

'Speak to the head of the Union.' Zipporah had long learned that the only way to get things done was to go to the top.

Another phone call, more words poured into the receiver. 'He says he will ask Bongile to look into the matter,' said Caroline, slipping the tattered paper back into her pocket. 'Maybe tomorrow we will speak.'

But the same day Caroline and the other cleaning women were called to the Chairman's flat and made to sign for receipt of a letter of dismissal:

Your services will no longer be required as from the end of the current month. You will be given what is owing to you, and will be dealt with fairly in terms of labour law.

Mrs van der Merwe had done her job well. The Trustees were triumphant, and the women desperate.

'Where is Bongile?' Zipporah ask. 'Why hasn't she been here? Why hasn't she phoned back? Let me see if I can speak to her – maybe we can still do something.'

She dialed the Union's number. 'Can I speak with Bongile, please?' The phone buzzed, and a woman's voice answered. 'Is that Bongile?'

'Yes.'

'It's Mrs Feigel here, from Heavenly Heights.' She heard the phone being banged down at the other end. 'I'm sorry,' she said to Caroline, 'but for some reason Bongile won't speak to me. You'll have to depend on solidarity. You must all stick together. Maybe you'll need to picket the building.'

'Mrs Feigel, The men are not standing with us,' Caroline announced a day later.

'What? What's this all about?'

'They have been given extra money. They don't want to stand with us. As long as they have extra money, they don't care.'

Bribery! thought Zipporah. The Chairman has bribed them! Split the forces! Divide and rule! An old but a very effective trick. I'm sure that Bongile was bribed too. A couple of hundred rands in the pockets and you can do what you want with people. But I can't prove it, and anyway, I'm an owner in this building. I have dual loyalties, am caught in a cleft stick. It's the end. I can't do any more. It's heartbreaking, but the women will have to go. I only hope the bastards who manoeuvred this will get their comeuppance!

And so it happened. The women left, manipulated by the Trustees, sold out by the Union representative, denied by their own. They were given a little money, which was supposed to keep them going for the rest of their lives. It was roughly comparable to what any of the owners in Heavenly Heights would spend in a month.

Caroline continued to work for Zipporah in a private capacity. She had been offered another job, working in a large household for a family with seven children, at three quarters of the salary she had been earning at Heavenly Heights. 'Don't talk to Jews,' said the prospective employer when Caroline told her about Zipporah. 'I don't like Jews.'

'For God's sake, don't take that job,' warned Zipporah. 'She'll work you like a slave, from early in the morning till late at night. You'll have to look after her seven children, and you won't be able to keep Sipho with you.'

So Caroline remained, doing piecework in the building. The other three women disappeared and weren't heard of again; Bongile, the Union representative, was no more to be seen. Dr James's own maid was severely injured in a road accident, and he had to do his own cleaning. When Zipporah bumped into any of the Trustees, she turned her back on them, and walked in the other direction.

One day, as Caroline was on her knees, washing the kitchen floor, she suddenly said, 'I want to get different work. I don't want to spend the rest of my life cleaning floors. I am going back to school, to get my matric.'

'Great,' said Zipporah. 'I'll help you where I can.'

'Thank you, Zipporah,' Caroline replied.

Dictator

AHMED ESSOP

It was seven in the evening when Senobia and her advocate husband, Kamar, entered the Steers Restaurant in Mint Road, Fordsburg. Kamar had had a long day in the Magistrate's Court in the city. Since the changes in the country the courts seemed even more demanding, and he wanted to dine before driving home to Lenasia. Zenobia had been visiting a friend for the day.

The restaurant had a gay atmosphere within and without. Along the wide pavement which had originally been a small park there were pendant lamps among plane trees, and tables and chairs where men and women were eating. Zenobia and her husband sat down in the restaurant beneath a chandelier. From the window they could see across the road where there was another restaurant. The waiter came up and they ordered. When they had finished eating they went to the cashier to pay and it was then that Zenobia saw him.

He was paying for two plastic tumblers of orange juice which he had bought at a kiosk near the entrance, counting small change methodically on the counter. He had much small change and as his eyesight seemed weak, he examined the nickle and copper coins with care before pushing them towards the cashier. So intent was he that he was oblivious of the people near him. Zenobia looked at the man: his hair was grey; his chin had a grey-black stubble; he was wearing a grey-blue safari suit. Then she recognised him – the safari suit, though faded, was the same one he used to wear when he came on his inspectoral visits to the school where she had taught five years before. How much the man had changed in appearance from the energetic conceited figure whose arrival put fear into the principal and junior teachers at Silver Tree High School in Eldorado Park!

As Zenobia looked at him she recalled the incident inspector D'Oliviera had been involved in with a retired lawyer, Mr Preston, who had been engaged temporarily by the Education Department.

The inspector had arrived at the school during the middle of the final term to return the English examination question papers to the teachers. He knocked on Mr Preston's classroom door and asked him to come outside onto the verandah. There he told him that he objected to the format of the question paper for the Grade 8 class: 'The Educational Bulletin requires paragraph-type questions and contextual-type questions on *The Wind in the Willows*, and you have only set the first type.'

Mr Preston told him that the Bulletin gave him a choice. It read: 'Paragraph-type questions *or* contextual-type questions may be set on the prescribed reading book.' This had infuriated Mr D'Oliviera who said that what the Bulletin said did not matter. He wanted both types. An argument had resulted. Zenobia and several other teachers came out of their classrooms and witnessed the altercation.

'You have no experience in teaching,' Mr D'Oliviera shouted. 'I am instructing you.'

'I have a choice,' said Mr Preston, a neatly dressed small man who selected his words with care, 'and I intend to exercise my prerogative.'

'You cannot. I will not let you.'

'Well, you have my decision.'

'You cannot make your own decision here. You think because you are a lawyer you can make your own interpretation of the Bulletin.'

'The wording is very clear. You seem to be distorting the meaning.'

'Am I? Am I? I will have you dismissed for insubordination.'

'Do as you please,' Mr Preston said firmly.

Zenobia had gone closer and addressed the inspector. 'Sir, this matter can be settled in the principal's office. Teachers and children need not be exposed to the dispute.'

'You keep out of this. This is not your business.'

'It is. This is a place of education. Not a market place.'

'What? What?' the inspector shouted, rushing towards the stairs and then to the principal's office.

Zenobia and the other teachers who had witnessed the dispute were offended. She spoke to them and told them that the inspector could not be permitted to behave unprofessionally and that they should register their protest with the principal and urge him to approach the inspector and advise him to make an apology. Mr Preston said that he, too, would lodge a strong protest.

After school Zenobia, accompanied by Mr Preston and several teachers, went to the principal. He was a tall, prematurely bald man who told them that Mr D'Oliviera was a difficult man to deal with and advised Mr Preston to change his literature question paper in accordance with his requirements. 'It's a minor matter,' he pleaded. 'You know he will never apologise and the matter will only become complicated. Please listen to me, Mr Preston, you are a temporary teacher and can be dismissed after a day's notice.'

Mr Preston said that he saw no reason to change his question paper and would not permit the inspector to dictate to him.

Two days later Zenobia heard a knock on her classroom door. When she opened it she saw Mr D'Oliviera and the headmaster.

'Mr D'Oliviera has come to inspect your work,' the headmaster said timidly. Zenobia surmised that the inspector had come to display his authority over her as her verbal thrust must have rankled within him.

'I will not permit Mr D'Oliviera to enter the room until he offers an apology to Mr Preston for his uncivil manners,' she said.

The inspector, finding himself repulsed, looked at an embarrassed headmaster who said, 'Let us go to the office,' and the two men walked away.

On the last day of the school year, six weeks after the inspector's visit, Mr Preston received a letter from the Director of Education:

After careful consideration of your insubordinate action in not carrying out the instructions of your superior officer, Mr T D'Oliviera, you are hereby dismissed in terms of your temporary contract. Henceforth your services will no longer be required at any school controlled by the Department.

Zenobia, whose appointment at the school was on a yearly basis, also received a letter from the Director:

You are hereby apprised that you will henceforth not be employed by the Education Department at any of the schools under its control for having prevented a superior officer of the Department, Mr T D'Oliviera, from conducting a legitimate inspection of your work.

When the inspector had finished counting the coins, Zenobia said, 'Mr D'Oliviera, I see you are short of cash. Let me pay.'

She gave the cashier a note and pushed the coins on the counter aside. 'Give these,' she said, 'to the beggars who come here.'

Mr D'Oliviera turned and saw an elegant, bejewelled, Oriental woman before him. Recognition came to him. He took the two tumblers of orange juice in his hands and went out towards the pavement and the street where his car was parked. As he walked his hands trembled, spilling the juice on his trousers and shoes.

The hand grenade

BEVERLEY JANSEN

The rain came down suddenly – just when Isaac touched the front gate to open it. He glanced back at their house. 'Ag what, I'm already outside, I may as well keep on walking. A little cold water never harmed anyone,' he said to himself. He tied the handles of the yellow supermarket bag in a knot and placed the packet containing his school books under his big green and yellow jersey.

As he walked across the field he heard a shrill whistle – Pheet! Pheet! Phee-ee-eet!' That was Abbie, his chommie, or Abraham Visagie, as he was known at the school. Isaac smiled.

It's a wonder that he is going to school on such a day. He doesn't like school as it is, but rainy weather makes school-going a much worse burden, he thought. But, then, it was Monday today. The day the teachers served barley-and-vegetable soup.'

He stopped, and waited for his friend. Abbie, a tall boy with an easy smile, wore long pants today. On cold days he always wore his grey school pants with the patches on the knees.

'Jus, my bra, did you do your homework?' asked Isaac.

'Homework? What homework?' Abbie frowned and shook his head.

They crossed the street at the corner near the Day Hospital. Then Isaac asked again, 'Did you do your homework, Abbie? You know how angry Meneer gets if we don't do our homework.'

'We had no candles last night and our electricity has been off for a while. No money, man,' Abbie said, putting his right hand in his pocket as he looked up at the clouds.

'Jong, Meneer is going to neuk you,' Isaac said and stared at him in disbelief.

Abbie stopped just before they reached the scholar patrol. 'He lives in a big house. He can push buttons and switch his lights on and off. We had no candles and no food so I did not do my homework.'

Isaac wondered if his friend was still going to be so brave when Meneer confronted him later in the class.

As they passed a clump of trees, Abbie suddenly suggested that they pull a skyf. They quickly moved into the short Port Jackson bushes and each lit a stompie. They pulled a few puffs while squatting on their haunches. Through the haze of blue-grey smoke they watched the children crossing the road at the scholar patrol and the grown-ups rushing to the bus-stop and taxi rank.

A group of children walked past without giving them a second glance.

Abbie flicked his finished stompie to the ground and stepped on it, while Isaac nipped his expertly between his fingers and hid it in his sock.

'These laaities keep them diknek – they want to tell a man where to walk and how to walk in the road,' moaned Abbie kicking a stone.

Just then they heard the siren and started to run. If they were not at the gate when the first siren went off, they would find themselves locked out for the day.

Once inside the school, they mingled with the other children and walked to their classroom where they lined up and waited for their teacher to arrive. They all looked in the direction of the teacher's staffroom and waited for Meneer to ring the small bell signalling the first period.

They waited for the bell to ring, but it didn't.

Just then Meneer came and shouted at the first group of children that there was going to be an urgent meeting. They shrieked with pleasure; an extra half hour to play.

Abbie and Isaac dashed to the bushes on the playing field. Time to pull another skyf. They walked towards the bushes singing a popular TV jingle. Behind the bushes, Abbie stretched himself on the grass while Isaac took the remnants of his stompie out of his sock. As he bent down, he noticed the round object under the bush. He pulled the egg-shaped thing towards him. 'Abbie, my bra, come check out this beweging here,' he said. Abbie turned on his side and whistled aloud.

'My chommie, you know what that is? It's a beweging the terrorists used to blow up the boere's buildings,' he said unable to conceal his excitement.

Isaac felt himself growing cold and numb.

'What are we going to do. Let's go tell Meneer,' Isaac heard himself say.

'No – no – no,' Abbie urged. 'It's our secret. Let's tell no one where we found it.'

They studied the hand grenade in silence for a while and noticed that a part was missing. Just then the bell rang and Abbie grabbed the grenade, put it in his pocket and ran off towards their classroom.

They quickly became bored with the early morning routine. Isaac glanced at the timetable, yes, he knew the pattern so well – Scripture, Maths and Reading. He threw Abbie a serious man-about-town look and moved his fingers across his line of vision. Isaac understood him to say: Are you watching this move?

Abbie took the object out of his pocket and nudged Badroe the Beast in the ribs.

'I say, Beastie, have you ever seen a beweging like this?'

Badroe did not say a word. Her mouth hung open. Abbie wished she would close it as the snot was nearing her lips.

'What? Where did you get it from?' she whispered hysterically.

'It's a grenade,' he menacingly replied, his eyes narrowed and his voice low.

Badroe rose and Abbie and Isaac knew that she was preparing to report the incident to Mr Smith, their teacher. They pushed her down in her seat and threatened by means of well-known signs what they would do to her during the interval if she did not keep quiet. Badroe knew better than to tell on them. They were, after all, the diknekke in the class.

During the interval the boys decided a good source of enjoyment would be to chase the girls around the playground. The moment they caught one of the girls, they would scare her with the grenade. The girls screamed in mock horror but enjoyed every moment of it.

As soon as they were back in the classroom Miss Reed, their English teacher, stepped inside. Now, this was one tough lady, not to be messed with. Her name suited her: thin as a reed, but what a voice. Some students said that she was an actress when she was young.

Today was poetry. Abbie and Isaac did not mind this aspect of the work as Miss Reed read well and loved to dramatise. She began by explaining that she was going to read them poems about children ... funny children, naughty children, sad children and happy children. They listened attentively. Suddenly Badroe put up her hand.

'Excuse me, Miss ... I have something to say ... it's about naughty children.'

Miss Reed stopped reading and waited patiently. And then Badroe brought out the whole sack of potatoes: 'Miss Reed, Abraham and Isaac have a war-thing under their desk. It can kill a person, Miss Reed.'

She took her bare hand and wiped it across the lower part of her face, leaving a shiny streak across her cheek.

Miss Reed rose from her chair and moved towards the boys. They did not argue. She held out her hand, and Abbie reached under the desk and placed the grenade in the bony hand. He saw Miss Reed's face go grey. She stood for a moment and then walked towards the door.

There was an unusual silence in the class.

The smaller, younger boys and girls did not say a word, the older ones shook their heads and the two friends now knew that they were in trouble.

On that particular day the man from Civil Defence had decided to visit the school. He came regularly and was busy discussing veld fires with the junior classes when Miss Reed entered the room. Slowly.

'Here,' she said. 'A boy found this in the grass.'

The man from Civil Defence did what he had to do. He told her to stand still. He took a book from the table and told her to place the grenade on the book. Then he walked towards the door. Only then did Miss Reed realise that the hand grenade was still dangerous.

What happened after that was a blur to the boys. The questions, the police vans, special police and bomb squad. And the endless questions. Even Miss Reed had to make a statement. The police wanted to make sure that there were no dangerous trouble-makers hiding under the shabby primary school desks.

Poor Abbie and Isaac. All they had wanted was some fun, just like in the movies. Instead they ended up in the school sick-bay drinking sugar water from an enamel mug and weeping their eyes out.

'It is like being in jail,' Abbie sobbed.

'Yes, for a crime we did not commit,' Isaac replied.

When the bell rang at the end of the school day, they held their breaths and listened for footsteps coming down the passage to set them free. At least Meneer never had the chance to ask for their homework.

Coming of age

DIANNE HOFMEYR

There's that heart-stopping moment when you've gathered momentum and there's no going back. The power of decision has been relinquished. You are hurtling towards a destination that can't be changed. The process is irreversible. One moment you are grounded. The next you are launched. Then that split second of being weightless, unrestrained, free ... followed by the all-powerful moment when a tautening of muscles, a lengthening of stretch gives you control again. When your body takes over.

This is how it is with diving.

Above me, water stains spread clouds of rust and ochre across the ceiling. Sunset clouds trapped in a rigid, white rhinoboard sky. In places the sickly green of the wall paint wavers into the white. I imagine warehouses piled to the roof with drums of official green paint ready to hand out to all hospitals and institutions. The country is drowning in green paint.

In the middle of the cloud stains, a ceiling fan cranks the heavy air in a blur of movement. If I stare at it long enough, I can will it to slow down. At times the dark blades seem almost perceptible like a propeller starting up on a plane. There's a visual reminder of a shape imprinted on the brain, even though the aeroplane is at full throttle and the blades are already a blur of action.

We sit there on the runway, Dad and I, and he goes through all the checks. The smell of insecticide is strong. I go along for the joyride. He goes for the money. He's in the crop-spraying business. He eases the plane slowly forward along the runway to the threshold. The controller gives him the go-ahead. Then a noise like a massive swarm of wild bees fills the cockpit. The bodywork shudders. The wings shake. Everything vibrates.

He releases the brake-stop. We rush forward but the runway seems to hold onto the wheels like sticky glue. His hands touch lightly on the control column. He keeps her centred. The knob-thorn branches reach out and almost scratch the belly of the plane.

We're airborne. Free. Independent. Weightless. Unburdened. Out in the atmosphere. Huge puffy clouds billow about our windows unfettered by the confines of a rhinoboard ceiling.

Diving is the same as flying.

The tension of the run-up. Every muscle pulsating. Heart throbbing. Nerve-endings vibrating. Then the moment of complete stillness before the rush forward. The pressure of the feet against the board. The arches raised. The metatarsals rising, pushing, forcing the body forward. The final lift. No turning back. The dive has started. You are airborne.

The fan fills the room with a sound that deadens and takes away the reality of everything. Both inside and out. The telephone is monotonous. Voices are muffled. From somewhere the long drawn-out sound of Silent Night, being sung over and over. Outside red-billed wood hoopoes cackling in the jacaranda. A Heuglin's robin calling and rustling in the carpet of fallen bougainvillea. The squeal of the swing in the children's play area that needs oiling. The crunch of car tyres on the gravel. Doors that slam. I know all these things. But I don't see them.

I see the ceiling with its trapped clouds and the whirring fan and the gold fringe of shivering lettering that says: MERRY CHRISTMAS, strung from drawing pins pressed into the ceiling above my bed.

And I see the faces that loom over me. Peer down at me. Too close. Invading my body space. Invading it, as if my body is inconsequential now.

'Time for your wash, now, love.'

And the green plastic curtains are zipped closed around my bed with the sharp sibilance of metal ring against metal ring along the rail. I smell the cheap deodorant and the whiff of Jik on her uniform. She pulls back the sheet and re-arranges my arms alongside my body.

I'm not dirty! I don't want to be washed! I plead with my eyes and the respirator pipe gurgles in my throat.

Her hands prod on. 'We don't want the family to arrive and find you smelly, do we?'

It's not a question. She doesn't wait for a reply.

There's a washcloth in her hands. She rubs soap vigorously against it.

'Just a little soap. The water's warm.'

She applies it to my arms. I don't feel the warmth.

'Under your arms now,' she cajoles.

Does she expect me to lift them up?

'There, that's better.'

For her? Or for me?

She works across my chest slowly as if she's enjoying it. Do I still have any definition in my muscles?

'And around Peter Pecker.'

Through my lashes I see my penis lying small between her thick, stubby fingers. And I imagine my scrotum all shrivelled up against me like a sea-anemone trying to escape invasion.

'Don't you worry. We do this all the time. We're used to it.'

Sure, you might be! But I'm not! I tell her with my face.

I clench my jaw until my teeth ache and the brace at the back of my neck bites into me and pulls at my scalp. I will my fingers to make a fist. But I don't think they do. Because when she's finished dabbing at me with a towel, she lays them out on top of the sheet again. They lie there as languid and useless as ever. The phone rings somewhere in another world. Silent Night strains on. Outside the window of the ICU, car doors slam and feet crunch across the gravel.

The dive started like thousands of others. With all the familiar tensions. As you step on the board, the feeling of a moth against your ribcage or a rat scrabbling across the ceiling. The sense of unease. Of knowing what the spectators demand of you. Of knowing what you demand of yourself. Then the moment of no return. The complete freedom as you launch yourself, knowing that with the smallest tautening the tumble can be altered. The supreme feeling of being in control.

110

Finally gravity takes over and the downward plunge begins. The sense of a sharp intake of breath as you go into the half twist. The pale blur of faces as the spectators crane their heads upwards. The knowledge that your timing has been perfect.

That day something different. Something out of place. No longer a sense of pale faces turned upwards. Instead the darkness of heads turned away towards the pool. A speck of colour in the blue below as you begin the tumble. Just where you should be entering the water, there's something else ... a child!

Why he's there or how he's got into the pool, is completely immaterial.

You are on your course of no return. No amount of muscle power is going to swing you back through the air and return you to the board like some rewind button on a video machine. In that split second you make a decision. You twist out of the dive. With every muscle straining, you pull aside to avoid the body that is bobbing around under you. In the panic, you overcorrect. And you know with a diver's, as well as a pilot's sense of timing and perception, that you've over-corrected. But you've run out of space and time. Except time to see the cement coping of the edge of the pool, swinging up towards you.

And you hear the spectators' scream.

Afterwards ... the green walls, a ceiling with the trapped clouds, a fan censoring the sounds and faces that loom.

My dad smelling of insecticide sweetened with brandy fumes.

'That was a good dive, son! Your best ever. At least it began that way ...'

'Shut up, Jack! This is not the time to speak about diving!' My mother's voice sharp and brittle.

Say it, Mum! Say it! I command her with my eyes and my chin clamps hard. Let me hear you say the word ... QUADRI-PLEGIC!

Instead she rearranges my arms along the sheet. How does she know I want them rearranged? Years and years of playing with dolls come in useful now. She avoids my eyes but I see tears in hers. I feel like a balloon that has too much air pumped into it! I want to shout ... it's not you, ma! It's me! I'm the one! Save your tears!

And then suddenly, I'm drowning. Just like I was drowning in the pool under the water until someone dived down to save me. Water filling my lungs and my arms useless and unable to thrust up towards the surface. The pipe gurgles in my throat. I need to sit up so that I can clear my lungs. I'm drowning in my own saliva. My lips struggle with words that are blocked by the respirator pipe.

'Nurse! Come quickly!' my mother shouts.

'What's the matter?'

My chest heaves. I feel the liquid filling my lungs.

'It's nothing! He's hyper-ventilating.' She pushes against my shoulders. 'Relax. Just breathe naturally. Don't fight the machine. Let it work for you.'

'Why's he hyper-ventilating?' my mother asks.

'It's nothing. Just tension.'

I want to shout ... I know the difference between tension and blind, bloody panic.

'He looks terrified ...' sweet brandy fumes from my father, '... as if he's struggling to breathe.'

'It's psychological. Of course he can breathe. The machine does it for him. He's got nothing to worry about. He just needs to lie there and relax.'

Fuck you! Fuck all of you! My lips twist silently around the words and a snort of phlegm comes from my nose as my throat constricts around the pipe. I can't even wipe my own snotty nose.

'What's he trying to say?'

'Come on, now. You have to behave. How can we help you, if you don't want to help us?' The cheap deodorant smell as she invades my body space. 'That's the trouble with these young quadriplegics. They try to fight it.'

'He turns twenty one tomorrow.' My mother pats my arm.

I've already become a 'he'. Someone without a name.

'Have to bring you a couple of beers, son. Feed them into you

112

through one of these tube things you've got running into your arm.'

'Shut up, Jack! Don't be so ridiculous!'

Later, the lights are dimmed. Finally the carol-singing has ended. The sounds outside have stopped as well, except for some crickets. Now in the silence the fan seems to accentuate the blips and pings of the machines hooked up to the patients. I feel the clamps at the back of my head pulling at my temples. I will myself to feel the weight of the counterpane against my body. My lips are cracked and dry. The fan wafts its breath over my face, insistent and irritatingly regular. Non-human.

I try to recall her soft breath on my face. I try to imagine the feeling of her smooth skin against mine. The lips that have covered my lips. I imagine the texture of her. I taste her with every shrivelled-up nerve in my body.

Suddenly under the tip of my left index finger, I sense the weave of the counterpane. My finger slowly plays over the bumps. I feel my heart will stop. This can't be happening. I re-trace a small circle. Explore the weave. Feel the outline of the hospital lettering. I force the muscles and tendons and nerve-endings of that single finger to co-operate.

I am centred once more. In full flight. Weightless. Free. I want to laugh out loud at the pleasure of it. Instead my pipe gurgles and I splutter.

'Have you got a problem?' The nurse hovers over me, too close to my face.

I stare back at her and try not to let my eyes tell my secret.

In the index finger of my left hand I have all the power of the world.

I hold back that knowledge.

Right now, I am the only one that knows that I've begun a process that is irreversible.

My body has taken over.

I'm airborne.

Free.

Independent.

The supreme feeling of being in control.

Housekeeping

ANN OOSTHUIZEN

I have fashioned this house so it fits my life as snug as a glove.
Paul knows this. He has turned the garage into his study.
Because the house is on such a small plot, it's close by, but not
quite attached.

'We've spent more than we can afford on this place,' he
says, lighting another cigarette. 'Those people who came with
Richard the other day – you took the woman upstairs, didn't
you?'

'She loved it. It reminded her of New Orleans.' She asked
had I been there? *In my mind*, I answered. *I've travelled – I
travel ... everywhere.*

'Richard told me they couldn't stop talking about it afterwards. They want to make us an offer.'

'Something I won't be able to refuse?'

'We could live in the bush. Or on the beach. Mozambique is
wide open – '

Paul is an ecologist. He's happiest when he's camping, far
away from streets, from the smell of towns. His work takes
him away for months at a time. He'd love to make a home
in a grass hut, set up a battery computer under a tree. I'm
attracted by his dream, but not quite, not quite. It is not
change that I want. Not now. Everything is just the way I want
it to be.

Built maybe a hundred years ago, my house has a wooden
veranda across the front, with white slatted railings on the
second floor. There's a front door and a bay window downstairs. The house stands tall in a plot so narrow that it could
link hands with all the other identical houses down the street
like a chain of cut out dolls in stiff white paper. Yet the upstairs
balcony is the only place from where you are aware of the

neighbours and can hear cars zoom into the city centre. In the small garden, the large blue-green banana trees, the tree ferns and tropical trees that grow dense green foliage and huge red flowers create an impression of stillness. By shutting out the middle distance, they reinforce the way the house looks inward at its own enchantment.

Paul takes the ashtray and empties it in the bin, washing it carefully under the tap. 'We'd have more money. You wouldn't have to work. You could ...'

'Could what?'

'Anything you like. Write. Paint.'

'Cook?' I tease him. We've had this argument before. I say that when he talks about liberating me from my job, it's just a smoke-screen for making me totally available to him.

'Did I say that? I never said that. You know I can cook quite well enough and besides ...'

'Who cares – there's enough fresh fruit about,' I join in, chanting his well-worn conclusion. We both laugh. That's where most of our arguments end.

In the small backyard, which is used by all our friends as if it were the real entrance to the house, I have built a square swimming pool and lined it with tiny grey tiles which give it the look of a natural feature. Large-leafed water plants, different ferns as well as a small waterfall which runs continually down the back wall into the pool and is part of its cleaning system, reinforce the impression that the visitor has entered an enchanted and ancient place. The back kitchen wall opens out with folding glass doors which slide away over large grey tiles flush with the surface of the pool. We are in a seaside town, so a cooling breeze blows constantly over the water and into the house, riffling the thin white lawn curtains downstairs, and making the wooden doors upstairs, with their panes of ruby and crystal glass, shut with a clatter and bang.

We are drinking white wine in tall blue glases, and I hear, during pauses in our conversation, the house creak and shift, getting itself comfortable.

I travel with my eyes across the wooden floors of the opened-up downstairs rooms, take the stairs with a bound, and imagine the bathroom luminous with old sea-green glass bottles, the three bedrooms tucked up all in a row, the wide passage where I prepare my lecture notes on the long shelves which serve as bookcase, table and desk.

'What about Greta?' I ask.

'You know Bob would love to have her live with him.' It's true. Bob is what Greta calls 'my biological father'. He's older than Paul, with thin greying hair and glasses that sit on the end of his nose because he can't be bothered to take them off when he's not reading. He's married again, with two younger daughters, but that doesn't stop him from being what Greta calls 'dramatic' every time she goes there. She says even if he has visitors, he opens his arms wide and bellows, 'Greta!' as if he hasn't seen her for years.

Once, overcome with adolescent shyness, she ventured to complain. 'Don't,' she whispered.

'Don't what?'

'Be so stagy. Like "Dr Livingstone, I presume"!'

'Now that really was staged!' he roared, and putting an arm around her, he announced to a roomful of American archaeologists, 'My daughter, Greta!'

She said she wanted to creep away, but there was nowhere to hide. Now she just smiles and endures his welcome. Probably she even expects it. I'm glad he loves her, but I wouldn't dream of giving her up.

My father sent me to university like an explorer. I didn't mind. The farm was in a lonely, cold part of the eastern Free State, where the mountains shut off the sun early in the afternoon and the sheep grew woolly and prosperous on their green slopes. I brought back suitcases of books that spilled out on the kitchen table. To please him, I was studying Philosophy and Psychology. He read all night. When he walked round the farm, Kierkegaard and Sartre, Freud and Jung entered into his own internal visions, and the ideas echoed back to him from the tall mountains and the arched blue sky.

Bob was my father's choice. Freed from home and farm and

116

his enduring love, I was discovering the erotic pleasure of my own sexuality. My father viewed me with compassion as if I were in the grip of a serious illness. When I brought Bob to meet him, they immediately got on in spite of Bob's English-ness. At any rate, by now, in his isolation and his reading, my father hardly knew what language he spoke or what nation-ality he claimed.

'He's the youngest professor at the university,' I boasted.

'Marry him.'

Flattered, uncertain, I did.

When we split up, all I knew was that I could not live with-out our daughter, Greta. From the moment she was born, she was a necessary part of my life. When Paul and I married, she was nine. Our wedding photograph hangs in our bedroom. A young girl, on her head a coronet of frangipani flowers, smiles between us. The photograph is oval, black and white, grainy from the enlargement, like an old-fashioned allegory, with Greta representing 'Hope'. The three of us are on a flat rock, encircled by a wild river, mountains rising up on all sides.

When Hans was born, it seemed only just that, as I had Greta, he should be Paul's. During the day, Hans slept in Paul's study. When Paul went running, he carried the baby in a papoose on his back. At six months Hans went for his first expedition into the bush. By the time he was two, he knew what it is to travel vast distances, to fall asleep under the stars and to be kept awake by the bright full moon. At three, he was a sturdy walker among the bitter-smelling mountain herbs, when they climbed for days in remote wilderness moun-tain ranges.

Hans is six now, Greta is seventeen. Hans and Paul, Greta and Una, Paul and Una: these are the strong bonds that keep us firm.

Paul is studying the fragile ecology of a remote inland lake. His living quarters on the hillside above the lake are becom-ing more and more elaborate. Several local families live there all the time and carry on his research while he is back in the city. Hans is still young enough to go with him on every trip, and Paul is even thinking of keeping him out of school for another year.

It's time for Paul and Hans to set off for their camp in the bush. When all the hustle of packing clothes and provisions and equipment is over, and the goodbyes have been said, and the four-wheel-drive rattles down the street, when Paul and Hans are gone, then Greta and I turn slowly back into the quiet house. It has been waiting for us.

'What will you do?' I ask her.

'There's that picture of the runner I want to work on. I've asked my Art teacher to supper. You'll like her.'

Later, I hear the soft murmur of voices downstairs. Asher is small-boned with huge dark eyes and thick shiny hair. We eat an enormous bowl of iced pink watermelon spiced with mint and crumbled feta cheese. The candles make circles of light, the corners of the room are treasures of mystery, the pool is silver in motion.

'I live with my family still,' says Asher. 'Like Greta.' She's making a joke, saying she is only a girl at home in spite of being a teacher, but my heart clenches, thinking how soon I must lose Greta. It's her final year at school.

'It's too far for Asher to go home by bus. I've asked her to stay the night. She can use Hans's room, can't she, Una?'

My room has red velvet curtains, dark sage walls. The double bed is high, with a brass railing. Paul's smell lingers on the pillow and on the satin sheets which caress my body. Why then do I listen for the creak of floorboards in the dark of the deep night? Do I imagine soft laughter? I am jealous of this woman, imagining that she holds my daughter in her arms, that Greta will find pleasure in her softly curved body, so different from the two of us, who are tall and skinny and long-legged. I can't sleep, and dare not switch on the light in case they think I am spying on them. I turn and turn.

At the first note of the dawn chorus, I slip out of bed. It is five minutes by car to the beach. My bare toes dig into the wet sand as I fly along beside grey waves, now turning silver in the low rays of the rising sun. The salt makes the sharp air

scour my lungs. Running back an hour later, the tide has covered the hard sand and I struggle to free myself from sinking
into the soft, clinging beach.

Home again, it is still not yet seven o'clock. I've picked up the
paper and some hot newly-baked croissants, and I set the coffee
pot before showering. When I return to the kitchen, they are
downstairs too. How could I be angry with such radiance? Greta
is brushing Asher's hair and plaiting it into a thick, dark rope.

It's Saturday morning. I wonder to myself if Asher will stay
another day, but it seems she has duties at home. When she
has gone, Greta shows me her latest painting – a large canvas,
the female figure, light as a feather, leaps across the diagonal,
arms up, head thrown back.

'What did Asher say about it?'

'The hair – she wants me to change it.'

'You'll try that?'

'Mmm. *She likes you*, Una.'

'Me?' I laugh and hug her. 'You're the beautiful one.'

Greta's hair spikes on her head. She's wearing very short
shorts and clumpy boots. I know how her heart beats small and
vulnerable.

'When you've worked on it a while, call me,' I say, and she
does. The figure is different now. Her hair streams out dark
and strong, changing the balance, not forward, not back. She
is suspended in her own field of force.

'Wonderful,' I say. We take our lunch and sit at its feet, ad-
miring.

Asher comes again the following week. I'm careful to stay
out of their way. I work upstairs and take myself off to the gym
and onto the beach for a long, tiring run. I'm missing the freedom to be with Greta whenever I want, the way it used to be
when Paul and Hans are away. I'm uneasy, careful before entering a room, afraid to overhear a conversation. I refuse their
invitation to eat with them. I've arranged to go out, and when
I get back, the bedroom doors are both shut. The next day,
Greta's contentment disarms me. I can't bear the idea of seeing her face hurt if I tell her I'm lonely.

But the next week Greta tells me she's not expecting Asher. She shows me a vague outline of a new painting.

'This figure in the centre – do you have time to sit for me?'

'I can't see if it's a man or a woman.'

'A woman – there are three women. The one you'll be modelling for will be draped. I need something stiff and heavy.' We settle on the stiff taffeta and brocade bedspread on my bed.

'Like this?'

'Turn your head a little. Perfect.' Greta works quickly, sketching in lines and planes, a shadow, bones. 'Just half an hour more, please.'

It's like old times. I dream out of the window, imagining the sea in the late afternoon, when the heat is waning and the light turns everything golden. 'Swim?' I ask. 'We could go to Sandy Cove.'

'Don't say anything yet, please.' But I can see she's tempted. 'You've put me off!' she laughs. 'Let's go.'

I snatch a costume and towels, pack cold chicken and furred peaches onto ice-cold bricks. A bright table cloth. Pale Chardonnay. Glasses. We drive away from the city on a road that cuts a narrow ribbon through dense fields of tall sugar cane. It winds around and through hills. When I turn towards the sea, the surface of the road is gritty with blown sea sand, and suddenly, over a dune, there it is.

We swim far out until the beach is only a line of white surf breaking. The water is calm and we lie in it, gently rising and falling as if on its breath. An infinity later, I dry my sticky, salty fingers and open the wine. Greta is sitting on her towel, her head tilted to catch the sun on her face.

'Do you miss them?' She doesn't look at me.

'Who?'

'Paul and Hans?'

'The boys?'

I should beware of such flip answers. Suddenly I'm clenched in a fear of what might become of them, as if by my negligence I could do them harm. I see Hans's hand waving in the car window, his two missing front teeth in an uncertain smile.

'Asher's coming next weekend. I want to paint the two of you together. You are mistaken, you know. We're not lovers. She says I'm too young. She —'

Greta is digging a hole with a piece of driftwood. She shoots out gritty bits of shell and wet sand. They fall in a damp spray on the white beach.

'What?'

Her smooth skin is lightly dusted with salt. Her short hair has dried in curly tendrils about her ears. She won't look at me. We have no rituals any more for daughters. After which we can say, 'Go, my daughter, you are a woman. The freedom is yours, take it.'

I remember my father's compassionate understanding of the fever in my body. He applied what he hoped would be the soothing balm of marriage. These days even that old remedy is out of fashion.

'I'm starving.' Greta reaches for the chicken and salad. 'Yum.'

Well, I guess food has always been a recommended substitute.

The next week, Greta makes pasta salad. 'Don't go away!' she mouths, using her arms to emphasise each word as Asher comes through the gate. I'm feeling foolish, but I'm limp and unresistant from the heat. Besides, these two women are so lovely. My own daughter, a flower about to open, Asher, a young rose. She brings me a pottery jar, as thin as a leaf. She has been experimenting with glazes.

'It's as firm as an egg!' I exclaim when I balance it on the palm of my hand. As warm too. 'Thank you.'

Asher smiles. Her eyes really are beautiful. As we sit round the table, Greta never stops sketching us. Now our two heads are intimate, serious, now bonded in laughter. The drawings are like a thermometer – you can see the fizz spark between us. *She likes you*, Greta said. I'm bolder now.

The night doesn't cool down. 'We'll never sleep unless we swim,' Greta urges me. I'm lazing over coffee and chocolate-coated ginger.

'Do you want to?' I ask Asher. She nods.

121

As usual we skinny dip in the pool before we go to bed. In the moonlight our bodies are ghostly, mythical. Our legs, our arms, our breasts, glimmer. We are three women with no one to spy on us. We loaf in the water. I let my legs float up as I lie against the ferny sides. Water bubbles tickle me. Greta puts her head under the fountain and laughs at the force of it when it hits her eyes.

As I walk to my room, the warm air dries my body. I know I will not lie awake alone tonight imagining floorboards creaking, whispering lovers. I'm waiting for Asher.

'... with naked foot stealing into my bed-chamber ...' I quote at her, opening my arms. The sheets are as slippery as whispers. They drape cunningly over her brown thighs. I bury my face in her thick hair, in her maidenhair. She runs her tongue down my back.

Greta is lazy in the early mornings, but Asher comes to the beach with me, and then I drop her at her parents' house.

'I've got to think about what happened last night,' I tell her.

To my surprise, the four-wheel-drive is in the parking place. The back door of the house is wide open. Hans careers into my arms. Paul, brown from days in the open, unshaved, his hair tied back with a leather thong, is struggling with rucksacks, tents, his camping trunk, specimen cases, portable computer, bedding, cool-boxes. He puts a tray of pawpaws on the kitchen shelf. 'Brought these for you. They were so cheap.'

He's hot and rough to my skin, and he tastes like stale cigarettes and an old bar. His dirty clothes are in an untidy heap on the kitchen floor. His entry has sent the wrong signals all over the ordered ambience of the house. As if in retaliation, he sniffs.

'Smells like a harem in here.'

I choose to be offended. I scoop up the dirty clothes and put them in the washing machine. Paul's boots leave circles of dust on the kitchen tiles. He notices my irritation, and picks up his books, papers, specimen jars in a gesture which is anger.

'I'll take these away to my kennel.'

'What?'

'My study. Woof. Woof.'

I refuse to follow, placate. Which leaves Hans, blond, tanned, quiet.

'Did you have a good time?'

He nods, staring at the floor, then makes for a sofa and sits quietly. He's too young to be this uncertain of my affection and I'm immediately stricken with guilt. I join him, and put an arm around his shoulders.

'I've missed you.'

'I don't want to go with him next time.'

'You don't want to go with Daddy?'

'No. I want to stay here with you.'

'But he needs you –' Am I saying that I don't? 'You usually have such a good time together … Did something bad happen?'

'No.' But there are tears now, silently making their way down his face. I feel his sense of abandonment. My strangeness on their arrival affected all of us. What have I been doing? I push Asher and Greta to the back of my mind.

We take his rucksack and his books and pencils up to his room. Look, it's still here, I'm saying to him. This is your place. The pictures he has drawn are on the walls, the flying birds suspended from the ceiling, his collection of shells on the windowsill. Everything is as he left it. I feel his relief. Now he's unpacking, showing me his pressed flowers, telling me about the fish eagle that cried like a baby, the pied kingfishers that hovered above the lake and then plunged into it with such deadly accuracy. 'Tiny birds, yet they move like bullets,' he exclaims, imitating them. I've missed him, I realise, hugging him.

I take Paul a beer, and sit with him in his study. Although we've put in a whole wall of windows, the room still gives the impression of a cave. It's the way his book-shelves are stacked right up to the ceiling, with, under them, the filing cupboards and specimen drawers.

'I can't go in there.' He means into the house.

'You've been away too much. What do you expect?'

Paul says, 'I've a meeting this afternoon. I may be home late.'

'I'll wait up for you.'

'Very late.'

So, when Greta comes back, Paul is out. Greta kneels down next to Hans, who has built an elaborate city on the livingroom floor. Without missing a beat, he absorbs her into his game. In the morning, when Greta greets Paul, she's cool with him, pretending to be late for school, preoccupied with making a fuss about where she left her school bag. Paul is reading the paper, but Hans turns his bowl of cornflakes upside down. There's milk and slimy bits of wet cornflakes all over the table.

'Damn it, Hans! You don't have to be so clumsy!' Paul yells, and Hans is suddenly shaking.

'I didn't do it!' he screams. And I rush to hold him. I focus all the love and energy I have on his wiry, squirming, shuddering body.

Paul is at meetings all day, so instead of dropping Hans off at his nursery school, I take him with me to work. He reads his books, draws, and after a while the students take him off to the cafeteria. Later, looking through the window, I see him lounging happily on the grass in a large group.

'It's the house,' says Paul. 'We're living on top of each other. Everything's too small – look at the pool, what good is that teeny thing? The garden is nothing. We're so crowded together, no wonder it doesn't work.'

Our conversations are like messages sent on carrier pigeons.

'You haven't said anything about Greta's new painting.'

'I hate it.' His violence shocks. 'Women – all she paints is women.'

Days later, when I come home from work, Paul is in his study. Greta is still at school. I walk through the house, calling, 'Hans … Hans …' but there is no reply. I find him in our bedroom. He's standing in front of the dressing-table mirror. He's wearing my red strappy dress over his blue T-shirt. It falls in a pool of colour onto the floor. He turns. His face is a mask of lipstick, rouge and powder. Two eyes, ringed with black mascara stare out, beseeching.

'Darling!' I sob. 'Let me help you with the make-up. You've put on too much. We'll have to get some of it off first.'

I use cutton wool and cold cream to clean his small, anxious face.

'Shall we do something together? What would you like?'

'Ice cream.'

'Okay. Let's walk to the café, and you can choose which kind.'

Later, Greta is home. I watch her setting out her tubes of paint. She turns to me, accusing. 'I thought you really cared about Asher.'

'I do.'

'You can't start something and then change your mind.'

It's a new feeling to have Greta scold me like this. She takes my silence as a question.

'I thought you were happy. That we were content.'

She begins work on her picture. Three women. It's not clear whether Asher is sitting on my lap.

'It's like the Leonardo in the National Gallery. Isn't that the one where the virgin is sitting on Saint Anne's lap?'

'Clever of you to spot it.'

Greta is the third woman. She's holding us together. She's willing us to fuse with her and through her into one fierce love. Her painted eyes seduce me to enter into this union.

'You played me – like a fish on a line!'

'You wanted it!'

'How do you know what I want? I'll say what I want!'

'You think you're the only one who's allowed to make things happen. You chose this house. You fixed it up. You get angry if we don't all fit in and play happy families. But if I decide to take control, I'm out of line. Way out!'

She's slashing paint over the women's faces. Her palette knife rips the canvas. There's a hole where my head was.

I can't see any more. I drag my body onto my bed. I must be ill because now I find I can't move my arms or my legs. I'm boiling. The sheets are in a tangle. They strangle me and I can't breathe.

Later, in a vision I see a cool farmhouse. My father is sitting on the veranda smoking a pipe. He nods at me.

Paul brings me mangoes, watermelon, pineapple, lychees,

pawpaw. Sometimes Hans lies next to me. Greta has taken herself off. My father sits on the end of the bed. I wish he wouldn't smoke in the house.

Paul is sleeping in Greta's room. She's staying with Bob, he tells me. She's fine, just that she feels she needs to work for her exams.

'Will she be all right?' I ask my father.

'She must make her own way now,' he says. He looks very wise, like an old man should.

'And Hans?'

My father begins to disappear. It is an answer.

Beautiful people

KEN BARRIS

I had lunch with Gill again, one of our regular dates. She was late. I passed the time with a boring magazine article on the Gender Commission, then something else on the abuse of women. This is a working-class problem, I thought wearily. Nothing to do with me really.

My brilliant friend Gillian arrived eventually. You probably have a friend like her. She's gorgeous in every way – brilliant skin, teeth, hair, eyes, the works. She speaks beautifully, so graceful and slightly, excitingly breathless, and to make matters worse, she has a bitingly clear mind. I've known and loved her since we were children, and deep down hated her for such outrageous success and beauty.

She picked at a Mediterranean salad and I scoffed down my chocolate mousse. 'It's all I'm having for lunch,' I said defensively. 'I won't have milk, won't even put sweetener in my coffee. The mousse here is an art form, an aesthetic experience, it's not greed you know, I love opera too.'

She shrugged, charmingly: 'Did I say anything? Do I care what you're eating?'

'No,' I conceded. 'You don't care what I eat.'

When the food was out of the way and I was stirring my coffee, she looked at me with those devastating eyes and said, 'Can you keep a secret, Shelley?'

'Of course I can, me a secret? I swear I'll only tell one person at a time, what is it?'

'Sands want to marry.'

My teaspoon ground to a halt. 'To marry,' I said carefully, 'you?'

She nodded, her face troubled.

I blurted out: 'Don't. Don't do it.' And regretted it instantly: 'I'm sorry, I shouldn't have said that.'

'No,' she said. 'You're right. I shouldn't marry him. It would be a real mistake.'

'Well, that's fine then,' I exhaled, relieved and just the faintest bit shaken.

'That's not the secret,' said Gill.

'What's the secret then?'

'The secret is that I think I'm going to do it.'

I looked at her in consternation.

It was the first time I could ever remember Gill looking helpless. She seemed trapped and – I thought at the time I was exaggerating to myself – stricken.

I had dinner with them not long after they were married, just the three of us. She was wearing an incredibly short, backless black dress. I kissed her on the cheek as I came in and whispered, 'What's with the outfit?' It was fairly cold, she had goose pimples all over and was obviously uncomfortable.

She looked embarrassed. 'Sands,' she said. 'He wants me to.'

I couldn't answer because just then he walked in, calling out: 'It's Shelley dear! Dear Shelley, our close friend!'

I gave him my bitchiest smile.

His real name was Urban Sanders. It was such an unlikely name that people called him Sands. He came from a Natal sugar-farming family and looked like the bad guy in a Wilbur Smith novel – hugely handsome in an ugly way, complete with thick coils of black chest hair, heavy shave on beefy cheeks, sensual and sardonic lips. He was twelve years older than Gill. Born wearing a tuxedo. Born to arrogance and money. On first meeting him I thought he was so corny I couldn't take him seriously, though I understood why she did. I knew about her social ambition. But as their relationship developed I was to see through the cracks in this impressive picture. His power over her would increase and with it his cruelty would emerge, growing in vigour and refinement. Now she had married him. ('You're not even pregnant!' I had stormed at her – 'are you?' But she wasn't, and I realised that she was in deeper trouble than she knew.)

'Here,' I said, thrusting a bottle of Chardonnay at Sands. He passed it absently to Gill and we went in.

The evening passed like a nightmare belonging to someone else: it doesn't affect you directly, but still unfolds with a horrible logic of its own that you can't escape. He treated Gill like a servant, making no comment on the meal she dished up (roast pork fillets in a ginger and honey dressing I can't resist mentioning, with scorched vegetables, too delicious), handing back his plate for more. Then he contradicted everything she said, often sarcastically, while at the same time awarding me with warm and exaggerated interest. She grew quieter as the evening passed, and I grew increasingly upset. No, I'm lying. My reaction was more complex than that, but I can't bring myself to talk about it right now.

The *pièce de résistance* (after the Dutch truffles and Irish coffee): Sands made Gill sit on his lap, in her tiny dress, while we discussed politics and he caressed her in the most intimate places under the black cloth; her eyes went moist and I didn't know what to do with mine. Once she looked up at me, pleading, but I didn't know for what. He saw my discomfort. He rested his chin on her shoulder and said, 'Don't mind me, Shelley, I'm just warming up the punda for afters.'

When I eventually left – after we mouthed the usual parting inanities to each other, as if nothing terrible was happening – I felt contaminated. By what? By complicity. I had to say to myself again and again that I would have walked out much sooner, in outrage loud and clear – but couldn't for fear it would rebound on my poor friend Gill. I cried myself to sleep that night.

Another lunch with Gill. It was our first meeting since that disastrous supper, and I knew things would be awkward. I watched her walk in. It was clear, even from her movement, that she was in pain.

'Are you alright?' I asked as she pulled out her chair.

'Why shouldn't I be?' she replied blankly.

But she looked – dull is the only word. I had never seen her look dull. I had never seen her in public with her hair bedraggled and needing a wash. It was upsetting; I ordered a fried Camembert starter with fennel and cranberry-sauce topping, and a main course of *pesce interno al forno con vinaigrette al pomdoro basilico*. And Gill? A salad, as usual, one of those designer lettuce smoke screens.

I leaned forward, trying to restore our intimacy. 'Gill, please. Listen to me. You can leave him, you know. Leave this number. Just walk away.'

She shook her head and after a pause said, 'It's not that easy.'

'But Gill why?' I protested, suddenly abandoning the restraint I had promised myself. 'Why do you let this happen? Why should such a strong person, such a wonderfully talented person let herself be –'

I was going to say: degraded, humiliated. Crushed. I stopped myself in time. I raised my hands helplessly: 'I'm sorry. It's not my business.'

Gill rested her hands on the table – held so still, so passive.

'Shelley,' she said, 'I can't talk about it. Just leave me alone.'

The fish arrived, a steaming colourful masterpiece. And a good excuse. I concentrated on it. A while later I looked up and saw Gill just sitting, quite upright, not eating her salad, her arms dangling at her sides. And then a horrible moment of insight arrived with the tartufo I shouldn't have ordered, between bites: at some obscure level, I was thrilled by what was happening to her. It made me feel well.

'Oh God, Gill, I'm such a piggy,' I wailed out of the blue.

She smiled listlessly at me. But I wasn't talking about eating. I hastily finished the ice cream and ordered cappucino.

I happened to drive past Gill's place quite near lunchtime and thought I'd take a chance and pop in. The door was slightly ajar, but there was no response to the intercom button. I went in.

'Hullo?' I called, 'anyone home?'

The house remained quiet. I wandered into the kitchen and

looked around. Sometimes you pick up the feeling of a house most accurately when it is empty: a dry sadness lapped at the shores of this one.

I opened the fridge to divert myself and began investigating. Before I knew it, I was at the *tres* designer counter working out what to do with a bagel, lox, black pepper, Stilton and various interesting pickles. I tried to slice the Stilton razor-thin; it crumbled greasily.

My breath suddenly sucked in as a moist male hand pressed the small of my back and crept up. My spine arched involuntarily and I shrieked, 'No Sands, don't do that!'

'What, Shelley, what? Me? Do?' he replied, thrusting his face over my shoulder. I felt the heat of his cheek radiating into mine. He reached round me and picked up the bagel. I couldn't move. I hated myself, I despised myself, I couldn't comprehend it, but it was true: I couldn't move. My back was still arched (but not quite as much as before). He lifted the bagel to his face, which remained thrust so comfortably and intrusively against my cheek, and bit off a piece.

'Here,' he said, mumbling round the bread in his mouth. He reached round and pressed the rest of the bagel against my lips, which he stroked with it.

'So round, so pink, so wasted,' he whispered.

Bastard, I thought, but my mouth opened and the bagel entered and the tip of my tongue touched salty crust.

A door clicked. We both heard it. He let go, too slowly, and we turned round as if in slow motion, as if underwater. There was Gill, looking from me to Sands and back.

'Hullo,' she said, contained, as if she hadn't seen a thing. Maybe (I thought wildly) she hadn't.

'Hello dearest,' said Sands absently, gesturing with the bagel. 'We were thinking about having lunch together.'

'No we weren't,' I said breathlessly. 'I was just about to go.'

Gill looked at the pile of food on the counter; I had collected more than one might think. 'Oh please don't,' she said. Her face, her eyes, begged me. This time I understood. She didn't want to be left alone with the monster.

I did stay. Slowly my trembling subsided. From time to time I caught Gill watching me speculatively. It was a most dreadful experience and I swore to myself (a thousand times!) I would never let Sands do this to me again.

He invaded my sleep. If I had lived in a more superstitious time, I would have accused him of black magic. I dreamed about him, dreams so compromising they're unprintable. I felt disloyal to Gillian, I ached with disloyalty. In one of the nightmares I invited them to a barbecue where I had half an ox turning on the spit, fat sizzling off and igniting into thick orange flame. Sands appeared behind clouds of black belching smoke – in the dream his name was Urban – grinning like the very devil, tempting me with bagel. And when I looked again it was Gill trussed to the spit, naked, so skinny her bones stuck out, her face sad and composed, no expression visible behind her Ray-Bans.

When I did invite them to a meal, it turned out even worse. No ox: I had a whole yellowtail butterflied under the grill, lathered with Ina Paarman's Peri-Peri Basting Sauce (I only appreciate sophisticated dishes when I don't have to make them), but I had taken the liberty of adding piles of chillie. The fish was tangy, done to a turn, blazing hot. Sands chewed his first bite tentatively and said, 'Marvellous, Shelley. For a woman cook anyway. The fish – this yellowtail is hot!'

'It is lovely, darling,' said Gill. I could tell it was too hot for her; she sipped her wine indelicately. Gillian never does anything indelicately.

Her voice was a trigger for Sands. 'Hot fish,' he remarked thoughtfully. 'Hot tuna. Now some of us are cold fish, aren't we, dear?'

'Cold fish?' I was stupid enough to ask.

'Yes, cold fish. Cold. As in frigid. As in bed. As in if you move just the teeniest it might destroy the magic.' He looked at Gill, over whose face a smokiness passed, and he laughed and nudged her crudely: 'Only kidding, my darling.'

He wiped his mouth with the back of his hand, then shoved in another forkful of yellowtail. It didn't stop him remarking loudly: 'Now Shelley dearest, on the other hand, is a hot fish.' He waved the empty fork at me and laughed: 'Hot yellowtail.'

Flames of embarrassment shot up into my cheeks, of desperate sorry anger. Perspiration broke out all over my forehead. I dabbed helplessly, opened my mouth in outrage but didn't know what to say.

'Pink yellowtail I should say,' continued Sands remorselessly. 'Passionate pink. Plumply passionate. Plump and pink, right down, all the way to –'

Gill looked down at her knees. Fish and sawdust – there was no difference in the taste.

'Beast,' I said in a low voice. It was all I could manage.

'Yarroo! Rotter! Beast!' shouted Sands. 'Ow! Leggo, leggo!' He fell off his chair, howling with contemptuous laughter.

It was then that something changed in Gillian. Most people wouldn't have seen anything, but I know her extremely well. She was trembling faintly, with rage.

I ordered a salad. 'Hold the vinaigrette,' I told the waitress. Gill couldn't make up her mind between *gesnetzeltes* and *eisbein*. Eventually she settled for the *gesnetzeltes*.

'Don't look at me like that!' she exclaimed. 'I'm hungry. I've been hungry for months without knowing it!'

But I couldn't take my eyes off her. 'Something's changed,' I said. I wanted to say: you're as gorgeous as ever and it's wonderful to see you like this again. But our old, easy relationship was gone. 'I know what it is,' I said instead in my practical voice. 'You've made up your mind to leave Sands.'

She nodded.

'Congratulations,' I added. 'When is the joyous event? Soonest, I hope?'

She glanced up at the corner of the ceiling and said, most whimsically, 'Ummm, it's too soon.'

I was thrown. More accurately, aghast: 'Too soon? How can it be too soon? Gill, he's –'

She rewarded me with a smile, but there was something terribly cynical about it that made me bite my tongue.

'Yes, it is too soon,' she insisted. 'I'm fishing, you see. When you do that, you have to be very patient.'

'Fishing for what?'

'For an idea. For the right one. It's not enough just to walk out. To leave quietly.'

We suddenly ran out of things to say to each other. Something about her manner made me feel sick with anxiety. I didn't know what she was contemplating. Was she planning some kind of disastrous revenge? I began to panic, but dismissed the thought as too lurid. Fortunately the food arrived: salad tasting of ash.

I continued to feel guilty and confused, and decided what Gillian needed was space and distance, specifically from me. I didn't contact her for a while, didn't hear from her either. Then eventually she did phone. 'Come for lunch,' she said. 'Next Sunday.'

'Gill, how nice to hear from you. How are you?'

'Fine,' she said flatly, discouraging further conversation.

I was very relieved, but still felt unsettled about our relationship – not to mention Sands – so I had a couple of gins and tonic before I left. When I arrived, no one answered the intercom. The door was ajar; I went in. 'Hulloo?' I called timidly. No reply. I found myself in the kitchen. There was no one there. It was very puzzling, with no meal prepared either. Had I mistaken the date? I searched in my handbag for my diary – I didn't know why but my hands were trembling – bare feet padded across the floor and there was Sands, wearing a gown of thick red towelling and little else that I could see. He yawned and stretched, exposing an offensive amount of coiled black chest hair.

'Shelley, Shelley dearest, what a surprise!'

My eyes shot back to his face. 'What's gong on?' I asked. 'Where's Gillian?'

'Going on? Nothing, nothing's going on.'

He padded across the tiles towards me.

I could only repeat myself: 'Gill – where's Gillian?'

He was right in front of me, intrusively close. The counter pressed into the small of my back.

'Sands,' I said urgently, raising my hands to push him away. My fingers touched his chest and I recoiled. 'Sands, don't. Please.'

He rested his knuckles on the counter on either side of me. 'Don't worry about Gill,' he said into my face. 'She's gone. She's left. No more Gill.'

My heart was pounding heavily enough to shake my whole frame, even before I understood. He raised his hand to my lips which he stroked, saying, 'So full, so round, so wasted.' Then slowly, slowly, my fingers fluttering helplessly, he turned me round and bent me over the counter, pressing my cheek down into cold Italian marble. Later he said, 'Of all the painters, it was Rubens who best understood sensuality,' and mouthed a humourless laugh.

But which little joke was the more cruel – his or Gillian's?

I think I understand my dazzling friend a little better now, something that was missing from my picture of her. Truly beautiful people are like gods who come down to the world of mortals for a while and play at being human until they're bored. Then they go, leaving things in better order than before.

Letitia's decision

MIRIAM TLALI

Letitia pulled the door carefully behind her. She turned the knob gently so that it clacked softly, locking without a bang. She moved cautiously – one step after another – slowly picking her way over the stony gravel road. The small shining multiple 'streams' were now digging deeper and deeper into the soil because of the flow of water during the rainy weather of the previous weeks. She had to be careful not to strain her right ankle. It was beginning to swell from the sprain she had sustained during the scuffle with her husband Bafana.

She had waited until it was dark outside. At that time, it would be better and easier for her to move out because the neighbours would not see her – especially the ever-prying Mma-Lebona, the old lady next door. She was thankful also for the fine drizzle which had begun to fall. No one would wonder why she had wrapped a neck-scarf round her head to cover half her face. Her knees were still shaky, but she had at last made a decision, a difficult, painful one. This time she would (like she often heard other women say) 'open up a docket' at the nearby Orlando Police Station.

At the corner where the street in which she lived made a T-junction with the Main Road, she paused and looked around before she hobbled across to the other side. She sighed, relieved that she had made it to that point. The hedges surrounding the yards and the line of trees along the broad avenue would provide additional shelter for her. She scampered along slowly, keeping to the shady areas and as close to the continuous row of fences as possible. As she walked along, Letitia reasoned with herself and came to the conclusion that life was in fact like a pilgrimage into the unknown. That a person's journey through life was like moving along a narrow pathway which meanders into a thickly-wooded endless expanse of land, where one is for ever wondering where the path may lead to. You just keep on stumbling along the road which now and again disappears as it winds and twists through the jungle, never knowing what lies ahead. Along this journey there were choices to be made, and these could be idled with calamities and uncertainties.

Letitia did not recognise any of the faces she saw moving in and out of the entrance of the ever-busy Charge Office. She moved in surreptitiously, hoping that no one who knew her would appear. How could she, Letitia, proud daughter of Kgoadi, ever have to wander over the threshold of such infamous precincts with her soul earnestly crying out to be spared from shame?

She took her place at the end of the queue waiting to be attended to. After some time, the people became fewer and Letitia was thankful that it would soon be her turn. Without showing any signs of suffering, she bravely endured the aches in her body not to attract any attention.

The stocky, bespectacled African policeman sitting behind the long counter signalled to her to draw closer. She noticed that the other constables, seated on either side of him, addressed him respectfully as Sarge. In her hazy mind and throbbing head she reasoned that 'Sarge' must be the short-cut word for 'Saejen' – Sergeant.

– What's your name? The man asked casually with a deep authoritative voice, reaching for a docket from a pile in front of him. He spoke to her in Se-Tswana.

She replied in a faint voice: – Letitia.

– Letitia mang?

– Letitia Mazibuke.

– What's your address?

– 4971 Mnguni Street, Orlando East.

– ID number? Do you have your pass with you?

Letitia pulled a folded piece of paper from a pocket in her overall and handed it to him. She explained:

– At the Pass Office they gave me this. My ID number is not yet ready. I applied for it last year.

The Sarge scribbled the provisional number and handed the paper back to her.

– What's your trouble?

– I have come to report.

– Report what?

– My husband.

– Report your husband? Report *what* about your husband?

– He beat me up ... Letitia stammered in a shaky voice. In her heart she wished that the Sarge would not ask questions in such a high-pitched voice. Why at the Charge Office of such a big Police Station did they not have private enclosed closets like the ones they have in the vestry of her church where she occasionally went for confession?

Her voice dwindled into a whisper and her arm was trembling as she pointed at her concealed eyelids, which now felt like pieces of semi-detached flesh hanging heavily over her right cheek. Almost inaudibly she added:

– Here ... and all over my body, my ankle ... also my left arm.

A threadbare shawl hung loosely over her shoulders. With her right hand, she tapped lightly over her chest, revealing that the left forearm was supported by a sling under the shawl. She kept wiping her eyes and sniffling into a blood-stained napkin.

The Sarge looked up more attentively at the woman before him. He seemed uncomfortable. After clearing his throat, he sighed, asking more questions.

Letitia tried to live up to her Christian beliefs. She believed in the sanctity of marriage. She was actively engaged in all church affairs, every Sunday morning wearing her Manyano uniform because she was a consecrated member of the Mothers' Union. She was a respected Mme-ca-thapelo – a woman of prayer. She sincerely believed in the power of the Word of God. But here she was, brutalised and virtually vilified before the eyes and ears of many. Has God forsaken me;

have my ancestors turned their backs on me? she asked herself. Too shattered to defend herself, she looked at the sergeant and shook her head slowly.

– Hm? he puffed inquiringly, raising his eyebrows, then looking at the document in front of him, he jotted down something. He repeated the question:

– Why, why did your husband do it?

– He wanted my money, Letitia mumbled uncertainly, selecting her words as carefully as she could so as not to offend the policeman.

– You must be aware that you are making allegations against your husband in an official statement and that you will have to appear in court before the Magistrate. You know that, don't you?

She nodded. Inwardly, she knew that she had made the decision and that she would stick to it come what may.

– How old are you?

– Thirty-three; I was born in 1953.

The sergeant stopped writing.

– Ya! he exclaimed.

He looked at the policeman on his right and then at the one on his left. After a pause he resumed his questioning:

– Why should your husband want your money; doesn't he work?

– He left work two years ago because the money he was earning was very little. He said he would rather run his own business.

– What kind of business does he do?

– He runs a pirate taxi.

– Do you want us to lock him up? ... Are you not afraid that he'll punish you for coming here to lay a complaint?

Letitia hesitated. She did not reply, but she reasoned with herself: If I say yes everybody here will say I am a traitor. So she kept quiet and bowed her head. A posture she had come to assume easily ever since she learnt to be respectful and submissive – first to her parents and elders in the extended family; later to all her teachers at school and to all people in authority, especially white people, and of course to her husband and all his relatives.

The Sarge asked:

– Where is your husband now? Is he in the line?

– No. He is not in the line.

– But you said he runs a taxi. That he is a pirate, didn't you?

– Yes. But now his taxi is not in working order. It's standing in the yard at the back of our house. He has been trying to fix it up. That's why he wanted my money.

– He wanted to fix up his car with your money?

– Yes. He always takes money from me … at the end of every month. If it's not for fixing up the car, it's for petrol. Now yesterday I decided that I was not going to give him any money any more. I wanted to buy the children clothes and shoes. The children are in Mafikeng. When the fighting started, and there was trouble everywhere, I took them away to Mafikeng to keep them in school.

An old flame

DIANE CASE

She was watering her ferns on the back stoep when he called her. She was engrossed in what she was doing – feeding the plants a mixture of half a cup of seaweed extract to a bucket of water. They looked rather poorly. She thought she might fetch a pair of scissors and trim them back, or perhaps they needed transplanting to bigger pots. Ferns had a habit of outgrowing their pots.

Yes, she decided. That was the reason for their lacklustre state. But she'd leave that for tomorrow. No, not tomorrow. Tomorrow she was going to church. She'd see to the ferns on Monday, or maybe Tuesday would be a better day. One never knew what a Monday could bring.

'Hettie, come quickly,' he shouted earnestly from the kitchen door. She swung around so fast that she bumped her knee hard on the old couch against the wall. It would surely leave a bruise.

'What is it?' she asked agitatedly.

'Come and look at the TV,' he said gleefully. She hated that look in his eyes – hated him, in fact. Still, she put her watering can down and waddled into the sitting room. The TV was blaring because Harold couldn't hear so well any more. Bishop Tutu's face flashed across the screen and was gone to be replaced by the newsreader with the sports news.

'What is it?' she asked again.

Laughter danced across his face and glittered from his eyes.

'You see,' he said slowly. 'The Truth and Reconciliation people will be in Cape Town soon. I thought you could tell them your story.'

She was still trying to understand what he had meant by that, was now concentrating on the weather, wanted to switch the TV off, couldn't stand the static at that loud level, when he let out the most offensive, belly-wrenching fit of laughter.

'But be careful,' he laughed as she left the room, 'that you don't make a fool of yourself.'

He followed her into the kitchen where she put on water for tea.

'These people are all heroes of the struggle,' he said, 'important people who sacrificed their freedom and their loved ones to end apartheid.'

How dare he? How dare he mock her?

'Nothing to nibble?' he asked as she shoved his cup of tea across the table towards him. She took the biscuit tin down and put it on the table. Greedily he took the packet of Marie biscuits out and proceeded to dunk them, one by one, in his tea with his ugly, crooked fingers. He might as well finish the packet because she wasn't going to eat any of them – not after he had fingered them all with his grubby hands. Did he wash them before he sat down? No! Did he ever wash them after he used the toilet? No! No wonder he always reeked of old urine.

'You must try it,' he said spluttering tea and biscuit bits onto the tablecloth. 'Perhaps there'll be something on the late news. You can claim compensation. Do it for the money. You can put it towards your trip.'

She rose to rinse her cup at the sink. She was not so sure that she would make the trip these days. Things were so expensive it was difficult to put a few pennies, or cents rather, aside. But she did long so to see her daughter and her grandchildren again. They had come over one year – a long time ago. The children must be big now – all finished school already. She missed them so. Still, her daughter had left the country to give them a better life away from the 'shackles of apartheid' as she had said. Hettie guessed it was for the better.

'Is there more tea?' he asked.

She poured the tea from her aluminium teapot into his cup – amid the biscuit bits – and she poured the milk straight from the fridge without heating it.

'You see,' he explained with the laughter still on his face, dancing in his eyes, 'if you can prove any injury or loss you will be paid out. But where's your injury? What's your loss? You're not a Steve Biko or a Chris Hani or anything.'

He lifted the cup to his lips and placed it down on the saucer again. And then he laughed uproariously.

'I'm waiting on your cup,' she said coldly.

He drank the tea quickly – his Adam's apple vibrating with every gulp. He sat watching her clearing the tea things away and giggled to himself. Eventually he stood up. 'I'm going to bed,' he said.

'I'm going to read the paper,' she said.

'There's nothing much in there,' he mumbled. 'It's not worth the paper it's printed on.'

She read of rape and murder, of robbery and housebreaking and she read about how young boys had been enticed to cross the border to be trained as guerrillas and how they were killed: a Vlakplaas joke?

We live in a sick society, she said to herself as she folded the newspaper again.

He was sleeping when she got to bed. His open mouth exposed his thin gums and his wizened face looked lost in the pillows. When she was young, she had always believed that older people were closer to God, due mostly to their impending deaths and the promise of Paradise – but he made her doubt that now.

Her knee throbbed in the darkness. She should have put a vinegar rag around it but didn't feel like getting out of bed. Perhaps she should lie on her back. She elbowed his snoring form away from her. As he turned over he laughed. Even in his sleep he mocked her. Renewed anger rushed through her. She desired to put her hand down his throat and wrench the laughter out of him so he would never laugh at her again as he had laughed at her tonight and that night, ten, eleven years ago.

She had been weeding her plants on the back stoep that day when she saw, with a start, the tear-filled eyes staring at her from behind the old couch. She had first noticed the puddle of 'water' – that's what made her look there. The child had put her finger to her lips, silencing the cry that nearly escaped from Hettie's lips. She continued her work, pretending that she had not seen anything. She heard Harold speaking in Afrikaans to someone at the front door. She smiled at the frightened girl and made her way inside the house. Harold closed the door.

'The police are looking for children,' he said, 'who were throwing stones at them. Why don't the bladdy children just go to school and learn their work? Leave politics for the politicians!'

Later, when Harold went to the shop to buy the newspaper, she had brought the girl into the house. She washed her face and gave her some sugar water and a clean pair of panties.

'Aunty, you will not believe what the police are doing to the schoolchildren,' the girl blurted out.

'I know, my love,' she said trying to comfort the child. 'I read the newspaper every night.'

'But it's not in the papers,' the girl said. 'The state of emergency forebids that type of information from being published. Do you know, Aunty, there are more than ten thousand children sitting in jails? Detained without trial?'

'I think you are mistaken, my darling,' she said to the frightened child.

'It's true, Aunty,' the child continued.

'You must hurry before my husband gets back,' she said, ushering the child towards the front door. 'Here is my phone number.' She hastily tore the flap from a used envelope and scrawled down the number. 'Let me know that you're okay. I'll pray for you,' she whispered to the child.

'Aunty,' the child said looking into her eyes, 'tonight people are going to burn candles on their stoeps for all the children being held under the detention without trial law. Will you burn a candle too?'

'Yes,' she said, anxious to have the child gone by the time Harold returned.

'Promise?' the child asked.

'I promise,' she said looking into her innocent eyes. 'You be careful now.'

'Who was that?' Harold had wanted to know when he returned in time to see her waving the child off.

'Just a girl selling things,' she lied. He excitedly explained that he had seen the police chasing children. She said she had heard the helicopters above.

The newspaper had a map of the Cape Peninsula with black spots marking 'troubled areas'. That was the total of the 'unrest' reporting. The state of emergency continued.

That night she was restless. She was worried about the young girl because she had not called yet. And she was worried about the young policemen. Eventually, after she had cleared the supper things away, she went to stand at the gate. It looked like Christmas. Every home had a candle burning on the gatepost. She rushed inside, fetched a candle, a jar and a box of matches.

Harold wanted to know what she was doing but she didn't answer him. Defiantly she lit her candle and placed it in the jar on the gate post. Defiantly she stood behind her flickering candle and prayed for the children – frightened children like the young girl – or any person held indefinitely in prison. It hadn't meant much to her before, but now it seemed ridiculous. How could a law exist that allowed for the detention of children accused of nothing – because that's what it amounted to. Therefore there would be no trial.

She didn't notice the policeman coming around the corner. He came to her gate and hit out with his truncheon. He knocked her candle off the gatepost and hit her across her arm, catching her on her elbow.

The candle flame had died and the shattered jar lay at her feet.

For the second time that day the eyes of youth had looked into her soul – this time steely blue and venomous. She stood transfixed as the policeman and his colleagues systematically made their way down the street, knocking the candles down.

Harold was watching from the bedroom window. His laughter humiliated her further. She wrapped a vinegar cloth around her elbow which was now bruised and swollen. Then she took a dustpan and handbroom and collected the discarded candle and slivers of glass from the gate.

The experience had stayed with her for a long time. Every time Harold had looked at her he'd guffaw: 'How's your elbow?' Yes, it had been a shattering experience. She wasn't sure whether she had lost something or gained something and she still sometimes wondered whatever happened to that young girl.

Harold turned around in his sleep and snuggled up to her. With one strategically placed seventy-two-year-old foot and one lusty shove, Harold was on the floor. Bewildered and mumbling protests, he got to his feet and climbed back into bed.

Hettie turned her back on him and pretended to be asleep.

The piano

JAMES MATTHEWS

Through the kitchen window of her council-built house in a township on the Cape Flats (incongruously named Silvertown by an omniscient member of an all-white Cape Town City Council), Mrs Samuels had an unobstructed view of a section of the lane. From where she stood she could check on passers-by. Each time a bus or heavily-laden lorry rumbled up or down the narrow street, the house shook violently and she cursed the council for building houses with one-brick inner-walls and trembling foundations. At this moment a loud rumbling drowned the Liszt piano concerto she was enjoying on the English radio station.

It was a lorry with an extra-heavy load. It created a St Vitus tremor which made a glass on the kitchen shelf develop an urge to change its position. Mrs Samuels rescued it seconds before it could land in a fragmented pattern on the floor. She glared at the offending walls. Her feeling towards the city council was pushed up a few notches more on the slide-rule of aggravation.

Silently she listed all the objections she had against the house to which she had at first come with willingness. It had meant an escape from the confinement of two stifling rooms in the overcrowded tenement house in the Bo-Kaap where she had shared a large kitchen with two other housewives. But the joy of moving into a house that did not restrict the movement of her husband, three daughters and herself, had soon palled against the long list of restrictions handed her, all making it clear that she was only an occupier and at no time could she look on this as a home of her own.

A movement from the lane caught her attention. Four women in white duster coats were advancing in the direction

147

of her front door. Her annoyance intensified as she recognised the one in the lead as Miss Carlisle, collector of rent on Monday mornings, and watchdog regarding the observance of council rulings.

Mrs Samuels' eyes became two pieces of flint chipping away at the approaching women.

She had purposely increased the volume of her set after Miss Carlisle had rebuked the other housewives for playing their radios at what she, Miss Carlisle, considered too loud a pitch. 'I don't hear any of my neighbours complaining,' was her reply when Miss Carlisle had insisted that she should comply.

She had also been the first to take in a visitor without asking Miss Carlisle's permision. The incident still filled her with righteous anger.

'And who is this?' Miss Carlisle had asked, pencil-thin eyebrows raised.

'She's visiting here.'

'You know well what the rules are about visiting, Mrs Samuels,' – the voice cold and impersonal.

Mrs Samuels had glared at the younger woman.

The object of their argument – her finger worrying the sock she was darning – sat fidgeting on the edge of her chair, conscious of the scrutiny of the white-coated white woman.

'Since when do I have to ask anyone's permission to have my own mother here for a visit?'

It was the start of a bloodless battle between the two of them, with neither giving any outward sign of the victories scored or defeats suffered.

Mrs Samuels turned and picked up a plate.

A sharp knock was followed by the rattling of the front door. Knuckles rapped impatiently a second time when the door refused to yield. Mrs Samuels deliberately wiped four plates and carefully placed them on the dresser. As she walked towards the door, drying her wet hands on her apron, she said softly, 'That should teach you to wait.' She recalled the many times she had been annoyed at the one rap, followed by the immediate opening of the front door. She had peevishly told her

148

husband just because they stayed in a council house it did not mean that they were not entitled to privacy. He always tried to soothe her, but she would not be denied.

She turned the key and swung the door open, blocking entry with her bulk. She stood firm, waiting for Miss Carlisle to make the first move.

No introductions were offered. When the silence stretched uncomfortably long, Miss Carlisle terminated it with a brisk clearing of her throat. 'May we come inside?'

It was an order veiled as an appeal. 'I've brought these ladies to have a look at your place.' Miss Carlisle, without waiting for a reply, led them around Mrs Samuels' imposing size.

Mrs Samuels ignored Miss Carlisle's glance at the radio. The four women moved towards the bedrooms.

A rumble in the region of her stomach indicated the hopeless anger filling Mrs Samuels. Then, as always in distress, she made for the kitchen to brew some tea. Her hands trembled as she lit the small pressure stove. With impatient gestures she watched the water come to the boil. After a few sips of hot tea, her anger subsided. The voice from the bedroom evoked only slight twitches of irritation.

'This is one of the better-kept houses,' Miss Carlisle's voice reached to the kitchen. 'After this, I'll take you to some others that are a veritable mess.'

The praise did not please Mrs Samuels. The impersonal manner in which she was referred to and the implied criticism of her neighbours increased her aggravation anew.

'You'd be surprised at the amount of inane things these people buy – huge stereophonic radio sets, refrigerators large enough to serve a hotel, washing machines, and some of them even own cars. The only deal they're not eager about is paying their rent. You might have observed as we came in that there's a piano in the front room.' Miss Carlisle's voice rose as she stressed 'piano'.

Mrs Samuels put down her cup with a sharp rattle, tea spilling over her fingers. What does she know about us? she asked herself. White bitch! She who has everything!

She stared at the four walls of the kitchen, seeking self-control in its pale-green colour-wash.

She thought back to the time she applied for the house. The many days she had to stand in an almost endless queue. And the many times she did not reach the office where they were interviewed in time.

Then the interview itself, the questions stripping her of all pride, and all the answers neatly written down on a form for anyone in the office to see. Next the inspection of their two rooms in Bo-Kaap by a woman, also white, who although kind, could not help wrinkling her nose at the many smells assaulting her nostrils. The agonising self-appraisal of their belongings and the trip to the furniture store later, to buy on the never-never system the necessary furniture so that their new neighbours would not look upon them as a family of no consequence.

She had been repelled by the clinical whiteness of the one-brick walls when they moved in. The harsh, white glare robbed the house of any warmth, making it what it was – a unit among hundreds of units composing the housing scheme – giving it the impersonality of army barracks or stables waiting to be filled. She would not rest until the walls were painted and transformed to indicate human habitation.

How could she explain to the women in their white duster coats that the radios, the refrigerators, overstuffed Chesterfield suites – even her piano – did not mean that they were stupid and easy prey for the salesmen whose hunting grounds were the council housing estates? That they were symbols of their self-esteem?

For most of them coming from slum areas, the move onto the housing estate was the first pull from the morass which often led to moral degradation, brought on by over-filled tenement rooms and children growing up on street corners. How could she explain that in a world where you were judged by the pigmentation of your skin, you could not display your ability? You could only prove your equality by filling your houses with whatever the stores offered?

The four women passed through the small lobby. She followed them to the front room. Aware of the eyes of Mrs Samuels and the rest of the family staring from behind glass-covered frames on the walls, three of the women, pen and pad in hand, tried to make an unobtrusive study of the room and its contents. Jesus Christ, hands outstretched and eyes beaming compassion, had a wall to Himself.

One of the women gingerly approached the highly-polished piano which took up most of one wall. She let her finger trail across the keys. A sharp tinkle filled the room.

She turned, face warm and friendly. 'Do you play?' she asked.

Mrs Samuels shook her head. A finger tapped a key. Again she was at a loss how to explain that it was not important to her whether or not she could play the piano – although she did hope that the two younger children would emulate the older one who was taking lessons after school. She had once seen a display in the window of a furniture store where a piano was the central piece, and the memory of it had remained with her. To her the ownership of a piano was indicative of what she wanted for her children.

'I also have a piano. I'm not that good playing it but I love what I get from it.'

Mrs Samuels looked at the speaker. Suddenly she was transformed from just another white face into an individual conversing with another, no barriers between them.

'It's time to go,' Miss Carlisle said, looking at the watch on her wrist.

The moment of contact was cut, but not lost, for the woman who had spoken paused at the door to give a friendly smile. Names were not exchanged.

Mrs Samuels gave a wry smile. She walked to the piano. With stiff fingers she tried to trace a melody on the black and white keys. Then she closed the lid with a sigh. Through the window she could see the four women entering another house. Slowly she went back to her washing.

The concerto on the radio ended in a crescendo of sparkling notes.

The scream

ETIENNE VAN HEERDEN

People referred to him as the irreproachable poet.

A man without enemies, who did not say much in public. He eschewed the literary scene and sat in his small room close to the Groenplaats, indefatigably writing his poems. 'The discreet engineer of the word,' a critic wrote about him. 'The quiet man.'

Furthermore, he avoided literary friendships. The literary scene was too small. He made friends in other circles – musicians, sculptors, painters like me.

'I'll not provide reasons why I wish to take my own life,' writes the irreproachable poet from Antwerp to me. 'But I insist that you visit me when you come to Europe again – if I'm still alive.'

His letter is accompanied by a coloured brochure from the Antwerp Zoo. I study it closely, momentarily distracted by the bright African colours in Belgium, but find no clues. After a while I throw it away.

With the poet you would never know: sardonic verses sometimes. Ironic. Mocking.

'You're no Catholic?' I write back lightly.

'The only mortal sin is to remain living when life has lost its poetry. Or, differently put, if poetry colonises life.'

Then I realise that he is serious. And that at the same time, he is again carefully designing and constructing.

I delay the visit to him. But his letters become more insistent. 'Winter's coming,' he writes in his shaky handwriting with the longtailed f's and y's. 'I hear you are coming to Amsterdam. Take the express to Antwerp. It's time for the last rites with Sabien.'

Sabien is unknown to me, but I choose a specific letter from the poet's handwriting and check it in all his sentences. Each time it looks different. His handwriting is deteriorating. The man who has always acted irreproachably is in trouble. The man without enemies is engaged in a struggle with himself.

'I'm coming in May. I hear the Antwerp station building is being restored to its former glory. Will we be able to find each other in the building rubble?'

'Meet me at the zoo gate, just next to the station.' The picture on the postcard is one of old trains steaming alongside the platforms.

Irritated, I think of the cold feeling in the palm of my hand that time when I scrunched up the full-colour glossy brochure.

'When Edvard Munch died,' the poet tells me when we stand with Coke cans in our hands in front of the American buffaloes' enclosure, 'he left one thousand and fifty paintings and thousands of drawings to the city of Oslo.

'His most well-known work is of course, *The Scream*, oil on cardboard, 91 x 73,5 cm, which can be seen in the Oslo Munch Museum. Munch made many variations of this scene of a person on a lonely bridge, with hands beside the face, uttering an open-mouthed scream of terror and despair.'

The buffaloes stand with their heavy heads hanging between their shoulders, looking at us. Perhaps they see through us, behind us, immeasurable prairies.

'At the end of his life Munch wrote that he had lived his whole life as if on the verge of a bottomless abyss. He had, he wrote, always suffered from intense anguish and tried through works such as *The Scream* to give expression to it. Without anxiety and illness, he wrote, he would have been like a ship without a rudder.'

The poet and I walk along a gravel path. We stroll quietly along the curve of the path which takes us through pools of sunlight and shade, with the crunch of the gravel under our shoes.

The poet is irreproachably clothed, in the black linen jacket he always wears, with his umbrella over his forearm and the elegant caution which makes him such a popular figure.

153

Shyness and self-confidence blend strangely in this man, I think while I walk beside him wondering about Sabien. Perhaps it is the discipline of poetry which leads to such a personality. At a distance elephants throw their shadows over bales of straw. Their trunks drag listlessly to and fro through stalks and dust.

'Few people know,' says the poet as we stop in front of the pride of the zoo, the Okapi. The animal lifts his head nervously. '... that Munch had a missing middle finger on his left hand. He had a stormy relationship with one Tulla Larsen, the daughter of a Nordic wine merchant. During an argument with her he mistakenly wounded himself with a gun. He refused anaesthetic during the operation in which the first digit of the finger had to be removed.'

We observe how the Okapi, delicate as a ballet dancer, tripples up and down nervously watching us. 'Munch wanted to be conscious to experience the operation.' The poet turns to me. He unhooks the umbrella from his forearm and leans upon it as if it is a walking stick. 'Sabien likes blood,' he says. 'Remember this when you are alone with her.' The Okapi is a restrained, finely-made animal. He is described on the plaque in front of his enclosure as a velvet creature. The head is dainty and too small for the body. Lovely stripes adorn his forelegs and hindquarters. He has a long tongue with which he cleans his eyes and ears.

'The Okapi only occurs in the Ituri forest in Zaire,' I read aloud to the poet from the brochure which we bought earlier at the zoo kiosk. 'The striped pattern on the animal's haunches is unique for each one – like a person's fingerprint. An international breeding programme photographs each Okapi from the rear and so keeps a record. The female animal is bigger than the male. The Okapi is the most recently discovered mammal – found round about the turn of the century by scientists in the former Belgian Congo.'

I look at the Okapi which bashfully turns its haunches to me. 'I would very much like to paint it,' I say.

'Munch refused anaesthesia,' the poet continues while a

154

group of school children with ice-creams run past us, 'because the curiosity of the artist, the obsession with deviation and pain, drove him. The experience of his own blood and pain during the amputation procedure remained with him for the rest of his life. It became far more than an hour of physical suffering.'

We wander further. The poet does not look like someone motivating his own death; more like a diplomat on a Sunday stroll.

'Just before Munch's death he allowed the hand with the shortened, crooked finger to appear in photographs.' The poet brings out to view a cutting from the *Vrij Nederland*. We bend over the cutting in front of the Egyptian temple, an imitation of a Pharaoh building where camels stand looking out like stiff mannequins. Pharaoh also keeps elephants – three morose, wrinkled mammoths in rooms of stone and ankle chains. The irreproachable poet and I stand and watch how one elephant unceasingly sweeps straw over the metal ring on his front foot.

'As if he is ashamed,' I say.

Four art students sit in the weak sunshine making images of the elephants. One uses charcoal, two water colour, and the fourth a lump of clay. Only the charcoal artist succeeds – the others produce blunt, crumpled forms – a pitiful heap of skin with a trunk, wrinkled and twisted in suffering.

But the poet again brings the cutting to my attention. On the black and white photo is an old man. It is 1943, one year before Munch's death. He sits in a large room, surrounded by paintings and next to him on the floor stands a mirror. The part of the room which otherwise would not be visible in the photo is reflected in the rectangular mirror and brought into view. Munch is looking ahead; thin, in an absent, morose and edgy attitude, with his hands on his knees, in an uncomfortable chair. The left hand with the crooked finger is displayed on his knee.

'See,' says the poet to me, 'it's all described.' He stuffs the cutting into my hand and stands with his back to me, looking at the elephants. The animals watch us. Then the poet turns. 'Sabien likes mirrors,' he says to me, suddenly urgent.

I look into his frightened eyes and hear the grinding of trains and the moaning fear of confined animals.

'I wonder how those exiles feel, the feathered and striped, there in the zoo,' I say to the poet as we walk out of the gate. 'A naked life: eating, passing water, defecating, sleeping and waking, mating, cleaning – everything in view of ice-cream eating children, wandering paedophiles, bored pensioners ...'

'As a child, Sabien was endlessly fascinated by Van Gogh's severed ear,' the poet relates as we walk past the station building. We cross the street to the block with the jewellers' shops. In display windows gold and gems are laid out in endless, glittering variations. Thousands of valuable watches show that it is a few minutes past eleven.

'There can be no doubt here about the time,' I joke. But the poet, withdrawn, wishes to continue his argument.

'In the streets of Antwerp and Brussels, or Amsterdam and Rome, you see young people with a nose ring, or even a series of rings high up on the ear. Mutilation reins nature in, confronts it.' We stand in front of a shop window looking at necklaces. 'It's like poetry. It restricts life. To create,' says the poet softly, while his breath fogs up the pane in front of him and I realise he is not seeing the gold pieces at which he is staring, 'whether it is sonnets or wedding cakes or bridges or sculptures that you create, to create means that you slam the metal ring around the elephant's foot.'

He sighs. 'Even there on the other side in the porno shop on the square there are photographs of women with jewels in their labia, or men who have had a needle put through the head of the penis. All that the needle artist has to watch out for is the urethra, an artery or two and a nerve.'

'Sabien?' I ask as he hesitates slightly. A bus roars past behind us. A light wind pushes through our hair. The tourists at the pavement café are sitting on deck chairs all facing the same direction. They are soaking up the little bit of sun.

'For Sabien,' the poet answers softly, 'the erotic and injury, desire and mutilation go together. She sees the moment of simultaneous pain and pleasure as a metaphor. And she understands that those unfortunate souls in the photos in the porno literature, and perhaps the director of the zoo, also feel that way.'

He takes my elbow. His hand closes around my arm. I cannot move this limb. He whispers close to my ear as if there are eavesdroppers in the middle of the city noise. 'Sabien's body is full of little holes. Some of the holes are already closing up. Others are fresh, or blocked with soap and sweat and skin residues. Sabien loves to adorn herself.'

I feel the poet's breath over my ear cartilage. His words scorch my cheek. I think of the porn shop opposite the station where like a space traveller you can go and sit in a chair and feed the meter coin after coin while you allow yourself to scroll through universes of flesh – lashes against pink bodies, blows and blood and distorted faces; flesh punished in the conjunction of guilt and pleasure, desire and penance.

The poet relaxes his grip, and I return to the glitter of the jeweller's wares. A light smile plays over his face. 'Watch out for Sabien,' he says. 'Her tenderness is deceptive. Come.'

We enter the shop, where he asks the jeweller to display the necklaces on the glass counter. The poet bends over the jewellery items which lie like sparkling worms. The jeweller gives the poet a magnifying glass, which he grips in his eye socket and with which he bends over the gems.

We wait while the poet with trembling hands lifts a string of gold and rubies and tests the weight. 'This is for Sabien's throat,' he says. 'And this ruby will lie against the little pulsing hollow in her neck.' He pays with shaking hands; carefully counts out the crumpled notes. I notice he handles the notes as if he is not familiar with money. He has the necklace wrapped in gold paper and gives it to me.

'Give it to her during your second meeting.'

The evening of the poet's death I visit the restaurant, De Elfde Gebod, near the cathedral. Inside images of saints decorate almost every open space. Images of Jesus, his disciples and Holy Mary, carved from wood or cast in plaster, stare at the diners.

I eat slowly, alone, and with attention narrowly focused on tastes and textures. I eat with the poet's mouth, and think also of the mouth of Sabien, the woman to whom the poet has committed me. I am amazed by the buzzing enthusiasm of the talkers, and by the Paisley patterns of cigarette smoke against the night air. My eagerness for Sabien rises with the roaring crescendo in the restaurant. I will have to find her; I can no longer put it off; I desire her; I do not know who she is and where to find her. Up till the end, when we said a hasty good-bye on the street corner as if we would see each other the next day, he refused to say any more about her.

'You will find her,' were his words, as he turned, and with his umbrella over his forearm walked into the city traffic.

I order various courses and drink too much. Finally I raise my glass to the empty chair opposite me. It is ten past eleven.

It is over.

I rise, pay, and walk across the Groenplaats. It is unexpectedly warm. Candles flicker behind restaurant windows. We are only three people in the brightly lit bus which weaves its way, rumbling and lurching, from stop to stop.

The driver watches me in the rear-view mirror when the bus stops on the Groenplaats a second time and I do not get off. We sit together in the lit-up, silent bus and wait while around us the city becomes even quieter and I imagine that I hear a single yelping bark of a wild animal, from far beyond the buildings on the station side.

The poet is buried, accompanied by leading articles and a television broadcast. I keep my distance, sit around in restaurants, wait for leads. I reveal to no one my presence in Antwerp.

'Never before have so many people attended the funeral of an artist,' writes *De Morgen*. 'He was a man without enemies,

158

who manifested his talent with a calm urbanity. His quietness, his civility, was an example to all in the cultural world. The poet is dead; long live the poet!'

Time is running out. I can wait no longer. In every woman who inadvertently looks at me on the street, I see a possible Sabien. I wait in the hotel lounge and ask repeatedly if there is a message for me. I continuously look to see if the phone in the hotel room is properly placed on its cradle.

But because I must return, I at last find my way to where the poet has, for sixteen years, rented the same little room on the top floor. I did not want to come here; I was, probably, afraid of what I would find. One could never visit him in his place because it was too small.

'Sabien ?' asks the landlady, leaning towards me with narrowed eyes. She is short-sighted and I do not come into focus.

'Yes, his mistress.'

She looks at me reprovingly. 'He's hardly cold and you want to come peeping into his life. The poet had no mistress, sir. He lived alone in his little room up here. No one ever came here. I knew him for sixteen years. He was celibate. He was not heterosexual, bisexual or homosexual,' she says with spirit, her hand working the door handle. 'Asexual. Celibate. His great love was his poetry. Once he said to me, "I share my body with words alone."'

I look at her hesitantly. She is going to shut the door in my face, I realise, and leave me there, with my passion for Sabien, with my unaccomplished task, with my duty to my old friend now committed to the earth.

I take out the gold parcel with the necklace and unfold the golden wrapping paper. I open the little box and allow the landlady to look at the necklace. 'The poet asked me to give it to Sabien after his death.'

She considers me appraisingly for a while. 'Come,' she then decides.

I walk up the creaking stairs behind her. The stairwell is dark and musty. We climb higher and higher, past various floors. The stairs give onto a single door, barely visible in the dim light. The landlady's breathing is laboured when she pushes it open and stands aside so that I can get past. I squeeze past her. I have to bend as the door frame is low.

'There is no Sabien,' says the landlady behind me while I look at the little bed with the dented pillow. One of the poet's hairs lies on the pillow. At first I want to pick it up, but then I decide to leave it there. He would have preferred that it disappears in a vacuum cleaner; I understand that now.

The coverlet is dark green. The writing table is small, with the uncomfortable, hard chair pushed right up against it. A small icon, Madonna with Child, hangs on the wall directly above the writing table. When the poet sat and wrote he would, on looking up, have looked straight into the eyes of the mother of the mutilated Christ.

The room is bare. The wardrobe has no mirror, only holes for screws and a shadow where once a mirror was fastened to the closet. I stroke over the screw holes with my fingertip and hear the landlady's breath behind me.

'He unscrewed the mirror himself,' she says. 'For no reason. It was a year ago. He carried the mirror down the stairs from here.'

I see the poet struggling down the narrow spiral, round the turns in the dusk, with the long mirror which reflects in turn his legs, his white knuckles, the stair railing and the ceiling.

I turn to the landlady with the box with the necklace in my hand. I lift my shoulders. She hesitates, then comes forward and opens the closet.

'Only this heap of porn magazines with, I must tell you, rather strange photos. This was the only small sin in the life of the late poet, I must add. He did not know that I knew about it. But one has to clean, even if the man does not want to allow you into his room.' She wipes the bedstead with her fingertip and exoneratingly shows me: dust.

Dust to dust, I think. 'He was such a refined man,' she continues. 'And then of course this pile of zoo brochures, all the same. He visited the zoo every day, and every day returned

160

with a brochure. There, there they lie, neatly piled up beside the pornography in the closet. Hundreds of brochures!' She shakes her head. 'One should actually return them to the zoo staff.'

'I don't want to look,' I say. 'You can lock up now. Take the necklace for yourself.'

'There never was a Sabien,' she repeats plaintively, with the necklace clutched in her hand.

I take a bus which transports me jerkily through the city. At the station I stand in the droning, massive building. I take a train to Schipol. And an aeroplane, back to Africa.

The aeroplane tilts into the warm air of the southern hemisphere. The horizon is red as the sun comes up over Africa. Flaming we glide into the airspace above Johannesburg. The aeroplane glows like a coal of fire.

The poet lived by his own hand, I think. And died by that hand.

In the lowing engines of the Boeing, in the hissing of the air vents in the passenger hold, in the radiant sun, the fidgeting and excited chatter of the passengers getting ready for the landing, in the humming city below us, from over the glistening curve of the globe, I feel the shuddering silence of the poet's scream.

Rough landing

SANDILE DIKENI

I have always had a love-hate relationship with air flights. I like them because flying is a nice experience, at least that's what most blacks who lack modesty say. I simply enjoy the attention I draw in a shebeen full of drunkards, demanding and claiming my friendship simply because of a short flight to Johannesburg.

Please forgive me also for a few exaggerations, about fictitious experiences while on a flight. I am referring to things like coincidental meetings with Mandela or, when I am feeling extremely creative, of the pilot giving me an opportunity to hold the reins because he got tired, or something. My boozing partners like the extras and I am fond of the free drinks that come my way accompanied by milk white teeth from shining black faces.

It is usually good times after every flight for black people like me.

It would have been nice if some white people were brain X-rayed before they were allowed to board a plane. In this way a lot of racist old timers and their cubs would be relieved of the agony of traumatising fellow passengers like me with their stares that pierce the black skin with ice-cold white grips, tugging viciously at it; demanding a reason why a baboon soul got onto such a thing as a Boeing, designed for the exclusive use of whites.

Since we left Heathrow Airport, the old tannie on the seat opposite, had been doing a good job at attempting to cause me discomfort. Under normal circumstances her 'ugly-kaffir' stares would have had me worked up. My brain ignored her, though, in its feverish journey, leading the plane back home, from where it indulged in various fantasies from bar rooms to bedrooms. The bedrooms especially were rolling leisurely in my mind. Of course none of them featured the old tannie.

I released the safety belt around my waist to give the brain more space. The brain flew straight away to the lady waiting at Cape Town airport. I had missed her tremendously. It is not as if my stay in Oslo was a nightmare – no it was quite delightful. So delightful, that I would have allowed South Africa to rot under the anger of people like the old staring tant Sannie – I had given her a name in the meantime. But the lady waiting at the airport had pulled me with her strength and warmth. I had this feeling that I was falling in love once again after three years with her. It was a good feeling. I pinched myself to verify if it was really me. I must have smiled unconsciously at the discovery, because tant Sannie threw me a 'now-he-is-also-going-mad' look. I ignored her and adjusted my seat to lean backwards.

My thoughts relaxed on a black futon. She lay on the bed with her hair covering the pillow. I thought her brown eyes looked nice. She was about to say something to me when suddenly: 'Please fasten your seat belts we are about to land.'

Whenever I would curse, I would think in Xhosa: 'Bloody bastard in cockpit, knows nothing about love, can't even give a person time to think.' The 'bastard' however knew a lot about Boeing 747s and landings.

She was stunning. With hair wild on her head, she gave me a smile that put her mouth in danger of tearing at the edges. Even tant Sannie could not help smiling – either from the relief of getting rid of me or from the contagious effect of her welcome. I ignored tant Sannie's sudden conversion. Instead I said, 'Hi, Lisa.'

The car moved too slowly from the airport. My brain was running very fast to the quiet of my room. The prayer emanating from my lips was a hope that my house-mate had gone to relax somewhere very far from our house.

'I missed you a lot,' she said.

'I missed you, too,' I responded.

We sat in silence. The car was slow. Too slow. She was telling me about her visit to Durban. My roving mind was kissing her hands, her eyes, holding her close to me, when Site C showed her battered squatter face and Khayelitsha, barren and dry in the sand-blowing distance, waved us away.

I cannot understand how such a place can have such high birth rates. It is as unromantic as reading an academic book. It is even worse when you have just arrived from Oslo. My voice thick with disappointment asked, 'Lisa, can we go to your brother's house?'

Strandfontein was not exactly the dream paradise I had mused about in the plane. A consolation to coloured middle-class aspirations, it showed signs of human habitation at least. Everything except Khayelitsha was fine.

It was late-night when they started getting tired of hearing about Norway. I was also getting tired of telling them about Norway. I was kneeling, leaning on the bed with Lisa in a horse-ride position on my back, the TV blaring some music, the sister-in-law and the husband, joke-fighting about their laziness, their eight-year-old son asking me complicated questions about Vikings.

Then he walked in. 'The garage door is open,' he announced in a 'I-am-about-to-commit-murder' voice.

'Thanks, Daddy.' The brother rose. 'Let me close it now.'

The father left immediately. We gossiped as soon as he departed. 'You are going to be thrown out of the house,' someone said, laughing. The telephone rang. Everyone could see the disappointment on the brother's face as he passed the message.

'Lisa, Daddy says you must come and fetch your clothes and leave his house right now.'

I winced. Here we go again, I thought. Once a kaffir, always a kaffir. When she came back with her clothes, the beautiful brown eyes were thick and soaked with tears. I could see the pain. Not knowing what to do, I paced the lounge. At last she stopped crying.

'I will never forgive them, for this, never.'

'It's okay, krokodilletjie,' I tried to console ineffectively.

Deep inside the gnawing fear was beginning to turn into

anger. For three years I had tolerated an unfair accusation from her parents that I was subhuman. An accusation born from a human attribute: love. I loved her like I would have loved anyone – anyone with a heart to return such love. A coloured, yes, because it is folly to deny the richness of her cultural otherness. It was an otherness that was healthy and willing to pour over into the empty patches of my upbringing, breaking down my own traditional dogmas. Anotherness willing to gulp from the satiated calabash of my own black African humanity, even when it was more often than not crucified for an alleged inferiority. I was helplessly angry. I became quiet.

The wind was daunting the uncomfortable silence between her sobs when he knocked.

'Go into the room,' she advised.

I went into the room to think.

He came inside and demanded to talk to her in private. I was thinking. It was not long before the voices became louder.

'He is not a kaffir, Daddy,' she defended in a loud voice.

'He is and I will also tell him directly in his face!' Daddy bellowed.

'Okay, tell him in his face,' came the answer, followed by fast small angry steps towards the room I was in.

'Please let me die, let me die,' I prayed.

I did not die and she opened the door.

'Lizo, come!' I was commanded. I dragged myself to the sofa and slumped on it.

There he was. A somewhat big man. A teacher and a principal. A father of teachers and lawyers. A coloured. A hater of Africans.

'Lizo, listen to me carefully. I do not hate African people. I am a father and Lisa is my daughter. And I care about her. If she gets hurt I will be the one to blame. Now I have some Tswana friends who came to me one day and they said ...'

The rest were clichés that said nothing except that I was a kaffir and that he felt that his daughter would be in danger if she had anything to do with a kaffir.

My anger climbed on the wind and flew away. A calm set in

my voice. My humiliation injected my body with humility. I became a powerful entity because I was convinced of how wrong this man was. I answered his claims in both languages that carried my social education. I felt hurt but powerful knowing that this man educated, no, trained, was inferior to me in all regards. He could not even speak my language whilst I spoke his in a quest to communicate my humanity to him.

I expressed my shared concern for Lisa's future but rejected the eagerness to make decisions for her. I complained about judgements made on me before my character was seen in action. I had shared my background and upbringing with coloured children who gave of theirs until both languages became just languages and not 'ours' or 'theirs'. I spoke of my love for his daughter and my wish to be known and to be accepted.

This narrative suggests that a patient listener was giving attention to my speaking voice. No! This narrative leaves out the interjections from the listener; it leaves out the further accusations: 'You are not a man. You are a weakling. Why didn't you come to see me?' It leaves out the daughter's response: 'Oh come, Daddy, you know you would not have allowed Lizo to come into the house.'

In the end the voices lowered themselves. The wind had calmed down. I think some human beings began to find each other.

Through the night we drove. Daddy, Lisa and Lizo. When we came to the house, my first step into the house was welcomed by a cerebral palsied bundle of beauty that hugged my African body. Lisa's sister. With tears rolling down her beautiful cheeks, she covered me with a love that knew no race or creed. She knew only Lizo the person. She was only fourteen years old but without fear. I had no misgivings when I promised that everything would be okay. Melanie's cerebral palsied brain knew it was going to be difficult, but she had hope. She had been hoping for three years that the secret affection she had for Lizo might one day be made public.

Eventually the mother gathered enough courage and was introduced to me. Her handshake was limp and as soon as she had done the required courtesy, she fled to her bedroom where she spilled her tears of racial hatred. That hurt, more than anything. Her hatred for my race was minor. She hated me for intruding into her perfect coloured life. I had stolen her coloured teacher husband, her teacher sons and daughters and even her cerebral palsied daughter. A coloured working-class woman, in South Africa, with nothing to live for but the pleasure of a racist-given status to be superior to something other than what she was. How to say to her that coloured is a mixture of white and African? I could not talk with her. When I left Strandfontein, the morning twilight was beckoning.

Back in Khayelitsha where I belong, with the whisky bottle going down fast, the sun was slowly climbing up in the sky. In the morning light I opened my mouth and laughed. Was tant Sannie smiling at the prospects of my adventure?

The divine one

COLIN JIGGS SMUTS

Now that apartheid is over and the New South Africa is here to stay, I, Divine, can look from the present back over the past and have a good laugh. All that Xhosa, Zulu, European, coloured and Indian, white, black and what-have-you classification crap is over now. You see, I was born in a squatter camp in Pimville. We moved for a few years to Doornfontein. Then they declared Doorie white and we had to move to Bossies: a proclaimed coloured area.

Now I can see it for what it was. But when we were kicked out of Doorie my sisters and I, we liked it. We had a big three-bedroomed house on the posh side. Not like the train houses below the railway line. At least there were people we could look down on. The only people better off than us were those who bought ground and built their own houses or added on to houses that were the same as ours. My father promised that one day when he made enough money he would enlarge the house or build us a big house where we would all have our own rooms.

That never happened.

The house was very crowded. You see there were eight of us. Three boys and five girls. So there was the boys' room and the girls' room. My baby sister slept with my parents until she went to school, then she joined us. My sisters and I used to dream of living in big, posh houses like those people in Bosmont where all the rich coloured people lived. We used to talk about it all the time. We even said, wouldn't it be better if we could stay like white people. We fantasised and played this game about which was our house when my father took us down Jan Smuts Avenue to Zoo Lake. We argued with each other about who picked the biggest and poshest house, and imagined how those people lived and how many servants they had. Oh, those were wonderful dreams.

Ma was very fair with straight hair. She could pass for white. Daddy was very dark with kroes hair. He looked like a native. Children in the neighbourhood used to call us Black & White whisky. We loved my father: he looked after us. But he was very strict. And he had a terrible temper. I felt sorry for Ma, he would beat her up if she did something wrong. But she got used to it and always took care that he wouldn't get upset with her. I felt sorry for my brothers because he gave them terrible hidings too. He wasn't so harsh with us girls, but then, we knew how to behave.

Daddy was a very busy man. You see, he was a business-man. He never worked for any white man like the other men in the township. He was his own boss, as he liked to say. He sold goods from home, and liquor. He had taxis and even had people working for him. He had white policemen for friends who used to visit our house and have a drink with him. But people were jealous: children teased us that Daddy ran a she-been and sold back-door goods and that he was a gangster. In high school one boy said my father was a sell-out and collabo-rator. My brothers beat him up so that no one dared say a thing like that about my father again.

You see there was no bottle store in the township and Daddy said he was providing a service. Most people would just take their bottles and go but some would sit in the yard and drink. Only those people he liked and were decent would be allowed to sit in the kitchen and drink. But it could be a nuisance over the weekends if we were having lunch, or late at night, when we were asleep and they would be knocking at the back door or on the windows. But Dad taught my brothers how to sell and deal with the customers. At night he just sold through the window.

'When I have made enough money,' he would often say, 'I will open up a bottle store and lounge.

He had good wholesale connections and bought goods and sold them cheap to the people and quite often on credit. He would have opened a shop but said the officials were so corrupt: they only gave licenses to their friends and families.

'You have to be fair with straight hair if you want a license,' he use to say.

Quite often if people who bought goods from him did not pay, he lost his temper and beat them up. Then they quickly paid.

Sometimes there would be fights with the other taxi operators and they could be rough.

'People are jealous of me,' Dad said. 'They're trying to take *my* routes and *my* customers. I have to fight them.'

He was arrested a few times. Once he spent a year in jail.

'My enemies gave false testimony against me,' he cursed, then boasted, 'but I survived the rotten bastards.'

Ma had a lot of money hidden under her mattress and she and the boys carried on with the business while he was in jail. Ma knew a lot about the business. When Daddy came out he was upset at first about the money and that she knew so much about the business.

'It's all the money you've given me over the years,' she explained, 'and I've saved it for a rainy day. Being married to you so long taught me a few things, you see. What did you expect me to do? Go out and work in a factory? With eight children to look after?'

He seemed to be proud of her but wouldn't admit it.

'I warn you,' he said, 'don't hide things from me again. See to the family and mind your own business.'

I loved Ma but I hated her for being weak and not standing up to him. I swore to myself that I would never allow a man to rule me like that. I would be like Daddy, the boss in the house.

He taught all my brothers the business. But he didn't involve any of us girls.

'You girls,' he said, 'you must find good husbands to look after you.'

You know, it's funny, all us girls were fair with straight hair like our mother, and all the boys were dark with kroes hair like my father. But I have this big flat nose with high cheek bones. I promised myself I would have plastic surgery one day, to give my nose a nice small shape. But you know, all of us, my sisters, too, we could pass for white. We could even go into a white cinema.

When we were in high school and boys started coming around, Daddy would chase them away if they were too dark. He said we were not going to marry any kaffirs or Boesmans. We had to go out with nice boys. You know, maybe that's why my eldest sister took so long to get married. She was very much in love with Trevor, but he was dark and Daddy didn't like him. She only married late in her thirties, to a much older chap who had been married before.

My other sister, Mary, married a priest. Daddy liked him, he's fair and good-looking. Only we all used to find it embarrassing. He preached on street corners and people would laugh. But he's left the church now and drinks a lot. It's more fun than preaching on the street.

Allison, my other sister, married a German. A real German, I mean. Klaus, her husband, is a carpenter, but soon after he got here he opened his own business and now employs lots of people. They got married in Swaziland and moved to one of those real big estates in the northern suburbs. Things were difficult in those days, so only some of us would visit them, those of us who could pass for white. But Daddy and the others didn't mind. Nobody wanted to spoil her chances and give them away. They could have been arrested under the Immorality or Group Areas Act those days. So mainly they came to visit us.

'What's wrong with these boere here? No culture. Uncivilised! They not white men, they white kaffirs,' Klaus would say with a thick accent when he was drunk. 'They must control the blacks, yes, otherwise everything will be kaput. But you people, you coloureds, you are just like white people, you civilised. Ja, control the Indians, otherwise they will own everything. Just like the Jews do now. You see the boere are just like the blacks, useless. Do you see them owning businesses? No, its either Englishmen or Jews. That's why I must come here from Germany to teach them. You know its easy for a white man here to open a business. But they too stupid. And they don't like to work, they just want to watch the kaffirs. To hell with them, now you all come to my house.'

But Allison would get upset and say, 'Please, Klaus, control yourself, you'll just get us into trouble.'

'Don't worry,' he would say, 'you are Mrs Beining now and I know the police, they my friends, they won't bother us.'

Klaus was a lot like Daddy. He could be brutal. Maybe that's why he and Daddy got on so well. But Allison knew how to handle him although he beat her up a few times.

My youngest sister, Greta, really worried us. She liked the township rough boys. Her first husband was stabbed to death in a drunken brawl. So what does she do, she marries another one of those same characters. She and her children have to keep running back to my mother's house because he's always beating her up.

But to tell you the truth, my brothers worried us. They all married dark, funny-looking women. And while all of us sisters wanted to stay in white or coloured posh areas, they prefer to stay in Eldorado Park and even Ennerdale, which is lower class than Bossies and far out of town. They all still run shebeens. It's legal now, and they call them taverns. They all deal in wholesale goods and run taxis. Just like Daddy, they say, we won't work for no white man.

You know, they and their wives only speak Afrikaans, just like the lower-class people in Bossies. It was a bit embarrassing when Ma insisted that we all have lunch together over Christmas. But she had to have it at her place then, none of us would agree to hosting it at any of our houses. And then we had to be nice to these funny woman they married and all the children they had. And it was irritating, we had to speak Afrikaans otherwise they didn't understand a word we said.

It's only Greta who seemed to get on with them. Maybe because her husband is of that type too. Me, Mary and Allison just treated the occasion as if we are doing a charitable job for poor people and try to be as nice as possible. Thank goodness we have now persuaded Ma to stop trying to do those family gatherings. If she wants them, fine and well, but it doesn't mean we have to all be there. Ma likes to be with us girls most of the time. In fact with me, I tell her what to do. She needs someone like that, especially after Daddy died. But I'm proud of my brothers. They are really self-made men, like Daddy.

Not like that stupid husband I married. He had everything going for him. He's fair, straight hair, his family was well-off. They even owned their own house in Doornfontein. They had cars and everything.

I used to admire them. Me and my sisters used to watch when they visited our neighbours in Doornfontein who stayed in the big house opposite ours. Daddy said the school principal who stayed there was a stuck-up-play-white Bushy. We went to the same school as his children and were friendly with them, but they never invited us over to play at their house. I hated them for that.

Terry, my husband, first fancied my sister Mary, but the Preacher Man got there first. She fell pregnant and they had to get married quick. It was only a few years later, just after I matriculated, that I met Terry at a dance and he started dating me. Daddy really liked him. He was from a middle-class family and he had his own car. Some people even said his family had white papers. We were all so excited that he was dating me.

He was a few years older than me, but that didn't matter. He was good-looking, seemed to have lots of money and was gentle and patient. He even started helping Daddy with the taxi and wholesale businesses. And he seemed to enjoy serving people in the shebeen.

We had first tried to hide the shebeen business from him, but he could see what was happening. He didn't seem to mind. And he was a real safe bet when Daddy had to transport some wholesale goods which were hot. The police never stopped him like they would have stopped Daddy, my brothers or the people that worked for him. Yes, he fitted in nicely with the family.

But *his* family was something else. Oh, his mother was so

difficult. I hated her. I could see she ruled the roost. His father was nice, I liked him. His two sisters were so stuck-up, they really went on as if they were English women from England. Jesus, their accents were so British. I put my mind to it and learnt to speak like the younger one and I can tell you, it helped me to advance my career.

His older brother just spoke money and went on as if his shit didn't stink. Terry's younger brother just spoke struggle all the time. I could see the whole lot looked down on us as if we were nothing. I hated them for that. But Terry was completely under my spell. He would do anything I wanted. He kept wanting to do it.

'No, we must be married first,' I said.

'Marry me then,' he asked.

'Only if Daddy says yes,' I told him.

He went to ask and Daddy gave his consent, but only after my twenty-first birthday which, thank heavens, was a few months away. I used to let him play with me, but would not allow him to put it in. Oh, I always wanted to do it, with other boys too, but after Mary got pregnant with the Preacher Man, Dad was really cross. He gave Mary and the Preacher Man a hiding they will never forget. In fact, if my mother didn't stop him and my brothers, they would've killed the Preacher Man. They were married a few days later and within three months the Preacher Man got the church to transfer him to Cape Town and we only saw them on holidays that time. They only came back to live in Johannesburg after Daddy died and the Preacher Man left the church.

After that, Daddy made the rest of us girls swear on the Bible that we wouldn't do it with boys until we were married. My eldest sister, Nettie, started crying hysterically when she had to put her hand on the Bible and ran to her room. This really made Daddy mad, especially when she locked herself in the bedroom. He went and fetched his sjambok and threatened to break the door down.

'You little tart!' he swore. 'Did you sleep with that bastard Trevor?'

'No, Pa. No, he wanted to but I didn't!' she screamed from behind the door.

'Well, open this door and come swear on the Bible that you didn't do it, otherwise I will kill you and go and find that bastard and kill him too.'

'Leave the child,' Ma pleaded, to no avail.

'Pa, must we go and find Trevor and bring him here?' Ernest asked.

We were all pleading with my father to leave Nettie. Ma ran to the room and phoned the priest who arrived a few minutes later.

After he'd talked to her, the priest told Daddy, 'Nettie has told you the truth. She has not had intimate relations with any boy. Mr Mackenna, as a Catholic you should rather come and see me when you have family problems than lose your temper like this. Will you all come to church on Sunday? And Mr Mackenna, will you come to confession for losing your temper?' he said in his Irish accent and left.

'Why did you call that goat?' Daddy asked. 'To embarrass me again, of course,' he answered his own question.

'I thought you were going to kill Nettie,' Ma said, meekly.

'Next time, I'll kill you too. I don't want anybody interfering in my affairs, understand?' he told Ma coldly. 'And you,' he glowered at us, 'stay away from the filthy boys. Wait until you are married. Is that clear?'

'Ja, Daddy,' we said in a chorus.

I never wanted to disappoint Daddy. So I made Terry wait until after we were married. But I learnt that I could control him with sex. He got it as a reward if he pleased me. He didn't get it if he didn't behave, except, of course, when I was randy myself and really wanted it. And it didn't take long for me to lead him on and he'd make love to me, just as I wanted it to be. And it taught me lots of other lessons on how to handle men. Oh, they do like sex, they are such jagse dicks. And all their prejudices fall by the wayside if they get it right with you. You can use men. You just have to know how.

Well, the wedding was in Botswana where his one sister

stayed with her white husband. The people were right, they did have white papers. That's why the wedding was there. My whole family wanted to come, after all, there was no apartheid there. But Terry said his mother didn't want a big affair. Besides his sister, only his father and mother were there, the rest didn't come. Maybe they thought I wasn't their class, they were always so full of shit. Even the struggle brother didn't come. And he was all over the townships preaching revolution. They are a strange family, my father and I agreed.

After our marriage, we moved to Malvern. It was white, but it was not what I had dreamt of. The whites there were not very different from the people in the townships. I think even lower class. They were more like the people in the train houses below the railway line in Bossies. But we were friendly to them, always inviting our neighbours over for drinks and sometimes having a drink at their houses.

Terry seemed to enjoy their company. He was a panel beater and they seemed to be like the types he worked with. He didn't have full papers as a panel beater, but his father had organised him papers as an operator and had got him a good job with a friend of his. Although they were white, it wasn't the company I wanted to mix with. But at least now I could move as a white person.

I changed my job and started working as a white person, with a white husband, living in a white area.

Oh, I had so many dreams and ambitions. But Terry's family, mainly his mother, stood in my way. I had to get rid of her influence. I would go off at him about how they hated me. A friend had told me that an aunt of his had called me Mrs Ples after the stone-age woman they had found at Sterkfontein Caves. What an insult! Just because my nose is not as straight as theirs.

I wanted another house. I had a nice job, flying all over the place. So I borrowed money from my father. We couldn't get a loan from the building society as we did not have the ten percent deposit. We bought a house in Robertsham. At least it was better than Malvern. A bit more upper class.

The only problem is Daddy died and he had borrowed the money from one of his friends who wanted the loan repaid. Ma couldn't help because Daddy never had a will, and besides, he never trusted banks and hid the money away somewhere and she didn't know where. And many people were coming to ask for money that Daddy owed them. My brothers couldn't help either as they were battling with their own businesses. And they had to protect Ma from those people who were threatening to take Daddy's taxis and demanding money for the wholesale goods he had bought from them. We were in a real fix.

Then Terry's father died and his old crow of a mother went to Canada to spend some time with her eldest daughter who had moved there to be as white as possible. I seized the chance, I knew there must be some inheritance due to Terry from his father. Why should the old crow hang onto it all herself? I tried to get Terry to contact his mother. He wouldn't. I then suggested he approach his rich brother. He turned us down after he heard what interest we were paying. I then suggested we go see the struggle brother. He was struggling on all fronts – politically, socially and financially. Another useless one.

In the end, I reached a deal with Daddy's moneylender friend that I would pay twenty-five percent interest. The bond rate was ten percent at the time. He normally charged forty percent, he said, but as I was Zim-Zim's daughter he'd charge less – that was my father's nickname. He was so fast with his hands, you never saw his fists coming at you, it was just like zim-zim and you were down, they said.

It was difficult. The moneylender said if we didn't pay on time every month he would be forced to take action. Maybe our furniture, maybe the house itself, or otherwise send his collectors to take care of us, especially my husband. 'We could give him a bit of a hiding to remind him, or perhaps a scar on his face with a razor, so that he won't forget to pay on time,' he said. Of course he might consider relaxing things if I was nice to him.

I turned on all the charm I could muster to get out of there.

I promised I would think about it. He told me that won't be difficult, I could even be nice to him now.

God, looking at the old miser, in his dirty, stinking clothes! I think his mother was black and his father something unclassifiable. His body was like a mapoza, fat and obese, with straight black hair and green eyes that seemed to turn yellow because of the funny smelling stuff that he kept chewing. And his house was so filthy, it gave you the creeps.

I had slept with men before. Lots of men, when I travelled for the company. I was my boss's favourite girl. I always controlled the situation and linked it to favours and my career. It was part of my job. I still liked screwing with Terry when I got home. It was a relief, I suppose. Terry was very understanding. He really liked his wife flying all over the country during the week. It also taught him to be a good house-husband. The outside-sex I saw as part of building my career. Oh, but you know what, I also had some affairs with some of the guys that I grew up with who have now become main-time, like successful businessmen, some even gangsters. Oh, I like doing it with them. They know how to take a woman. Just like my father knew and my brothers know how to take a woman, I imagine. You know none of this namby-pamby business, like Terry, my boss and those other white men I had slept with, but to really possess you and do it with you. Until you have been well and truly done! You know, I had met one or two boere salesmen on my trips who had what it takes. But there was no way I was going to sleep with that evil-looking, smelly, obese moneylender!

It took all our resources to pay that stinking shark every month. We were reduced to living on fish and chips when we could afford it, otherwise on brown bread with pilchards or bacon. It was only after his mother returned from overseas and I got Terry to riot about his inheritance at the family gathering to welcome her back.

His mother couldn't stand the scene with the rich brother and the struggle brother and Terry shouting at each other. The upshot of it was that she paid off our debt to the moneylender and lent us the money to take out a bond with the building society. As far as I was concerned, she would never see that money again. It was part of Terry's inheritance. However, I didn't realise his rich brother was keeping the books. I only started realising my dreams when that old crow of a mother of his died. Then I really started my thing.

You know, we have owned no less than fourteen homes. And most in the northern suburbs. Yes, it did wonders for my career, having addresses like that. Oh, it was what I had always dreamt of.

Sometimes we found ourselves staying next to prominent Nats and we had evenings at their places and even voted for them. Post ninety-four we stayed next to prominent ANC officials and wined and dined with them and voted for them in the local elections. It was divine.

At some of the places we stayed little over a year, others less, but it was a marvellous experience. When the bond repayments became too much, we just sold up and moved on. When nasty people like Terry's brothers and sisters asked us what we were doing, asking why didn't we get settled in one place, I told them, 'It's part of our business; we buy and sell houses and we always make a profit.'

They were just jealous, like lots of people from the townships, jealous that we were doing so well, staying so far north and all that.

Ah, but Terry, he was such a failure. After his mother died I suggested he leave the firm he was working for and open his own business or find a better job, something more smart and respectable than being a grease monkey. Something that I could be proud of. But was he useless. He under-quoted, and when I tried to help and gave a decent quote, it was rejected as too high. Klaus got him a job as a salesman with some German company that he had dealings with. There he was, smart suit, company car. 'Honey,' I said to him, 'I'm so proud of you, you got to go for it, make a smash of this. Don't forget, you are the one, the main one, this is for yourself. Be like my Daddy, be sharp, look after yourself.'

Three months later he was arrested for theft.

He was selling goods, not invoicing them and pocketing the money, bringing in small returns for the company and not being able to account for all the goods he had taken. I had thought he was doing so well. He was flush with money, drinking with the boys and telling me he's being as sharp as Daddy. The monkey did not take note that the storeman was keeping records of what he was taking out and returning and that the sales department was noting his sales returns.

I didn't have money to bail him out. I ran to Klaus.

'I do him a favour, I introduce him to my friends, they give him a job and he disgraces me as a thief, they think I am a thief too. He must sit. They're saying coloureds are just like blacks, the only thing they know how to do is steal,' Klaus said, making it clear that he was not going to help.

But his rich brother came to the rescue. We bailed Terry out and payed the firm back for the stolen goods and they dropped the charges. The only problem was when it came to the inheritance, the rich brother charged the loan, bond and bail and payout all to Terry's share and we ended owing him. Of course, he will never see the money, the crooked bastard that he is.

Terry tried going back to the panel-beating workshop. They wouldn't take him. I said what is he worried about, only bums do that job now. He tried welding. It hurt his eyes. Eventually he got asthma. The doctor said it was stress. I told him it was the years of working on cars, the fumes from the chemicals, spraying, grinding and the welding gave him the asthma. He believed me.

With only me working, I couldn't afford a maid. Terry took over all household responsibilities: cooking, cleaning, doing the shopping, you name it. It was marvellous, I had achieved my goal, I was complete master of my house, with my husband doing whatever I wished, like my Ma used to do for my father, I was like him, the Boss!

The only problem was that he still expected to sleep with me and I couldn't stand him in bed and next to me. I mean, you don't sleep with your maid, do you? Maybe that's why my father had jolbokke. I had to get a life. It was becoming stifling. I needed a man equal to my standing, one who was ambitious, a go-getter, someone who wanted to be something in life, not a useless bag of potatoes like Terry.

Well, I divorced him. Kicked him out. Let him go back to that stuck-up family of his. Let them look after him, like I did all these years. Those brothers of his got involved and I had to agree to some things. But let's see if they get it right. They don't know me or my connections. I'm Zim-Zim's daughter and don't mess with me. You know, that Terry is such a weakling. When he found me in bed with my lover, he walked out and came back early the next morning, dead drunk. When he woke up and wanted to speak, I demanded a divorce and that he move out of the house immediately!

I met my lover, now my new husband, through Klaus, his cousin. He's recently arrived and much younger than me. He's fascinated by his blonde African woman, as he calls me. I never had plastic surgery as I always wanted to do. Could never afford it. He loves my flat nose and my high cheek bones. He's divine. He always wanted an African woman, he says. Had no idea that African women could be fair and blonde and have African features as well, like me. He adores me. My natural features have finally paid off.

Let me tell you, I have never been interested in politics. Apartheid meant nothing to me. My father always said the whites are bad but the blacks aren't any better. But I like what's going on now. It's time for opportunity, if you got the know-how, like me.

You know our family name is Mackenna, you know, like Scottish. But it's actually, I think, Sotho or Tswana – Makene. I'm going to change it to Beining-Makene or Makene-Beining, it's so in at the moment, cute, to proclaim your African heritage. I wonder why we used to want to be so white or like fair coloureds. Ah, it's good now to look like me. Now I have a genuine white man, not a play-white, and I can be myself, Divine.

Lady, that's the rules

RAYDA JACOBS

Sabah arrived at the bank her mother had recommended, and stood for a moment studying the instructions on the steel door. Banks had come a long way since the sixties when she was there last. Not all banks, but this one certainly. You couldn't enter just by walking in. You stepped into an inner cubicle, where boxed in by glass slabs, you waited for the red light to change to green, pulled on the handle, then stepped into the blue and chrome interior of the bank. A robber might have his chance with a teller, but would think twice about being trapped in a glass booth on the way out.

Inside the bank, the line-ups were long, a row of tellers behind bullet-proof glass on the left, consultants in cubicles on the right. She joined the line for the consultants and presently a girl with the name tag Esmerelda pinned to the lapel of her navy blue blazer finished with her customer and motioned for her to take a seat.

'I'm a returning resident. I'd like to open an account and transfer my money from Canada.'

'How long have you been out of the country?'

'Twenty-seven years.'

'You need a letter from Home Affairs.'

Sabah smiled.

'I have dual citizenship. Here's a letter saying so. And here are my South African and Canadian passports.'

Esmerelda picked up the letter.

'The letter's six months old.'

Sabah looked at Esmerelda. Esmerelda was a plumpish woman in her forties who looked like she'd had too much porridge that morning and now regretted it. It was going to be a long morning, she thought.

'It is, but it doesn't alter the fact that I'm a South African as well as a Canadian citizen.'

'You need a new letter, miss.'

'Listen, Esmerelda, forget the letter. I shouldn't have mentioned the letter. Here's my South African passport. I want to open an account.'

Esmerelda picked up the passport and studied it.

'This is an old I.D. number. They changed them when they came out with the new I.D. book. Do you know what's a I.D. book? It's an identity document with your picture, identity number, and driver's licence. If you buy a firearm, that would be registered in there, too. Everyone must have a new I.D. book.'

'I realise that, but I've just arrived. An I.D. book isn't first on my list. In the meantime, I want to open an account and transfer my money from Canada. Before the season changes, Esmerelda.' She laughed to show she wasn't upset.

Esmerelda didn't share her humour.

'The best thing is to go to Home Affairs and first get your I.D. book. When you have it, we can open an account.'

'Home Affairs takes three months to process identity documents. Isn't my South African passport good enough? I want to open an account, not sleep with the manager.'

A bright spot appeared on Esmerelda's cheeks.

'You don't have to get huffy with me, miss.'

'Do you think you could go and ask whoever's in charge of returning residents whether a South African passport's good enough to open an account in this bank?'

Esmerelda kicked back her chair with a flourish and went off. Sabah leaned back and closed her eyes. One week back in the country. How often did a returning resident step into the bank to open an account? And how many of them would even have a dual citizenship letter for Esmerelda to be so familiar with it that she could say a letter was too old to be of use? It didn't matter how old the letter was. Her birth certificate was more than forty years old. It didn't change the fact that she was born on March 10th.

Esmerelda returned and placed the letter and passports in front of her.

'The manager says you need a fresh letter. You'll also have to fill out a form for the Reserve Bank. The application's two hundred and fifty rand.'

'What?'

'You're bringing dollars into the country. The Reserve Bank keeps track of all monies coming in.'

'I bring money into the country and I pay for the privilege? I've never heard of anything so ridiculous!'

Esmerelda smiled. She was starting to feel better.

'That's the rules. Also, if we have to fax your bank in Canada to transfer the funds, it's thirteen rand and sixty-eight cents. There's a cover page, and a page with the message. That would come to,' she hastily wrote down numbers on a scrap pad, 'twenty-seven rand and thirty-six cents.'

Sabah wanted to smack the look off her face.

'Does your bank do anything for its customers, Esmerelda? Do they have incentives or services to make you choose one bank over another, or are they all the same because they know they have no competition?'

Esmerelda's smile grew deeper. 'I can give you the name of the manager if you want to complain.'

'Don't bother. I'll take my business elsewhere.'

The morning with Esmerelda depressed her and she left there for her brother's office. Wasiq said they should try his bank and the next day he went with her to the main branch at Wynberg where she explained her position to a girl in Foreign Exchange.

'I should tell you miss, what's your name – Karen? I should tell you, Karen, I've been to another bank and was given a long story about the Reserve Bank and a letter from Home Affairs. I don't know what the big deal is about opening an account if a person has a South African passport.'

Karen was a fresh-faced blonde who knew her job.

'When you left the country twenty-seven years ago, did you fill out a form at the bank and tell them you were emigrating?'

'No.'

'Then you don't need a letter from Home Affairs. We can open an account right away.'

'Are you serious?'

'Yes. If you didn't sign any forms when you left, you didn't officially leave.'

'It's as simple as that? Why didn't the other girl ask me that question?'

Karen showed a row of polished teeth. 'Maybe she didn't know. We listen to our customers.'

'Wasiq, did you hear? They listen to their customers.'

Wasiq was in the chair next to her and smiled that smile he reserved for his audience at Manenberg's when the crowd roared after his rendition of 'Take Five' on the tenor sax.

'However, there's no getting around the two hundred and fifty rand for the Reserve Bank.'

'That's a lot of money for information I'm happy to supply for free.'

'How much money are you bringing into the country?'

Sabah scribbled a dollar amount on a scrap of paper and showed it to her.

Karen smiled.

'For that amount, I'm sure we can work out something.'

'What do you mean?'

'Well, the money's not here yet, but when it arrives, perhaps we can do something with the rate.'

'You can do that?'

'If it arrives on a Friday, especially. We can keep it in abeyance until the Monday and see what the rate is on that day. If it's in your favour, we'll give it to you. Of course you won't get the two days' interest, but you'll have the opportunity to choose. Even a slight change in the rate can result in a few thousand rands' difference. It will make up for the two hundred and fifty rand charge.'

Sabah looked at her. She was young. Sharp. The girl at the other bank didn't have her smarts.

'You haven't checked with your manager.'

'I don't have to.'

'And the fax to have the money transferred?'

'Nine rand a page, but we won't charge anything in this case. We would like to have your business.'

'Karen, I'm very impressed with this bank.'

Karen smiled. She knew she had scored points and started to explain the various accounts. Half an hour later travellers cheques had changed hands, and an account for the incoming funds had been opened.

'Well, that's that,' Sabah said to her brother when they were out in the car. 'I can't believe it all went so smoothly.'

'And seeing as it did, I think we should go to Home Affairs while our luck holds and apply for your I.D. book. You have to get it sorted out anyway. Feel like some hot chips? I know this place not far from here. They make the best.'

'One packet, we'll share.'

'One packet's too little. I'm hungry.'

'A packet and a half, then. I don't want all that grease in my arteries.'

'You and your arteries. Canada's changed you, man. Remember how we used to buy those fresh cream doughnuts and eat two at a time?'

'And I could eat a chicken sandwich right after that,' Sabah laughed. 'And still weigh in at a hundred and ten. Now, one piece of chocolate and it's hip city.'

They arrived at the take-away restaurant, and Wasiq asked for a packet-and-a-half of peri-peri chips.

The girl, a frizzy-haired assistant with four missing front teeth, looked at him as if he had asked for the keys to the Challenger.

'A packeta-'n-half? I dunno how many extra chips to give.'

'Half of one packet.'

The girl shook her head.

'I have to ask Mr Singh.'

'You have to ask if you can sell us one and a half packets of chips? The chips is four rand. You give us a few extra. You charge us six.'

'I have to ask.'

'Forget it,' Wasiq said, turning to go.

'No, don't forget it,' Sabah cut in, nodding to the people waiting patiently behind them. 'Let her get him.'

Mr Singh was a short, fat, Indian man with six strands of hair combed from one ear all the way over his speckled dome to the other.

'What's the problem?'

'We'd like some hot chips, please,' Sabah said, 'more than a packet, but less than two. We're not hungry enough for two packets. We'll pay for the extra chips.'

'I can sell you a parcel.'

'What's a parcel?'

'Viennas and chips.'

'We don't want viennas, just chips. All we're asking for is one and a half packets. We'll pay the extra.'

Mr Singh moved aside and pointed to the chips bubbling in the fryer.

'Lady, you know how much it costs to heat this fryer? You want to see my 'lectricity bill? If I do it for you, I have to do it for everyone.'

'What're you talking about? You sell chips. You make the rules. Humour us, Mr Singh, please. You're not losing money, just being creative. All we want is a packet-and-a-half.'

'Lady, buy two packets, I'll take what you don't want,' a man said in the line that had grown behind them. He had a nervous tic and the corner of his mouth twitched as he spoke.

'I appreciate that, but there's a principle involved.' She turned back to the owner. 'Are you giving us the chips?'

Mr Singh wiped the sweat off his forehead with the back of his hand.

'Sorry, I can't do it. It's one packet, or two.'

'I don't believe it,' Sabah said.

The man behind them lost control.

'Give de woman de focking chips!'

Mr Singh looked at the man with the tie glaring at him and gathered himself upright in an effort to make himself taller.

'Look, here.'

'No, you look. We stan'ing here focking ten minutes. Give de woman de chips!'

'No he can keep his chips,' Sabah said angrily. 'He can stick it over his bles. Do you think you're the only one who makes chips? Fry that attitude, man. It stinks from here to Gauteng!'

Wasiq pulled her by her arm out of the store.

'What's the matter with you?'

'I've had it with this third-world turtle mentality. First the woman in the bank, now this. Like fucking sheep. If you hold a bag of oats in front of them, they'll all run over a cliff.'

'You're in the Cape, girlie. Wait till you run into affirmative action. That's really going to sit in your craw.'

'You mean that wasn't it this morning in the bank? The woman didn't even know to ask a fucking question. Shit man, I said I was giving up swearing. I've done nothing but cuss since I got here.'

'Let's go eat before we hit Home Affairs.'

'Nah. I can't take the government this afternoon.'

'Get it over with. You'll feel better after you've eaten. I promise you, it's not as bad as people say.'

After a high-carbohydrate lunch and two cappuccinos, they headed for the Home Affairs office in Wynberg. Sabah, somewhat restored, explained to a girl with a mane of sun-bleached surfer's hair that she had lived in Canada for twenty-seven years and wanted to apply for an identity document.

'No problem,' the girl smiled pleasantly. 'Fill out this yellow form here, have two photographs taken. Do you have a driver's licence?'

'A Canadian one.'

'Oh. We can't put that into your I.D. book. You should have it converted.'

'What do you mean?'

'You go to the Traffic Department, have your licence converted, then return here and we'll incorporate it into your I.D. book. You can have your pictures taken at the side of the building. There's a photographer in a caravan parked in a driveway.'

She had her picture taken and was at the Traffic Department within the hour. There, she went straight to a lady with a stiff bouffant and pointed spectacles, called Mrs Marais, smoking a cigarette behind a thick glass barrier. Mrs Marais listened to her relate what the girl at Home Affairs had said, then let out a slow, poisonous stream of smoke and sighed heavily.

'They don't know what they're talking about at Home Affairs. You first apply for your I.D. book. When you have it, you bring it here with your Canadian licence, pay forty rand, we convert it, you take it back to Home Affairs and apply for a new I.D..'

'You don't mean that.'

'I do.'

'You mean I apply for the same document twice?'

'That's right.'

'It doesn't make sense. Why don't I have my licence converted first as the girl said, then take it to Home Affairs to have it incorporated into my I.D. book? The system can't surely be that ill-conceived.'

'I've worked here twenty-four years,' Mrs Marais smiled with the same tired expression as the girl in the worn calendar on the wall. 'Believe me.'

'Who pays for my gas to drive up and down, my time, the forty rand?'

'Lady, that's the rules.'

'The rules? I'm tired of the rules. People keep telling me about the rules. Who makes these rules?'

'You can write a letter to the ANC. It's a free country now, anyone can say anything.'

'The ANC made this rule?'

'Listen, let me call Home Affairs in Cape Town. I know someone in the office there. I'll hear what he says. It's not everyday we have someone coming in with a Canadian driver's licence.'

She and Wasiq stood at the counter and watched Mrs Marais blow smoke circles as she nodded and sighed into the mouthpiece. 'He wants to talk to you,' she said, handing the receiver to Sabah.

'Lady,' a guttural voice boomed in her ear, 'this is Mr van der Westhuizen. Home Affairs in Wynberg's got their wires crossed. Mrs Marais is right. You first get your identity document, then get your licence converted, then go back to Home Affairs with both documents and apply for a new identity document.'

'Mr van der Westhuizen, even to you, this must surely be a ridiculous rule. Isn't that rather like feeding the bull before slitting his throat?'

'Someone made that rule, miss. There's a reason for it.' He laughed awkwardly.

'That's what scares me. What if I don't do it?'

'Well, miss, if you want your identity document ...'

'And it's your way or the driveway.'

'I beg your pardon?'

'Never mind.' She handed the phone back to Mrs Marais. 'So I go back to Home Affairs.'

Mrs Marais nodded sympathetically. 'Why did you come back?'

'I like to be punished.'

Mrs Marais returned her documents.

'It's not so bad here. Give it a chance. In no time you'll get used to it.'

'In no time I'll get used to street children, too. I don't want to.'

Out in the car she leaned her head in her hands.

'I'm not going to Home Affairs.'

'You are.'

'No.'

'It's two o'clock. Let's see the thing through. We don't want to do this again tomorrow. With luck, we can get the damn thing over with.'

'Luck? We have no fucking luck.'

At Home Affairs, Wasiq filled out the forms and they joined the throng of people waiting in line. Three of ten clerks were at their stations to attend to forty people, the wait so long, mothers sat on the floor breast-feeding their babies, while children ran up and down making a noise.

At three thirty she finally stepped up to the counter and laid out her forms. The clerk was a young, no-nonsense woman with the stub of a cigarette burning between yellowed fingers. She drew the last, precious poisons into her lungs, examined the documents, made several ticks, then looked up.

'It says here, divorced.' She pointed to the box where Sabah had made a tick. 'Do you have your divorce order? I need to verify that you're divorced.'

Sabah crunched her toes together in exasperation. Of all the things she'd thought might be asked, this wasn't one of them. She forced herself to be calm.

'Miss, I've had a rough day, you don't know how rough. I don't carry my divorce papers around in my purse. Do you? Tick off 'never married', I don't care. Please. If you don't do it, I'm not coming back. I can't. I won't.'

The clerk looked down at the form. A frown appeared in the freckled space between her eyes. Without a word, she scratched out 'divorced' and ticked off 'never married'. She never looked up. It never happened.

Sabah was stunned. She looked at Wasiq. A government employee with guts! They couldn't believe it.

The clerk stamped the documents and handed them back to her.

'That line over there. For your fingerprints.'

'My fingerprints? Why?'

'Everyone has to do it, miss. It's the law.'

'Oh no, man, not that, too. My fingerprints are a personal thing. It's like my period, it belongs to me. Not even the F.B.I. has it. Why should I give it to Home Affairs?'

The clerk was already looking over her shoulder at the next applicant. The Home Affairs office was the war zone for liberalised, expatriates who couldn't come to grips with the reality of being back home. She was tired of all these lofty, returning residents flocking back telling her how things were done in other countries.

'If you don't have your fingerprints taken, you won't get your I.D. book.'

'But in Canada –'

'This isn't Canada, miss. Now please, if you don't mind. This office is closing in twenty minutes. There's still a long queue. Next?'

The person behind her, a well-dressed woman with a tan, smiled understandingly at her before moving up to take her place.

'Don't take it so hard. I returned last year after fifteen years in Australia. This is my eighth trip to Home Affairs. They wrote me to say I owed them forty-three cents. It cost them eighty cents to mail the letter. Welcome back to South Africa.'

A brother with perfect timing

RUSTUN WOOD/KAREN WILLIAMS

The pick-pick-pick of the axe handle followed them through their dreams to this. Picking over bones; picking over scabs; picking over what they had left behind when they came back – full circle – to this South Africa.

There was Matthius; and there was Miles; and there was the history of their story waiting for them.

Matthius picked up his camera one night in London, on the hazy edges of coke and scotch, and headed back to hear the pick-axe thudding over the Free State earth, to that bag of bones Miles had become, during his last journey home.

It was still dark as each in turn turned around, sighed and tried to push the clammy edges of nightmare away from the present.

Nothing could come to rest the night before.

Not Matthius, not Bongi, not Matthews Phosa, not Zolani nor that bag of bones they shared between themselves as the restless night turned to morning.

Matthius turns: hoping he would never have to wake up to a morning like this again. Ever. He watches as the last of Jo'-burg's sunrise shadows move from his bedroom: revealing squares and corners where just now the darks of moonlight had hidden his whispering fears. Today.

In one of the revealed corners now stands – looking back at him – his video camera already set up, as well as a photographic camera with extra supplies. Four weeks back in South Africa, and today he *has* to get out of bed.

Matthews Phosa had called him last night. They had a last-minute chat about this morning. What might be found.

'Yes, it's okay. I've spoken to Miles's family,' Matthius said.

'And …?' Phosa asked.

'They were cool about it,' Matthius reassured him.

(Much bloody cooler than any of his so-called damn comrades were, since he'd come back, he wanted to say.)

This would be the third or the fifth … or was it nearing tenth? … grave excavation for Matthews.

They've started teasing him about it too. People in ANC circles said: he was doing a better job finding bodies of slain guerillas and bankrolling the lavish township funeral business, than he was getting time to run his province, or even be head of the ANC's legal affairs.

Dredging his poet's heart across the parameters of South Africa's memories and farms, to find and excavate another mass grave of anti-apartheid soldiers killed and buried in secret.

Everyone knows there was war: but now there are only the families to own up and claim the bodies.

'But ja,' Matthius assured him. 'Things should be going off cool today.'

Snapshot: after the apartheid security raids in Harare, and Gaborone.

Now that he is dead, they can talk very little of Miles, but only of the things they always secretly used against him. Like he smoked too much bhang. Like in Lusaka he was always going off wandering by himself, intellectualising …

None of this matters to Matthius now.

He walks up Fulham Road, coat collar turned up to the icy London wind. It is getting dark under the street lamps, the lights are casting shadows on the pavements and over the bleak faces of people passing him, who do not look up.

I wonder, Matthius thinks to himself, I wonder what these people think will happen to them if they should look me (and each other) in the eye? What do they think? That Britain will crumble?

He walks up the stairs to the flat entrance, rings the door-bell.

'Who'zit?' a muffled voice bellows from inside.

'Zolani, open the fucking door.'

Next door a lace curtain stirs.

'What?'

'It's me, dammit. Matthius. Open the fucking door!'

Muffled feet shuffle to the door – Zolani talks to someone at the other end of the passage, then fiddles with the locks clumsily, while muttering under his breath.

'Open this fuckin' door now, Zolani!'

'Wait, wait, I'm coming – Jissis man!'

'Open this fucking door now! – open it!'

'Heera! What's your problem, broer .. looks like you want to wake up the whole neighbourhood …'

But before Zolani can open the door wide enough to let him in, Matthius wings it open, slamming Zolani against the wall, before grabbing him by the collar and shaking him and banging Zolani's head against a wall hanging.

'What the fuck is going on?'

'Hê, hê, hokaai – wag broer! What's happening now? Take your hands off me.'

'Who the fuck killed Miles, hê? Who?'

'Eh, wait wait … calm down chief … just wait a minute … Look I'm really sorry about Miles: I know you and him were big buddies … and that … But the man is dead – and there is nothing any of us can do about it. He was probably too busy intellectualising so the Boere caught him.'

Matthius takes a step back, gives one final shake to Zolani's collar, breath flaring through his nostrils, before giving Zolani one final punch, turning and heading back up the street.

Outside, the lights have come on, people are walking hurriedly past, collars turned up – not looking at this man with tears streaming down his cheeks, face contorted, saying loudly: 'fuck, fuck, fuck'.

It is Miles's darn lopsided, crooked smile that pushes him out of his nightmare. Matthius now turns for one last time, swinging his legs out of bed, before planting his feet on his bedroom floor. He ruffles his hand over his head and tries to remember the dream that had just woken him up.

This is the morning.

Scuffling around and looking for a lost cigarette butt he was sure he left at his bedside last night, he tries to focus on the exact dream he has just left behind.

The telephone rings. Between searching for the cigarette and automatically reaching for the ringing phone, he stops. Waits. Then decides to let the answering machine pick it up.

Whoever would want to talk to him this morning, can wait till he's in the mood – whenever.

'Matty – you there?' David's distinct British voice cuts through the booziness and probably druggy sounding timbre of his voice.

'Matty – Matty it's me: David, dammit. Pick up if you're there. Matty!'

The urgency and pleading of the last word is lost in the sheer exhaustion of will that David is going through now. Matthius considers calling back to London, but then finds the cigarette he's been looking for, and starts another search. For a lighter or for matches this time.

This is the morning.

Miles would have loved this South Africa. E-kha-ya. Phosi. Huistoe.

Matthius focuses quickly to get a snapshot of the two tsotsis swaggering across the road: holds the frame; smiles as the camera shutters hold the moment.

Ja, this one he will definitely use in the film.

'Smiles for Miles.'

The angry wind of early morning is less noticeable here in the city centre, he thinks as he signs himself into Bank Building where Zolani is holding his press conference.

Matthius makes a mental note to come earlier the next

morning, to try to get the same shot but with better, early morning lighting. He gets his identity tag.

When he walks into the sunny conference room, Zolani has already started his address to the gathering of journalists.

Matthius sets up his camera. But the picture just won't focus.

Zolani, now Mr Dube, talks at length about the new economic policy. Being in the same room as Matthius is making him nervous. He did wave his hand when Matthius came into the room, but from behind the eye of his video camera lens, Matthius knows that the last meeting they had in London could only but make Zolani nervous.

Zolani coughs, smiles slightly and then makes a sweeping gesture in the direction of Matthius's camera eye to punctuate his point.

'So, as you can see, ladies and gentlemen of the press, while in the short term, it might seem as if the new macro-economic policy means a possible further devaluation of our rand, in the long term, it is the surest way to restore investor confidence in our economy.'

Pompous fucking fart, Matthius thinks. Only last time, that time before their last meeting in London, 'pompous fart' would have been meant as a joke. The best of their drunken nights was when they would sit, hours into their brandy bottles, giving themselves ministerial posts when they took over.

A real joke then: an exile joke that lasted more than thirty years. And look at them now, Matthius thinks to himself, while he tries to get a clearer shot. Look at them now. Fucking taking over – and how.

Only when everyone around him fidgets with their bags, packing up equipment and putting their notebooks away, does Matthius realise the press conference is finally over. But this footage is nothing he can use.

Zolani is hurriedly making his way to the door, bantering with some financial hacks.

'Eh, Zolani, broer, I was wondering if we can get together

197

sometime, man. I'm making this film, and I want to talk to you about it,' Matthius cuts into his path as Zolani is heading for the door.

'Ja, sure sure chief. Sure. Give me a call so we can make a plan. I'm in a bit of a hurry right now, but give my secretary a call and then I'm sure I can find a few minutes to spare. Nice seeing you man, I've gotta run now, but ja, be in touch.'

Freeze frame.

What would Miles look like as a bag of bones? The four-hour Jo'burg to Free State drive has Matthius digging and burying and then re-digging the bag of bones waiting for him this morning.

The eternity of the sky is choking him here. He's only now finally gotten into the pulse of Jo'burg's wretchedness and flash-quick violence. And now this: four hours of the choking serenity of farmland and sunflowers and wheatfields, and skies and skies belonging to people who still think they're lords of this white-hard country.

'I don't see why – I really don't know why you're doing this,' Bongi's voice next to him in the car interrupts his visions of blood across the wheatfields.

Now he can't remember why he asked Miles's sister if she wanted to drive with him to the exhumation.

Or how they've come to this stone-cold silence between them. This after nearly twenty years of being friends, and occasional lovers.

'I mean, I really can't see what's so important to make a film about him now. You know and I know he wasn't all war hero. Or is that exactly what you want, Matthius: some *real* hero with clay feet?'

He concentrates on the consistency of the tyres turning on the road while he decides if it's anger or vile hatred he now feels starting at the back of his neck.

'Fuck you, Bongi. Fuck you and your prissy little professional exile martyr friends. Stupid fucking bourgeoisie.'

The splatter of Bongi's unsaid answers hangs between them,

resting on the whirr of the tyres. For Matthius, his vision returns to bombs between the sunflowers; blood across the wheatlands. He waits: hoping goddammit, that she would answer.

But this journey is taking Bongi back years and years of blood memory between brother and sister: to a more forgiving time than what she is prepared to allow to this grave of bones waiting for them now.

Let Matthius have his petty victories, she thinks staring at the road stretching out before her.

As Matthius shifts gears and then leans forward to turn on the car radio. Bongi turns; looks out the window trying to remember when this land belonged to them ... When this foreverness of wheatfields and sky, and yes, goddammit, this *South Africanness* of the landscape was theirs: their dreams; their hopes; their bitterness to fight over and fight for?

Now their twenty-year exiles' dream is holding the bones of her brother. And how many farmers didn't conspire in renting out their farms as graveyards? Driving now with the sting of Matthius's anger still hanging between them, Bongi sees her dream still in the clutches of unyielding whiteness. And to think that this is her country too.

This is the landscape she so much wanted to taste that first night in their camp in Lusaka. It was a night both she and Miles thought would never come: the certainty that gave reward to the fear and the decision to run away; the contacts with the comrade who came to recruit them; then finally leaving home without telling their mother; crossing the border, and still not being sure they were not going to be shot by the South African police. Then this: here.

'Miles,' their few strands of conversation now echoes in Bongi's head.

'Hamba, Bongi. Just walk,' Miles's strained tone was enough to silence her as they made their way through the bush past the edges of Mafikeng and Mmabatho, and to where they were going to cross into Botswana.

Their contact had dropped them off what seemed like at

least two hours ago, but if Bongi looked at the watch Miles had given her for her birthday, her very first watch, she knew it was only about forty-five minutes ago.

'Miles?' Five minutes had elapsed and perhaps, if the time was going as slowly as this, perhaps, she thought, they'd never get there.

'Shaddup, Bongi. No, what is it? What the hell is it now?'

The word 'hell' showed Miles's tension – his vitriolic swearing was directed at everybody he knew or came across, but now he spoke as sharply to his sister.

'Miles, Miles what if …'

'Bongi, no what-ifs! We're almost there and if you stop talking we can get there quicker.'

Then, as if to ward off any possibility of her starting to cry because of fear and his sharp words, he added a gentle 'okay?' to punctuate his sentence.

Now driving here through this stretch of farmlands and sky, she remembers how that three-hour walk had made her hungry for colour. The stealing through the dark to meet their lift to the border; and the endless walk of trees and clay earth until they got to their camp; and then fear and excitement and utter disbelief made her wish she had just stayed at home – and not made this choice of no-turning back.

There was no colour after that walk. The comrades were friendly, but there were no familiar scraps of colour when they finally left Botswana and reached Zambia. And she didn't know her place there.

That first night in their camp in Lusaka she'll always remember for the quiet that rested underneath the calls of the night birds, the turning and mumbling of her recently-met comrades, and the freedom songs through the night.

Lying on her camp bed, Bongi wondered what in all this strangeness would become familiar to her with time. But her thoughts were interrupted by the soft whistle she heard first, before she heard Miles nervously changing from one foot to the other.

There it was again: that soft whistle they used to make to each other as children.

200

She turned over, and tiptoed out of the barracks for young girls. And there he was: her lopsided brother shifting from one foot to the other.

'Miles, you supposed to be asleep.'

'Ja, I know. I just wanted to see if you're alright.'

'Well, now you've seen: So go back.'

'Okay, okay. Cool it. Anyway I also just wanted to give you this.'

And there it was from in the folds of his pockets, which he must have had since they crossed the border. A bright red (but gummy-soft from being in the heat of his pockets) watermelon slice.

Finally, back here driving across the wheatfields, her answer comes.

'You've forgotten what it is to have a heart, Matthius. Just so bitter.'

It is now the rough edges of freedom hymns that are sticking in her throat, desperately wanting to be spat out like watermelon pips. Bongi swallows.

This is a grave – this is the grave; and here she is twenty years later, again feeling the tears and longing and sadness like that other time when she desperately tried to swallow down her fears with the gummy watermelon piece. This is irretrievable now.

The flash of the sun momentarily hitting Matthius' camera lens, hits her sharply in her left eye. She winces. Damn you, Matthius. Wanting another spectacle of this too?

The freedom song is picking up – carried on the urgency of Miles's sister's voice. Their mother, always small and sometimes frail, now looks even more folded into herself.

Matthius, shielding his eyes from the sun, searches in his pocket for his box of matches he was sure he put there before leaving his flat this morning. He finds the box. Lights the cigarette. Inhales.

He looks over at the crowd: Many of his former comrades,

he is sure, are embarrassingly aware of his presence. Bongi he can see out of the corner of his eye: looking in his direction, and then hurriedly looking away when she is aware that he's seen her.

Matthius sees an outbuilding at the side of the gathering. He walks over to go and finish his smoke in the shade. Reaching the small square building, he turns his back to the wall and slides down until he is sitting on his haunches.

The crescendo of singing, and soft wailing is reaching him clearly now. He searches in his pocket for another cigarette, and his box of matches. But footsteps and a shadow reaching over from his side startles him just as he manages to finish lighting the cigarette.

'Oh, it's you.'

Matthius looks up at the voice and straight into Zolani's face. He says nothing; doesn't take a drag from the cigarette.

'What do you want today, now Matthius. Pick over these bones too? Is this art enough for you?'

Matthius now takes a drag from the cigarette, before replying.

'No, Zolani – just looking out for a friend – a friend and brother: who, as we say – just lost his head along the way.'

While Bongi was longing for a taste of colour, it was fear making Miles walk faster through the bush. He knew a no-going-back when he saw it.

Inside his pocket was the watermelon slice he had meant to give to Bongi last night already, even before they had run away: a token to wish her well on whatever they were going to. But it all got forgotten with the excitement and fear, and then meeting Matthius at the agreed place.

And whose idea was it that they could trust this man with his deep silences? Matthius Zondo. How he'd changed since those times they would race each other back from school or piggyback each other just for the hell of it, because they knew that as two lanky adolescents, they could only but fall.

'So,' Miles tried to prod the first night Matthius was back.

'So what's it like, broer?'

But they, whoever these people were that had taken his lanky friend away, now gave him this man whom they had taught how to hold back.

'It's … it's uhm – you have to be there to really know. That's why I came back for you.'

What had happened to hello? To heita? To hoezit, broer? What language had they put in his friend's mouth? It had changed him: that sure-footed belief, even more so than having any gun in his hand (and what did he do with it, and who did the kill?) ever could.

'So what do they make you do? – I mean what have you been up to,' Miles said haltingly. The image of his best friend piggybacking on his back, with an AK over his shoulder, shooting at everyone they could see, kept coming into view over his chosen words.

Miles fished in his pocket for the crumpled cigarette he'd stolen from his uncle's pack earlier that morning, before going off to school. He had to have some token of showing Matthius he, too, had moved on since his friend had one day just upped and gone. Miles wanted to show this familiar stranger things happened here, too.

Matthius now learnt how to hold back.

'I've come for you, Miles,' Matthius said ignoring the cautious strand of Miles's conversation.

Now it was Miles who was holding back; holding out on this unfamiliar friend.

But now Bongi was falling behind again in the group, and Miles had a hard time keeping up with Matthius walking in front of them, and his sister's soft whimpering was coming to him from further and further behind.

'Bongi, come on. You've got to walk faster, or we're going to get lost.' The earnestness in his voice betrayed his own terror at the journey, but also at this stranger, once his friend, now leading them: at his fear about what could happen to them.

It's raining softly now; and this is a morning Matthius does not *have* to get up to. That is behind him now.

He opens his eyes from his restless night of sleep; and then immediately shuts them again. Today he does not have to move. Today he has to do no more than just lie here. No film; no excuses; no Bongi; no damn dead Miles. Not today.

The quiet, masquerading as Matthius's early morning loneliness settles into the house. He turns; sticks his hand out to fumble for a cigarette and finding none, instead lights up the half-smoked joint left over from last night.

A perfect bag of bones. That's what he was. One day silly Miles who wanted them all to conk their hair just in case they were caught by the Boers during one of their missions into South Africa.

'Ja, chiefs,' Matthius can still hear him saying now, 'we're now the original gangsters – taking over from those boys from Sophiatown in the fifties. Besides,' he'd continue with his lopsided grin, 'when those Boere get you, the best you can be is a good-looking corpse.'

Now, with the dagga settling into the comfortable corners of his brain, Matthius wants Miles here now, dammit. Just to say to him. Ja broer, good-looking corpse: as if anyone would ever be able to recognise you after the South African security police got a hold on you.

But what timing he had. Miles …

The phone rings; and Matthius runs through all the possible names of people who would want to talk to him. Dammit, not this morning. The ring stops as the answering machine picks up. Matthius waits, looking at the machine, for the voice that doesn't come. Instead it's a cough that comes just after the sound of the beep. Then a short pause: then:

'… Uhm, Matty, – it's me – me – it's me – David. Matty you there? Well, maybe not; but Matty? Matty if you're there, please pick up the phone. Matty! Uhm, it's David – please call me, I'm at home. Yeah? I'll be waiting for your call.'

Miles had the timing that could freeze the seconds in the heart of a bomb. Perfect, timing. Now, looking over the last photographs he has of Miles after Miles settled into Maputo, Matthius remembers their lessons in combat. Miles's steady fingers showing him the notes that gave life to the black wires and the red wires and the steady tick-tick of their weapons of hope.

Miles's fingers over his, separating the wires, while talking gently into Matthius' ear: 'Sssh, timing broer, timing'. Talking at once to Matthius and the clock at the heart of the bomb, Miles who would whistle Dollar Brand's 'Manenberg' while they learnt to put together this clock that was to bring them home.

Miles's fingers went on to other things: more bombs; missions; crossing the border; learning the noises of the bush and his gun by pitching them to any Abdullah Ibrahim score he was currently whistling in his head.

And, now, looking over Miles's last happy pictures in Maputo, Matthius remembers how his fingers went on to cradle his camera, helping him catch the images of other people's lives between his hands.

After moving to Maputo, before his last mission that would take him into South Africa, Miles became more of his namesake Miles Davis, than Dollar, really. The timing turned happy and cocky and edgy at the same time. Much more 'Tutu' than 'Water from an Ancient Well'. Perfect, Timing.

It is a calm you feel when you first wake up in Maputo. A calm; and not the wonder you went to sleep with. Smell it. Everywhere. After twenty-five years of war, it is the wonder of What now? Where to now? These are the questions he goes to sleep with and wakes with. And it is a wonder that turns to calm for those who stumble into Maputo, wondering how much this can become home.

Now Matthius sees why Miles's smile grew so comfortably on him here. Here it is again – starting at the corner of his eyes; stretching to the cocky angle of his head; and exploding in his busy fingers. This is the smile that started with Miles here in Maputo; and spread across his photographs of Ruth First, too. The last batch of photos Miles had sent to him: showing the whole group of them who revolutionised the world, and who finally came to know peace.

It's in Ruth's face, too. The joy of her riding her bicycle at her now-home; the way she let her hair go frizzy as the calm too worked its way into her.

It was that peace that Miles wanted to take to his mother's house. It was that calm that could make him stop the heartbeat of a bomb.

Milk and honey galore, honey!

GOMOLEMO MOKAE

Themba Mlotshwa could not disguise his contempt for the men seated around the table he was about to serve.

'Sies!' he frowned, placing their meals before them. 'You people think this is Canaan, the land of milk and honey?'

The men, all foreigners, laughed.

Chief Adegboye Onigbinde, the genial Nigerian in regal, flowing white robes was the most amused.

'Come on, brother!' he patted Themba on the back playfully. 'Cheer up! You don't wish to bite the hand that feeds you, do you? We are all Africans. This is our continent.'

The other diners nodded their heads. Even Francois Matumba, the French-speaking Zaïrean, seemed to get the chief's drift.

Themba glanced in the direction of the office of the restaurant-owner and manager, Ebrahim Patel. The coast was clear.

'You're not feeding me, you're feeding that leech!' he replied. 'For all I care he can go back to India when you return to whichever holes you have crawled out of.'

'Come back Idi Amin, all's forgiven,' Margerine Chavanduka, the Zimbabwean journalist, guffawed.

This infuriated Themba.

'I'm serious. Strue's God: if all you illegal immigrants went back to your countries those of my people who're now out of work would get jobs.'

The Nigerian dipped his right hand into his jacket pocket. Then he flashed his new South African I.D. in the waiter's face.

'Ag, it's a fake,' Themba waved him away with his right hand.

He strongly believed people of Chief Onigbinde's ilk were devious. In fact, he suspected the Nigerian was not really a Chief.

To Themba, Onigbinde and his boss, Patel, were two sides of the same grubby coin. He detested Patel's opportunism in naming his restaurant 'OAU'. What's African about this Indian curry that I'm serving one of these illegal immigrants? he wondered inwardly.

However, Themba Mlotshwa's misgivings notwithstanding, Ebrahim Patel's restaurant did seem like the Organisation of African Unity; catering for diverse African culinary tastes. Patel, a recent arrival to the country from India, had a nose for business. As soon as he saw the innumerable African immigrants from Kenya, Zaire, Malawi, Zimbabwe, Mozambique and other parts of the continent in Hillbrow, he had a brainwave: why not open a restaurant to satisfy these people's nostalgic palates?

Black South Africans only had themselves to blame for the glaring absence of their indigenous dishes on OAU's menu.

In the beginning Patel had tried to cater for them, offering local fare like mala-mogodu – explained as 'tripe'; mopani worms and bogobe ba ting, which is sorghum-flour pap. He was casting pearls before swine: the natives were unimpressed.

His clientele were the aliens. On most days you would find the restaurant filled with a motley crowd from farther north in a kaleidoscope of traditional dress, the diners' languages as varied as their tastes in dishes. The table which Themba was serving was a microcosm of such heterogeneity.

'The new South Africa doesn't need shady characters like you,' the waiter informed the Nigerian. 'You people are tricksters. Every second Nigerian wants to pass himself off as a Chief.'

'There are only a few "Indians" in Nigeria,' Margerine butted in. 'Too many "chiefs", with just a few "Indians",' she chortled.

Themba was about to say something about Nigerian druglords when the Chief replied, flashing a gold tooth.

'My brother, my countrymen and I will be more than happy to go back home as soon as you people have returned our culture.'

François Matumba was not the only one at the table with a

208

confused look. He looked at the Chief, waiting for him to elaborate.

'You black South Africans are very fond of wearing dashikis and other West African garments when you attend functions calling for "traditional dress". That is our traditional dress, not yours. When we leave, we leave with them.'

The story of borrowed robes had the other diners in stitches. Themba shrivelled in his kaftan.

'Though I must say their "First Lady" does look fetching in them,' Chief Adegboye Onigbinde whispered to the Zimbabwean journalist between spasms of laughter.

The Nigerian's 'threat' gave the traditional doctor from Malawi an idea. Dr Looksmart Banda smiled, his sparkling white teeth illuminating his dark visage. In broken English, he let Themba know he and other Malawians would not mind leaving the country. But where would black South Africans – including many of their politicians – go to be examined by 'the floor X-ray': the bones thrown on the ground? Everyone knew Malawian inyangas were considered the most potent in the whole of southern Africa, if not the entire continent.

Margerine joined the fray. Zimbabweans would not mind leaving either. But black South Africans would have to 'return' the help Mugabe's government gave to the liberation movements during 'the struggle'.

In English worse than the Malawian's, Pedro Baloi, the immigrant from Mozambique, said something to the effect of 'ditto'. Samora Machel had been of inestimable help to the liberation movements. Black South Africans had to reciprocate by now accommodating immigrants from Mozambique.

Themba was about to retort that they cannot compare the plight of refugees from an apartheid South Africa to that of 'unpatriotic Africans who left their independent countries', when François began to speak, in French, which was Greek to all of them but the Nigerian Chief; Onigbinde was nodding his head in agreement.

'What's he saying now?' Themba enquired from Onigbinde. 'Just goes to prove my point!' he told the Zimbabwean hack,

Margerine. 'Must French now be our twelfth official language in order to accommodate the likes of him? Jussus! You people think this is the land of milk and honey!'

The Nigerian translated the Zaïrean's warning to Themba and his fellow diners: South Africans should be careful lest they kick out their next president in their zealousness to get rid of illegal immigrants.

Themba, Looksmart, Margerine and Pedro were puzzled. Was the Zaïrean perhaps suffering from delusions of grandeur: viewing himself as a possible successor to Madiba?

Chief Adegboye Onigbinde expanded: Napoleon Bonaparte was not French, but a native of the island of Corsica.

'Our Francophone brother would know about that, wouldn't he?' Margerine laughed.

'But he's right, you know, look at what Napoleon did for France,' the Chief said seriously.

'Until Waterloo, that is,' the journalist from Zimbabwe continued mirthfully. 'Though I do get his point, Kenneth Kaunda is said to be of Malawian descent yet ...'

'That's right!' Dr Banda shouted with pride.

'... he went on to become president of Zambia. On the other hand, his successor Frederick Chiluba is rumoured to be Zaïrean.'

The Chief remembered that Uganda's president Museveni was from Rwanda and Ghana's JJ Rawlings's a half-Scot.

Pedro said something incomprehensible, but Margerine thought he heard him mention the name of his president, Robert Mugabe.

'He says your president is originally from his country,' the Nigerian Chief decoded Pedro's remark for the Zimbabwean. 'He was reportedly taken to Zimbabwe by his parents when he was a young boy.'

'You see, brother,' Onigbinde turned to Themba, 'we are all Africans. We all belong here. Who knows, you might be looking at your next president.'

'God forbid,' Themba muttered. He told them that as it seemed foreigners stood a great chance of rising to the top in

Zambia, they should flood that country and not South Africa. They were 'stealing' jobs from his people.

'In fact,' Margerine shot back with a wry grin, advisedly putting an emphasis on the 'in fact' – 'In fact, it's your leader who should consider that option. Over here he's unlikely to ever become the country's president.'

'Don't be so sure, brother,' Onigbinde told Margerine. 'You should know from Joshua Nkomo's experience that "Home Affairs" is a good omen. He was minister of Home Affairs in Zimbabwe, now he's the president's right-hand man – a heart-beat away from the highest office in the land!'

Themba wished he had his traditional weapon on him. He would use it to wipe the smirks off the faces of the unwelcome interlopers.

He was about to walk off when the diners stood up all at once and made for the other exit out of OAU. The waiter turned around. His eyes fell on Colonel Krappies van Wyk at the entrance, the feared leader of the police squad whose brief was to rid Hillbrow of all illegal immigrants.

Themba smiled to himself. His suspicion that Chief Onigbinde's I.D. was false was being proved founded. He would not be running away from Krappies and his cronies if it was not. 'Bon voyage, fellow Africans!' he mockingly waved at the Nigerian and company as they scuttled.

'Domkop!' Colonel van Wyk barked at the waiter. 'We have come for you, not them.'

The Colonel whistled at one of the policemen accompanying him. 'Japie, come in with that lady.'

Themba recognised the lady as his wife – wife to Lesotho citizen Tsepo Moloto – alias Themba Mlotshwa, the Zulu waiter.

She had come to look for him in South Africa because the last time she and their four children had heard from him was seven years ago.

A Question of identity

PHIL NDLELA

It is a chilly Saturday morning. After fourteen hours on the plane I am still jet-lagged, dazed and a bit homesick at the end of a gruelling first week at the City University of New York's Graduate School. It's been a hectic week of culture shock, a persistent and unabating snowfall, shuttling from building to building filling out forms and carefully selecting courses relevant to my academic discipline. I am still in bed and savouring the latest news from *The New York Times* and the *Boston Globe*. The front pages of both publications are full of details on the much publicised investigation into President Clinton's private life.

As I get up to rewind the O'Jays 'Family Reunion' on my CD player, I receive a surprise phone call from Sazi, a friend in East London. He sounds so upbeat and exuberant on the line: it is his first transatlantic call! So the whole thing is a milestone of sorts to him. He asks me a bunch of questions about the trip to the USA; the courses that I have chosen for the Spring semester; and about life so far in the US.

'Brother, what I am going through here is a baptismal of ice,' I say. 'It's been snowing heavily all week, and you know how I hate the cold.' I tell him that the people here tell me that the weather is likely to remain nasty until at least the beginning of May. 'Life is pretty tough and the people generally are as cold as their weather. If you speak English with a foreign accent they tend to think that you are naïve and dumb. There is no sense of community here. You are rejected and spurned by your fellow black brothers and sisters. This is a very weird and tough place to be. I don't think I have the guts and staying power to endure this culture, brother. I find it too complex and confusing. I itch and long for my roots already.'

212

'Hang in there, brother, don't quit. Don't forget the extract from Psalm 37 that Mbongwe read out on the eve of your departure,' Sazi advises me.

I thank him for his words of encouragement and undertake to fight on. We exchange goodbyes and hang up. Before getting under the covers, I put on the late Bob Marley's 'Buffalo Soldier' and keep rewinding it until I doze off to sleep.

If you know your history
then you would know where you coming from
then you wouldn't have to ask me
who the 'eck do I think I am ...

I am suddenly jolted from my slumber by the persistent buzz of the telephone. Who could that be, I think as I lazily pick up the receiver. It is Nonnie, the Graduate School's international student advisor. She tells me that Professor Makapela, a political exile who left the country in 1976 at the height of the students' uprisings against Bantu Education, would be more than happy to meet me in his home this evening. He is a distinguished Professor in Political Science. As Nonnie and I talk, I can sense that she has a lot of respect for this South African.

'You know, Ken, the entire university community here regards Professor Makapela as an authority on the black struggle in South Africa. He is a highly influential academic who also advises the provost on exchange linkages with relevant black South African universities.'

After a lot of persuasion and some arm twisting from Nonnie, I finally agree to meet this distinguished Professor and his family, even though I have mixed feelings about it. Nonnie's husband will pick me up at 6 p.m. and drop me off at Makapela's residence. It's a deal and we hang up.

Back to Psalm 37. Mbongwe is one of the mainstays of our Black Methodist Church in N.U. 13, Mdantsane. He is a highly eloquent, unassuming and no-nonsense kind of preacher. He is forthright, solid and frank. He is a very shrewd and highly perceptive preacher who has a penchant for invoking parables and David's *Psalms* in his fiery sermons. Dark as a coal, short and heavily built, Mbongwe is an indefatigable middle-aged man who could easily spend two hours behind the pulpit devouring and dissecting the Word of God. He is a marvel to watch. The idea of preaching seems to be in his veins, his entire system. He does it effortlessly.

At an emotion-filled prayer meeting held at my home before I left, Mbongwe based his sermon on Psalm 37 verses 5 to 7. Reading out aloud from his Xhosa Bible to the massive congregation who came from all over the Eastern Cape to bid me farewell, he concentrated on:

Yiyekele kuye indlela yakho,
Ukholose ngaye; wókwenzela.
– Leave your way to Him,
And trust in Him, he will help you.

The Congregation kept nodding and urging Mbongwe on with 'Ewe, Tata; ewe, Nkosi yam, Thixo wam!' – Yes, Father; yes, my God, my Lord! – as he armed me and warned me of the daunting impediments that were likely to dog me in my mission.

'I urge you to have faith in God and to invoke Him alone in moments of doubt and hardship. Work hard everyday and be a good ambassador of your country – do not fail us. We hope that you will come back more enriched in order to serve your country and your church better. May God bless and prosper you. May all your aspirations and dreams be fulfilled. Amen!'

As Mbongwe left the pulpit, Nomji, in her deep, warm and seductive voice led the congregation into a spirited and moving rendition of Hymn 221 from the Methodist hymn book:

Ewe, Nkosi, mandihlume
Ndibe ngoxakathileyo;
Ndizamele, ndiphuthume
Konke okulungileyo
Iz' ingabi nakuphikwa
Yonk' imilo kwanemikhwa …

– Yes, Lord, let me grow
And bear fruit;
Let me strive for, and bring
All that is good ...

It was a colourful spectacle with members of the congregation stomping their feet, clapping their hands, whistling and ululating in unison. The atmosphere was electric. I looked at my mother and saw tears rolling down her face. She is a very resilient and unemotional kind of woman by nature, but she looked subdued, totally overwhelmed and moved by the occasion. She was probably contemplating and trying to figure out what three full years would be like without seeing her favourite son.

I glanced at Mbongwe. There was a broad smile on his face. He looked contented and seemed to be at peace with himself and his God – the mission had been accomplished. As my father stood up to thank the congregation, I thought: I am going to miss this sense of community and abiding spirit of African humanism. It was a grand send-off.

The phone buzzes. It is 6 p.m. and Nonnie's husband is waiting downstairs to drive me to the distinguished Professor's residence in Harlem. We exchange greetings. I hop in and we drive straight to our destination. It's hard to strike up any kind of conversation with this man. He is the extreme opposite of his wife Nonnie who is a very warm and endearing conversationalist.

As we enter the residence, we are met by a huge, smiling and broad-shouldered gentleman. 'Professor Mathew Makapela Ph.D. Harvard University,' he immediately calls out as he stretches out his arm to welcome me. 'Meet my wife, Professor Thembi Makapela Ph.D. Yale University,' he continues.

As the obviously proud Professor and his wife lead me to their posh and impressive lounge, I can easily tell by his walk and manner of gesticulating that this balding bastard is a country bumpkin.

His equally proud wife keeps on saying 'Yeap' each time her husband, proud as a peacock, makes a point. She looks like an old-fashioned lightning bird in her exotic and over-elaborate make-up, curly wig and high-heeled shoes.

I think they make a perfect match.

I take a glance at their beautifully painted walls and to my surprise see two huge portraits of America's former Republican Party presidents, Ronald Reagan and George Bush. Is this man a genuine black South African or an imposter? I wonder. While the husband and I talk casually about the weather and my academic programme at the Graduate School, the wife retreats to the kitchen and comes back with two glasses of orange juice.

I do not feel comfortable with these folk.

Professor Makapela goes to his study and comes back with two lovely daughters whom he introduces as Neo and Thabisa.

'Molweni, Neo and Thabisa. Ninjani?' I ask.

'What's that?' Neo responds, laughing. 'Dad, could you please tell your friend that I don't understand these weird African words that he's saying. He must speak English if he expects some response from me.'

'Okay!' her father says, 'that's no big deal, kid. I haven't spoken Xhosa for ages myself. Not since I decided to cut off these narrow tribalistic tendencies and immerse myself in a language that has an international currency.'

Will I endure this crap and hang out with these completely uprooted and assimilated bastards for three full hours? I ask myself. At this point, Professor Makapela goes to the refrigerator and comes back with two glasses of beer and offers me one – which I politely refuse.

'Try American beer, brother. It is the best beer in the world. You guys in South Africa should stop drinking mqombothi and imbamba. Those traditional African beers are primitive and unhealthy.'

I'm pretty incensed and scalding inside and I hastily respond, 'Mr Makapela ...'

'No, *Professor* Makapela,' he corrects me.

216

'I am sorry, Professor Makapela, I don't drink liquor. It would be foolhardy of me to start doing so in a foreign country. Trying out American beer is not part of my mission here.'

'You should flush out and undo the narrow and rigid African mentality that seems to pervade your psyche. Beer and red wine are good for your health – you really need them,' he informs me, looking me straight in the eyes.

I just tell myself that I am not going to respond to this crap.

After gulping down a couple of cold beers, the proud Professor from Harvard continues with his attempts to edify me: 'I'm actually extremely relieved that you are not taking any graduate courses in my Department because the standard of South African education is disgustingly low. I believe in the maintenance of academic standards, and if you were in my class I'd probably have no option but to fail you. I know that the system in that country doesn't prepare students well for graduate school. What I admire most about the system here is that we deal with self-motivated students who come well-prepared.'

'Wouldn't it be fine then if you could take your expertise to South Africa and contribute towards the development of the under-educated black child?' I venture to ask.

Not one to run short of words, the haughty professor has a ready reply: 'The people back home are too naïve. They would be easily intimidated by my qualifications and high level of scholarship. They would also refuse to pay me a competitive salary and accord me privileges that I'm entitled to here. I would never return to a country where my status and achievements would be compromised. I didn't spend all these years at Harvard for nothing. Any job that they could offer me in South Africa would have to be commensurate and compatible with my credentials. They would also have to offer my wife a tenured professorial position because she has a Ph.D. from Yale – a top university. We have been very fortunate in a number of respects in this family because we obtained our Ph.D.s from America's two premier universities. I'm afraid any notion of going back to South Africa is out of the question at the moment.'

He pauses to catch his breath before rambling on.

'We have just qualified for a green card – that's quite an achievement, you know, because it opens up many opportunities and options for me and my wife. We are well respected here. We've made friends with people who are in strategic positions in government. As a matter of fact, I've just received an invitation from President Clinton asking us to join them at the White House for the dinner that will be held in honour of British Premier, Tony Blair, who will be on an official visit of the country next week ...'

'Tell him about your forthcoming book, honey,' interjects the wife.

Professor Makapela takes off his glases, wipes them, and beaming from ear to ear he continues, 'Thanks, honey. Oh yes, I have just finished writing a book – a compelling book that depicts the macabre violence and the political situation in South Africa since the attainment of liberation. It is an open and forthright account of the anarchy that now continues to plague the country. Armed robberies, corruption at Government level and the rape of women and children are some of the issues that I tackle head-on in the book. You should make an effort to procure it. It will be launched next month at the W.E.B. Dubois Library in Amherst, Massachusetts. I'm terribly disgusted, no, to tell you the truth, I'm pissed off by the situation in South Africa. I used to be proud of being South African. Not any more ...'

I look at my watch and realise that it's 12 p.m. I politely ask that I be taken back to the dorm.

On our way there, I'm treated to the late Elvis Presley's music. Professor Makapela keeps reminding me of how great and phenomenal Elvis was. He goes on to tell me how different and superior his sound was to the crap played by Hugh Masekela, Fela Kuti and Miriam Makeba.

'I tell you, man, what these guys are playing isn't genuine art at all, it's political tracts.'

At 12.30 p.m. Professor Makapela's posh and expensive BMW stops in front of the dorm.

218

'Thank you very much, Mr and Mrs Makapela, for inviting me to dinner. Thanks also for the wonderful discourse ...'

Before I can continue, I'm interrupted.

'*Professor* Makapela. I would appreciate it if you could address me as such. That's my designation. Okay?"

I apologise, close the passenger door and wave goodbye. I shake my head in disbelief as I take the elevator to the fourth floor.

What a wasted evening, I think to myself. I'm angry with myself for spending my precious time with these pompous and completely assimilated snobs. As I get between the covers I find myself invoking the words of the late Malcolm-X: 'You are not an American. You are an African who happens to be in America.'

In the middle of the night the phone rings. What on earth has happened? I think. Gingerly I pick up the receiver. It is Sazi. 'Listen,' he says. 'I don't know what the time is on your side, but I'm on my way to work and Mbongwe asked me to give you the following advice from the Scriptures, Proverbs 17 verses 27 to 28:

'Umntu onengqondo uyawakhetha amazwi akhe, kanti ke nomntu oqondayo uhlala epholile.
Kanti ke nesiyatha sicingelwa ukuba sisilumko ukuba asithandi ukuthetha; kaloku umntu othuleyo ubalelwa ukuba yingqondi.'
– Someone who is sure of himself does not talk all the time. People who stay calm have real insight. After all, even a fool may be thought wise and intelligent if he stays quiet and keeps his mouth shut.

'Listen, Sazi,' I say, but he interrupts me.

'He wants you to know the following as well.' I hear my friend turn some pages, then he laughs and reads:

'Ngaphezu koko, lutsha, nasi isilumkiso: Ukubhala iincwadi ezininzi yinto engaphele ndawo, kanti ke nokusoloko ufunda kuyawuqoba umzimba.'

– My son, there is something else to watch out for. There is no end to the writing of books, and too much study will wear you out.

'That's written in Ecclesiastes 12 verse 12. Now tell me, Ken, what did you do last night?'

Just another Monday

MIKE NICOL

Emancipation Day was a Monday: 1 January 1838. It was raining. These are facts. I could say that it was probably not raining so much as drizzling, that kind of light summer rain that
hangs in the air and beads on your clothes. I could say water
dripped from the eaves of the flat-roofed houses and from the
oak trees; puddles probably formed in the streets, muddy
puddles mixed with horse dung; the mountain ghosted at the
back of the town. I could say all this but I've no way of knowing if it's true, except that I've walked in Cape Town on such
days when it's humid and the sky is grey and high and the
sound of the city is muted by the damp.

So the rain, the drain and trickle of it, the tick tick tick of
drops against the windowsill, is a way of imagining what it was
like on that Monday one hundred and fifty-nine years ago.
Picture it: in Table Bay the ships ride at anchor facing into the
north-west breeze; a small, choppy sea beats against the tide-
line in a scurf of offal and faeces and kelp. On such days,
without the south easter to blow off the humid fecund stench
of sewage, the town stinks. In the elegant white houses on
the Heerengracht and in Grave Street, in the warehouses of
Long Street, in the Waterkant taverns and the brothels at the
bottom of the town, the stench of human waste wafts in-
escapably.

But listen ...

Listen ...

Listen to the gurgle of the rain, to a faint hissing behind
the muffled sound of the waves. Even the seagulls are quiet.
The town is waking: a damp, dripping town. New guards have
come on duty at the castle sprawling near the shore, they look
across the Parade towards the Commercial Exchange and ris-

ing beyond it the Groote Kerk, but as yet there's no one about on this dull day.

Yet in the kitchens of the grand houses there are women lighting fires, bringing in buckets of water, sweeping, preparing food, bundling washing, emptying chamber pots; and soon there will be men slipping out barefoot from backyard rooms to go fishing, or to the market gardens, or to their leather shops, or to their carpentry stores: but they are the ghosts on this day and in this story, they are dim figures glimpsed yet not quite seen. Once they had been slaves. This is indisputable.

But for the rest, of course, I'm guessing: reinventing, trying to recreate something about that day.

There are a few facts about this particular Monday in a newspaper called *The South African Commercial Advertiser*. They amount to very little: just a handful of disparate details really. Not much, but something on which to base a reconstruction, something to go by.

So:

Imprisoned in the castle were 'several persons' who had been caught the previous afternoon 'in the act of stealing wine from the stores of the Widow Bam in Grave Street'. I see them dressed in tattered clothing, shoeless, the one with three fingers missing on his left hand (they'd been crushed while he was building a merchant's house). Another, a fisherman with breath that stank like a gannet colony; another, a Portuguese sailor; the fourth a potter from Madagascar, now crazy. Their fate is unrecorded, their lives only part of this day because they decided to steal wine from the Widow Bam.

Who is opening her bedroom shutters to let in the grey light and feels the rain on her skin and smiles at its coolness. What a relief after the dusty south east winds and the hot days of December. Protect us, Lord, from thieves, she prays and looks down into the street where Mr Hyde, hunched on his horse, goes slowly towards the centre of the town.

A street away in his house on the Heerengracht, William M Billingsley balances his glasses on his long nose, gazes out at the rain and sighs to his wife: 'I don't know, Mrs Billingsley, how we're supposed to run a shop in this town. Who is going to venture out on a day like today? If it's not wind, it's rain, if it's not wind and rain, it's heat. And this smell, it's worse than the Thames.'

'Don't fret so, Mr Billingsley,' says Mrs Billingsley, 'the weather will clear.'

In his shop Mr Billingsley has a stock of 'fine bright Yellow and Brown sugar, cocoa nuts, and Tamarinds'. This is first-grade produce from Mauritius bought the previous week when a ship called the *Transit* put in to sell some of its cargo.

Round the corner from Mr Billingsley's store, in Short-market Street, Mr R J Jones, the auctioneer, opens his shop with not a thought to the rain. He has thoughts only for the work that must be done, the goods to be sold.

'Good morning, Mr Jones,' calls out a voice and the portly auctioneer turns to see Mr Hyde, who is now leading his saddlehorse, coming up the street towards him. 'What a wetness this day is,' he exclaims.

'Better than the wind,' replies Mr Jones, sucking at his teeth.

'True,' agrees Mr Hyde, 'better than the wind.'

'And what can I do for you, Mr Hyde?' says Mr Jones.

'I'd like you to auction this trojan, Mr Jones,' says Mr Hyde. 'He's done what I needed him for but there's years in him yet that someone could put to good use.'

'As you say, Mr Hyde,' says Mr Jones, patting the horse on its flank which shivers with a run of muscles. 'I've got another going under the hammer this Saturday but two's always better than one.'

'I'm obliged,' says Mr Hyde, 'I'll bring him round first thing in the morning.'

And the two men part.

In his office Mr Jones sits down to write some adverts for the Wednesday edition of *The South African Commercial Advertiser*:

'To be sold by Mr Jones on the Parade on Saturday next a

Bright Chestnut Horse; his passes are very good and is particularly recommended as an Officer's Charger as he stands fire.'

And:

'At Mr Jones' Sale on Saturday next, 2 cases, consisting of 40 lbs White & Black ostrich feathers, to be sold to the highest bidder.'

When he's finished Mr Jones calls out to his apprentice that he's going to the *Advertiser* and won't be long.

'If anyone comes looking for me, Titus, you sit them down and keep them seated,' he adds, and then is gone into the drizzle.

Outside the newspaper offices at 11 St Geroge's Street he raises his hat to the Honourable Judge and Mrs William Menzies with their baby son, Oswald, swaddled in white taffeta, as they hurry to the church.

'What a start to the new year,' says Mr Jones.

'Indeed,' replies the judge, 'but nothing a few bottles of that St Julien claret you've got for sale couldn't put a brighter tinge to.'

'There're still a few cases left, judge, but it's going fast,' smiles Mr Jones. 'And some Uitenhage butter too, if Mrs Menzies is interested.'

'I'll be by,' says the judge.

St George's Church bells ring loudly through the rain. There are baptisms to be done: a cross of holy water to be signed on the foreheads of Oswald, and of Louisa, the daughter of George Harrison Esq. of the Mauritius Civil Service; and of John Robert, the son of Mr James Scott.

An hour later, as they are leaving the church (the drizzle continues although the sky is brighter), the Widow M Smuts (born de Kock) – still in mourning, the rings below her eyes as black as her dress – goes in at the newspaper offices. Mrs Menzies nudges her husband.

'I wonder what she's going to do now that her house and garden have been sold?' she says.

'I've heard she has family at Stellenbosch,' replies the judge. 'Or somewhere out in the country.'

224

The truth is I've no idea if the Widow Smuts had family in Stellenbosch or anywhere else for that matter. Nor do I know why she was widowed. Maybe her husband died in his sleep. Maybe he succumbed after a short illness. Maybe he fell from his horse and cracked open his skull. But no matter how he died: why did the Widow Smuts want to sell her house? And why did she want to get rid of everything, including the people her family – she – had once owned as slaves? I don't know. All I do know is that she placed an advert in the Wednesday edition of the *Advertiser* which said she was going to sell by public auction her 'Mahogany wardrobes, chairs, stinkwood tables and bedsteads with bedding complete, an hour clock, glass and earthenware, and, if not previously disposed of, the Indentures of some clever male and female Apprentices.'

Apprentices?

It's like this: after the Emancipation Decree was enacted on 1 December 1834, slaves became, for a period of four years, 'apprentices'. Only on that wet Monday 1 January 1838 could they really call themselves free. Well, free but not free.

So what happened to the Widow Smuts's apprentices?

They're lost in history.

But.

But here's a possibility, albeit one of many: they could have fallen into the hands of a man called L Twentyman.

Now there's a name to conjure with. L for Larry. Larry the loan shark. Larry the Lip.

And Twentyman? It's not a made up surname. There are people called Twentyman in today's Cape Town telephone directory.

But Larry the Lip is a slimeball. Polished shoes but dirt under his fingernails. Blue eyes but a tinge of grey on his skin. Jackets of good cloth but dusty to the touch. A ready smile but his lips are too thin and the smile seems a sneer.

For some months Larry the Lip has been buying 'on liberal terms, for Cash, Slave Compensation Claims'. His 'liberal terms' are less than the colonial office will pay to slave owners, but Larry the Lip offers hassle-free cash. He can relieve the Widow

Smuts of those 'clever male and female Apprentices' with a smirk and a wink and a flick of dirty fingernails counting the notes. And perhaps he does.

Surely on that Monday his lips would have been drawn in a permanent grin as he adds up the Slave Compensation Claims he's bought. Lying on his desk is the previous Saturday's newspaper that says 'Claimants for compensation under the Slave Abolition Act have been offered the whole amount of their claims ...' For Larry the Lip this is good news indeed. He bundles the claims into a bag and goes out into the rain without even noticing it, heading for the colonial office.

Here's an irony: this very office is the old Slave Lodge, all renovated and limewashed with not a trace of a hundred and eighty-odd years of slavery leaching from its walls. And in it the governor, Sir Benjamin d'Urban, glances at his advisers and says: 'Well. That's that.'

'Then we can get the budget published, Governor?' asks an adviser.

'As soon as possible, whenever that will be,' says Sir Benjamin.

'On Wednesday, Governor,' says the adviser.

'Good,' says Sir Benjamin.

The colony's budget comes to a 'Sum not exceeding £144,038 7s. 2d. to the Service of the Year 1838.' Part of it makes allowance for repayment of slave compensation claims.

The exact clause reads: '... for the Unfixed Contingent Expenditure to be incurred by the Special Justices, who have been appointed under and by virtue of an Act passed in the 3rd and 4th Years of the Reign of His late Majesty, William the Fourth, entitled "An Act for the Abolition of Slavery throughout the British Colonies": for promoting the industry of the manumitted Slaves, and for compensating the Persons hitherto entitled to the services of such Slaves, a sum not exceeding £3,158 6s.'

There's no telling how much of this is due to Larry the Lip who even now is being let in at the heavy street door.

In the afternoon it stops raining and the sky and the town gleam in a white light. Slowly the wind swings from north west to south east. In Table Bay the first stirrings of the breeze draw the captains from their cabins and over the next few hours some twenty-seven cutters, schooners, brigs, and barks set sail: their damp canvas filling, the water slapping at the bows, the timbers creaking. Five of them are going whaling, the rest are headed for such far flung destinations as Mauritius, Sydney, London, Madras. As they leave an American ship called the *Indian Chief* puts in 'for refreshments'. She's been whaling in the south Atlantic and has on board some 2 600 barrels of oil.

Late afternoon. The stench over the town has been shifted by the freshening south easter. The sun has gone behind the mountain; the town lies in shadow. The puddles have already dried.

In an inner office at *The South African Commercial Advertiser*, the editor sits with pen and paper putting the final ringing words to his editorial. All day he's been honing the sentences, giving his declaration the gravity demanded by a new year. Now he's finished. He puts down his pen, flexes his fingers and for the first time feels the day's humidity.

How do I imagine him: a big head, heavy eyebrows, his hair brushed back and receding at the temples, full sideburns and moustache but his chin is shaved. A tall man yet he has long delicate fingers, unhaired. He dresses severely in black. His shoes are crusted with mud and sand. He has small eyes, eyes that are not in proportion to the size of his head.

He looks down at his handwriting: it is large, the words sprawling across the pages.

'In rain and fruitful seasons,' he reads, 'and all those blessings which men are accustomed to ascribe immediately to Providence, the Colony has, during the past year, enjoyed the full and unmixed influences of its excellent climate. It has suffered neither from extremes of drought nor of moisture, the crops, though luxuriant, have been unscathed by Rust: the

227

winged plague of locusts has spared us; no disease has spread amongst the cattle or sheep; nor has any epidemic touched the inhabitants.

'From one extremity to the other of our immense frontier, from the Atlantic to the Indian Sea, approached or touched by numerous independent tribes of natives in different stages of barbarism, Peace has been preserved unbroken, save by occasional alarms or incidents that only served to show the watchfulness of government and the competence of those arrangements for defence which the ill-disposed have thus been taught to respect, and on which the Colonists as well as our neighbours now feel that they may completely rely.'

He glances up. The breeze coming in the open door has eased the stuffiness in the room. It riffles the pages on his desk. He reads on, crossing out a word, adding a better one, until he reaches the last paragraph with its resonating cadences, an acknowledgement – the only one I can find – of this day: 'The Apprentice and his Master have accommodated themselves to their new relations to each other with a pliancy most creditable to both. Exceptions, no doubt, can be advanced to this general remark ... but if offences between Master and Apprentice be regarded comparatively with offences between owner and slave in times past, a prodigious balance of good treatment, obedience and industry, will fall to the credit of the new order of things.'

Ah, the new order of things!

It was Emancipation Day: 1 January 1838. But to tell it, you'd have thought it was just another Monday.

Black swan
RACHELLE GREEFF

Tannie Elsie gets out of the way when one of her chickens has to be killed. And her voice over the Blydskap farmyard – *kom ounooi se kiepies, kom* – is silent.

Chicken meat never passes her lips. Eventually not even the weekly Sunday chicken pie at Silwerblare, the old-age home in the town, to which Tannie Elsie's only son, Raoul, impatient to change things on his inherited Boland farm, brings her.

On Raoul's fortnightly visits to his mother, he notices how the untraceable network of calcified arteries confuses her. Every time he leaves her behind in the chair beside her high bed, he feels as if something precious has been stolen from him.

Mercifully, it's the same disturbance of the mind which cushions Tannie Elsie from any knowledge of her son's penultimate action on earth: the removal and placing neatly together – just as she taught him – of his two slip-on leather slippers. She bought these slippers on her first and last overseas journey, in Firenze on the Ponte Vecchio. She bought them, counting and recounting the lire, and carried them home to him, because of his weakness for beautiful things.

Raoul is a collector of collections. He reads, he travels, he buys. He discovers how to make magic with money in places other than in the Blydskap wine cellar and the town branch of Boland Bank.

Who would ever know what sparks off a new collecting urge. Apparently from nowhere he fixes on Emile Gallé glass vases, then suddenly he is in love with Bohemian wine carafes, and then, almost overnight, he indulges in early recordings of Maria Callas. Some of the collections, like the Art Nouveau candlesticks, are extensive. Others modest, such as the single golden Fabergé egg in his safe.

In the course of the seventies, when bloody ink spills from the hands of the schoolkids in the ghettos, Raoul collects black swans.

There was a time, long ago, when Raoul, too, was a student. At that time, as he completes his agricultural degree, two of his university friends ask if he, flamboyant and generous, would be the godfather of their expected baby. They christen her Lea.

To mark the day, Raoul gives the baby a silver chatelaine wrapped in tissue paper. The late-nineteenth century Scottish chatelaine has seven minute functional objects on seven diminutive chains: a heart-shaped perfume holder, an embossed thimble, a pill box, a pencil in a silver sheath, a pincushion, a whistle and a tiny pair of scissors in a holder.

But over the years Raoul and the young parent couple see less and less of each other, though the attachment remains. When he visits, it is always unannounced. He arrives either in his imported American Lincoln Continental or in some other polished veteran car. Lea's young mother loses her heart to the 1933 Derby Bentley. When Raoul is there she moves lightly. Glides to the bedroom, flutters back. Smells differently. The years of motherhood and matrimony peel from her face. Outside in the street the children buzz and swarm around the vehicle. Nobody dares touch because you respect the possessions of others. In the movies, one of the older boys explains to his young audience, people drive around in cars like this.

Sometimes Raoul brings godchild Lea gifts. Once, from Spain, a Toledo bangle inlaid with gold and enamel. Barely ten, she receives a bottle of Joy, but the pretty container gives her more pleasure than the Jean Patou perfume.

'Remember now, just a whiff,' he admonishes her as he bends to where she is playing on the floor.

With time the godchild and her parents see even less of him. From her parents' whispers Lea deduces that he drinks. A life without God and church, in which marriage, too, is dishonoured, is inevitably unacceptable. Then there is an accident: Lea overhears from the passage outside her parents' bedroom door. Her father's face, between the door and the jamb, is a mask of simultaneous sympathy and disapproval. He tells her mother how the car rolled on a dirt road along the West Coast. Raoul and his passenger crawled from the wreck unharmed, she only in a bra and slip, he in underpants. The glass splinters of a bottle of Dom Perignon stuck like prickly pear thorns in their clothes, which, along with a sack of fresh crayfish, were hauled out of the back of the Cadillac Eldorado Classic. 'Sies. People who came past,' tells the father as if he had been there himself, 'covered them with blankets and things. You'd better get him out of your system.'

Lea could hardly imagine her godfather sitting bloodied in a blanket next to a dusty road. Things like that do not happen to movie-star people, people who always smell good and have eyes that look as though they are outlined in pencil.

Then, unexpectedly as always, Raoul turns up again. It's Saturday afternoon and Lea's parents and neighbours are listening to rugby commentary around the kitchen table. The accident is not mentioned. He places a couple of bottles of KWV between the ashtrays and glasses of beer on the table, and comes to greet her – she is twelve now – in the bedroom. On her grandmother's oak wardrobe pictures of women cut from magazines are stuck with diagonal strips of Sellotape. Among them Sophia Loren. He smiles:

'Have you ever seen me stick pictures of beautiful women on my wardrobes and walls? No, if you *have* to do that, stick them on the inside of your cupboard door. So that people won't see.'

Lea doesn't tell him that the inside of her cupboard doors are already decorated with animal pictures from the Weetbix box. Her pleasure in her pictures is spoiled thereafter. When her friends go mad over pop stars, not a single poster of the Osmond Brothers or the Rolling Stones is found on her walls.

Much later, in Lea's third year at university, Raoul fetches her for a meal. It is 1976; her twenty-first was a week before. He takes her to a restaurant in a Cape Dutch homestead with a

National Monument plaque next to the double front door. Here she is given a menu without prices and tastes trout for the first time. It is a world apart from the places on campus with their wooden benches where she and her friends order plates of chips and Tassies by the glass.

The waiter waits patiently while Raoul tastes the wine. He rolls it in his mouth, head slightly back and tests it lightly on his palate, before he, with mild distaste but still smiling, returns it to the waiter:

'Sorry, not mature enough. This one should have the aroma of an experienced woman, I'm sure you understand.'

'Naturally, sir. Our apologies.' The waiter leaves with the unacceptable bottle cradled in the ample white starched cloth over his arm, as if consoling it. He returns with a second choice. While Raoul lingers over this one too, the waiter does not move a muscle.

Lea sees, more clearly than ever, how different Raoul is from her father and uncles. She was never allowed to call him Oom, to her parents' initial indignation.

He enjoys her student stories and in turn tells of his own days long ago on the same campus, when he was a member of the clandestine men's ensemble which, in black cloaks and masks like birds of the night, serenaded the tender and susceptible female students.

'If I could have my life over again, I would change many things,' he murmurs dreamily. 'Like make music, maybe sing, rather than make wine. Like …' Across the tablecloth he takes both her hands in his. He strokes her fingers one by one, slowly, thoughtfully, his unfinished sentence flickering between them like the candle.

At the end of the evening they sip port in front of the restaurant fireplace. They are alone in the gently lit room, sunk into a plush sofa. Raoul does not touch her this time, only shifts his eyes from the leaping flames to her pale profile: 'So my godchild is no longer a girl sticking up posters, is she? Did she change overnight?'

It is late, and by way of an answer Lea stretches her arms

behind her head and yawns. Unaware that to her godfather's connoisseur eye she resembles a cat.

It is during the leisurely return trip in the Borgward Isabella Coupé that Raoul tells Lea about his imported swans: the whereabouts of the New Zealand breeder, permits, inoculations, and, in the end, the impatient wait. About money and costs, in any context, he never speaks. 'Did you know that a swan has only one life-companion, mates always with the same swan? Don't you also find it astounding?'

She doesn't.

The male and female take turns, he explains, to hatch the eggs. Often their nest of plants drifts like an island on the water.

Raoul's farewell kiss is not in itself strange. But this time he holds his godchild somewhat longer, closer, against him. Time in which his tongue teases her lightly. She knows only the ineptness of the trembling male students. This masterly caress is shocking.

The house-committee member on duty at the front door suddenly pretends to be deeply immersed in the textbooks around her.

Soon the empty vineyards and the white-washed labourers' cottages on the farms around the campus stand etched against the sky: the colour of cold ash. It is winter. The whites are nervous. The blacks restless and riotous. And at night the hostel is guarded against *die swart gevaar* by male students. Lea quietly refuses – unlike most of her giggling hostel mates – to pass coffee and rusks through the burglar-bars to the commando of adolescent bravados.

At this time she reads the short one-column story, tucked away between reports of the unrest, in a newspaper. She carries it inside her like a secret. In order to understand, she does not phone her godfather or her parents, she goes to the university library at dusk one evening. It is quiet in here, the students are required to be back in the safety of their hostel by early evening. She is looking for something, anything, on swans. As if to lay something to rest. But this bird is foreign to Africa and there is little information.

The ritual courting dance of the swans, the godchild discovers, is referred to as a victory ceremony, an apt description befitting of the swan's monarchical connections. For centuries, swans have been gliding on royal waters, or have been served up, lavishly garnished, on solid silver trays and carried, by not fewer than four lackeys, into the banqueting halls of rulers. In her imagination Lea sees their elegant neck movements on the water, the slender heads stretched high, the graceful lifting of the body till the one breast presses against the other while they call and trumpet loudly, crossing their necks rapidly to and fro as if fencing. Their wings unfold three feet on each side and beat exuberantly on the water in this erotic fanfare.

But unlike the white swan's, the pas de deux of the black is silent.

It is doubtful whether Meisie, wife of Job, farmworker on Blydskap, and domestic help in the sprawling homestead kitchen, knows this when she prepares the black swan with cloves and onions and potatoes, dished onto enamel plates alongside thick slices of bread which she has kneaded and baked herself. They wash the swan down with jugs of sweet Lieberstein shared out in their dop mugs, and through the open door throw the bones to the dogs that scavenge around the labourers' cottages. Between the greenflies and houseflies and snot-nosed little ones, these creatures live on the skimpy leftovers from the workers' pots.

Meisie uses some of the softest feathers to restore some body to an old flattened pillow.

When the police turn up two, three weeks later at the labourers' cottages on Blydskap, there is not a downy feather to be found.

Job, who caught the swan on Baas Raoul's dam one Saturday evening and killed it, was given away by a co-worker. Baas Raoul's reward had been irresistible.

234

In the local magistrate's court Job is found guilty on a charge of theft and his sentence is eight hundred rand or eight hundred days. Baas Raoul says he can pay off the money in instalments of five rand a week, deducted from his weekly wage of ten rand.

Before Job steps down from the dock, he has the urge to interrupt the magistrate to say he regrets that he killed the swan because the bloody thing was tough, even though it filled their bellies.

The surviving swan becomes so lonely that Raoul, already deeply involved in a subsequent fad and not keen to import a new bird, moves her from the dam to the big square swimming pool near the house. Though he seldom swims in the pool it is always sparkling.

And the swimming pool is where Raoul turns up one Boxing Day evening, a few years after the swan episode, in his silk dressing gown, to remove his leather slippers – his mother's gift – and place them neatly beside each other.

He steps down onto the pool's first step of hand-painted Italian tiles, each the size of a postage stamp, from where he would fall into the water after the shot. He has planned this for a long time with the same attention to minute detail he bestows on his collections. Doing it in the pool would spare his home.

Inside the house, a woman, his only enduring craving, dreams on unaware in the Sotheby's acquisition of 1976. It is nearly time for Raoul to bring her her early morning fix, always in a different espresso cup.

She walks to the verandah after she awakes without the smell of coffee. Outside the dawn fondles the land of the man she loves. O heavens, she thinks seeing the stained water, the damn pigs have been in the pool again.

After she finds Raoul face down in the water and after the S.A.P. van and the S.A.P. hearse have driven up and purposefully down the farm road between the oaks, she orders the workers to pump out the water. Before neighbours and family and friends in slow cars laden with flowers and questions and sandwiches creep along the avenue towards the homestead where the pool is glistening like a giant turquoise.

Job, still unsteady from the previous day's festivities, stands and watches how the discoloured swimming-pool water sinks into the earth of the orchard where Blydskap's harvest of yellow Kelsie plums shine through the green leaves, just like the Christmas decorations on the tree on Baas Raoul's stoep yesterday, where they, for the last time, received new overalls and aprons from him.

N2

ZOË WICOMB

They argued all the way from Stellenbosch.

Something odd as they sat around the table toasting Jaap's prize-winning pinot noir – later she thought of a spiked drink – slipped into what she had described to her girlfriends as a nice 'n easy relationship. A lovely evening it was too, with the mountain just taking colour, and in her hand the crystal flute with those divine little beads jostling at the brim.

Now for this barbarian, she had smiled into Jaap's sunburnt face, you must fill it right up, almost to the brim, yes, just so, so I can watch the suicide leap of the bubbles. No half glass for me.

As a child Marie loved weddings. Then grown-ups sipped from wide-brimmed coupes at darling little ponds of champagne. She supposed it hadn't been real but what did she care about such snobbish distinctions, méthode champenoise sounded grand enough for her; it was the effervescence that counted. She watched the sparkles rising from the bottom in a stream of light, and bubble at the brim. Oh, there was nothing like it, bubbles that hurled themselves at her, that couldn't wait to be taken. That's what's best, the moment before, when for seconds you are queen of a world of pleasure that awaits. Marie saw herself fixed in a photograph, with glass held to lips moist with expectation, chin – still young and firm – regally lifted, but there you are, who can resist greed, even when you know that that moment is best, that the actual thing falls just short of its promise. Like sex, she supposed, and surprised herself by casting a resentful look across the table at Harold.

Harold, only half-focused on the still life of crystal, liquor and lips, was asking about vines cultivated on higher slopes, about the heavy sandstone loams, and so caught that ugly look with puzzlement. Was she bored? Uncomfortable about something or other? Not that her demand for a full-to-the-brim flute was not charming. He half-smiled, solicitously. No wonder she felt cross, not knowing what to make of such a hybrid look.

Yes, sex. She would have liked to have said it out loud. That's what people like Harold with all their talk of politics don't think of, that there are now all kinds of freedoms. Just think, that a man who had sat in prison for decades, no champagne, no sex, was the one to push the country into the twentieth century, into the civilised world; she had been to Amsterdam where they made no bones about these things. Now everyone here at home could talk about it, see it on television, read about it in magazines, even in poems. No need any longer for men to make sinful trips to the Wild Coast or Sun City, it was all there to be had at home. And what's more, for women as well. Sex between all kinds, although she would have drawn the line there, perhaps taken one step at a time, no good being too advanced, even stepping ahead of England, but that's freedom for you, just as De Klerk said, freedom is unstoppable.

All of which prolonged the moment of anticipation, for the glass was still held to her mouth while she pondered liberation, until Harold, now attentive, watched the composition come to life: the glass pressed against cherry-red lips parted, the liquor spurting. Behind her, the sun was dipping fast, drunkenly, in the usual gold and reds, and then the light, how the light ricocheted from the crystal as she tilted it to her lips. The something flare of lightning ... beaded bubbles something at the brim ... Marie thought of lines that were once, perhaps, recited at school; she couldn't quite remember.

It was getting late. From below in Idas Valley the smell of location woodsmoke rose, and the skelbek of a drunk woman could be heard above the distant beat of kwela music. It was time they went home.

Drink up, said Harold, still smiling. Only one glass for him; he was driving. Jaap pushed a bottle across the table. To lay down. Ag, no man, what's the use of a prize winner if you can't pass it round.

And again, Drringcupp! Crass like the skelbek that drifted on to the terrace, his voice cut through the first sifting of frangipani as the light drained quickly, helter-skeltering after an already-sunken sun.

She turned to Jaap, What a beauty you have here – has she said that before? – top marks from me.

Oh, I can't take all the credit. I've got some first-class men working for me. My manager, he can tell just the right moment to irrigate, that's crucial you see, and I've even got a chap here from Idas Valley who knows everything there is to know about hanepoot.

He smiled, shyly for such a big man who stretched comfortably, brown arms flung out as if blessing the table. But the table too had had it. Others had left their traces on crumpled napkins; the cloth was stained with wine; and beside the posy of wild flowers an oyster canapé lay capsized, its crushed stern flung to the edge, to the printed border of guinea fowls craning their speckled necks onto the table. Marie folded her napkin, placed it over the scrap of pastry. Postprandial sadness flitted across her face.

Time we went, Harold announced in a first-time voice.

Ah, she thought, a spike of jealousy. That's what it was, jealous of Jaap who travelled to Europe once, twice a year with his estate wines. And oh yes, what if she were not ready to go, what if she did not think it time, but coming as it did, belatedly, the thought slunk off. So she looked deep into the empty glass, spun the stem, set it down, and pinged with her perfect nail against the crystal. Which made the men rise. Their chairs scraped against the stone paving of the terrace.

Ja-nee, said Jaap, that motorway is no joke in the dark. I see those squatter people have started throwing stones from the bridge again, something in this morning's Times about the N2. Kapaah! he beat together his large hands, also onto a Merc it was, but on the other side, coming from Cape Town. Luckily it hit the back.

Marie thought of the three wild men. On the N2 that morning, as they drove to Stellenbosch, the black men leapt naked, except for skimpy loincloths, out of the bush, ran across the dual carriageway, jumping the barriers, and disappeared into the bush on the other side. Their faces were covered in grey clay. They may have carried shields and spears.

Ag what can one do, she shrugged, there's nothing to do other than brave it out. That's now the new life for us hey, just braving it out on that chicken-run.

Jaap's kapaah! hands fell, See-you-soon, on her shoulders. Then she felt quite sober.

Princess's boy, the eldest, it was not that he did anything in particular, he just was funny, different from other children. Mrs Matsepe could not put her finger on it. Òh, that Themba was deep-deep, which may have made for a charming little boy, always with his head tilted asking funny questions like an old man, but now that he was no longer little there was a strange brooding air about him that surely would bring trouble. And what can you do, you can pray and pray to God to keep the children safe, but that's life, nothing but trouble, nothing to do, just the business of braving it out.

Funny how children grow overnight, and for that matter a boy who doesn't eat much. Even over the big days, Christmas and New Year, just like that turning fussily away from all the special food, and still shooting tall and broad into his eighteenth year, a good-looking boy with Princess's firm chin and deep black skin, so that she wrote to her sister to say how fine he looked, nevermind the strangeness that had already started to set in, she supposed, when his voice finally broke.

Princess wrote to say that yes, Themba had written, Themba now wanted to go back to school, start where he left off in Standard Six, Themba wanted to be a photographer. And in the envelope was twenty rand. Twenty rand, òh, the girl must be mad sending big notes in the post with all these skelm postmen who sit in the dunes with the mailbags and a tube of glue, going through people's letters before delivering them, late in the day, when the sun is already sitting in the middle of the sky. But miracle of miracles, the money slipped past the hands of those skelms which is something to be thankful for, and another thing, at least Themba didn't want to be a postman.

But still, Mrs Matsepe was hurt. The boy was her own since so-so high, since before she herself had children. Why had he not spoken to her? If only she had thought of it first, that he should go back to school, that they could manage again now that things were getting better. But Jim said, and Jim too was no less than his father, Jim said it was only right, it was only respectful that he should write to Princess first, that he appreciated having two mamas, that he should test out his ideas on paper before blurting out things that might come out wrongly. That was when she stopped listening. Having given her this bullshit wisdom he would in any case expect her to speak to Themba. Which was just as well. Only last week when she complained about the boy's strangeness Jim of all people came up with such a kaffir-idea that she just had to shake her head.

About this Themba business, he said, I thi-ink … and then stared deeply into his mug as if she had nothing better to do than stand around waiting. As if she were not about to take her life in her hands as she did every morning before sunrise, squash herself into a show-off taxi that would hurl itself recklessly all over the N2, as if driving people under cover of pounding music into a death of steel and fire were better than delivering them to their places of work. Not for Mrs Matsepe. She adjusted her beret, that was her name, that's who she was, since the day she decided to hell with laws and in-laws and came to the city after Jim, her lawfully-wedded husband. No, after all those troubles – and now also Jim with a head full of foolish ideas – she would survive any taxi-ride to get to her Greenoaks Nursing Home where she was in charge of all the cleaning girls. No, for her it was nice to get out to Rosebank every day, nice to be spread out amongst trees and purple flowering bushes, away from the noise of the motorway, from the filth of Crossroads. She would not give up hope that they'd get away; it was just a matter of time.

Jim cleared his throat to continue, but then the blue work

van hooted, and without grabbing his lunchpack he rushed off. So now he'd have to spend money on slap-chips. It was she, Mrs Matsepe, who got up early, got everyone ready for the day, packed his bread with peanut butter and a nice sprig of parsley she took from the Greenoaks garden. She admired the way cook put a curly bit of green on the dinner plates, made everything so nice and appetising, but that man of hers was too stupid. It was not till night-time, in the creaking bed, whispering so as not to wake the children, and worried about Themba who was not yet home, it was not till then, and with an elbow nudge from her, that he returned to his thought.

Themba must go to the bush, to initiation, it's the right way to turn him into a man, help him over this difficult business of growing up. He must go into the bush. She could tell from his voice that his heart wasn't in it, but still, she really didn't expect such a backward idea from a Christian man. What could have got into him.

The bush, she exploded, call that strip along the N2 a bush? Just a rubbish scrap of trees left there to keep our place out of sight.

Yes, but it's still our bush, that's what we've made of it; we must make do, it's all we have for the young ones to go to, to become men. Even the students have started going to the bush.

As if that meant anything. Mrs Matsepe snorted. Those students were toyi-toying fools, always going on strike, loafing about at weekends, doing those terrible things to girls in the hostels and then talking rubbish about roots and traditional culture. She supposed that that was what Themba wanted to be, a student.

I'm saying to you now and I won't say it again, Jim. No people of mine are going to have anything to do with such backward things. A pretend bush in Town, that's the very last I want to hear of it.

But now, with Themba back at school, now a young man, who carried on scowling and shrugging his shoulders and going about with others who looked as if they carried guns, she did not know what to think. What if she were wrong? If it were

242

the only way to pull him right should she not think again about initiation? If the boy himself were to ask, would she not say, yes anything?

But Themba said nothing. Themba did not speak; he sat with his head buried in books.

For a few seconds before he braked sharply, the car hobbled as if the road had grown potholed. Marie raised her eyebrows and turned away disdainfully. The last straw, said her look.

So now I'm responsible for the behaviour of the car, he said.

I said nothing at all. I don't care who's responsible, but I would like to get back to civilisation. This is no place to get stuck in the dark.

We're not stuck, he hissed. Then, resolving to be patient, it was after all no joke for a woman to find herself in the middle of nowhere, It won't take a minute, just a puncture, just a matter of changing the wheel. I got the spare checked just the other day. He opened his door a fraction, and in the light leant over her to scrabble in the cubbyhole for a torch. Marie shrank into the corner, her head turned to look into the moonless night.

Themba heard the screech of the car coming to a halt just yards away. He had made himself a hideout in the Port Jackson bushes, had cleared the space of rubbish blown from the houses, and had dug out with his hands something of a dip in which to settle himself comfortably. Here he often sat in the dark, with the smell of earth not quite smothered by petrol fumes, the sound of the traffic a steady woosh and hum, and through the screen of reeds and bushes his eyes followed the flashes of light and the sleek shapes of cars sailing by in the black night. Behind him, Crossroads was drowned in darkness.

Themba sat up, squatting to see the yellow light spill onto the shoulder of the road, the light on the woman's cropped yellow head. He watched the man wrenching at the handbrake, swinging his long legs out onto the tarmac, and in another pool of propped torchlight, opening the boot and lifting out a jack. Themba could see that he hadn't done this before, not on the chassis of this car. The man groped for a place to fit the jack, looked about ruefully for a second then slid on his back under the belly of the car, a silver beauty of a Mercedes Benz, yes he'd found it, the jackpoint. Now he reached for the wheel-brace to loosen off the nuts.

In the intimate interior of the car the woman's yellow head was bent over a handbag in which she pushed things about, groping for something at the bottom. Another flash of light within that lit space, then a glowing circle of red as she drew deeply from a cigarette. She stared straight ahead. A car rushed past. For a second her face shone white and still.

Fuck. Fuck. The voice cracked into the night so that Themba started, losing his balance. The man threw down the brace in a rage, then picking it up again, pushed with all his might, with clenched teeth, at the nut that would not budge. The woman's head was turned, towards the bush; she had heard a branch give as he toppled on tensed ankles. Oblivious to the angry grunting of the man, her hand groped in the bag while her eyes flitted in search of the invisible branch.

Themba squirmed with guilt. For spying on them, for not helping the man. But it was not his fault that they had landed right there at his private place, displaying themselves in their own light, acting out their business in slow-motion it seemed, before his eyes, and hearing Mrs Matsepe's voice to keep away from white people, to keep out of trouble, he hesitated.

Then he stood up, parted the branches noisily and walked straight out on to the road. The man's back was turned. The woman was out of the car in a flash, like a movie star, kicking open the door; her gun clasped in both hands was trained on him. He held up his hands, stuttered, Hô-hôkaai lady, I'm just coming to help, get the wheel loose so we can put on the new one lady. Stupidly betraying himself as spy.

In slow motion the hands were lowered, a slow smile twitched on her face as she looked him in the eye, the moody boy's eyes, ag he was only a kid, and her lips settled, smiling, Yes, sorry, you know what it's like on the N2 ... The man was taking the gun out of her hand, pushing it casually into his own back pocket, smiling energetically at Themba.

244

Ag man she's just a bundle of nerves, and pointing to the wheel, it's these bladdy nuts, you can have a go if you like but I've been trying all this time you know.

We must put something by the front wheel, the boy said. Themba picked up the torch to search the ground and pointed the light at a suitable stone. A moment's hesitation before the man bent down to pick it up himself. With the front wheel wedged, he tried again and shook his head. He watched the boy straining against the brace. Just his luck that the boy should be the one to shift the nuts. I think, said Themba, as if he hadn't managed it, they'll perhaps come loose under the jack. Together they pushed aside the clutter in the boot, the toolbag, an old rug and what looked like a brand new Nikon camera, shifted these to lift out the spare, and in a jiffy the car was jacked up, the old wheel off, the new one fixed.

Themba was wiping his hands on his trousers as they got into the car. The windows rolled down simultaneously. Together they spoke their scrambled words of thanks, then her voice above his, laughing, It's so good of you I don't know what ... and the man's, Yes, that was a devil of a wheel, thank you man, and one day I'll be the one to roll a stone out of your path hey. Again the noise as their voices merged, and the key turned and the Merc started up and it was as if from a distance, joining the gibberish of thanks, that he heard a thin sound coming from an unknown place inside and distinctly the words, Please sir, madam, have you please got some rand, then the scramble in pockets, in the handbag, and two sets of white hands dropped the notes – Yes of course, ag shame man, sorry we just weren't thinking – into the bowl of his very own prosthetic hands.

The hands were on fire. Themba stuffed a burning note into each of his pockets, felt the fire running down his legs and back up through his body so that he sprinted home with the repetition of his own voice in tinny echo, Please sir, ma'am have you please got some rand, some rand, some rand ...

Mrs Matsepe dropped her dishcloth right there on the floor and followed the boy, a streak of fire she could have sworn, into the room where the youngest was already asleep. Themba whipped the money out of his pockets, two twenty rand notes, and threw them on the bed.

It's for you, he whispered, from the people on the road. I helped them change a wheel.

And they gave you money?

Themba dropped his eyes. Some rands, some rands, some rands, echoed in his head. He said slowly, watching his hands curve once again into a cup: I asked for the money. From mlungu in a Merc. I begged.

With her eyes fixed on the boy, on the face twitching with shame, Mrs Matsepe took the notes, folded them together, then tore them carefully, into halves, into quarters, into eighths, and again, into tiny scraps of paper that looked nothing like confetti as they floated onto the bed.

For love
ELLEKE BOEHMER

It's the pop-popping of the tractor engine in the far garage that
nudges him awake.

His mouth throbbing and the electric heater beside the bed
already glowing, which is a kindness of Susan's.

Can't begin.

Can't begin to get out of bed these days without the room
warm, and breakfast cooking. Fleshy smell of the bacon bringing its strong pink taste against the back of his mouth. And
Edward warming up the tractor in the far garage.

Tongue tender and lumpy. Funny. What he keeps noticing is
how this old age of his brings a shrinking of horizons, no opening, no clearer understanding like you might've thought. This
mouth and its sores, cancer, but operable – the world has
shrunk around the pain that is this mouth.

Once they said he was the ablest man they had, wiry, sharp-
eyed, tough-headed, Chief Forest Warden for the government
plantation company. He spent the long days in high crow's-nest
towers, racing watertrucks down rocky roads after tell-tale
wafts of smoke, and always the cluster of black guys hanging
on behind.

A time ago. Now there's just Edward, him and Edward the
tall flat-faced Zulu, working the smallholding. Edward who's
this minute astride the tractor seat, eating the bready pap his
woman, girl-friend, will have carried out to him, and waiting.
Where's the boss?

Morning, boss. I thought boss was never coming.

Named for a king. That's what he tells him, kind of steady
joke, when they walk the back fence planning their work.
Named for a king, even though no king of that name has ruled
in Edward's lifetime. In his own lifetime, when he was hardly

knee-high, less than a pipsqueak. King of my lands, Edward, he says, a compliment he knows is a hidden arm grip.

What could I ever do without you?

All this, the cauliflower plots, Susan's kitchen extension. Edward's own two-room hut, the dog run along all four sides of the property, the water tower and its look-out post between the syringa trees (the look-out for old time's sake), everything they had to make and fix when him and Sue bought this place using the early retirement package – all these things are the work of Edward's hands, these things him and Edward have planned, thought about together, walking the back fence.

I thought boss was never coming.

Helpmate. It crosses his mind to say this sometimes, even to Sue, like here over his mug of breakfast tea and his bacon sandwich softened in milk; he very nearly wants to say, but can't quite manage it, can't quite. Speaks with difficulty anyway.

Helpmate.

Closest, next to my brother he must be. Must be, just about, the closest mate I have.

You can say these things nowadays and almost not surprise yourself.

Named for a king and as bad as madam, he says, walking out to the tractor and Edward sitting waiting, smoking a roll-up, the tractor engine muttering. As bad as madam, you, forcing me out to work everyday, to shift these bones, when it's soft and comfortable beside the electric fire, and I could be dozing, nursing this stupid mouth.

Tongue aching with every sound he speaks.

Which is also why he likes this Edward. Without even a word Edward gets down and he climbs into his place, the cupped seat warmed. Plough up the cauliflower field today, plant next week, the two of them know without saying. Edward doesn't waste words, doesn't waste his breath to use his voice more than necessary. Even the girl, woman, he has living with him, is well-spoken. She says 'Morning, how are you?' in English. Once Edward told him – they were standing at the west end of the smallholding, they could see her sitting against the wall of the hut with a newspaper – he told him, she has matric. He said it like another man might say, her family owns a farm in the Biggarsberg.

Careful with words in the way some people are careful with money. On election day a few years back they drove together to the high school where they had a polling station. Susan went alone to vote in town. He offered to talk him through that ballot paper like a Christmas streamer, long as an arm, stupidly colourful, full of Third World guff.

Edward let him say his say, then, thank you boss, but no thank you boss, Edward said; thank you boss, I know what I'm voting for. Didn't waste his words.

Then they queued to vote in silence, walked up to the booths side by side in silence. He heard Edward's pencil click on the ledge where he dropped it, after putting his cross.

Edward, the man says, sticking his head into the stuffy dark of the hut, the smell of bananas and rat poison.

A reflection, his own face, winks across the mirror hung on the wall.

It was always going to be the woman trouble, matric or no matric, he should've foreseen. A policeman squeezes past him into the room. An excellent man like that, he says to himself shifting to one side, it had to be the woman to bring him down. Ten days now Edward's been gone, the hut locked, the curtains drawn tight, and the woman AWOL too. It's been four days he himself hasn't really bothered to get out in the morning, mouth torn to pieces by these sores, no one round to get the day's work started. The woman was always going to mean trouble, it was clear as a blue sky from the start, it had to be her, the hair twisted into those American plaits, the newspaper reading. 'Morning, how are you?'

Edward himself didn't let on there was anything the matter. Maybe just lately he was, well, more correct than ever, more careful, almost whispered to speak. But they didn't discuss the change – wasn't his business. The one real sign, the one mention, that was when Edward said, my woman – or was it wife he said? – my wife has gone to visit with relatives in Empangeni. After the man told his neighbour this detail early this morning, the tractor still silent in the far garage, the neighbour persuaded him to call the police.

Can't begin to say what could've happened, the man tells the two policemen, one black, one white, useless bunch of no-hopers that they are, took seven hours getting here. Edward'll have followed the woman maybe, he says, hoping the pair'll leave as soon as formalities are over. No, it's impossible, he repeats, can't begin to say what's happened.

But the officers insist on 'taking steps'. First step was breaking the lock on the hut door. That was one of J H Massey's most expensive padlocks, the man said, and his mouth pulsing with pain as the saw – Edward's best saw – grated through the shiny steel loop.

The shadows in here hang thick as wood smoke.

Note on the bed, says the white officer. He reads, hands it over in silence, ruled exercise-book paper.

But the message isn't for their eyes, they shouldn't be reading this, these words printed neatly in pencil.

To Margaret Magubane. How can I live without you?

Can't begin to speak. If he opened his lips and the cool air suddenly touched his sores, the pain would shake his skull like a leaf.

You think this means she's coming back? says the officer, the idiot.

It means he's dead, the man just manages to say.

Can't live.

She returned, just the once, to collect his things and the wages still owing, for funeral expenses. Her hair was unplaited but the city pose unchanged, the hip thrust out, the face held up to the sun, slightly squinting.

He couldn't handle it, she said. He always knew I had the other man, two sons by him.

The body hung from the deodar tree heavy with corruption, a shimmering crust of teeming flies. More than three weeks after the death it was, the spot that well-hidden, a mature plantation thick with trees. The police called, come identify.

He recognised the overalls, and the photo in the pocket. Of her. Smiling into the light.

The noose was her black pantyhose knotted together.

That hip thrust out.

I don't know what I can say, he said to her now, can't understand.

Life goes on, she said, I got children to feed. She seemed to thunk herself in the stomach. I got a new job, she said.

He died for love, the man said. For love.

The woman raised her face to the sun. Maybe, she sighed, a huff of exasperation.

But he said it again to himself, and again. This straightforward young man, ordinary good-sort black, he killed himself for love.

As if saying it would make clearer what beggared belief.

Rose
NORMA KITSON

She's frail now. Her eyes, once deep, complex and dark blue, turn to me with faint entreaty, a pale, yellowish tinge rimming the empty blue. And where she once walked with an impatient flouncy clicking of heels, she now shuffles along unsteadily as if all the certainty of her past life has led her only to ultimate vacillation. And her mouth – that smooth, shiny, bow-shaped, patent-leather red slash, once capable of pert, stinging remarks – now stutters and strains, the lips filleted with a thousand tiny wrinkles etched with still carefully applied lipstick. Her once thick black hair, slicked with soft shiny curls, has thinned, and the reddish tint shows sparse grey roots.

That once arrogant, World Olympic Bridge winner, poker player, trendsetter, squabbler with her five sisters and friends, is no more. Only an occasional outburst of frustrated, stuttered irritation evokes – nostalgically now – my childhood fear and awe of her tremendous power as she scattered children, servants and husbands to go about her important business, and then guilty memories surge: how could I have been born, awkward and ugly, to shame such a shining, deft, beautiful mother.

But now my mother has grown very old.

Fate has dealt her the worst blow. She cannot get her words out. Some cerebral trickle – or stroke of retribution – has disconnected her voice from her thoughts. Except when she's talking to the cards. Then she's fluent!

Playing cards: Bridge, rummy, canasta, poker, klaberjas – anything as long as it was cards – has always been my mother's preoccupation. As a child, I longed for her attention, for her interest, but she was always just going out for a game: a brief kiss, a strong whiff of Chanel No. 5, a final pat to her hair and a twist to a bow, flounce or pleat in front of the mirror before she swept out, full of purpose, leaving me bereft in the big house.

Or she was staying in. Then, in lounging pyjamas, or the latest satin-feathered housecoat or trendy slacks, she'd entertain her card-playing visitors in the purple lounge or green card-room and, for some reason, I'd get deeply nauseous helping the maid with the exquisite tea-trolley laid with glittering silver and the latest fashion in four kinds of cakes. I'd help wheel it in and was allowed to say 'Good afternoon' to the visitors and hand round the cakes, and then, answering my mother's slight frown, I'd leave them to it, sometimes lingering irritatingly in the doorway, listening to the incomprehensible chatter of 'Three Spades', 'Four Hearts', 'Four Spades', 'Pass' and understand that this was the most important language in the world.

Well, that was all a lifetime ago, and now, a Bridge-player myself – though I swore as a child I'd never play cards and would always give my children the first priority of my attention – life has come full circle. Our roles have somewhat reversed and my old mother looks to me for love and comfort. Now she shudders when she looks in her mirror, loathing the self she has become, and I try to reassure her and tell her she looks lovely.

Her only comfort is still a good old game of cards, and at K-Rummy she's as sharp as ever she was, and when she's playing, she's back to her old self. We sit across the card table with new Bicycles (my mother wouldn't dream of any other – or an old pack) for long, tedious hours.

'Don't you do that!' she says with uncharacteristic fluency, to the Queen of Hearts. And, 'nice to see you, my boy,' to the Jack of Diamonds.

She has a natural sympathy with the male cards and a spiky irritation with the women, though she appears to have a relationship of some kind with every card in the pack. She goes to the pack and flicks up a card. Her face twists with distaste:

'Get off, you bitch! Go away!' she says to the Black Widow – the Queen of Spades – as she deftly slots her into the neat fan in her left hand. Her fluency with this family is remarkable bearing in mind she cannot even get out a comprehensible 'Yes' or 'No' to my query as to whether she wants a cup of tea.

We play on. Now my mother is excited. She has melded a five-card run, lays it down with a sort of flourish from the past, and looks up at me, words straining to come. I know what she wants to say, as she sticks on 'D-d-d'.

'That was very good, Mom,' I say, filling in for her, and she lowers her head to her fanned-out cards and says to the Nine of Diamonds she has just picked from the pack: 'I knew you'd come to me, darling. You're my little middle-pip!'

I am beginning to get a cramp in my right leg, and my back feels the strain of sitting for hours playing K-Rummy with my old mother who is unable to talk to me, who can only talk to the cards. As I look at her concentrating, trying to outwit me at the game, I am overwhelmed with feelings of love for her. I flex my leg and stretch my back. I will play K-Rummy with her forever if it makes her happy. With a pack of cards in her hand, my mother can still face the world with confidence and she can still beat all-comers.

The day draws on. It is nearly time for her supper. My brother, David, will soon arrive and his warmth will flow over both of us like a healing balm. Perhaps old Auntie Sellie or Tookie will send a maid over with some gefilte fish or lemon stew, or Fenella, Minna or one of the 'girl' cousins will pop in for a quick visit – a whirl of perfume, high heels and wearing the latest fashion in a trendy colour.

Some family traditions have changed over the years. We were all stuck in Durban by invisible glue, facing the wrath of Grandpa David and then Uncle Joe if we so much as considered leaving our hometown for longer than a week or two. Now we are spread around the globe. Some cousins left to escape conscription into the white army, others in fear of the post-apartheid blood-bath they had for so many years expected as inevitable, and some who just didn't fancy living under black rule.

254

I wonder if Uncle Solly has given up his shiksa 'seketry'. He has grown quite bald and his shoulders stoop. Rachel's neigh and nagging has got worse with the passing years.

Our youngest uncle, Jerry, now in his seventies, is frail and has retired from his lingerie and dress factories and his son, David, has taken them over. (There are now so many Davids in the family – all the males born after Grandpa David's death were called after him.) Auntie Fay, is still given to blowing her nose and maintaining she is in delicate health though there is no doubt she will outlast the lot of them.

Most of the aunties are now widows and have moved from their luxurious villas and houses on the Berea to beautifully-appointed flats overlooking a Durban that has mushroomed into a huge city and completely changed its character into a busy black metropolis. Many old stores, have gone. The elite shops have moved out to the suburbs.

My old aunties look lost amidst their gorgeous old-fashioned decors, ornaments and clothes, wearing the styles and make-up of yester-yester-year. They have never heard of gender equality, think the very worst of women's liberation and still laugh unbelievingly at the word 'lesbian'. They have out-grown the world and keep to themselves in comforting insula-rity, frightened of the increased violence and frequent mug-gings.

With Uncle Joe's death, shortly followed by Auntie Pearl's, the spine that attached our vertebrae to Durban and to the family's unwritten but numerous strict rules, has gone. Now our friendships are not restricted to some few other Jewish families – some cousins have even married out of the faith!

Friday night suppers for the whole family are no more. Archie Bellman rules the family roost and he never liked the family get-togethers. He is now the head of the vast financial empire. The male members of the family go to Archie's office when they need money to develop their schemes, and his office is also the venue for the confabs and hullaballoos. Now the women play no role. The aunties have been excluded from family confabs and the female cousins don't seem to care.

Archie refused to take over Uncle Joe's house in Ridge Road and instead still lives in his designer house which Fenella has never liked.

Gwennie escaped to Australia and rich Lionel who inherited his father's businesses and estates, has divorced his famous film-star wife and, in his forties, lives like a teenager, dating young girls, lighting candles and dimming the lights in his chromium-and-black-glass flat, drinking bottles of French wine and playing seductive music on his music-centre.

For years no one in the family has spoken to Uncle Izzy. He was thrown out when he divorced Auntie Tookie and married Beryl, even though Auntie Tookie got her own back by marrying Beryl's husband, Natie. But Tookie never looked happy after Izzy left and Natie passed away a couple of years after their union.

Uncle Basil died, flying his plane into a mountain. He'd been warned that the weather was bad but, being Uncle Basil, he never listened to a soul and his major error of adopting our cousin John made paupers of his own children, Gwen, Ralph and Anne. From the time cousin John left to go back to Greece, Auntie Dolly got thinner and frailer and now, in her nineties, resembles a river reed.

Auntie Sellie still lives her life for Fenella and Fenella is still in love with Archie, who seems to be on every committee that counts. Uncle Reuben has been dead these ten years.

Vinegary Auntie Bea never knew she had ruined her daughter's life. Even on her deathbed, and as a fussy interfering grandmother, she was urging Minna to correct her behaviour and advising her on cooking, decor and child-rearing.

In her ripe old age, Auntie Betty left Durban to live in Chicago commuting from one city to another to be near her grandchildren. Cole died of AIDS.

After years of living in England, I have come back to my roots. I have returned to a strange new country at last ruled by its majority. Apartheid has officially gone. It is more alive than ever.

Durban. Home. How I have longed for it! How big and beautiful it has become. I have missed my family: my aunts with their multi-coloured eye-shadows and beautiful crochet work, their outlandish flower arrangements, their pedestrian talk, their barbed comments. And I have even missed my dominant, aggressive uncles with their boxes of Black Magic chocolates and the rich, warm umbrella of security they exuded. All the things I left home for, I longed for during the twenty-five years of my exile: the Friday-night suppers, the family confabs, the heat, the sea, the warm blue of the night, the heavy sub-tropical flowers, the elephant at Mitchell Park, the Indian market, Grey Street and the gloss of West Street.

The houses down steep Marriott Road have gone and now towering blocks of flats overlook the racecourse below. Along Musgrave and Essenwood Roads, the martingulu bushes have been replaced by high walls: every house is walled, barred and gated. The beachfront has been changed to accommodate the motorist, flea-markets abound, and the hotels now stretch so far up the coast it is only a matter of time before they reach the Blue Lagoon. That trysting place, where the estuary of the Umgeni River runs into the Indian Ocean, is no more. No longer does a keen Indian waiter rush out to your car, parked at the end of the pier overlooking the jet-black sea, to attach a tray laden with hot-dogs and milkshakes. Now it's just a little drab shop selling sandwiches and boxed cold drinks. The Edward Hotel, that ritzy paradise, now plays third fiddle to the Maharani and the Elangeni.

Durban North stretches for miles, and Burman Drive is no longer the monkey-infested malarial swamp where Dad took us on Sunday afternoons. Now the outskirts of Durban boast enormous shopping centres and mega-markets and flaunt all the suburban glory of lush gardens and beautiful tree-lined streets. And Pinetown, where my brother, David, lives, is no longer a garage selling take-away curries, with a few Indian homes dotted around the hills. Now Pinetown, too, is a huge spreading residential area with enormous blocks of flats and housing estates. The centre of Durban has changed too. The shops in West Street are unrecognisable. Greenacres has gone, and even Payne Bros.

This is Thekwini – white Durban – rich, with acre-big homes, tennis courts and swimming pools, where the people enjoy every privilege and every facility is provided: libraries, gleaming rows of shops, theatres, cinemas, sports grounds. In Thekwini each family has two or three sleek new cars and the houses are painted glitter-white. No, not every house, not every family. There is also evidence of growing white poverty. South Africa is beginning to show its class structure more clearly these days.

I walk the hot, steep streets of Berea alone. The once oh-so-grand Caister Hotel is now a lodging house. The corner shop where Alison bought her weekly Peppermint Crisp, and David his bulls-eyes or lucky packets, is now an estate agency advertising hundreds of homes of whites fleeing a liberated South Africa. Now and then a domestic in uniform and pinny with the inevitable Victorian maid's cap, passes by carrying, in plastic bags, the madam's shopping, and a silent group of black people and a couple of white-haired pensioners wait patiently for the Mynah bus to the plush Musgrave Centre or town. There are no whites abroad in the streets. The houses seem dead behind their walls. Thekwini has the feeling of a graveyard.

Just over Ridge Road, where Uncle Joe's house still stands flanked now by high-rise flats, there is another world. No walls. No facilities here: few libraries, theatres or cinemas. It is the thin dividing line of Overport between white and Indian Durban.

Past Overport into Sydenham and Asherville is the world of the Indians, a rich world of tarred and sand-track roads and a mix of houses: from the small and lopsided with a pawpaw tree sticking out here and there, to trim homes with banana palms in laid-out gardens, and others, grand and painted in beautiful startling colours. Chock-full shops line the main streets, spilling their wares onto pavements, and broken, chugging cars share the roads with slinky new and old third-hand models. This is a packed world of people, where the men greet each other warmly and fondle children's heads, women converse over the hedges and the children play together and cross back and forth into each other's homes. It is a world of warmth and reality and it draws me.

The black world is remote. You can't see where they live, love or eat. Row upon row of buses and 'emergency taxis' line the Thekwini streets waiting to get rid of the workers from the white world at dusk and return them in the early dawn to serve white industry. Do they ever see their children in the sunlight?

After cooking and washing up the three-course evening meal for the madam and the master, the domestic workers will leave the gleaming kitchens and lock themselves out of the stately homes to eat their mealie-meal, and then flake out in their ill-lit one-room shacks beyond the gardens, rising, with the first barking of the dogs, to prepare breakfast and clean and dust and wash and iron and polish and raise other people's children – for three or four hundred rands a month.

But, of course, now that 'apartheid is over', black people are free to buy houses on the Berea, tear up their passbooks, eat at the Royal Hotel, go on holiday to Sol Kerzner's Lost City or buy a block of flats on the seafront. And now they have even put their crosses on the pieces of paper and have voted, overwhelmingly, for an ANC government.

The Freedom Charter, the historic programme, for which I fought for over forty years (and was thus made an outcast by my Durban family and white South Africa) has been eroded in the cause, they say, of practicality and necessary compromise. And yet, it is said that South Africa is free.

Now any black South African knows she is free to buy herself a Rolls Royce or dine at the Ritz in London, or marry van der Merwe – who has violated her for years.

Now you will never meet any white, any member of our family who was pro-apartheid – except Archie, of course, who rants about South Africa becoming another Tanzania because black people, according to him, have no skills to rule and are innately corrupt. But the rest of the family have faded, like their views, old and reclusive.

I have been forgiven for my political priorities. They misunderstood, they said. Now that it doesn't matter, I am something of a hero in their eyes. 'We always knew she was the clever one,' they say.

But there is terror abroad. The whites fear black encroachment as much now as they ever did.

Yet the black world lies in the distant townships and rural areas, beyond view. Their meeting places and homes are unseen, except now and then, on the rims of Durban, you pass a poor shanty town which could be in Somalia, Bangladesh or Ethiopia.

At the rendezvous of victory

NADINE GORDIMER

A young black boy used to brave the dogs in white men's suburbs to deliver telegrams: Sinclair 'General Giant' Zwedu
has those bite scars on his legs to this day.

So goes the opening paragraph of a 'profile' copyrighted by
a British Sunday paper, reprinted by reciprocal agreement
with papers in New York and Washington, syndicated as far as
Australia and translated in both *Le Monde* and *Neue Züricher
Zeitung*.

But like everything else he was to read about himself, it was
not quite like that. No. Ever since he was a kid he had loved
dogs, and those dogs who chased his bicycle – he just used to
whistle in his way at them, and they would stand there wag-
ging their long tails and feeling silly. The scars on his legs were
from wounds received when the white commando almost cap-
tured him, blew up one of his hide-outs in the bush. But he understood why the journalist had decided to paint the wounds
over as dog-bites – it made a kind of novel opening to the story,
and it showed at once that the journalist wasn't on the side of
the whites. It was true that he who became Sinclair 'General
Giant' Zwedu was born in the blacks' compound on a white
man's sugar farm in the hottest and most backward part of
the country, and that, after only a few years at school where
children drew their sums in the dust, he was the post-office
messenger in the farmers' town. It was in that two-street town,
with the whites' Central Hotel, Main Road Garage, Buyrite
Stores, Snooker Club and railhead, that he first heard the voice
of the brother who was to become Prime Minister and President, a voice from a big trumpet on the top of a shabby van. It
summoned him (there were others, but they didn't become
anybody) to a meeting in the Catholic Mission Hall in Goodwill

Township – which was what the white farmers called the black shanty town outside their own. And it was here, in Goodwill Township, that the young post-office messenger took away the local Boy Scout troop organised by but segregated from the white Boy Scout troop in the farmers' town, and transformed the scouts into the Youth Group of the National Independence Party. Yes – he told them – you will be prepared. The Party will teach you how to make a fire the Government can't put out.

It was he who, when the leaders of the Party were detained for the first time, was imprisoned with the future Prime Minister and became one of his chief lieutenants. He, in fact, who in jail made up defiance songs that soon were being sung at mass meetings, who imitated the warders, made pregnant one of the women prisoners who polished the cell floors (though no one believed her when she proudly displayed the child as his), and finally, when he was sent to another prison in order to remove his invigorating influence from fellow political detainees, overpowered three warders and escaped across the border.

It was this exploit that earned him the title 'General Giant' as prophets, saints, rogues and heroes receive theirs: named by the anonymous talk of ordinary people. He did not come back until he had wintered in the unimaginable cold of countries that offer refuge and military training, gone to rich desert cities to ask for money from the descendants of people who had sold Africans as slaves, and to the island where sugarcane workers, as his mother and father had been, were now powerful enough to supply arms. He was with the first band of men who had left home with empty hands, on bare feet, and came back with AKM assault rifles, heat-guided missiles and limpet mines.

The future Prime Minister was imprisoned again and again and finally fled the country and established the Party's leadership in exile. When Sinclair 'General Giant' met him in London or Algiers, the future Prime Minister wore a dark suit whose close weave was midnight blue in the light. He himself wore a bush outfit that originally had been put together by men who lived less like men than prides of lion, tick-ridden, thirsty, waiting in thickets of thorn. As these men increased in numbers and boldness, and he rose in command of them, the outfit elaborated into a combat uniform befitting his style, title and achievement. At the beginning of the war, he had led a ragged hit-and-run group; after four years and the deaths of many, which emphasised his giant indestructibility, his men controlled a third of the country and he was the man the white army wanted most to capture.

Before the future Prime Minister talked to the Organisation of African Unity or United Nations he had now to send for and consult with his commander-in-chief of the liberation army, Sinclair 'General Giant' Zwedu. General Giant came from the bush in his Czech jeep, in a series of tiny planes from secret airstrips, and at last would board a scheduled jet liner among oil and mineral men who thought they were sitting beside just another dolled-up black official from some unheard-of state whose possibilities they might have to look into sometime. When the consultation in the foreign capital was over, General Giant did not fidget long in the patter of official cocktail parties, but would disappear to find for himself whatever that particular capital could offer to meet his high capacities – for leading men to fight without fear, exciting people to caper, shout with pleasure, drink and argue; for touching women. After a night in a bar and a bed with girls (he never had to pay professionals, always found well-off, respectable women, black or white, whose need for delights simply matched his own) he would take a plane back to Africa. He never wanted to linger.

He never envied his brother, the future Prime Minister, his flat in London and the invitations to country houses to discuss the future of the country. He went back imperatively as birds migrate to Africa to mate and assure the survival of their kind, journeying thousands of miles, just as he flew and drove deeper and deeper into where he belonged until he reached again his headquarters – that the white commandos often claimed to have destroyed but which could not be destroyed because his headquarters were the bush itself.

The war would not have been won without General Giant. At the Peace Conference he took no part in the deliberations but was there at his brother, the future Prime Minister's, side: a deterrent weapon, a threat to the defeated white government of what would happen if peace were not made. Now and then when he cleared his throat of a constriction of boredom, the white delegates were alarmed as if he had roared.

Constitutional talks went on for many weeks; there was a cease-fire, of course. He wanted to go back – to his headquarters-home – but one of the conditions of the cease-fire had been that he should be withdrawn from the field, as the official term, coined in wars fought over poppy-meadows, phrased it. He wandered about London. He went to nightclubs and was invited to join parties of Arabs who, he found, had no idea where the country he had fought for, and won for his people, was. This time he really did roar – with laughter. He walked through Soho but couldn't understand why anyone would like to watch couples making the movements of love-making on the cinema screen instead of doing it themselves. He came upon the Natural History Museum in South Kensington and was entranced by the life that existed anterior to his own unthinking familiarity with ancient nature, hiding the squat limpet mines, the iron clutches of offensive and defensive hand-grenades, the angular AKs, metal blue with heat. He sent postcards of mammoths and gasteropods to his children, who were still where they had been with his wife all through the war – in the black location of the capital of his home country. Since she was his wife, she had been under police surveillance, and detained several times, but had survived by saying she and her husband were separated. Which was true, in a way; a man leading a guerrilla war has no family, he must forget about meals cooked for him by a woman, nights in a bed with two places hollowed by their bodies, and the snuffle of a baby close by. He made love to a black singer from Jamaica, not young, whose style was a red-head wig rather than fasionable rigid pigtails. She composed a song about his bravery in the war in a country she imagined but had never seen, and sang it at a victory rally where all the brothers in exile as well as the white sympathisers with their cause, applauded her. In her flat she had a case of special Scotch whisky, twelve years old, sent by an admirer. She said – sang to him – Let's not let it get any older. As she worked only at night, they spent whole days indoors making love when the weather was bad – the big man, General Giant, was like a poor stray cat, in the cold rain: he would walk on the balls of shoe-soles, shaking each foot as he lifted it out of the wet.

He was waiting for the okay, as he said to his brother, the future Prime Minister, to go back to their country and take up his position as commander-in-chief of the new state's Defence Force. His title would become an official rank, the highest, like that of army chiefs in Britain and the United States – General Zwedu.

His brother turned solemn, dark in his mind; couldn't be followed there. He said the future of the army was a tremendous problem at present under discussion. The two armies, black and white, who had fought each other, would have to be made one. What the discussions were also about remained in the dark: the defeated white government, the European powers by whom the new black state was promised loans for reconstruction, had insisted that Sinclair 'General Giant' Zwedu be relieved of all military authority. His personality was too strong and too strongly associated with the triumph of the freedom-fighter army for him to be anything but a divisive reminder of the past, in the new, regular army. Let him stand for parliament in the first peace-time election, his legend would guarantee that he win the seat. Then the Prime Minister could find him some safe portfolio.

What portfolio? What? This was in the future Prime Minister's mind when General Giant couldn't follow him. 'What he knows how to do is defend our country, that he fought for,' the future Prime Minister said to the trusted advisers, British lawyers and African experts from American universities. And while he was saying it, the others knew he did not want, could not have his brother Sinclair 'General Giant' Zwedu, that master of the wilderness, breaking the confinement of peace-time barracks.

He left him in Europe on some hastily-invented mission until the independence celebrations. Then he brought him home to the old colonial capital that was not theirs, and at the airport wept with triumph and anguish in his arms, while schoolchildren sang. He gave him a portfolio – Sport and Recreation; harmless.

General Giant looked at his big hands as if the appointment were an actual object, held there. What was he supposed to do with it? The great lungs that pumped his organ-voice failed; he spoke flatly, kindly, almost pityingly to his brother, the Prime Minister.

Now they both wore dark blue suits. At first, he appeared prominently at the Prime Minister's side as a tacit recompense, to show the people that he was still acknowledged by the Prime Minister as a co-founder of the nation, and its popular hero. He had played football on a patch of bare earth between wattle-branch goal posts on the sugar farm, as a child, and as a youth on a stretch of waste ground near the Catholic Mission Hall; as a man he had been at war, without time for games. In the first few months he rather enjoyed attending important matches in his official capacity, watching from a special box and later seeing himself sitting there, on a TV newsreel. It was a Sunday, a holiday amusement; the holiday went on too long. There was not much obligation to make speeches, in his cabinet post, but because his was a name known over the world, his place reserved in the mountain stronghold Valhalla of guerrilla wars, journalists went to him for statements on all kinds of issues. Besides, he was splendid copy, talkative, honest, indiscreet and emotional. Again and again, he embarrassed his government by giving an outrageous opinion, that contradicted Government policy, on problems that were none of his business. The Party caucus reprimanded him again and again. He responded by seldom turning up at caucus meetings. The caucus members said that Zwedu (it was time his 'title' was dropped) thought too much of himself and had taken offense. Again, he knew that what was assumed was not quite true. He was bored with the caucus. He wanted to yawn all the time, he said, like a hippopotamus with its huge jaws open in the sun, half-asleep, in the thick brown water of the river near his last headquarters. The Prime Minister laughed at this, and they drank together with arms round one another – as they did in the old days in the Youth Group. The Prime Minister told him – 'But seriously, sport and recreation are very important in building up our nation. For the next budget, I'll see that there's a bigger grant to your department, you'll be able to plan. You know how to inspire young men ... I'm told a local team has adapted one of the freedom songs you made up, they sang it on TV.'

The Minister of Sport and Recreation sent his deputy to officiate at sports meetings these days and he didn't hear his war song become a football fans' chant. The Jamaican singer had arrived on an engagement at the Hilton that had just opened conference rooms, bars, a casino and nightclub on a site above the town where the old colonial prison used to be (the new prison was on the site of the former Peace Corps camp). He was there in the nightclub every night, drinking the brand of Scotch she had had in her London flat, tilting his head while she sang. The hotel staff pointed him out to overseas visitors – Sinclair 'General Giant' Zwedu, the General Giap, the Che Guevara of a terrible war there'd been in this country. The tourists had spent the day, taken by private plane, viewing game in what the travel brochure described as the country's magnificent game park but – the famous freedom fighter could have told them – wasn't quite that; was in fact his territory, his headquarters. Sometimes he danced with one of the women, their white teeth contrasting with shiny sunburned skin almost as if they had been black. Once there was some sort of a row; he danced too many times with a woman who appeared to be enjoying this intimately, and her husband objected. The 'convivial Minister' had laughed, taken the man by

267

the scruff of his white linen jacket and dropped him back in his chair, a local journalist reported, but the Government-owned press did not print his story or picture. An overseas journalist interviewed General Giant on the pretext of the incident, and got from him (the Minister was indeed convivial, entertaining the journalist to excellent whisky in the house he had rented for the Jamaican singer) some opinions on matters far removed from the nightclub scandal.

When questions were asked in parliament about an article in an American weekly on the country's international alliances, General Giant stood up and, again, gave expression to convictions the local press could not print. He said that the defence of the country might have been put in the hands of neo-colonialists who had been the country's enemies during the war – and he was powerless to do anything about that. But he would take the law into his own hands to protect the National Independence Party's principles of a people's democracy (he used the old name, on this occasion, although it had been shortened to National Party). Hadn't he fought, hadn't the brothers spilled their blood to get rid of the old laws and the old bosses, that made them *nothing*? Hadn't they fought for new laws under which they would be men? He would shed blood rather than see the Party betrayed in the name of so-called rational alliances and national unity.

International advisers to the Government thought the speech, if inflammatory, so confused it might best be ignored. Members of the cabinet and Members of Parliament wanted the Prime Minister to get rid of him. 'General Giant' Zwedu? How? Where to? Extreme anger was always expressed by the Prime Minister in the form of extreme sorrow. He was angry with both his cabinet members and his comrade, without whom they would never have been sitting in the House of Assembly. He sent for Zwedu. (He must accept that name now; he simply refused to accommodate himself to anything, he illogically wouldn't even drop the 'Sinclair' though *that* was the name of the white sugar farmer his parents had worked for, and nobody kept those slave names any more.)

268

Zwedu: so at ease and handsome in his cabinet minister's suit (it was not the old blue, but a pin-stripe flannel the Jamaican singer had ordered at his request, and brought from London), one could not believe wild and dangerous words could come out of his mouth. He looked good enough for a diplomatic post somewhere ... Unthinkable. The Prime Minister, full of sorrow and silences, told him he must stop drinking. He must stop giving interviews. There was no mention of the Ministry; the Prime Minister did not tell his brother he would not give in to pressure to take that away from him, the cabinet post he had never wanted but that was all there was to offer. He would not take it away – at least not until this could be done decently under cover of a cabinet reshuffle. The Prime Minister had to say to his brother, You mustn't let me down. What he wanted to say was: What have I done to you?

There was a crop failure and trouble with the unions on the coal mines; by the time the cabinet reshuffle came the press hardly noticed that a Minister of Sport and Recreation had been replaced. Mr Sinclair Zwedu was not given an alternative portfolio, but he was referred to as a former Minister when his name was added to the boards of multinational industrial firms instructed by their principals to Africanise. He could be counted upon not to appear at those meetings, either. His director's fees paid for cases of whisky, but sometimes went to his wife, to whom he had never returned, and the teenage children with whom he would suddenly appear in the best stores of the town, buying whatever they silently pointed at. His old friends blamed the Jamaican woman, not the Prime Minister, for his disappearance from public life. She went back to England – her reasons were sexual and honest, she realised she was too old for him – but his way of life did not recover; could not recover the war, the third of the country's territory that had been his domain when the white Government lost control to him, and the black Government did not yet exist.

The country is open to political and trade missions from both East and West, now, instead of these being confined to allies of the old white Government. The airport has been extended. The new departure lounge is a sculpture gallery with reclining figures among potted plants, wearily waiting for connections to places whose directions criss-cross the colonial North-South compass of communication. A former Chief-of-Staff of the white army, who, since the black Government came to power, has been retained as chief military adviser to the Defence Ministry, recently spent some hours in the lounge waiting for a plane that was to take him on a Government mission to Europe. He was joined by a journalist booked on the same flight home to London, after a rather disappointing return visit to the country. Well, he remarked to the military man as they drank vodka-and-tonic together, who wants to read about rice-growing schemes instead of seek-and-destroy raids? This was a graceful reference to the ex-Chief-of-Staff's successes with that strategy at the beginning of the war, a reference safe in the cosy no-man's-land of a departure lounge, out of earshot of the new black security officials alert to any hint of encouragement of an old-guard white coup.

A musical gong preceded announcements of the new estimated departure time of the delayed British Airways plane. A swami found sweets somewhere in his saffron robes and went among the travellers handing out comfits with a message of peace and love. Businessmen used the opportunity to write reports on briefcases opened on their knees. Black children were spores attached to maternal skirts. White children ran back and forth to the bar counter, buying potato crisps and peanuts. The journalist insisted on another round of drinks.

Every now and then the departure of some other flight was called and the display of groups and single figures would change; some would leave, while a fresh surge would be let in through the emigration barriers and settle in a new composition. Those who were still waiting for delayed planes became part of the permanent collection, so to speak; they included a Canadian evangelical party who read their gospels with the absorption other people gave to paperback thrillers, a very old black woman dry as the fish in her woven carrier, and a prosperous black couple, elegantly dressed. The ex-Chief-of-Staff and his companion were sitting not far behind these two, who flirted and caressed, like whites – it was quite unusual to see those people behaving that way in public. Both the white men noticed this although they were able to observe only the back of the man's head and the profile of the girl, pretty, painted, shameless as she licked his tiny black ear and lazily tickled, with long fingers on the stilts of purple nails, the roll of his neck.

The ex-Chief-of-Staff made no remark, was not interested – what did one not see, in the country, now that they had taken over. The journalist was the man who had written a profile, just after the war: a *young black boy used to brave the dogs in white men's suburbs* ... Suddenly he leant forward, staring at the back of the black man's head. 'That's General Giant! I know those ears!' He got up and went over to the bar, turning casually at the counter to examine the couple from the front. He bought two more vodka-and-tonics, swiftly was back to his companion, the ice chuntering in the glasses. 'It's him. I thought so. I used to know him well. Him, all right. Fat! Wearing suede shoes. And the tart ... where'd he find her!'

The ex-Chief-of-Staff's uniform, his thick wad of campaign ribbons over the chest and cap thrust down to his fine eyebrows, seemed to defend him against the heat rather than make him suffer, but the journalist felt confused and stifled as the vodka came out distilled once again in sweat and he did not know whether he should or should not simply walk up to General Giant (no secretaries or security men to get past, now) and ask for an interview. Would anyone want to read it? Could he sell it anywhere? A distraction that made it difficult for him to make up his mind was the public address system nagging that the two passengers holding up flight something-or-other were requested to board the aircraft immediately. No one stirred, General Giant (no mistaking him) simply signalled, a big hand snapping in the air, when he wanted fresh

271

drinks for himself and his girl, and the barman hopped to it, although the bar was self-service. Before the journalist could come to a decision an air hostess ran in with the swish of stockings chafing thigh past thigh and stopped angrily, looking down at the black couple. The journalist could not hear what was said, but she stood firm while the couple took their time getting up, the girl letting her arm slide languidly off the man; laughing, arranging their hand luggage on each other's shoulders.

Where was he *taking* her?

The girl put one high-heeled sandal down in front of the other, as a model negotiates a catwalk. Sinclair 'General Giant' Zwedu followed her backside the way a man follows a paid woman, with no thought of her in his closed, shiny face, and the ex-Chief-of-Staff and the journalist did not know whether he recognised them, even saw them, as he passed without haste, letting the plane wait for him.

GLOSSARY

aanslag – onslaught
baas – (white) boss
beweging – literally: movement
bhang – marijuana
bietjie pap – here: little weak
biltong – strips of dried meat
bladdy, also: blerry – bloody
bles – bald patch
boere – here: Afrikaners
Boesman – here: dark-skinned person with frizzy hair
bra – brother, comrade
broer – brother
casspir – armoured troop-carrying vehicle
chommie – from English *chummy*: mate, pal
dagga – marijuana
die swart gevaar – the threat of black nationalism
diknek – tough guy
dominee – parish priest in Dutch Reformed Church
domkop – fool
donga – dry, eroded gully
dop – wine given to workers as part of their pay
ekhaya – home
fyndraai – orgasm
hanepoot – variety of muscat grape
hê hê hokaai, wag broer – ho ho hold it, wait brother
heera – represents Afrikaans pronunciation of *Here*: Lord
heita, hoezit broer – hallo, howzit brother
hokaai – exclamation usually used to halt animals
huistoe – going home
inyanga – traditional healer, herbalist, diviner
ja, also: jas – yes
jagse – randy
jislaaik – exclamation equivalent to *heavens*, *unbelievable*, etc.
jissis, also: jissus, jussus – represents the Afrikaans pronunciation of *Jesus*
jolbokke – good-time girls
jong – here: expression of exasperation

kaffir – derogatory term for black person
kaffir-boetie – abusive reference to white person friendly with black people
kak – shit
kiaat – a southern African hard wood, teak
klaberjas – type of card game (piquet) in which the jack of clubs is the
    highest card
klonkies – here: small black boys
knoppiesdoring – knobthorn (wood)
kom ounooi se kiepies, kom – come missus' little chicks, come
kroes – frizzy
krokodilletjie – term of endearment; literally: little crocodile
kwela music – penny-whistle music
laaities – young guys, adolescents
laksman – here: fiscal-shrike
lekker little plek – nice little place
lekkerkry – sensual enjoyment
likawaans – leguaan
manne – men
mapoza – policeman, night watchman
meneer – mister, sir
mlungu – white man
oom – uncle
pampoen – pumpkin
poes – cunt
shebeen – drinking establishment, often in private home
shiksa – non-Jewish girl or woman
shul – synagogue
sjambok – whip
skelbek – here: abusive shouting
skelm – crook
slap-chips – hot fried potato chips
sommer – equivalent to *just, simply, for no reason*
stompie – half-smoked sigarette, kept for later use
strue's God – as true as God
tannie – auntie
Tassies – (cheap) Tassenberg wine
tauza – actions prisoners have to perform during full body inspection to
    reveal any object they might have hidden in or on their bodies
terr – terrorist
toyi-toying – quasi-military dance during which knees are lifted high
tsotsi – young black gangster or hoodlum

NOTES ON THE CONTRIBUTORS

KEN BARRIS is a Cape Town-based short-story writer and poet who lectures in Communication Studies at the Cape Technikon. His fiction includes *Small Change and Other Stories*; *The Jailer's Book* and *Evolution*. His poetry appears in *Advertisement for Air*. He is the recipient of The Ingrid Jonker Award for Poetry, the Vita/Ad Donker Award for Short Stories and the M-Net Award for Fiction.

ELLEKE BOEHMER is a novelist, short-story writer and literary scholar in Post-Colonial Studies at Leeds University in the UK. She is author of the novels *Screens Against the Sky* and *An Immaculate Figure*. She has edited *Altered State? Writing and South Africa and Empire Writing: An Anthology of Colonial Literature*. She is author of the critical study *Colonial and Postcolonial Literature*.

SANDRA LEE BRAUDE is a fiction writer and founding editor of the literary journal *herStoriA*. Her publications include *The Windswept Plains*, a collection of short stories and poems, and *Mpho's Search: The Story of a Streetchild*. She is the recipient of the First Prize of the First International Conference on Story and Metaphor, Budapest, 1992.

DIANE CASE is a writer of fiction and children's stories, and lives in Cape Town. Her publications include *Madam, this is Annie* and three novels for teenagers – *Albatross Winter*; *Love, David* and *92 Queens Road* – all of which were MML Young Africa Award-winners. *92 Queen Street* also earned her the Percy Fitzpatrick Award.

ACHMAT DANGOR is a novelist, short-story writer and Chief Executive Officer of the Nelson Mandela Children's Fund. His publications include *Waiting for Leila*; *Bulldozer*; *The Z Town Trilogy*; *Private Voices* and *Kafka's Curse – A Novella & Three Other Stories*. He is the recipient of the Mofolo/Plummer Award, the Vita/Cosmoplitan Story Award and the Herman Charles Bosman Award for Fiction.

SANDILE DIKENI is a poet, print and radio journalist based in Cape Town. He is the arts and culture editor of the *Cape Times*. His work has appeared in local and international journals and newspapers. His poems are collected in *Guava Juice*.

AHMED ESSOP is a retired educationist, short-story writer and novelist. His stories are collected in *The Hadji and Other Stories*; *Noorjohan and Other Stories* and *The King of Hearts and Other Stories*. His novels include *The Visitation* and *The Emperor*. His is the recipient of the Olive Schreiner Award for Fiction.

GRAEME FRIEDMAN is a psychotherapist and fiction writer living in Johannesburg. He is the co-editor of *A Writer in Stone: South African Writers Celebrate the 70th Birthday of Lionel Abrahams*. His novel, *Fruit of the Poisoned Tree*, which won the Macmillan Boleswa/Pace Writer's Competition in manuscript form is due for publication in 1999.

NADINE GORDIMER is a novelist, short-story writer and essayist who lives in Johannesburg. She is the author of 12 novels, the most recent being *The House Gun,* and numerous volumes of short stories. Her essays appear in *Black Interpreters*; *The Essential Gesture* and *Writing and Being*. Her numerous awards include the CNA Award, the Booker Prize, the French International Award, the Nellie Sachs Prize and the Nobel Prize for Literature.

RACHELLE GREEFF is a short-story writer, novelist and columnist who lives in Cape Town. Her first collection of stories, *Die rugkant van die bruid,* won the CNA Debut Award. She has since published a second collection, *Onwaarskynlike engele* and a novel, *Al die windrigtings van my wêreld.* Her magazine columns have been published in *Spektakels en mirakels.* She is the recipient of the M-Net Bursary for Creative Writing and the Sanlam Award for Fiction.

DIANNE HOFMEYR is a fiction writer and art teacher from Cape Town now living in London where she works as a freelance travel writer. Her novel for teenagers, *Boikie You Better Believe It,* won the M-Net Award for Fiction as well as the Sanlam Gold Prize for Youth Literature. Three other novels have won awards and *Blue Train to the Moon* was nominated as an IBBY Honours Book in the Netherlands.

PETER HORN is a literary scholar, poet, short-story writer and critic. A selection of his poetry from eleven separate volumes – including *An Axe in the Ice* and *Rivers that Connect Us to the Past* – appear in *Poems 1964-1998.* His collection of short stories, *My Voice Is Under Control Now*, earned him the Alex la Guma/Bessie Head Fiction Award. His essays are collected in *The Writing of My Reading*.

MAUREEN ISAACSON is a short-story writer and journalist living in Johannesburg where she is books editor of the *Sunday Independent*. She served as the research editor for two publications, *Fifties People of South Africa* and *The Finest Photos from the Old Drum*. Her short stories are published in *Holding Back Midnight and Other Stories*. She is a recipient of the 1997 Book Journalist of the Year Award.

276

BEVERLEY JANSEN is a poet and short-story writer living in Cape Town. Her work has been published in anthologies such as *Voices in a Garden* and *iQabane* as well as in local literary journals.

RAYDA JACOBS is a short-story writer and novelist who now lives in Cape Town after an absence of twenty-seven years. Her publications include a collection of stories, *The Middle Children*, published in Canada, and two novels, *Eyes of the Sky* and *The Slave Book*. She is a recipient of the Herman Charles Bosman Award for Fiction.

NORMA KITSON is a fiction writer who was born in Durban and left South Africa to settle in London, when her South African citizenship was withdrawn because of her involvement in the anti-apartheid struggle. She now lives in Harare, Zimbabwe. Her publications include the autobiographical work *Where Sixpence Lives*. Her stories and reviews have been published in anthologies, journals and newspapers in Britain, the USA and Zimbabwe.

BARRY LEVY is a journalist and fiction writer living in Australia. He left South Africa in 1984 when called up to serve in the army. His publications include *The Glazer Kidnapping* and a novella 'Farewell to Mrs Eels' published in the anthology *Scenes from Another Day: New South African Writing*. He is the recipient of the Anning Barton Memorial Award for Outstanding Journalism and the Australian Human Rights Award for Journalism.

JOHNNY MASILELA is a journalist who worked for the *Rand Daily Mail* and the *Pretoria News*. He is now a freelance writer and lives in Pretoria. His first collection of short stories is entitled *Deliver Us From Evil*. A second, *A Place of Mud Huts*, is in preparation. Various other stories have been published in journals and anthologies.

JAMES MATTHEWS is a poet, fiction writer and founder of the publishing house Blac. He lives in Cape Town. His poetry is published in *Cry Rage*; *Pass Me a Meatball, Jones*; *Poisoned Wells and Other Delights* and *No Time for Dreams*. His fiction appears in *The Park and Other Stories* and *The Party is Over*, a novel.

DAVID MEDALIE is a short-story writer, anthologiser and literary scholar. He lectures in the English Department at the University of the Witwatersrand. His stories appear in *The Shooting of the Christmas Cows*. He is the editor of *Encounters: An Anthology of South African Short Stories* and is a recipient of the 1996 Sanlam Short Story Award.

GOMOLEMO MOKAE is a medical doctor, playwright, scriptwriter and fiction writer living in Mmabatho. He writes in Setswana and English. His publications include *The Secret in My Bosom*. He is a recipient of among others, the Bertrams V.O. Literature of Africa Award, the English Association Award, the National Arts Coalition Award and the African Heritage Literary Award.

PHIL NDLELA is a fiction writer and academic lecturing in the Department of English at the University of Fort Hare. Awarded a Fulbright Scholarship to study in the United States, he is writing a doctoral dissertation on *Black South African Writing 1950-1985*. This is his first published story.

MIKE NICOL is a poet, novelist and freelance journalist living in Cape Town. His poems appear in *Among the Souvenirs* and *This Sad Place*. His novels include *The Powers that Be*; *This Day and Age*; *Horseman* and *The Ibis Tapestry*. His non-fiction includes *A Good-Looking Corpse: The World of Drum*; *The Waiting Country* and *The Invisible Line: The Life and Photography of Ken Oosterbroek*.

ANN OOSTHUIZEN is a novelist, short-story writer, translator and editor. After years of exile in the United Kingdom she returned to South Africa in 1991. Her novel, *Close Up*, was the winner of the Bertrams V.O. Literature of Africa Award. She is a member of the editorial collective of the journal *herStoriA*.

PETER RULE is a fiction writer living in Pietermaritzburg. He is programme director for the Natal Adult Basic Education Support Agency. His short stories have appeared in several South African journals and anthologies. He is co-author of *Nokukhanya Luthuli*, the biography of the wife of Albert Luthuli.

COLIN JIGGS SMUTS is an educationist, fiction writer and former Director of the Open School, living in Johannesburg. His involvement in educational programmes for children from the South African townships resulted in *Two Dogs and Freedom* and *In this Land*, made up of writings and drawings by childern. His fiction is published in *Nights of Immorality*.

TANIA SPENCER is a freelance photographer and journalist living in KwaZulu-Natal. Her poems and short stories have been published in various newspapers and journals. She is currently working on a photographic project on street children in South Africa.

MIRIAM TLALI is a short-story writer and novelist who lives in Johannesburg and Lesotho. Her novels include *Muriel at the Metropolitan* and *Amandla*. Her stories are collected in *Footprints in the Quag* and *Soweto Stories*. In the late 1970s she contributed to the genre of popular history through her column 'Soweto Speaks' in *Staffrider* .

ETIENNE VAN HEERDEN is a writer of fiction and a literary scholar in the Department of Afrikaans at the University of Cape Town. His novels include *Toorberg* (translated as *Ancestoral Voices*), *Casspirs and Camparis* and *Kikuyu*. A selection of his short stories appear in *Mad Dog and Other Stories*. He is the recipient of the CNA-prys, the Rapport-prys and the Hertzog-prys. He is editor of the internet literary journal *Litnet*.

ZOË WICOMB is a fiction writer and literary scholar born in South Africa and now teaching English and Creative Writing at the University of Strathclyde in the UK. Her short stories have appeared in journals in South Africa and abroad and are published in *You Can't Get Lost in Cape Town and Other Stories*.

RUSTUN WOOD/KAREN WILLIAMS is a journalist and writer living in Johannesburg. Her stories have appeared in two anthologies, *The Invisible Ghetto* and *Worlds Unspoken – The Vintage Book of International Lesbian Fiction*, and in American journals such as *Sinister Wisdom* and *Common Lives*.

ACKNOWLEGDEMENTS

Thanks are due to Sandra Lee Braude for providing material from which stories were selected and included in this anthology, as well as to all the writers who submitted work.

Special thanks must also go to Annari van der Merwe of Kwela Books for commissioning and enthusiastically assisting Lesley Beake with preparing the manuscript for publication. Also to Clive Hanekom who kept track of everything.

'At the rendezvous of victory' by Nadine Gordimer was originally published in *Something Out There*, Viking Press, New York. © 1984 Nadine Gordimer.

'The finger of God' by Graeme Friedman was previously published in *herStoriA*, Vol. 4 No. 2, August 1998.

'Housekeeping' by Ann Oosthuizen was previously published in *herStoriA*, Vol. 5 No. 1, April 1999.

'N2' by Zoë Wicomb was previously published in STAND magazine, New Series Vol. 1 No. 2, June 1999.

'The scream' by Etienne van Heerden was translated from Afrikaans by Jane Rosenthal; in this story extensive use is made of an article which appeared in *Vrij Nederland* 57:16.

In 'A question of identity' by Phil Ndlela the Xhosa quotations come from *The Bible in Xhosa* (New Translation) © 1966 Bible Society of South Africa; the English quotations come from *Holy Bible Good News Edition* © 1976 American Bible Society.